LA CROSSE PUBLIC LIBRARY
LA CROSSE, WISCONSIN

WAS IT A RAT I SAW?

WAS IT A RAT I SAW?

SUE PERRY

A Perfect Crime Book
DOUBLEDAY
NEW YORK   LONDON   TORONTO   SYDNEY   AUCKLAND

A PERFECT CRIME BOOK
PUBLISHED BY DOUBLEDAY
a division of Bantam Doubleday Dell Publishing Group, Inc.
666 Fifth Avenue, New York, New York 10103

DOUBLEDAY is a trademark of Doubleday,
a division of
Bantam Doubleday Dell Publishing Group, Inc.

All of the characters in this book are fictitious,
and any resemblance to actual persons, living or dead,
is purely coincidental.

Grateful acknowledgment is made for permission to reprint the following:

Excerpt from "Not A Second Time." Words and music by John Lennon and Paul McCartney. Copyright © 1963, 1964 by Northern Songs. All rights controlled and administered by MCA Music Publishing, a division of MCA Inc., New York, NY 10019 under license from Northern Songs. Copyright renewed. Used by permission. International copyright secured. All rights reserved.

Excerpt from "Moon River" copyright © 1961 by Famous Music Corporation. Copyright renewed 1989 by Famous Music Corporation.

"Lady Doctor," by Graham Parker, copyright © 1976. Excerpted by kind permission of Graham Parker and GEEP Music, Ltd.

Excerpt from "Unsatisfied," by Paul Westerberg, as performed by the Replacements. Copyright © 1984 by NAH Music.

BOOK DESIGN BY TASHA HALL

Library of Congress Cataloging-in-Publication Data
Perry, Sue.
Was it a rat I saw? / by Sue Perry.
p.   cm.
"A Perfect Crime book."
I. Title.
PS3566.E7169W37   1992
813'.54—dc20   91-38116
                                    CIP

ISBN 0-385-42238-5
Copyright © 1991 by Sue Perry
All Rights Reserved
Printed in the United States of America
May 1992

1 3 5 7 9 10 8 6 4 2
First Edition

for my parents

ACKNOWLEDGMENTS

For their comments and support in the writing of this book, many thanks to: Willard Carroll, Ruth Gribin, Peter Hankoff, Bill Hickey, Julie Hickson, Will Huston, Christine Madsen, Dave Madsen, Kate Miciak, Wendy Pratt, Julie Robitaille, Deborah Schneider and Dean Stefan.

Special thanks to Julie Hickson for the title.

*The people and events in this book are fictional.
The split brain phenomena, however, are factual.*

CONTENTS

PART ONE	The Average Evoked Potential		
	Chapter 1	Excitation	3
	Chapter 2	Inhibition	35
	Chapter 3	Confabulation	53
PART TWO	Kindling		
	Chapter 4	Type One Error	79
	Chapter 5	The Fixation Point	107
	Chapter 6	Neglect	126
	Chapter 7	Symmetry Breaking	140
	Chapter 8	Cerebral Dominance	156
	Chapter 9	Acute Disconnection Syndrome	180
PART THREE	Synesthesia		
	Chapter 10	Habituation	205
	Chapter 11	Completion	232
	Chapter 12	Reductionism	261
	Chapter 13	Fight or Flight	289
	Chapter 14	Strange Attractors	307
PART FOUR	Chaotic Dynamics		
	Chapter 15	The Falling Sickness	341
	Chapter 16	The Dichotomy	367

	Chapter 17	*Chimeric Faces*	380
	Chapter 18	*Grand Mal*	404
PART FIVE	*Epilogue*		
	Chapter 19	*Lucid Dreaming*	427
	Bibliography		435

WAS IT
A RAT
I SAW?

PART 1

The Average Evoked Potential

Electrical activity in the brain that is characteristic of a particular stimulus or effort is called an average evoked potential.

CHAPTER 1

Excitation

"I saw a banana," Tommy said with complete assurance.

"Great," Dr. Clare Austen replied. "Now with your left hand, draw what you saw."

A right hander, Tommy fumbled to get the pencil positioned in his left fingers. Clare studied his face as he commenced drawing. The right side of his face definitely looked worried. Did the left look a little smug? Falteringly, his left hand sketched a clock face.

"Well," Tommy paused, then continued in a rush. "See like I told you before I can't draw for shit especially with my left hand. Some banana, huh?" After two-point-something seconds of consternation, he tossed the pencil down. "I was confabulating again, wasn't I? Or anyway the *left* side of my brain wa—"

"Dammit Tommy, if you don't stop reading the literature you're going to make yourself absolutely useless to me." Clare slouched deeper into her chair; the orange plastic creaked and sighed.

"I stopped when you told me to last time, I swear, that was a term I picked up before. Don't fire me, I love being your victim."

She resisted the urge to correct him. He was her subject, not her victim; and she couldn't fire him, his participation in these experiments was voluntary. But if she said more, he would tease more. And he had to stop teasing. Even her current assistant—one of the dimmer bulbs—noticed an unclinical air in the lab when Tommy Dabrowski was the subject of Clare's experiments.

Victim indeed. She studied his long bony frame that looked tense even in relaxation, the smooth pale skin that was whiter than the lab coat he insisted on donning, the cool gray eyes that were several shades darker than usual.

"What's wrong?" she inquired.

"Why I read all those brain books. I just. Wanted to understand what was happening to me, for once. I didn't think about how it might screw your research if I was too aware of what you were testing for."

"I know. It's okay, I think. Did reading the books help?"

"The more I read, the less it seemed like anybody could explain anything about my brain or anybody else's."

"That about sums up the state of the research."

"Anyway, in some ways it's better not to know. Bad enough before when <u>dzzz</u>," he pantomimed a body being electrocuted. "Then when I start thinking about those guys who went in there and <u>whap</u>." He motioned, his hand an ax splitting a log. Or a skull. "But hey. At least I got to meet you, right?"

Their eyes met. "Is that what your seizures felt like?" Clare asked softly. Many patients described their epilepsy in short circuit or electrocution terms. Sometimes she wondered if that was only because their doctors had. "They really felt electrical?"

Tommy's most deadly smile flickered: he'd noticed her refusal to flirt back. But he let it go and replied, "Before I'd pass out, having a seizure felt like I was plugged in, all of a sudden, not just electrically though. I can't really explain it."

A door slammed. They looked toward her office adjoining the lab. "Found one, Professor Austen!" Steve the lab assistant appeared, brandishing a lighting element for the tachistoscope, the special rearview projector Clare used in her experiments.

Clare and Tommy withdrew physical inches, emotional light years. "Way to go!" Tommy congratulated Steve, he of the too-beady eyes and too-full mustache.

"They need help upstairs. Hurry." Steve ran out, then back in to deposit the lighting element on the edge of a table. He was halfway out the door again before he realized the element had fallen to the floor. He took a step back.

"Just leave it, Steve." Whatever was happening upstairs had undone his chronic phlegmatism and was thus worth a look, help needed or no. So she and Tommy followed Steve to the labs on the third floor, an area Clare usually tried to avoid.

In the stairwell, streaks of fresh blood made the tile steps slippery. There were thick red patches on the walls as if someone had ricocheted off them. Clare wondered whose blood was now oozing into the treads of her shoes. From the floor above, she heard yelling, pounding, cursing.

She exited the stairwell into one of her personal versions of hell. She was distantly aware of Steve and Tommy running ahead, Tommy returning to where she stood frozen, fighting the need to flee. Something bumped her foot. A black cat lay against her shoe, legs splayed, panting. Its head was shaved; wires dangled from electrodes implanted in its skull. When Clare lifted the creature, it hissed unconvincingly. Murmuring comfort, stroking fur gently, Clare slept-walked forward into a disaster zone.

All down the long hallway, countless cats, guinea pigs, mice, rats, rabbits—full of implants, incisions, surgical alterations—were crawling, running, crouching in terror. Dozens of humans in lab coats dashed around, corralling the experimentees.

The lab was in ruins: overturned cages, shattered glass, scattered instruments. Pools of chemicals on the floor, blood swirling in interesting chaotic shapes. Apparently every lab on the floor was in similar shape. The stench of formaldehyde was almost as strong as the animals' fear. In one corner, a rabbit huddled, taut, mouth open in a silent wail; silent because its vocal chords had been cut to curtail excess noise in the labs.

". . . His arms were raw up to the elbows but he just kept at it. He smashed a computer screen with his fist . . ."

". . . Thank God we relocated the primates . . ."

". . . I yelled 'what the hell are you doing' and he came at me like he wanted to kill me. I had to hit him with a beaker . . ."

". . . We'll never be ready in time for the symposium now . . ."

". . . He looked like a surfer, didn't he? We came out of the staff meeting and he practically knocked me down. I chased him but he had too much of a lead . . ."

". . . These animal *rights* maniacs should all be—"

"No." Clare interrupted. "It couldn't be them. They would have removed the animals before they destroyed the labs." Were her hands shaking, or was it the cat they held?

A group of white coats stared. She knew them but couldn't recognize them. One of them took the cat from Clare. "Look how frightened the poor thing is."

Another regarded Clare. "You're right. They'd make sure we couldn't salvage anything."

Yet another concluded, "So we're dealing with a deranged surfer? I'd prefer the activists."

Nearby at floor level, something screamed. Everyone jumped. Clare backed away from the group. "I've got to get back."

"Thanks for your help, Dr. Austen."

"Sure. Anytime."

Heading back down the stairs, her lab assistant Steve seemed energized by the experience. As he spoke, his hands flapped and swooped like bats at sunset. "I got twelve of them. One of the rats had part of its skull removed and the tiniest implants inside. The precision of the work is really impressive. I hope this doesn't ruin their data, some important work being done up there, especially by McGregor's people . . ."

Tommy murmured, "You okay?" Clare replied with a curt nod. He touched her shoulder in a gesture of support that for once had nothing to do with making time. She felt a rush of affection that petrified her.

As they stepped back into her lab, Steve concluded, ". . . and they should all get thrown in prison."

"So there's proof that animal activists were responsible?" Clare was surprised.

"Well, no, but I heard Dr. McGregor himself say that, after all, it was only a matter of time." Steve gloried in saying the great doctor's name. How quick he was to accept the stated, to revere the proven.

He resumed babbling as he installed the new tachistoscope lighting element. Tommy took his lead from Clare and sat silently.

Thanks for your help, Dr. Austen . . . Sure. Anytime. What a coward she'd become. Scientists opposed to vivisection were tremendously unpopular. But perhaps if she made her views known she might convince others—an other—to try different research strategies. She knew all the for-the-benefit-of-mankind arguments. In her nine years of higher education and ten years as a researcher, surely she'd heard them all—from the self-righteous and the self-aggrandizing to the thoughtful and the noble. She appreciated their persuasiveness, particularly the one that saw vivisection as Darwinism in action. To Clare it was simply a class struggle and her sympathies were fully with the oppressed. But by the time she'd formed this opinion, she'd learned what outspokenness could do to a GPA; a tenure request; a lunch in the faculty dining room.

The look in the eyes of those hallway animals.

Clare made herself stop picturing them. What about this deranged surfer anyway? A rejected graduate applicant run amok? An advocate of—

"Uh?" Steve had replaced the bulb and needed further instructions.

"Let's continue." She pushed all else from her mind. Research would now resume into hemispheric organization and lateralization, pre- and post-commissurotomy, on subject Tom Q, as Tommy was known in Clare's published research.

Tommy was seven when he suffered his first epileptic seizure. An electrical storm raged through his head, knocking him unconscious and hurtling him across the floor. The older he got, the worse the seizures became, despite modern medicine's best efforts to block the attacks. A year ago, the seizures were deemed life-threatening. A host of specialists recommended the last resort: brain surgery. Since Tommy didn't want to die at twenty-seven, even though there <u>was</u> a precedent for it among rock musicians, he agreed to have a commissurotomy, with the hope that after it was performed, his epileptical storms could not travel as far, nor wreak as much damage.

For a few patients, the surgery quells the epilepsy entirely. Which leaves these individuals quite lucky, if they haven't also incurred brain damage during the risky operation. So far Tommy seemed to have become one of the lucky ones.

The human brain, like that of many other animals, in part consists of near identical-looking halves, the left and right cerebral hemispheres. Each has primary domain over half the body. Connecting the hemispheres is a thick bridge of nerve fibers, the corpus callosum, or central commissure. Via this bridge, the two halves of the brain communicate, sharing what its half of the body is sensing about the world, avoiding duplicate or contradictory responses. Without such communication, the experiences and memories of each half of the brain could diverge, creating wholly separate consciousnesses in the same head.

Commissurotomy severs this bridge, terminates those communications. Yet on a day-to-day basis, split brain patients function very well. Their brain hemispheres adapt, find new ways of learning what the other half is doing.

In labs like Clare's, however, split brains were temporarily robbed of their adapting abilities and experiments were conducted suggesting how very different each brain hemisphere is. So different, that she was increasingly convinced that every brain has at least two separate consciousnesses, often in conflict. On bad days, Clare was sure the brain was designed to foster indecision, mixed feelings, confusion.

"Clare?" Tommy's voice was so gentle, he must think she was brooding about the upstairs lab incident she was actually refusing to consider. "I can't see the dot."

"Hold on," Clare replied, "Steve has to dim the lights first. Steve? Steve." Shame that Steve was graduating this quarter. She'd really hate to lose him.

Eventually the lights dimmed. Tommy stared straight ahead, his solemn concentration in conflict with his deliriously messy jet black hair, so blatantly dyed, it was an in joke. She admired the intensity with which he could focus his attention as he stared at the fixation point.

Even after commissurotomy, the eyes and ears of split brain patients still transmit information to both brain halves, as occurs in "normals." However, sensory inputs can be isolated so that only one side of the split brain receives them. Today, Tommy would stare at a fixed point in the middle of a screen, where a projector called a tachistoscope would flash an image for about 1/100th of a second, far from that visual midpoint, so that it registered in only half his field of vision, and thus was visible to only one side of his brain. In this way, Clare could test each hemisphere on what it had seen and on how it could articulate that information.

The experiment itself probably wouldn't tell her anything new about brain organization. But studying Tommy's brain over time, from the month before his operation until some years after it, would show her what changes, if any, occurred in the way Tommy's brain processed "reality," now that the hemispheres were split and his epilepsy calmed. This might tell her something about the brain's ability to revise and ad lib the way it does business. And that might be quite interesting information to have.

Two pictures flashed on the screen. Tommy's left hemisphere was shown a cow. Tommy's right hemisphere saw a winter scene with snow-covered home and trees, kids on a sleigh, a snowman in the yard. "Did you get that, Tommy?"

"Roger."

"Now I'm going to show you more pictures. These will stay on the screen as long as you need to study them. Steve? Okay Steve. Steve."

Eventually four drawings appeared, shown to both sides of Tommy's brain: a carton of milk, a tricycle, a rose bush, a snow plow. Clare placed a pointer in Tommy's left hand, the hand controlled by his right hemisphere. He held onto her fingers until she cleared her throat in warning.

"Looking at these four drawings," Clare said, "tell me which of them, if any, are related to the flash images you just saw."

"The carton of milk is related since I saw a cow."

"Anything else?"

"Nope," Tommy said, while his left hand raised the pointer to the snow plow.

"Why did you point to the snow plow?" Clare asked innocently.

Tommy's right hand snapped fingers nervously, drummed the table, then quieted. "You ever walk through a cow field? It wouldn't hurt to have a snow plow moving ahead of you."

"Of course, I didn't think about that." She ignored Steve's chuckling. Tommy's expression was bland, although his left eyebrow lowered in frown mode.

"Let's move on. Next one, Steve."

Amazingly, a flash of images occurred as soon as she requested. This time, a blank screen flashed to Tommy's left hemisphere and a picture of a gun flashed to Tommy's right hemisphere. "What did you see?" Clare asked.

"Nada."

"Here are four drawings to peruse at your leisure." A horse, a banana, a car, a gun. "Do any of these match the picture you saw a moment ago?"

"I didn't see anything," Tommy insisted, as his left hand pointed to the gun.

"You're pointing to the gun. Does that mean you saw a gun?"

"No, I'm pointing at it because I wanna know, who draws these things anyway?" The left side of Tommy's face, controlled by his right brain, grimaced while he spoke. Clare had seen this effect in split brain patients before: half the face frowning to indicate that half the brain was mistaken. It never ceased to amaze.

"What if I drew that picture, imagine how hurt I'd be, Tommy."

"Imagine how I'd have to make it up to you."

She could feel Steve's attention. "Now with this next one, I want you to follow the instructions you see on the screen."

"Could be dangerous," Tommy grinned.

"Please fixate on the point, Tommy."

Once again, a blank screen was shown to Tommy's left hemisphere. Flashed to the right side of Tommy's brain were the words GET A JOB and an evocative sketch of a young man in a suit and tie being shown to a work cubicle.

Tommy grunted. His left hand covered his eyes.

"What's wrong, what did you see?"

"Nothing. I just felt sick all of a sudden. I don't know why. C'mon, this is boring, flash me a pic this time for a change."

"Next, Steve." Exactly the same images flashed, this time reversed. The GET A JOB scene went to Tommy's left hemisphere, the blank screen to Tommy's right.

Tommy emitted a similar grunt, followed by "Get a *job?* Forget it, you don't pay me enough to follow those instructions."

"So what did you see?"

"Some poor sap in a suit taking a gig so he could grovel for coins."

Tommy's aversion to gainful employment might be unique, but otherwise his reactions had been foreshadowed by numerous other split brain experimentees.

Like 95% of all right handers, the left side of Tommy's brain was dominant for language. That is, it controlled speaking, comprehension of speech, reading and writing. The right side of Tommy's brain had other specialties.

Each time Clare asked Tommy what he had seen during the flashes of images, the left hemisphere was the only brain half that could speak. Tommy's language centers were aware only of what his left hemisphere saw. Those images and no others. And that hemisphere insisted that what it had perceived was all that could be perceived.

However, Tommy's right brain had also been a participant. And although, since the commissurotomy, it couldn't communicate directly with the left hemisphere, nor get access to Tommy's speech centers, it still controlled half his body. So when Tommy's left hemisphere claimed he had seen only a cow, and chose a carton of milk as the related image, Tommy's right hemisphere used its hand, his left hand, to point to a snow plow, because the right hemisphere had seen a snow scene.

Like other tested left hemispheres, Tommy's had trouble admitting it didn't know all the answers; had a lot of trouble with the possibility that something might be occurring that it didn't understand; and would always, ardently insist that its world view made sense.

When Tommy's languaged left hemisphere was uninformed, it bluffed, guessed, and outright lied to give the appearance it was still on top of the situation. Tommy's left hand pointed to a snow plow—aaah, to shovel the cow shit, the left brain claimed. Its desire for order and understanding is that strong, some neuroscientists posited. Its need for control is that powerful, others speculated.

When Tommy's left hemisphere saw nothing, Tommy's right had seen a gun. And although the right hemisphere couldn't say so, it could certainly indicate this through pointing. Again, the left side used its language and reasoning abilities to manufacture an excuse for Tommy's pointing at the gun. Who draws these pictures anyway? the left hemisphere claimed it wanted to know.

Then, when Tommy first glimpsed the GET A JOB command, it was with his right hemisphere, which had enough language ability to comprehend the scene—and to react. Certainly, the right side had no delay in its visceral reaction to the heinous order; and through means still mysterious to neuroscience, it transmitted its strong emotional reaction. Thus horror and disgust filled both sides of Tommy's head, although his left side couldn't explain its bad feelings until it too saw the horrible picture.

Clare could no longer count the times she'd witnessed this process with split brain patients. Yet it still gave her the chills. What affected her most was the utter conviction when the left side told its tales—confabulating, as it was sometimes called.

Why this occurred, no one knew. Neuroscience wasn't even sure why each brain hemisphere controlled the opposite side of the body. In the process of finding a few meager answers to questions about how the brain works, neuroscientists mostly unearthed even bigger mysteries. They were so far from answers, they were rarely sure which questions they should be asking. The more they found out, the less it turned out they really knew. The bigger their body of knowledge, the smaller it seemed. Neuroscience, the fun house of the western world.

"New test," she informed Tommy. "I've placed a box of objects behind the screen. Reach back here," she guided his left hand, "and tell me what you're touching."

Tommy briefly touched a spoon. "I don't feel anything. There's nothing in the box." In split brain patients, touch sensations went almost solely to one side of the brain.

"Now use your right hand."

Tommy's right hand groped behind the screen. "Here's a hand, here's something feels like a spoon, did you put it in here, is this your hand?"

"Pinch it and see."

"Ow. Hey what's going on!" Tommy yanked both hands back into view, nearly knocking over the screen in the process.

It had been a mean thing to do, in the interest of science or no. With his hands behind the screen, Tommy's "disconnection" was so strong that he really didn't know he was touching one hand with the other. It understandably gave him the creeps. He looked scared. She resisted the urge to touch him. "Can you manage another one?" After a moment Tommy nodded. "Left hand behind the screen again and tell me what you find."

Reluctantly, he put his hand behind the screen. This time, he grabbed a comb. Felt it thoroughly. "There's nothing in here again," he said with annoyance. Then his fingers began flexing the comb's teeth. The noise was unmistakable. "Oh. A comb."

Clare had done the comb test month after month with Tommy. This was the first time his left hand had attempted to cross-cue.

Cross-cuing: when the nonverbal hemisphere relayed clues about its knowledge. In this instance, the right hemisphere had used the unique sound of a comb's teeth to transmit information; there were a vast number of other ways a brain might cross-cue, using both sensory and emotional cues. Some brains became more adept at this over time. Others never displayed the technique at all. Tommy's cross-cuing ability had been late to appear, but recently his right hemisphere did seem to be taking more initiative. Cross-cuing was the bane of the valid split brain research result. One went to great lengths to eliminate it from data. Clare had begun studying it of itself, however. Cross-cuing was too damned interesting to simply eradicate.

"Is that all?" Tommy demanded.

"Let's do one more. What else can you find in the box?"

With his left hand he hefted a pair of scissors. With his left hemisphere he responded, "A pencil."

"Do you know that or are you guessing?"

"It's a pencil. I'm sure of it."

"Pull both hands into view again. Look in your left hand. What are you holding?"

"Scissors. I was touching the point, that's why I thought I had a pencil."

"Sure you weren't guessing?"

"Get stuffed."

Subject as usual displays hostility when left hemisphere is caught confabulating. Interesting note: sometimes Tommy was aware of confabulating, sometimes not.

Bright light poured into the lab, momentarily blinding Clare. The door to her office had been opened. In the doorway loomed a figure in silhouette.

"Who's there?" Clare's voice quavered. She was upset at the intrusion and at her inability to identify the hulking shadow of the intruder.

"It's Cynthia Bates," the intruder replied.

"Mrs. Bates. I'm happy you're feeling better." Cynthia Bates, another of Clare's split brain subjects, had canceled her last five sessions, with last minute messages that she was ill.

"I must speak with you I'm so sorry to interrupt but. Please." In her voice was more than the usual faint trace of English accent—which meant she was agitated.

Not much was being accomplished today: Tommy's session had been a string of interruptions. If only Mrs. Bates had shown up in time to draw Clare away from the incident upstairs. "I'll be back," Clare told Tommy and Steve.

"Want me to keep going with the tests?" Steve asked eagerly.

"No thanks, Steve, I think you've both earned a break." And she'd seen what harm Steve could do to an unsuspecting set of data.

"I am sorry to intrude," Mrs. Bates called over to them.

Tommy grinned at her. "Stop by anytime."

Mrs. Bates smiled. Tommy could make any woman within fifty yards feel better.

Outside, Clare and Cynthia walked in silence, through the old section of campus, where aged Spanish buildings exuded taste and stability. Above doorways, scripted letters were carved in stone, proclaiming each building's intellectual specialty: Geological Sciences, Mathematics, Particle Physics. Clare liked the continuity and incongruity here: twenty-first-century science conducted in nineteenth-century elegance.

I will do great work here. The certainty had surged through her when she first walked onto these grounds. Nearly fifteen years later—long after she'd lost the ability to feel certainty—walking here still gave her a serene sense of purpose. But the tonic had no effect on Cynthia Bates.

"What *is* the matter?" Clare demanded. "You look awful." And that was tactful. Mrs. Bates's eyes were shadowed by more than one sleepless night. She had a broad-shouldered, six-foot frame, usually held at full height with complete assurance. Now she hunkered over like a teenager on a date with a jockey. Her clothes, always so neat and correct, were replaced by a crumpled sweatsuit. Her previously lush, silvering hair today looked like worms had crawled through it.

"I look that bad," Mrs. Bates said tonelessly, then announced, "It hasn't stopped. In fact it's getting worse. I can't control it." She clutched her left wrist with her right hand.

A month after commissurotomy, Cynthia Bates had first experienced an unsettling side effect. Her left and right hands would behave in contradictory ways.

This relatively rare phenomenon was written up frequently in popularized accounts of split brain research. One commissurotomized woman, it was oft reported, buttoned a blouse with one hand while the other hand unbuttoned it. And there was a man whose left hand reached to strike his wife, while his right hand tried to stop him.

While it was merely uncommon for patients to experience this phenomenon, it was quite rare for the condition to persist. With Mrs. Bates it had continued for over a year now. At first she tried to ignore it, joke about it. All her doctors and scientists assured her there was no cause for alarm. But over the last months she seemed increasingly panicked.

"What exactly has happened?" Clare put as much calm into her voice as possible. "Here, let's sit." They were in the Mall, a courtyard filled with precise arrays of roses, scattered magnolias, and occasional students. They settled onto a stone bench.

"This hand's a troublemaker!" Mrs. Bates declared, shaking the captive wrist. She stopped abruptly. "How absurd this is." She freed her wrist. She and Clare watched with trepidation, but the liberated left hand simply flexed and stuffed itself in Cynthia's purse.

Clare couldn't help it. She laughed. Fortunately, Cynthia joined in, then moaned, then explained. Ironing yesterday, while her "good" hand arranged one of her husband's shirts, the "bad" hand used the iron to burn a hole clean through the fabric. Then the bad hand spilled coffee on a client at work. Not spilled, tossed was more like it. And her little ones are always terrified: she'll intend to do one thing, then that hand does another, at which she gets furious and—well, she acts insane and she's starting to wonder if she is. Insane. *Why* did she get the operation, when she'd been perfectly happy with her seizures, too?

"You had the operation so you could live a normal life and not be a prisoner of your seizures. I believe I'm quoting you pretty much exactly."

"But I still have blackouts, little ones anyway. I still can't drive, we still must drill the children on emergency procedures. I've merely lost the good part of the attacks." Her tone had been angry but now conveyed a sense of enormous loss.

Tests done by electroencephalograph (EEG) had revealed that Mrs. Bates's epilepsy began in her right parietal lobe, the upper rear section of her right hemisphere. The electrical disturbance swept across the central commissure to the left temporal lobe, above her left ear. Many epileptics with temporal lobe seizures report mystical experiences. Right before Mrs. Bates blacked out, she would experience sensations of profound calm, a cosmic sense of peace and universal well-being.

Mrs. Bates dragged her fingers through her hair; the skin at her temples stretched taut. "I'm sorry. I know you can't possibly understand. Just more proof I'm bonkers—longing for an epileptic seizure."

"You're in good company there. Dostoevski said he'd rather die than lose his."

"I didn't know that. It must be especially hard, being an epileptic and a dancer."

Clare had no response.

"Do you know that man?"

Clare looked in the direction Mrs. Bates indicated, into the recesses of one stone portico. In the late afternoon sun, the arched pillars cast wide shadows, obscuring the view. Clare saw no one.

"He's gone now. But the way he was watching you. I just wondered if he was someone you knew. What frightening eyes."

Clare looked again but she saw no one. Then a flash of orange caught her eye and she smiled at the approach of a small dark woman in tangerine silk.

"What a lovely surprise," Dr. Lalitha Rao greeted Clare in her soft distinguished voice, a melange of accents chronicling her past: from Bombay to London to Vienna to Los Angeles.

"It's been too long," Clare agreed. She introduced Dr. Rao to

Mrs. Bates. Lalitha extended her hand. Cynthia's eyes flicked over her, then away; she ignored the offer of goodwill.

"Forgive my intrusion." Lalitha met rudeness with warmth, took a step away to indicate she wouldn't interrupt for long. "We must make time to get together, Clare. If not at Thanksgiving, then surely by Christmas."

As Clare nodded and started to reply, Cynthia blurted, "I'm so sorry!" then told Lalitha pleadingly, "My mother hated the Pakis. I heard so much of it as a girl, my first reactions always seem to be hers, not mine."

"Hated the what?" Clare demanded.

"The Pakistanis," Lalitha replied, her dark eyes flashing. "You're absolutely right, Cynthia, such early prejudices are so hard to escape. My own just flared, as I was raised by a family in which both Pakistanis and English were disdained."

Clare, still feeling insulted by proxy, marveled at Lalitha's never-judgmental nature, then worried about Cynthia's mental state, for now she beamed and said giddily, "Thank you for sympathizing and what a beautiful piece that is. Silver and marcasite? And shaped like a parrot? I've never seen anything like it."

Lalitha touched the antique hair clip through which one length of her thick black hair was swept. "It was a gift from a dear friend. I wear it every day." She and Clare exchanged a smile: it had been Clare's birthday gift to Lalitha, last spring. "Now I'll leave you to this glorious afternoon."

Lalitha bid them a brisk, warm farewell, then Clare turned to scrutinize Cynthia, who was intent on hunting a pack of Virginia Slims in the depths of her purse. "It is exceptionally pretty today, isn't it? Pasadena is so lovely, the months when one can see the sky." With one hand, Mrs. Bates planted a cigarette in her mouth. The other hand plucked it out. Her mood disintegrated. "Somebody put a demon in my head."

"Let's not get medieval," Clare warned, forcing herself to forgive her patient's treatment of her friend. "You know, it could be that your hand is just trying to help. And we really ought to stop talking like it's got a will of its own. It may be the operation caused a bit of motor control damage to your right hemisphere. It could even be that your "bad" hand used to do the tasks it's now trying to do, but once received more instruction than it's getting now. None of these possibilities is dangerous."

"But I imagined hurting—my children, my darlings. I'd never done that before. What if—"

"You can't blame your life on your seizures, Cynthia. Nor on the operation that reduced them."

"You're right. Maybe things aren't entirely happy at home. My medical problems have been such an intrusion, it's hard to know what's what." She waved her hands. "I so wish I had a quorum here. Thank you for being so patient with me. And please thank your friend, also."

"I will. And I'll see you tomorrow at nine?"

"No. I won't be back." Before Clare could respond, Cynthia continued in a well-rehearsed rush. "I must stop reminding myself that I'm a freak. I've got to stop thinking about my head. This seems the only way I can be—normal. I hope I'm not causing your experiments too much trouble."

It would wreck nineteen months of work. But the woman radiated pain. And fear. "We should both think about this more," Clare said evenly. She needed time to decide just how much she would push Mrs. Bates to continue. And whether she should also pressure her to get counseling.

They parted company at the entrance to Neurobiology. As soon as Clare stepped inside the building, her eyes stung and teared, her vision blurred; the air reeked of the chemicals spilled on the ravaged third floor. As she ascended the stairs to her floor, she heard a shuffling walk behind her. She paused, the shuffling paused. She continued, the shuffling resumed. Topping the stairs and rounding the stairwell corner, Clare stopped and turned to look behind her. The lights strobed when she blinked. A form loomed in front of her. She stepped back; it kept coming right at her.

Throwing an arm out for protection, she connected with something that rattled. Now, she saw the man, bespectacled and surprised.

"I do apologize," the man said, stepping around her. "I'm a little absorbed." He continued on his way, reading a sheaf of papers as he shuffled along.

When Clare reached her office, her heart was still beating hard and she felt like a fool. On her carpet were brown caked footprints. Clare fit her shoe into one of them. Great. She'd tracked blood in from the third floor. She entered her testing room, to find Tommy cracking up and Steve turning red. "What's so funny?"

"Steve just told me a scientific joke." Tommy explained between laughs, "about the four F's of animal behavior. Feeding, fighting, fleeing, and reproduction."

That old thing. But Clare had to laugh too. Tommy's laugh was infectious, the Ho! Ho!s of a hysterical Santa. Steve skulked out to the bathroom down the hall. "I'm ready for more scintillating experimenting," Tommy declared.

"I detect a note of sarcasm."

"Sometimes I'd like some material that was a little more demanding. It's always 'See Dick run, jump Spot jump' kind of stuff."

"I don't think you appreciate the enormity of what happens when you read 'See Dick run.' How do you know those words? What about 'See Dick run into the sea'? Does that confuse you? Why not? When you were a baby saying 'Da da'—"

"No way, I hated my old man."

"Whatever you were saying," Clare continued firmly, "the greatest scientific minds on the planet can't explain exactly how you did it. It takes millions of neurons firing, impulses we can hardly measure, with chemicals we can barely name. You just shifted in your seat. The chair scraped the floor, it was loud, you ignored it. Some time in the past your brain learned that noise, learned not to care about it. You heard it now 'unconsciously'— it didn't register in your attention. But your brain is still on top of the situation in case you decide to care later. How does that habituation occur? Where is the memory that says this scraped chair noise can be ignored? Some people have searched their whole lives for where your memories are stored. Can't find a single damned one. And did you know that you have areas of your brain deep in here," she touched the side of his head, "that make plans to react, before this part of your brain," she touched his temple, "even decides it wants to react? Meanwhile, other parts back here," she reached around to the nape of his neck, "are taking care of your breathing, heartbeat, minor details like that. Do you realize how incredible all that is?"

"Yeah I realize," Tommy replied. She was only inches from him. He moved no closer but she felt enveloped, then surrounded. The warmth of his skin, the desire to—

She pulled away fast as in burned. His smile was half mocking, half regretful. "Good reflexes," he said.

"What time is your wife coming?" she replied.

"Said she'd pick me up about five. What time is it?"

"About that time."

"Clare—"

"Don't." She cut off his sigh with, "I'll see you out." For reasons better left unperused, she didn't like Tommy's wife coming into her lab. But Clare couldn't get Tommy to leave unless she lured him away.

She left her alleged assistant a note. *Steve, go ahead and wrap up.* Then she and Tommy walked down the arched hallway, a bit too close together, so that they bumped randömly into each other as they progressed.

Someone appeared at the far end of the hall and they moved imperceptibly farther apart. The toxic air had mostly cleared; Clare watched the approach of a tall muscular man wearing two-hundred-dollar running shoes. "Hey Andy," Tommy greeted him.

"Great to see you two again," Andy Stuart replied; and somehow made the line sound sincere.

"Hello, Andy, it's good to see you too." Clare mostly meant this. After all, she'd heard he had a new job. But previously, Andy had worked for the extremely solvent Tekassist, the company that provided the campus labs with research animals, transported them, and could also be hired to feed and water them.

Yet somehow, Andy had always been likable. She could even tolerate his fitness fetish, since he'd confided that okay he'd gone overboard but he'd been such a lumpy weak kid. Clare had met other Tekassist people. They were not likable. But Andy even showed concern for the critters he delivered. Perhaps that was why he'd quit.

"How do you know him?" she asked Tommy, once Andy was past them.

"He's a supervisor at Bianca's gym. I think they might be fooling around."

Clare had no valid reason for being so happy to hear this, so refused to acknowledge it. "You mean Betsi with an *i*, don't you?"

"Give her a break." Tommy's reply was sharp.

"I just never met anyone who changed her name every six months, that's all," Clare backpedaled.

"Me neither." Tommy displayed amusement and appreciation.

Clare began counting the terra cotta tile stairs to the first floor. Someone had cleaned up the blood in the stairwell.

"When Bianca goes through changes, if her name doesn't fit anymore, she changes it too."

"Whatever works." Clare looked up. An undergrad passed them on a landing. Even in Tommy's quick glance was enough content to make the girl look away, then lean over the iron banister to appraise him as he continued downstairs.

"Sorry I got on your case," he told Clare. "What happens is, it jazzes me to make you jealous of Bianca, which makes me pissed at myself so I get pissed at you and all of a sudden I'm protecting my wife because around you I want to forget I've got one."

Around me or any other female. "You seem to be doing a pretty good job of forgetting. I'm the one having problems with it."

"I love a woman who goes for the jugular." Tommy clutched his and stumbled down the remaining stairs. Two astrophysicists, exiting a lounge on the ground floor, looked alarmed, then stared at Clare.

"You imbecile," Clare hissed. How she could possibly be attracted to someone so idiotic. So juvenile. The really annoying thing: he was funny too. "I'm going back. See you next time," she called down.

"Clare. Wait." He loped back up the stairs.

"Hi Tommy, am I late?" Betsi—er Bianca—appeared on the floor below. "Hi, um," she greeted Clare. For someone who had to learn so many new names, she sure had problems recalling Clare's.

Clare was drawn to stay, to study the couple's greeting: finding signs of imminent separation in that brisk peck of cheek; losing all hope when Bianca tousled Tommy's hair in that intimate way. Was Bianca having an affair, or did Tommy just want Clare to think so? Tommy insisted he and Bianca were more like siblings than lovers. But wasn't Clare more the sibling type than Bianca?

In some magazine makeover, Clare would be the before to Bianca's after. Clare's hair straddled brown and blond, and was cut blunt and practical to minimize upkeep. Bianca's roots were the same color but the rest was bleached white, unkempt yet ultra chic and probably requiring hours of daily maintenance.

Clare's eyes were sometimes brown, sometimes green. Bianca's were an unforgettable jade that could only be contacts and were a real argument for artifice. Clare swam the absolute minimum laps to remain healthy and mobile as she aged. Bianca taught aerobics and was the model in print ads for a swank new fitness center, Le Gym.

Bianca had announced her current job by saying, 'I'm so glad Tommy had that brain operation. Otherwise he wouldn't've been here getting tested at the school and I wouldn't have seen the ad on that bulletin board downstairs for Fitness Instructors Wanted.' She now said, "How'd the experimenting go today I think I'm getting a shin splint I hope I don't have to miss work."

Tommy had once told Clare that Bianca, then known as Betsi, was in awe of Clare's intelligence. Bianca would quiz Tommy for hours about their lab work; she'd go on and on about how cool Clare was. Bianca was purportedly tongue-tied in person, because she felt so stupid by comparison. Clare wasn't sure she believed this. But, awfully enough, Bianca did seem to like Clare.

"Are you coming to Tommy's gig tonight, he really wanted you to come." Which made Clare feel like Tommy's favorite third-grade teacher. "He talks about you all the time, the work you do here, he really admires you."

Fleetingly, Bianca's eyes said she knew something was happening between her husband and his scientist and it scared her. Then the moment was gone. Clare shrugged it off. Tommy didn't really treat Clare any differently than he did other women; and Bianca wasn't the type to see Clare as competition.

"I forgot he—ah, you," Clare risked a glance at Tommy, her first since Bianca had joined them, "were playing tonight. I'm not sure I'll be able to make it."

"There'll always be another night." Tommy put an arm around his wife and as he led her away, looked back to Clare. "You'll still be on the list. Plus one, right?"

"Oh wow I almost forgot," Bianca cut off Clare's reply. "I'm real sorry about your friend that got offed."

"What are you talking about?"

"I heard some people discussing it outside. God I thought you knew. I didn't want to be the one."

"Bianca," Tommy said, "you'll get your Oscar, okay? Cut the crap and tell her what's going on."

"It was a Dr. . . . Haffer? . . ."

"There's a Dr. Haffner, but I barely know him."

"Oh—I figured, since you're in the same department."

All us scientists look alike. "He died?"

"He was mur-r-r-dered, in his house. His wife got home from work and found him. They say his head was split open like somebody ran over a watermelon, his brains were all over the place and the fireplace poker was still—"

"Thanks for sharing those details with us." Tommy stopped her.

"But why would anyone kill him?" Clare remembered Haffner as a mild shy man who got embarrassed when nodding hello in passing.

"It was a daytime burglary. He came home while it was happening and they got him."

"They? There are suspects in custody?"

"No. Nobody. I dunno why they think there was more than one."

"Maybe it was the same guy as upstairs," Tommy said.

"There was a murder upstairs? *Here?*"

"No it was—" Tommy looked at Clare. "It's a long story, I'll tell you later."

"It was definitely a burglary?" Clare demanded.

"Yeah the TV was gone and some stereo stuff but not all of it, that's why they think he interrupted a crime in progress."

Clare was holding her breath. She exhaled. After a long moment's silence, Tommy gestured good-bye and once again led Bianca away.

"Glad you didn't really know him," Bianca called back cheerily.

"Right." Clare took the long way back to her office. The building's hallway was a rectangular loop connecting offices along four corridors. On the exterior side of the hall were windowed offices occupied by secretaries and assistants. On the interior were the windowless research offices with adjoining labs. Clare's office was in the southwest sector of the building, but now she walked northeast.

When Clare was faced with events too big or awful to immediately confront, walking gave her time to prepare. The third-floor hell, what to do about Mrs. Bates, what to do with Tommy, the must-have-been-dreadful demise and discovery of Dr. Haffner: Clare would have to walk to Mexico to put all this in perspective, but strolling the halls was a start.

Usually, Clare renewed inspiration with this particular walk. She never ceased to enjoy the beauty of the building; the patterned tile alcoves, the vaulted ceilings, the wrought iron fixtures. Plus, the sense of intellectual activity all around would invigorate her. But tonight she was aware only that the building was silent, seemingly deserted, its occupants having either left for the day or taken a dinner break. Briefly, Clare felt spooked to be alone.

No, there were undoubtedly researchers behind some of these oak doors, immersed in their findings, sitting in rooms black save for a pool of desk light and the weak underdoor light from the corridor—a seepage always brighter with daylight. Clare remembered many times, fighting some inexplicable set of data, she'd look up to rub her eyes and know it was dawn because she could see beyond her desk.

Somewhere nearby there was a faint scraping of metal against metal, then a thunk like a bat hitting a metal ball. Clare stopped. Had the sounds been ahead or behind her? They were noises she'd never heard in this building. She resumed walking.

She rounded a corner. The new corridor was just as empty but less bright. A light was burned out down the hall, past Dr. Colton's office. Colton. Though his name conjured very mixed emotions, with a slight smile she recalled sitting on his ancient green couch, watching him scowl and grunt as he read her papers and proposals. He'd insisted on reading while she waited, the more freshly to attack her, she supposed. But the rare, brusque "good work" from Dr. Colton was worth more than the wall full of plaques/certificates/awards she'd earned elsewhere in her academic career. It still hurt to recall the long period when he'd stopped speaking to her. They'd achieved détente in the years since, but sometimes his strained politeness felt worst of all.

An unexpected chill hit her right side. KEEP DOOR SHUT DOOR LOCKS AUTOMATICALLY WHEN CLOSED. Inside a shallow alcove, an emergency exit door was propped open with a metal strut. Didn't that door just lead to a fire escape? Why would anyone be out there at night?

By the time she might reach a phone to call campus security, whoever was out there might have escaped. Or caught up with her. If it wasn't just somebody admiring the view of the night sky. Did she want to find out for sure? She could open the door, see who answered when she called.

That was how certain players in horror movies acted. The ones with the bit parts.

What she could do. Tiptoe over there. Push the door open just enough to kick the strut out. Slam the door shut and thus locked. If Whoever was out there legitimately or innocently, she'd hear a "Hey! Let me in." If not, the intruder would be stuck and would have to jump to the ground. No doubt thinking very dark thoughts of Clare. But Whoever wouldn't know she had done the locking out. Right?

She heard a scuffling of shoe against metal outside. Heading inside.

Quickly, Clare crossed the corridor, kicked the strut, slammed the door. She felt pressure from the other side, briefly, as if someone tried to hold the door open, then let go. She waited a moment, hoping for a pounding on the door. She heard a creak, as if the someone outside had shifted weight. The someone was waiting. She waited too, some ninety seconds that felt like all night. Her heart thumped in her ears, so loudly she wasn't sure she could hear another creak. Eventually she felt the emptiness of the corridor at her back, stepped soundlessly away from the fire door, and retreated at a healthy pace. She'd call the campus police from her office.

Ten steps down the corridor, a latch turned and a door opened. Still in fight-or-flight mode, she jumped measurably. "Dr. Colton. You startled me."

"Oh hello Clare. Going home? I'll walk out with you."

"I should use your phone. There's someone out on the fire escape."

Dr. Colton paused in his efforts to deadbolt his door. He moved in a permanent stoop, attacking the world from the same position in which he vanquished his experiments. "On the fire escape? For what purpose?" He sounded impatient.

"Well—lurking, I think."

Colton studied her a moment, then strode to the door and shoved it open, threw his head outside and looked left right up down. "Nobody there," he said. "Are you alright?" His head tilted sideways to free the boyish shock of white hair from his eye, the better to regard her suspiciously, just as he had during the bad times post-mentorship, pre-détente.

Reduced to adolescence by his patronization, Clare rolled her eyes. She wanted to tell him about the man on the third floor, but the lab animals in the hall weren't a scene she wished to describe to Colton. She ghoulishly considered hitting him with Dr. Haffner's murder—but it had no relevance. Anyway, any attempt to justify herself would only make her appear more of a hysteric to Colton. And so she said nothing.

They backtracked down the corridor and had just passed his office door when they found themselves walking on glass. Clare looked up. The darkened light was not burned out as she'd previously thought. The opalescent fixture and the bulb were shattered into minute pieces that scraped like pinheads underfoot. Likewise the next fixture, forty feet down the corridor.

"Perhaps your lurker is a vandal too," Colton said. This could be his apology for thinking she'd imagined the presence on the fire escape; or it could be sarcasm.

Clare switched to an easier subject. "I hear the Nobel committee has turned serious attention to you. I'd say it was about time. Long overdue, in fact."

Colton exhaled sharply. "Prize is hardly worth much any more, not since they gave it to Smith, Härdel and that bunch." Competition had always cramped Clare's style; Colton thrived on it. He was driven to do more for neuroscience than Einstein had done for physics. And appreciation by his peers—colleagues, rather, he didn't see many equals—meant almost as much to him as making landmark discoveries.

"What are you working on?" She'd read the annual Biology report, where researchers sketched the parameters of their next year's work; but everyone knew how secretive Colton was and expected his sketch to be inaccurate and evasive. She didn't expect a real answer now. Still, it was standard procedure to inquire.

"New direction. Most important yet. Perhaps you'd like to see the new setup."

"I'd—like that. Very much." Clare was stunned. Even his archest rivals, Smith in Chicago and Härdel in France, would have coveted such an invitation.

". . . down to see the setup and he said he was speechless," Colton was saying with great pride. "Everything I've done has been merely preliminary compared—"

"Wait a minute. Did you say you were with Dr. Haffner today?"

"Yes, but only to give him a taste of the unattainable." Colton chuckled. "He's not completely stupid, Clare. It's wrong to snub him simply because his work is derivative."

"I'm not accusing you of slumming, sir."

He blinked. Then she told him about the burglary/murder, and he sniffed, as though this proved Haffner was incompetent. "Must have happened when I dropped him off. Hmmph."

"You'd better call the police. Perhaps you saw something that—"

He waved her off dismissively. "I saw nothing. Haven't got the time for pointless police questions."

Could anyone ever convince Stanford Colton he might be mistaken? They reached Clare's office. Steve was gone, after straightening, darkening, and locking the lab—but leaving the tachistoscope on, flashing 100-millisecond bursts of light. Another lighting element would meet an early death. Only 23 working days to Steve's winter quarter graduation.

Clare collected papers for work at home, if she didn't go to see Tommy play. Dr. Colton used her phone to call Security about the smashed light fixtures outside his office that needed repair right away; and oh, yes, the fire escape door may have been left open.

As they headed to their cars, Clare tried again. "Because there was a burglary in progress, you may have seen a car that didn't belong in the neighborhood, or—"

"Neighbors would know that better than I. What are you working on?"

Compared to Colton, mules were eager to please. To avoid a pointless battle, she sketched her current experiments.

When she mentioned Cynthia Bates, Colton interrupted. "Bates, she's that striking woman with the sad eyes?" Clare was surprised he remembered Cynthia Bates. As a neurosurgeon, Colton had performed the commissurotomy; but as an elitist, he rarely recalled his patients. "Bilateral for language, isn't she?"

They'd reached Clare's '86 Nova. She tossed her briefcase on the seat, leaned on the open door frame. Yes, tests showed that for Cynthia Bates language production and comprehension centers were not solely in the left hemisphere. (Hmm, perhaps this relatively rare patterning was related to her "troublemaker" hand.) With another subject, Dabrowski, left-lateralized for language, there was interesting evidence of reorganization. If only he would stop analyzing process. His expectations about the purpose of each experiment stood in danger of—

"Bates came looking for me today," Colton interrupted musingly. "And yesterday. Know what that could be about?"

Clare got in her car, rolled down the window, meanwhile giving a rundown of Cynthia's acute disconnection syndrome and the woman's reaction to it.

"Suppose I'll have to take some time to talk to her." Colton's tone said: waste some time to talk. But she'd caught him grimacing with sympathy during her description of Cynthia Bates's fear. Still, he'd never admit to a good deed. "So Dabrowski wants to conduct his own research? Get rid of him. Get some cats. Work like yours, human subjects aren't worth the variations."

What an impossible man. "Good night, Dr. Colton."

"Yes." And he was gone, intersecting with three exiting scientists as they all headed for their cars. The others greeted Colton respectfully; warily.

Clare's keys were in her pocket. Which meant she had to undo her shoulder harness, fish out her keys, redo the seat belt, hunt the ignition key. By the time she was ready to start her car, Colton was driving out of the lot.

In the acerbic November night air, she heard another engine start. Across the street, a car without lights pulled away from the curb and made a U-turn across a cement divider, turning on its lights once the maneuver was completed. It now headed in the same direction Colton had taken. The car was noticeable only for being so nondescript. Few cars in LA had so few distinguishing features. Colton drove through a yellow light. Car X accelerated to do the same. Then both cars were lost from view.

It would be of no use to try to warn Colton that someone might be following him. Following Colton. What the hell was going on? Could—

Suddenly Clare was thrown sideways, so violently her shoulder harness snapped tight, yanking her upright. From outside labored breathing filled her ears. Fingers groped for her throat. Futilely, she pulled at the hands, feeling thick calluses on the fingers. She grabbed her briefcase, slammed it out the window, connecting with her attacker's face. His grip slackened; he took a stumbling step away.

Straw blond hair and mustache, both in need of trimming. Blood poured from his gaping mouth; it looked like she'd knocked out a couple teeth, too.

After reeling back, he took a step toward her. For an instant she looked into eyes like black holes. Time expanded and it was hours before she got her car started and gunned into gear. She released her parking brake and lurched out of the lot and onto the street.

Most terrifying of all was his utter silence, even when her briefcase smashed his face.

Clare was relieved when she started shaking; it released some of the pressure inside her. Thank God she had her car today; although she certainly wasn't going grocery shopping now. *Why was she thinking about this she must be in shock.*

It was all she could do to drive: observing the street and traffic patterns required more concentration than she could muster. She should pull over but the prospect of stopping made it hard to breathe.

Her route home took her in the same direction Colton had gone. Two blocks away, she spotted Car X parked, the tip of the driver's nose illuminated while studying paper in map light. Tourist X, lost by moonlight. If only she'd melodramatized her attack, too.

Surely her attacker had also been the one to destroy the animal labs. What had they called him? The deranged surfer. She recalled those deep dead eyes and had trouble finding the road once again. Fortunately, she only had a few blocks to drive.

Car X had pulled back into traffic, behind her. She made a sharp right turn. Car X continued along the boulevard. Clare did not feel relieved. Once before she had been sure everyone was out to get her. It had heralded the most terrible time of her life.

Left at the next block and she was home. She parked questionably and ran across San Pasqual Avenue, some part of her calming at the first view of her apartment complex, the Villa San Pasqual. She sprinted past peach stucco apartments, mint green scrolled metal railings edging the exterior stairs and balconies.

Striding briskly up the stairs to her apartment, Clare heard a familiar faint jingling. She turned to greet Jessie, a tortoiseshell cat with collar ID jingling. Clare, who had lived with Jessie for seven years, knew the cat didn't like to be held while outside; but tonight would have to be an exception. Clare plucked her up and continued toward the apartment. Jessie purred but held herself stiffly.

Clare dared a glance out to the street. Car X cruised slowly down San Pasqual. Clare stepped from floodlight into shadow, fumbling for her house key, straining to make out Car X's license number. She was too far away, but thought she discerned an odd bright background color—an out of state plate? A Pasadena squad car came up the street. Driver X flagged the policeman, conversed a moment, then turned around and drove off. False alarm, then. No villain would make special effort to attract police attention. Clare was convinced of this by the time she and Jessie were inside with the lock turned behind them.

CHAPTER 2

Inhibition

The lights were on inside her apartment. It must mean that—
"Robert is I mean you're home early," Clare greeted Robert as he exited the kitchen, toweling his hands. They smooched hello.
"I decided it was time I fixed you dinner."
"Decisiveness. I like that in a man." Clutching Jessie, she inspected the pot on the stove. Jessie leaped away as though in mortal danger. Vegetable stew. In a bowl nearby was the sauce, so spicy that Clare's eyes stung after sniffing at it. "Dangerous. Is it the cashew hot sauce you invented last spring?"
"It may be similar." Robert was a theoretical physicist. On campus, he was the most precise human being. In the kitchen, he could never duplicate a creation because it didn't occur to him to note ingredients. In both arenas, he came up with astounding things never before imagined. "What?" he demanded as she stared at him.
"You," she replied, smiling and shaking her head at the

Brooks Brothers collar under the CAUTION! CHEF AT WORK! apron. Both were swap meet finds.

He tugged his wire rims, a gesture he used when pleased or nervous. "Clare . . ."

"I need to make some phone calls." Clare backed into the living room. Robert came to the doorway to listen, as she tried to deal with the afternoon's events.

First she called the campus police. By the time she explained different pieces of why she was phoning to umpteen answerers in a quest to reach those directly in charge, Robert had heard about her attacker and his similarity to the man who had destroyed the third-floor animal research labs; the presence on the fire escape; the shattered second-floor hallway lights; and the man who may have been watching her while she talked with Mrs. Bates.

Then she called the city police and Robert learned about Dr. Haffner's murder and Colton's possibly being the last to see him alive, but not wanting to waste time conferring with the authorities.

The campus police were glad she had called. The Pasadena police were not: Lieutenant Beaudine, the man in charge of the Haffner investigation, was out and no one there understood why she was calling.

When she got off the phone she walked toward Robert in the kitchen doorway. "And how was *your* day, dear?" she tried to joke.

Instead of speaking, he held her. She clung to him, so tightly. His slow steady heartbeat resonated inside her. "You weren't hurt?" She shook her head and, to her disgust, started to cry. Unlike most men she had met, Robert was not rattled by this. "Were the lab animals—injured?" he inquired next. She shrugged. "Not anymore than usual," he translated for her. "I'm sure there's some motive for this man's actions and they'll catch him soon. In the meantime, you'll just have to be careful. Although it doesn't sound like he's out for you personally."

Robert's particular brand of reasonableness could ease any crisis. Clare remembered the time Robert had talked a very hostile fellow out of taking their wallets. She smiled. Robert sighed. He still had his arms around her but was no longer holding her. "Why didn't you tell me all this when you first came in, instead of making small talk and phone calls to strangers?"

Clare stepped away, walked into the kitchen, Robert following at an awkward distance, every move so self-conscious, they could be onstage in an amateur domestic drama. "I wanted to pretend life was normal for a minute, I guess," she told him, unsure whether this was the truth. When he said nothing, she turned to face him. Confrontation ahead. All she really wanted was for him to hold her again. Instead he stirred the stew. She thought back. Had they fought this morning? She couldn't recall.

"I know I've been immersed in my work lately," Robert said with his back to her. "Out of commission, as you've so aptly put it." Initially, part of their attraction had been of the So I'm Not a Freak After All variety. Both were devoted to, obsessed with, their research, but unwilling to let that consume their lives. However, Clare proved better able to juggle than Robert was. Or less able to maintain her drive. Friction intermittently ensued, beginning as skirmishes, lately turning holocaustal. If only he could see that none of this mattered right now. "I can't promise it won't happen again. But look, I'm busting myself now. That's an improvement, isn't it? I'm trying to change, I swear I'm trying."

"I know you are." What else should she say? Oh have you been ignoring me again? I didn't notice; I'm too preoccupied with this married unemployed rock musician ten years my junior. Anyway, the work vs. love ethic wasn't their only source of problems. Not that Clare could name the other sources. Nor explain how things could be as good as they ever were, one moment, and then . . . Was this phenomenon attributable to death throes? Growing pains? Temporary technical difficulties?

Ultimately she blamed herself. She kept hoping she was going through a phase. Looking at Robert, she saw a catalog of all that was good and true. But she felt nothing. She thought she remembered a time when she did feel toward him, but more and more she suspected this was a false memory.

"Dinner," Robert decreed. "You'd better set the table. Or. We could eat in bed."

They'd first lived together in a one-room "bachelor." The bed adjoined the toaster oven and a ritual developed of fixing meals while undressing one another; feeding while pleasing each other. When they moved to their current one-bedroom-plus-dining-alcove, they felt separated until they started dining between the sheets again. Gradually they acclimatized and now ate at the table, except for special or restorative occasions.

At one time, he wouldn't have had to ask; certainly, this hesitancy in his voice was new. Had she done this to him? Not a subject she could peruse at this time.

"We'd better stick to the table, aren't we going out afterwards? Remember, one of my patients is performing tonight. You did say you wanted to go."

"Oh sure the musician. Well sure. If you want. I thought we'd stay home, I can't remember the last night we were both home without work or guests."

Clare bristled. "Who said I don't have work?"

"Then why are you going out?"

She opened the silverware drawer with such force, the utensils slid to the back out of view. "I thought you wanted to go too."

"I do unless you'd rather go alone."

She felt as transparent as a slug's trail. "We don't have to go at all."

"I'd rather stay home and talk some—"

"I am _talked out_." She spat the words. "We discuss _endlessly_ but—"

"I meant that you should talk about what happened to you today."

"I'm not ready for that now. Maybe when we get home."

"No. Then you'll be too tired, then you'll have been thinking about it so much you need a breather, then it'll be last week's news, why am I dredging it up now."

"You're in a terrific mood for comfort and soul-searching."

"We'd better eat or we'll miss the show." He spooned stew into her bowl. "Tell me when."

"Stop," she said.

During their meal, they discussed their research and they reparteed with Jessie, who was always talkative when they ate though it was never clear why.

Toward the end of the meal, the phone rang. When Clare answered, she thought she could hear breathing on the other end, but no matter how many times she said hello, there was no response.

Robert took the phone. "Who is this?" He replaced the receiver. "They hung up."

"I could have handled it myself, thank you."

"Oh for christ's sake."

They were excessively polite as they cleaned the kitchen and dressed. This got them running late. Then the Pasadena Freeway was blocked by an accident.

It was the first freeway ever built. Quaint to contemplate, dangerous to drive. The off ramps and on ramps could be as brief as fifty feet, with stop signs. One floored the accelerator to merge; one floored the brakes to exit. Apparently a recent driver or vehicle had not met the challenge. The result was a three-car collision—nothing serious, but traffic was slow before the accident and skittish after it.

For the next several miles, Caltrans had the left lane closed, performing inscrutable repairs. Caltrans was always working on the highways, yet they never got much better. Perhaps the state transportation agency's real purpose was to slow traffic. This it accomplished brilliantly. Tonight, Clare and Robert were stuck in first gear all the way to the Hollywood Freeway.

At last they could pick up speed—and squabble about which

exit to take. Robert was right but Clare was driving. (She always drove out; Robert didn't drink so he could drive home.) Clare's choice of turnoff put them through two pointless miles of stop-'n'-go. "We needed to know about another nine Thai restaurants to try some time," Robert said.

"You want to say 'I told you so' so why don't you just do it?" Robert was nearly always right in their disputes; the least he could do was win more graciously.

"What, when you're always on me about being more tactful? Oh. Turn right."

"Do I go under or over the road blocks?"

The stretch of Sunset Boulevard encompassing the club was blocked to all traffic. Mostly lower-class kids liked to cruise nearby Hollywood Boulevard. Primarily affluent adults would complain of congestion, crime increases, potential gang violence. The LAPD would cordon off Hollywood. The cruisers would drop south two parallel blocks to Sunset. Local adults would complain. The LAPD would cordon off Sunset. The cruisers would dwindle. The road blocks would go into storage. Within months, the locals would be complaining about cruisers on Hollywood Boulevard, once more.

Tonight, Clare and Robert became victims of this endless cycle. They bickered about which side street would have sooner yielded a parking place, then stomped the four blocks to Club Lingerie in testy silence. Clare was unnerved to realize how comfortable she felt arguing with Robert.

They were nearly ninety minutes late. If they were lucky they might catch the end of Tommy's set. The club's doorman ignored Robert's inquiry about which band was up next and cocked a thumb to his right without making eye contact. The bouncer was ogling the cashier, who ran her tongue over her boudoir pink lips in reply. The cashier found Clare's name on the guest list, and stamped the inside wrist of their left hands without glancing at them or interrupting her flirtation with the bouncer.

"I give it until lunch tomorrow," Robert assessed the budding romance.

Clare laughed. They looked at each other for the first time in hours. What they saw made Robert tight-lipped, Clare sad. She took his arm as they climbed three steps to the club. Why couldn't she just keep loving him; why couldn't she stop wondering if she still did? After meeting Robert her life had felt correct for the first time. Then she'd started having doubts. Which came first, the doubts or the problems?

"What time does your watch say?" Robert shouted above the PA system, which blasted a beat that might have been reggae.

Had they crossed into an earlier time zone, coming west from Pasadena to Hollywood? They were an hour and a half late but the room was nearly empty and those present had the air of the just arrived, purchasing inaugural drinks. It was only an hour until the late show was alleged to start yet the early show had not commenced.

Clare liked the club though. Surveying the plank and brick walls, she tried to recall when she had last ventured someplace new around L.A., excluding restaurants.

A flurry of activity from the back of the long narrow room: five pairs of arms were waving, five faces regarded Clare and Robert. But Clare didn't recognize any—oh, there was Bianca, wearing a man's pinstriped jacket, tight belt, and stiletto heels.

Clare and Robert wound their way around the knots of patrons to the back stairs, which led to a mezzanine. On the stairs stood Tommy's wife, another woman, and three men. The woman and one of the men were idly massaging each other's muscle tone. All but Bianca casually surveyed the room for worthy prospects. It took Clare a moment to determine what was odd about this group: they were all stunning. The men were tanned, lean but muscular, chiseled. The woman almost made Bianca look plain.

"I kept trying to get your attention but I couldn't so they helped me," Bianca greeted Clare. "Glad you could make it, they should be starting in another half hour or so. These are people I work with, I could introduce you except nobody remembers names at these things. But who's *this*," she demanded, appraising Robert.

Clare made the introductions. As Bianca had indicated, there was something incredibly attractive about Robert. The unassuming way he slouched, which accented his lankiness; the careless part in his hair, which was salt and pepper since age twenty-three and always a bit too long and thick; the air of timelessness which perhaps was due to the stylish but outmoded sports jackets he loved finding at thrift stores.

Bianca shook Robert's hand carefully. "Now I'm not so worried about what kind of experimenting my husband does with the doc here." She smiled a smile that said she hadn't worried in the least. "If you ever want to commiserate, give me a call."

Robert was the original open book. In a matter of seconds his face registered surprise, embarrassment, flattery, confusion. He finally settled into amusement, as he concluded that Bianca was quite a character. Clare realized that it would never occur to Robert, even fleetingly at three A.M., that she and Tommy or anyone else might . . . It would never occur to him not to trust her. "I could use a drink," Clare announced.

The waitress's attention was difficult to get: Clare and Robert were so out of their element as to be invisible. Bianca flexed an eyebrow and a waitress in a red lace bodysuit was taking their orders. "Bring 'em around back," Bianca instructed her, then told Clare and Robert: "C'mon and say hello to Tommy. Since his operation he gets real nervous before he goes on. He could use a distraction. Don't wait up," she advised her gym friends, then led Clare and Robert across the room, down three steps, left under a neon clock, back through a narrow hallway.

Clare looked at the clock, marveling that she was the only one marveling at how late the show was. Looking down from the clock, she glimpsed a man staring at her. As he turned away, light silhouetted his nose and chin. It was the driver of Car X. No it wasn't. Now she wished she'd stayed home. She hadn't felt this suspicious, this sure of evil portents everywhere, since her breakdown.

Bianca and Robert had disappeared. But a black curtain to Clare's left swayed slightly. Clare peeked behind it, saw Robert's jacket. She parted the black cloth, which was sticky, and stepped inside. The dressing room had the dimensions of a cigar box and the ambiance of an ashtray. It was even more dimly lit than the club proper. The chair best for reading was farthest from the sole track light. The sofas best for conversation had their backs to one another.

Sprawling around, nursing beers and/or cigarettes, were three guys in the last stages of terminal boredom. Tommy lay on a shag throw rug, propped on his elbows, dismantling a small, bright-colored apparatus. "Oi Tommy," Bianca began.

Without turning around Tommy said, "Look what I found in the trash in the alley."

Clare said, "What we don't want to know is why you were rooting in the trash."

At the sound of her voice, Tommy rolled onto his back and beamed a grin that made Clare take a step back. "Hey you made it."

"Hey we did," Clare replied.

Getting to his feet, Tommy regarded Robert. "You must be Clare's uh you and Clare live together, right?"

"For over four years." Robert spoke with the same sense of wonder he'd first had.

"Shit, we've been married longer than that," Bianca noted.

"In other words you were still minors when you got married." Clare was only partly joking.

"Naw but it is true we couldn't drink legally at our reception."

Clare winced.

"Our marriage was really depressing," Tommy said, "it was like a week or something after Lennon got assassinated."

"And Tommy felt real guilty because he'd written Lennon off as a cow," Bianca explained.

"You'd think I would've learned. I did the same thing with Elvis. I just really bought into 1976. And I mean, punk was right, mostly. But not about everything. Or everyone," Tommy concluded morosely.

"I'm sure they'd both understand. You were so young then; everybody misjudges old folks at that age," Robert told him sincerely.

"Thanks." Tommy nodded and extended his hand. "Tommy Dabrowski."

"Robert di Marchese," Robert took Tommy's hand.

"Alright. For once they told us the truth in school. America *is* a melting pot," Tommy proclaimed. "No, I get it, your name used to be Smith but you changed it to be more colorful, right?"

Poor Robert. He was so sensitive about his name. Roberto Giovanni di Marchese had considered a change to Bob Martin because flamboyant was the last sort of name he wanted. Favorite social status: fly on wall. Observing all, observed by none.

"Your hair's got a lot of gray in it," Tommy added. Robert blinked. "See, since my operation," Tommy explained, "I wash out when I meet somebody. I can learn your name and I can learn your face but I can't put them together. Maybe Clare will explain it to you, she won't tell me why."

"Tommy, if anybody figures out why that occurs, you'll be the first one I call."

"Must have been pretty frightening before you realized what was happening," Robert sympathized.

Bianca yawned and left the room.

"Yeah it was," Tommy acknowledged. "I thought I was pretty jaded. What *next*, you know. But that one got me. Clare really calmed me down though. She showed me statistics to prove it happened to most of Us. And she told me this trick for getting around it. I can still connect features with names. So I'll be able to recognize Robert di Marchese—mind if I call you Roberto? Really a cool name—anyway, I'll recognize you when I see your hair. Hey Trish." The new visitor was the gorgeous female gym instructor who had been standing with Bianca out front. The woman gave a vague nod and flopped on the sofa tight against one of Tommy's bandmates.

The waitress delivered Clare's Bohemia and Robert's Poland Water. Tommy insisted on putting the drinks on the band's tab, although it was clear from the expression on his band's face that these drinks were cutting into the total discount allotment for the night. Tommy caught Clare catching the band's disgruntlement. "By the second set they're usually too wiped to play right, anyway," he shrugged. "It'll be nice to have them conscious both sets for a change."

"Is that—" Robert gaped and stared at the object with which Tommy had been tinkering when they came in. "A Bullwinkle clock." He dived to the floor to examine it.

"Clock radio," Tommy bragged. "Doesn't work, but there's gotta be a way to . . ." He joined Robert on the floor.

Clare sipped her beer. If this were a fluffy French cinema piece, Tommy and Robert would become and remain friends, even after Robert learned she and Tommy were lovers. No. Robert and Tommy could but she and Tommy weren't. Nor would they become. At that moment she made her decision. It left her disappointed yet relieved. Her sin would only count with Catholics—it remained solely in her heart.

Tommy had been using a screwdriver to show Robert what he'd tried so far. Now Robert took the tool and Tommy alternated watching Robert's progress, then Robert, in much the same way that Clare always caught herself studying Bianca.

It was convenient that both men had their backs to her. She rarely got the chance to unabashedly stare at Tommy, except in profile illumined by tachistoscope spillover. In this light, his finely hewn features, already as beautiful as they were handsome, looked ethereal. He wasn't as spectacular as Bianca. The A bomb is less devastating than the H bomb. His legs were awfully skinny, a fact accentuated by their length and his skin-tight black pants. Plus, he had the beginnings of a spare tire around his middle.

Actually, these and other alleged flaws only made him more accessible. As did his affability. Only half the men in a room dared to openly stare at Bianca, but every woman within miles felt comfortable coming on to Tommy. Still, there was an aloofness, a guardedness. What you see is not nearly all you get, the message radiated from him.

Robert likewise had that unknowable quality. She wouldn't ever comprehend Robert completely and that had long tantalized her, made their connections that much more profound. Ah Robert. Did she want to know more?

Maybe maintaining long-term interest was like Zeno's arrow, a mathematical paradox called the dichotomy. Zeno had pointed out that the distance between an arrow in flight and its target can always be divided in two. The arrow can complete half the distance and still have half to go. But then that remaining distance can be halved, and again the arrow can complete half its journey and still have half to go. Although the half distance remaining may become infinitesimally short, in theory the arrow will never arrive at its target because it always has another half distance to go.

And yet arrows do arrive at their targets. There is a point where what's left to travel becomes irrelevant, where all the distances add up to a particular length of journey which can be determined in advance. Had she and Robert reached their target? Was hitting the same target with Tommy a foregone conclusion?

"It just doesn't work like that," Tommy insisted heatedly. For one horrible moment, Clare thought she had spoken aloud. No. Tommy was still occupied with the clock radio, and upset by some repair effort Robert was making, yet unable to articulate what bothered him. Apparently his right brain—which was better at spatial relationships and at comprehending the forest over the trees—knew what to do, but couldn't explain. Could only transmit its frustration to his languaged left brain.

Robert handed him the screwdriver. Tommy took it with his right hand, as his left brain was generally preferred for activities requiring agility. None of this was unexpected. But then Tommy's left hand cupped itself over his right, to guide the screwdriver's progress. "Tommy!" At Clare's startled tone, both men regarded her with concern. "Ah, which hand are you using, there?"

Tommy looked. "Both of them. I always do that."

Did he? Damn. She didn't know. Whether he always did that. Whether she could believe his saying so. Perhaps his left hemisphere was confabulating, since acknowledging the novelty of this situation could mean something alarming, i.e., outside its ken. She'd have to check her videotapes to see if they held unnoticed incidences of this phenomenon. It wasn't something she was testing for. (If only she could invent a way to truly do everything at once.)

As a long-standing trait, Tommy's double-handed attack was interesting but not terribly unusual. But if it was new, it raised a wall of questions. Did this indicate a strenuous effort to cross-cue? Reorganization? A change in hemispheric dominance? Tommy was grinning at her. "More split envy, huh?"

"I guess that's what it amounts to." It was a standing joke between them.

Tommy had always been horrified by the differences between his brain and others'. Then he began contemplating commissurotomy. The idea of having a head *that* different. Even if experts claimed that nobody would notice except more experts, it'd still be capital W-E-I-R-D. What was that, nobody could guarantee results? Possible side effects may include brain damage? Thanks but no thanks guys.

Meanwhile his epilepsy began to act more like a serial killer than the mugger it had been before. What turned him around was the time Clare confessed that she was always Just This Far from having herself commissurotomized, so curious was she about the possible results. She envied him every effect, impulse, reaction—and gradually he began to look forward to reducing the seizures, whatever the risks; to testing his weirdness; finally he was teasing Clare that he had all the fun . . .

"Okay, you're on, let's go, move it." A club official breezed in. When the band wasn't on stage before he could exhale, he acted like it was their fault the show was so late.

"Could you keep this with you, Roberto, the room isn't exactly secure." Tommy handed the Bullwinkle radio to Robert.

"Honored," Robert accepted it.

"But I'll keep this," Tommy laughed, taking the screwdriver. "Where'd you learn home repairs, anyway?" Robert shrugged good-humoredly. Tommy looked around to check his band's progress. One taped a set list to a guitar, one limbered fingers prior to gripping drumsticks.

"Where's Harry?" Tommy demanded of the room at large. He kept looking at the vacant sofa. Apparently Harry was the six-foot-plus chubby blond who'd been the target of Trish the gorgeous. She was likewise no longer in evidence. Tommy studied the closed bathroom door. He stalked across the room and threw it open, interrupting serious drug activity between Harry and Trish. Trish assumed *l'attitude blasé*; Harry looked pissed and worried. "You're out of here," Tommy said icily. "Permanently."

The blond grimaced. "Aw Tommy, don't get amped, we were just—"

"You've had too many warnings. That's it." Tommy slammed the door, shutting them inside the john.

The drummer rubbed his stubbled scalp. "We could use a bass player, you know, let him finish the gig at least."

Tommy did not quite yell. "He plays like Madonna when he's loaded."

"I didn't know Madonna played bass." Sometimes Robert did not know when to become a bystander.

"She doesn't," Tommy snapped. "Mark. You're playing bass. Go borrow one." Mark handed his guitar to Tommy and went in search of the bassist in the headlining band. Tommy strapped on his own guitar, after putting Mark's carefully away.

"Ladies and gents. Please welcome Black Diamond," a PA voice requested. Ensuing polite applause gave way to hoots when the crowd saw no band.

"Asshole," Tommy said to no one in particular.

He and the drummer led the exit from the dressing room. The two hustled up the length of the club and onto the stage. By their second number, Mark the bass né guitar player had joined them. By that time, Clare and Robert had made their way toward the front of the sparse audience. She looked around for Driver X but saw many and none who could be him.

Not long into the set, the ousted Harry left with Trish, looking barely ambulatory yet very smug. Clare was glad Robert held the precious clock radio; something on Harry's face made her fear for the band's belongings back in the dressing room. Half expecting to smell smoke, Clare returned attention to the music.

Even when it was just Tommy and his drummer playing, the effect was powerful. Tommy came from the chain saw school of guitar licks. The drummer's grandfather was probably a big Keith Moon fan. Their playing styles offset an innate innocence in the melody lines. Which in turn offset the lyrics' possession of a sensibility that knew a lot more than it cared to. Tommy's speaking voice was a smooth tenor, but his singing was lower, with an evocative rasp that only certain blues singers and chain smokers usually obtain. And he was so sexy and likable on stage that by comparison, he was an automaton off. His band members seemed just a bit intimidated by him—just enough.

A few years before, Tommy had been a sensation on the local

scene, before his seizures housebound him. He exuded a celebrity's aura, but Clare suspected he'd had it before he became known on the club circuit.

Tommy had been in bands for well over a decade, starting at age thirteen with a garage punk outfit. He'd once told Clare that nothing phased him on stage, except the prospect of ceasing to play. Tonight, the arrangements floundered now and again, as Mark the guitarist fumbled with his bass responsibilities and Tommy combined rhythm with his lead playing. But the meager audience was noisy in its approval. And Tommy was clearly transported by the whole experience.

Robert shouted in her ear. "He's better than I expected. His use of minor—"

Clare brushed her ear as though to shoo a mosquito. Robert loved to critique concerts, movies, art exhibits, while in attendance. Clare hated the distraction.

When Tommy played certain leads, his concentration on his guitar work caused him to stop singing. The other two would fill in, creating odd fragmented harmonies. Someone in front of Clare yelled to a companion: why didn't they move to New York if they wanted to do that avant shit. He moved forward to toss the dregs of his drink at Tommy and yell, "You suck!" Tommy thanked him and turned up his amp. Even more than usual, Clare admired his dauntlessness.

Tommy had resisted commissurotomy until he was sure he'd die if he didn't have the surgery. Didn't it take separate parts of his head to write lyrics, write music, put them together, employ both hands on his guitar, while singing . . . What would remain?

Before a split brain operation, each brain hemisphere is numbed in turn and then the patient is tested to see if language abilities are still functional. This determines which side of the subject's brain controls language. In 90% of the testees, only one hemisphere is responsible. And nearly 100% of the time, the other hemisphere orchestrates musical abilities and appreciation.

Neuroscience holds language to be the most important contributor to an individual's normalcy and happiness. So, during the commissurotomy, when the surgeon has to choose one hemisphere to fold and spindle in order to expose the central commissure for severing, the prevailing wisdom is to leave the language hemisphere alone.

Tommy, however, had demanded that they safeguard music before language. Eventually, the neurosurgery team had to agree —it was the only way he'd have the operation.

Since then, he'd explained to Clare, when he played a song learned just prior to his operation, his right hand had trouble with its pick work. But if he watched that hand, he could *feel* what he was doing wrong, and never stray too far from correct playing. Tonight, Clare assumed it was during these songs that he stopped singing mid-word and studied his guitar work. She hoped nobody ever told him he did this. Self-consciousness might freeze him. And with his current technique, his guitar playing was fine and his singing lapses had an endearing quality that few seemed to mind.

Belatedly, Clare noticed that directly in front of the stage, Bianca and her cohorts were demonstrating just how good dancing could be if you really Had It.

All too soon, the set was over. Clare and Robert were too old to wait for the second group, much less Tommy's second set; so, after giving the band time to towel down, they went back to say good-bye. The headlining band was occupying the dressing room and resenting all space taken by Tommy's people. Tommy thanked Clare and Robert for coming out, but his attention was elsewhere. Someone had piled his band's belongings, then peed on them. Robert handed over the clock radio, then he and Clare made a quick exit.

Driving home, Robert, who preferred early Miles and all Coltrane, was complimentary toward Tommy, his clock, his music. Now that Clare had decided she could absolutely not have an affair with Tommy, she felt safer appreciating him and enthusiastically concurred. As they parked and walked upstairs to their apartment, Clare was consumed with determination to really make Robert-and-Clare work out.

Robert proclaimed it too late to make love. She undressed in front of him, as seductively as possible. He began to lecture her on making her getting-ready-for-bed procedures more efficient. Yet by the time she was in bed and ready to sleep, Robert was switching on his bedside lamp every forty seconds, making notes on tomorrow's work. She suggested he trust his ability to remember, or write in the dark.

"How stupid of me," he said in his most acid voice. "I see now. Only you are allowed to disrupt our lives."

"What's that supposed to mean?"

"It means I'm sleeping in the living room." Robert's light went out. A few minutes later came the squeak of the Hide-A-Bed unfolding.

She lay in the dark and heard labored uneven breathing, felt thick fingers at her neck. She tried to flee but lay frozen, unable to scream. At last she dragged herself upright and convinced herself she was alone. Considered crawling into the Hide-A-Bed with Robert. Stared into the dark. Sank back to her pillow.

Jessie, who had been disturbed by Robert's note-taking, now returned to bed and curled up purring next to Clare's ear. This provided the tonic for Clare to forget it all and fall asleep.

CHAPTER 3

Confabulation

Clare awoke to the sensation that someone was watching her. Jessie sat erect and solemn beside Clare's pillow, the tip of her tail twitching. The apartment had a silence it only attained when Robert was gone. She looked toward the clock. That was gone too. Jerk. He'd taken the alarm into the living room with him, then hadn't bothered to wake her. And now, judging by the sun edging the curtains, she was very late.

He hadn't bothered to feed Jessie either, of course. Damn. It was nearly eleven A.M. She'd hoped to be at her desk by ten: she had so much to do and wanted to be home before dark. When Clare reached the kitchen, Jessie was waiting silently next to her dish. From all available evidence gathered in the seven years Clare had known Jess, the cat never meowed when she wanted something.

This was not a good day so far. She was out of cat food, except for this bagged sample that had arrived by mail, who knew when. Clare poured the pellets into Jessie's bowl. Cute:

little mice and birds, though the colors were autumnal. She hoped that wasn't Red No. 5 in there—wasn't it outlawed? Probably not entirely—and it would figure if the manufacturers were getting their investment returned by using the dye on pets and third worlders.

Clare set the food down and stepped back. Jessie looked at Clare. Sniffed the food. Drew her paw along the floor next to the bowl: out then back, out then back—the same motion she would use to bury shit. She looked at Clare again then left the room. Damn. Hunger strike and Clare didn't have time to negotiate.

There were those who claimed Clare spoiled her cat. Actually Clare thought of Jessie as a companion, not a high-maintenance belonging. Jessie gave her a lot; in return, Clare thought it only fair to be prompt and considerate with the few things for which Jessie depended on her. Jessie never let Clare down. But Clare did occasionally fall into the double-standard behavior of "owner" to "pet." Clare was running late so the cat would have to eat bad-tasting food or go hungry until dinner. Vowing to make it up to Jessie, Clare rushed through her morning preparations and out the door.

Her office was unlocked and Tommy sat in her chair, his black Converse high tops on her desk. "What are you doing here? How did you get in?"

"Great to see you too. There was a guy sitting at your desk when I got here."

"What guy? What did he look like?"

"About my height but more meat on his bones, brown hair, glasses, and he was wearing the uniform—in fact he looked a lot like this guy."

Clare turned. Dr. Sid Stein hovered in her doorway, hands in his lab coat pockets. "Morning, Clare, I asked the guard to let me in here earlier, I—"

"You what? And he did it?!" Clare tried to glare but looked away; the way he squinted one bulging eye, magnified behind his thick glasses, she felt trapped on his microscope stage, looking up the wrong end of the tube as he studied her.

"I needed those printouts I loaned you."

"You told me I could keep them until next week."

"I was wrong. But I couldn't find them and felt bad about searching."

"Then I came in," Tommy interjected, "and made him feel really bad about it."

"Basically he chased me out." Clare handed over the printouts. "Sid Stein," he turned to Tommy. "I'm a colleague of Clare's, as I said. Pharmacology."

"Tommy Dabrowski. Commissurotomy."

"How's it going?" Sid sat on the edge of Clare's desk.

"Not bad. Learning a lot. I'm going into business for myself. Brain surgery clinic in my garage. You got any customers be sure to send them my way. My rates are definitely competitive and there'll be a little something in it for you."

Sid laughed. "I'm sure we can work something out."

"You're encouraging him," Clare warned.

Sid stood up. "I'll get these back to you this afternoon." He waved the printouts.

"Monday will be fine," Clare replied. "Good-bye, Sid."

"Later." Tommy waved good-bye. Possibly before Sid was out of hearing range Tommy told her, "You ask me, he was snooping. Turning over a lot of stuff too small to be hiding those printouts."

"He always was nosy." Clare sighed.

"I hope it wasn't coming to hear me play," Tommy said.

"Don't talk in riddles today. Please?"

"That put you in such a scuzz mood."

"No. No, I'm glad you invited me. Did you really fire your bass player just like that?"

"It took me a while to decide but once I did that was it, except for the aroma in my change of shirt. So what's with you today? You and Roberto have a fight?"

"Why are you here? Are you and Bianca having problems?"

"Naw, she was off working out before I got up. Anyway we never have problems; we've known each other too long. I came because I wanted to see you. Let's go sit outside, this fluorescent shit's getting to me. I've got brain damage, you know."

"No you don't and I've got a lot of work to do."

Tommy stood, shut the door, crouched to meet her eye-to-eye. "Work later. I'm really happy you came last night. My playing's fucked up, I can't keep a band together, it's all disintegrating, but I really enjoyed last night, knowing you were out there."

Clare didn't feel sorry for him; she knew he'd persevere. He'd told her about the last few years. With his medical dilemmas, his bands kept breaking up, his shows kept losing momentum. His career—hah! what career. He lost most of his audience and bookings when his epilepsy started canceling gigs at the last minute. And there were those loyal fans who didn't return when he resumed playing after his commissurotomy. Apparently they'd mostly liked the possibility of his having a seizure on stage. "It's been really tough for you. I admire how—"

"I don't want to talk about that shit," Tommy said. "And neither do you." He leaned in to kiss her. Their lips grazed. She jerked away. Tommy made a show of losing his balance. She ignored it.

"This can't happen." Clare heard the harshness in her voice. "Face it, we're really only talking about fucking. And that's hardly reason to break up a marriage or—well, Robert and I might as well be married." She wished he wouldn't stand so still. And so close. "We can't let anything happen between us."

"It's already happening, Clare. It's not going to stop just because you tell it to."

"Of course it will. *I* will. You'll still have every other female in the universe coming on to you, you'll hardly notice I stopped. Forgive me. That was a low blow."

"People come on to me." Tommy shrugged. "Men and women. Sometimes—okay, usually—I reciprocate. Makes them feel better, makes me feel alright too. But it doesn't mean anything and I think you see that. Whereas—you mean a lot to me."

"But why? You've got the most beautiful wife in—"

"Like that's what matters. And like you're the elephant man. Look. You haven't tested me for ESP but I don't think I've got any. I don't know if we're going to screw our marriages then go 'what a mistake how could I be so blind.' I see just as much chance we mess this up and say the same thing. You start worrying about all that you end up like Howard Hughes with his germs."

"I think you're making a—"

"You want me to back off? All you have to do is say 'Tommy I'm in love with Robert, please leave me alone.' Go on, say it. Robert's a cool guy, you won't destroy me. Say it." Tommy leaned in close to her again.

"Fuck you."

Clare bolted from her chair, putting distance between them. She'd thought she could suggest a pact to view each other strictly as researcher and subject, henceforth. Talk about dream worlds. She was clutching her arms against her abdomen; she willed herself to release the protective posture. "I don't know what will happen with Robert and me. I do know I want that decision to be separate."

"I get that, okay." Tommy flopped in her chair. "You want to know you left Robert because of Robert, not me."

"*If* I leave Robert, yes, I want to know that you and he were separate issues."

"You're deluding yourself but I can accept that too."

What she couldn't bring up lest it make her seem less resolved: what about Bianca? Tommy never mentioned leaving her. Was Clare to become the Other Woman? Was Bianca one of those unfathomable Forgivers who would just wait until Clare gave up? No, Clare didn't dare factor Tommy into any equation. If she left Robert, it would be because of Robert.

"You have to stop this, Tommy. I'd love to sleep with you but it would be a big mistake. Still, when I'm around you I get persuadable. Don't give me that look. I don't want to be persuaded."

She would have to swap him for some other subject she wasn't yet studying. It would be a fairly easy trade to make. Few commissurotomy patients had right hemispheres that understood as much language as Tommy's did—and thus testing them was more frustrating and often less revealing. Clare could trade Tommy for one of the "stupid" right brains. The other researcher would wonder fleetingly, but not really question a fate turned kind. Clare could make do with the new subject and settle her dilemmas without the confusion of Tommy's provocative presence.

The way Tommy watched her, she knew he knew. This was the last time they'd be seeing each other until it didn't matter anymore. She made it official: "I'm going to have you assigned to another researcher."

"What about our experiments?"

"I'm almost done with this phase—I'll figure something out." If she lost Cynthia Bates too, she'd really be set back. But so be it.

"Okay I can take a threat. I'll be—"

"It's not a threat. It's the way things have to be."

They exchanged stares. "So now what," Tommy finally said.

"I've got quite a lot of work to do."

"Yeah. You mentioned that." Tommy walked to his jacket, tossed in a corner on the floor. "You want to see my journal this week?"

"Yes, let me look at it." Recently, it had occurred to Clare that Tommy's exceptional knowledge about his condition might prove a help, not a hindrance. Frankly, she was amazed that more of her patients didn't learn all they could about their neurological status. In any event, with Tommy it seemed hopeless to enforce clinical naivete, as if he were a jury sequestered during a sensational trial. She still tried to dissuade him from reading about other experiments. But she'd also got him started keeping a journal, observing himself and jotting down any changes of habit/technique/ability/method.

Usually she and Tommy sat side by side on her couch to go over the journal. But now: "Thanks. Can I send it back to you?"

"Ho-kay. See ya." And he was gone, shutting the door too quietly behind him.

When she stopped staring at her desk, she leafed through the new journal pages. *If I'm talking I can't pour milk with left hand.* Clare read further. He'd written a song this week, the first since his operation! *Before when I felt a song coming on, I would find paper and the pen I bought at Graceland, the one where you can make Elvis slide across the lawn. I would write lyrics until I heard some music in my head. This would usually happen during first verse. If music didn't come by end of second verse it wouldn't come at all that day.*

Since my operation I'd write words but their rhythm was off and I never heard any music. More and more I got scared about this and I stopped writing because it made me feel kind of sick. But I had this gig coming up so I practiced some older tunes. There was this one tune I kept $#@%ing up.

Clare laughed: Tommy was aware this was for posterity. She couldn't read more: she already missed him and he probably wasn't even out of the building. Still she felt relieved, which suggested that she'd made the right choice. Still . . . *You're $#@%ed up, Austen,* she told herself.

Fortunately, she did have a lot of work to do. *You could be in the forefront but you consistently backwater yourself!* The words rang so clearly, Clare jumped. But Dr. Colton was not in her office, not reprising their long-ago argument. She grimaced, imagining Colton's reaction to her trading Tommy and possibly allowing Mrs. Bates to quit testing. She admired Colton's ability to believe he ruled the world. Yes, her work was crucial—to her: she could not survive without it. But not if. But not when.

She'd met only one person who really fathomed her position. And now she was thinking of leaving him. Was life really possible without Robert's stalwart presence? She considered walking over to watch him teach; he was one of those rare profs who consistently inspired curiosity and enthusiasm. Observing him in the classroom once led to her seducing him in his office, to his bafflement and delight. She smiled but felt very sad. Could such good times ever be retrieved?

She opened her briefcase and found a note scrawled to herself last night at home. LT. BEAUDINE—HAFFNER. This time, she reached the lieutenant at the Pasadena police station.

She knew certain linguists who should study Beaudine. His ability to transmit meaning through inflection was astonishing. Not to mention irritating. After she explained that Dr. Colton was perhaps the last one to see Dr. Haffner alive—except for the killer—and perhaps had seen something that could turn into evidence, but felt himself too busy to deal with the police, Beaudine responded, "So this Dr. Colton asked you to call?" With those few words Clare learned that he thought she was a meddler and an ambulance chaser. After she reiterated Colton's concern about wasting time, he inquired, "What do you personally know about Haffner's murder?" Now she was a crackpot <u>and</u> a suspect.

She suggested that perhaps it wasn't a burglary, perhaps Haffner was killed by the same man who destroyed the labs and attacked her yesterday. "You were attacked yesterday?" That she was calling about other matters clearly made her mentally questionable, at best.

The lieutenant asked every possible question about her conversation with Colton and about her attacker. Curtly he then explained the reasons burglary was currently presumed in Haffner's death: missing items, a neighbor who saw three strangers in the vicinity just before the murder, and evidence that at this point had to remain confidential. With complete lack of inflection, Beaudine thanked her for her concern and advised her to talk to someone about her parking lot attack. Clare hung up feeling humiliated and alone.

She spent the next several hours in desk-clearing operations, with no recollection of what she'd tossed in her OUT pile by the time she'd grabbed the next IN stack. Now it was nearly five and almost dark. She began packing up. There was a knot in her stomach, because she'd skipped breakfast and forgotten lunch. No, she'd heard a noise. She realized what it was when it came again: a shuffle of shoes outside her door. "Who's there?" she called.

The doorknob turned, the door slowly opened. As the shoes took a shuffling step inside, all the lights went out. Clare groped for her tape dispenser, the heaviest item on her desk, while keeping ears cocked for advancing feet. The lights came back on with searing intensity.

"Always did like a dramatic entrance," Tommy said. She dropped the tape dispenser. It dented the desk with a thud that barely penetrated through the pounding in her head.

"You don't look so hot. Are you mad I came back?"

"No—well, it depends."

"On what happens next, right?" Tommy laughed briefly, tugged at his hair. He seemed almost as nervous as Clare felt. "Can we go somewhere and talk?"

"You can walk me to my car." She collected her things, if not her thoughts.

They headed out, their steps echoing. Early Friday evening, even the building's most workaholicked residents were absent. They walked a corridor, turned a corner, walked a corridor, turned a corner, all without speaking. They completed a circuit and were passing Clare's office door when Tommy spoke.

"I'll go without a fight. On one condition. If you change your mind, you tell me—however long from now that may be. I know, you figure I'll find some new game right away. I won't. That I can prove to you."

"All you'll prove is that you love a good chase."

She was walking by herself. She turned to find him standing with his face screwed into a squint, as if she were miles away and he couldn't quite make her out. "You don't think much of me, do you?"

She walked back to him, touched his cheek. "I suppose I want to make sure you feel as rotten as I do."

"Forget it, I've never felt better." They almost smiled and resumed walking. Corridor, turn a corner, corridor, corner.

They were on their third circuit when the lights went out again. "Which way's fastest to your office?" He linked his arm through hers.

"I'm not sure anymore." As he hurried her down the hall, "It's just a power outage."

"It feels wrong."

Before Clare could reply, a darker presence loomed out of the dark in front of her. A great force hit her in the chest, knocking her breath out. She staggered sideways, hit a wall and skidded painfully to her knees.

"Hey asshole!" she faintly heard Tommy yell. She was going to pass out from the pain in her lungs. Fighting to stay conscious, she dimly perceived Tommy's shadow lunging to grab the dark form that had thrown her aside.

In a flash of light, metal glinted. The attacker's arm drew up, then plunged forward. "Knife," she tried to yell. Tommy's shadow raised a protective arm, his voice cried out, his shadow collapsed against the opposite wall. She crawled frantically toward him. Meanwhile feet ran out onto the fire escape, tripped down the stairs, jumped to the ground, stumbled away.

Why was she crawling? She stood, but could not straighten. Each step came with a piercing but diminishing chest pain. Soon she intersected with Tommy, who was likewise groping toward her. They held each other a moment, needing touch to confirm the other was safe. Tommy groaned. His left side was wet, sticky, and he used his right arm to cradle his left.

"He got me," Tommy said unnecessarily. "You alright?"

"Reasonably. Can you walk?"

"Yeah yeah I'm not mortally wounded or anything. But I think I have to cancel my gig next week."

Tommy stumbled. Clare put her arm around his waist to support him. "He went that way so I vote we go this way." In the too-quiet building they could hear running feet downstairs, authoritative voices yelling about getting the lights back on.

Meantime, it was slow going in the dark. Although reason should tell them there was nothing to bump into, they stepped hesitantly, progressed microscopically. "I think I've got matches in my pocket." Tommy fumbled for them, twisted, groaned, cursed. Clare would have to get them from his left front jeans pocket; his injured side.

"Oh for God's sake," she said as her fingers got stuck. "Couldn't you get these pants any tighter?"

"Mmmm, that feels good," Tommy replied.

"You'd better not be lying about the matches." Tommy giggled; Clare found the matches. Half the pack was soggy but the rest was usable. She lit a match, held it aloft. Briefly they regarded each other. Then she led the way down the hall.

Tommy stumbled, bounced against a wall. Clare caught him on the rebound, dropping the match. "Man I got to sit down soon," he said. She got Tommy straight again, paused to light another match. In the flare of ignition, Tommy discovered, "Here this door's open. Hello anybody?"

Clare helped him inside the room, flicked the light switch. There was no electricity in here either. She leaned Tommy against the door frame in order to light another match.

That threadbare Kashmir carpet in the entry room. She knew this office. "Dr. Colton?" Her voice was too weak to reach the inner office door, which gaped open, greater darkness within. Clare struck another match. She had trouble moving slowly enough to keep the damn things from blowing out.

The new light flared. Tommy said, "I think I see a couch in there." Columbus sighting land.

"There used to be one past the desk."

Sheaves of paper and stacks of printout overhung files and bookshelves, casting long jagged shadows by match light. Clare kept her eyes on Tommy, who was teetering. As she neared the desk, the give was different beneath her feet. The carpet felt—odd. Another step—it felt downright soggy.

"Aw fuck," Tommy breathed. And just before she dropped the match in horror, she saw it too. A man's body, collapsed beside the desk, one hand still gripping the desk top, as if he were about to pull himself erect. But the way his arm twisted at the shoulder: he wouldn't be standing again of his own accord.

The sound of shoes running along the corridor outside; authoritative voices close at hand. A flashlight beam hit the glass of the office door. But the sounds passed without stopping. The feet and voices faded into the distance before Tommy or Clare recovered enough to call for help.

Clare lit another match, took a step closer. Had Dr. Colton had a heart attack? Her foot sank in the rug with a liquid squelch. From this angle, she could see Colton in profile. His eyes were open, his face frozen in outrage.

A mechanical hum vibrated deep within the building. The lights went on.

One hand clutched his abdomen. A red stain encircled the area. Blood seeped between his fingers. The closer the carpet got to him, the redder it became. There were red blots on papers on the desk. The desk lamp had fallen to the floor and its beam spotlit the blood as it left his fingers and hit the carpet.

"Oh man," Tommy moaned, and fainted.

The floor rushed up to meet her as she knelt beside Tommy, loosened his collar, brushed hair from his forehead. In making sure his breathing was regular, she touched her cheek to his face; discovered he'd regained consciousness when he kissed her ear.

By the time the Pasadena police arrived, the paramedics had checked Tommy over, bandaged his arm, and were preparing to trundle him off to Huntington Hospital to confirm their diagnosis: muscle injury, just missed an artery, no broken bones.

Clare's sternum was already bruising but otherwise she felt fine. As much as she could feel. She was inside a balloon, wafting atop a long string, her body at the other end, the world down there too. No, she was fine, she insisted to the paramedics, uncertain how to explain about the balloon. Tommy kept staring at her. She knew she should stop folding her fingers against her palms, studying the way the skin would stick for a moment, with his drying blood as an adhesive. She looked up when she heard a cop being dispatched to accompany Tommy to the emergency room, get his story, and return him when the hospital was through with him.

Clare was not allowed to go with him. "You his wife? Significant other? Stick around, he'll be back." Chairs now lined the corridor. Clare took a seat, as instructed, and the balloon slowly floated down toward her shoulders.

The men from homicide were not pleased to hear that the blood trail in the hall was Tommy's; nor that the browning patches on their clothes and skin were also Tommy's blood; nor that the shoe prints in the bloody carpet were solely Clare and Tommy's, so far.

The man in charge: Clare's new friend Lieutenant Beaudine. He orchestrated the murder evaluation meticulously, while questioning Clare down the hall, in a secretary's office. "And now we meet," was Beaudine's reaction upon learning her name. He didn't suit his jaded telephone manner, though. He looked like an overgrown kid: tall, freckled, stocky, with clear blue eyes and ragged red hair. He reeked honesty and disappointment the way some men wear too much after-shave.

He wanted a word-for-word recreation of the conversation she'd had with Colton the day before; and a detailed description of the man who had attacked her in the parking lot. "That wasn't him in the hall tonight," Clare told him.

"You sound certain." Beaudine spoke without inflection tonight, which made Clare hear subtext in every syllable he uttered.

"This one was much taller, around six feet. The deranged surfer couldn't have been more than five-four."

"You keep calling him that. Makes him sound like a comic strip."

This startled her. Beaudine watched her eyes as she thought it through. She studied her hands and explained, "Calling him that—defuses him. His eyes. They were more terrifying than anything I've seen tonight."

"Is that right." He'd lost interest. He now had her describe the evening's events *ad nauseam*, asking incessant questions. Her answers were recurringly delayed, as one underling or another brought him information on slips of paper. But she eventually told him about her walk with Tommy, though not how many times they traversed the corridors, nor what they discussed. Beaudine grunted when she told of Tommy's "just sensing" something was wrong when the lights went out. He grunted again when she explained why they had entered Colton's office. He scrutinized her while she described finding Colton's body.

Then she backtracked. She told Beaudine about the nondescript sedan Car X, maybe tailing Colton, maybe tailing her; and described what little she could of the driver and the car. She also recollected the presence last night on the fire escape; Colton's finding no one outside; the shattered hallway lights. As for the state of yesterday's third-floor labs, that she could recall vividly; and she could repeat the overheard bits of conversation verbatim, but was not sure who had said what; she could only recite the names of scientists she knew to work up there.

Then she answered seemingly random questions. No, Colton didn't use the secretarial pool. No, he'd stopped employing assistants supplied by the school, oh, five years ago now at least.

Enemies? He wasn't Mr. Congeniality but everyone at least respected him.

She suddenly recalled Colton's saying Cynthia Bates had wanted to see him. She wondered, belatedly, why Mrs. Bates hadn't mentioned this when Clare saw her yesterday.

"You remembered something." Beaudine intruded on her thoughts.

"Ah—no. I was just trying to imagine how someone could do this." She would tell him about Mrs. Bates; but first she would warn Mrs. Bates. In the woman's current fragile state she needed all the buffering she could get.

That flexing of Beaudine's jaw said he didn't believe Clare's last answer, but he went on to other subjects. No, she wasn't knowledgeable about what sort of research Colton had been doing. As far as she'd heard, Colton no longer used the lab adjoining his office. Rumor claimed he used several labs, all off campus. Could he have been doing defense department work? She doubted it but wasn't the one to ask.

Beaudine now consulted slips of paper and his palm-sized notebook. Yes, she did know about the burglaries in this building four months ago? No, she couldn't name anything of value in Colton's office, although that rug was worth something if they could get the blood out. How did she know Colton? She explained how he'd been her mentor, over twelve years ago. She didn't tell everything. It really wasn't relevant.

Ultimately, reluctantly, she found herself liking Beaudine. He was cautious and thorough.

"Why are you smiling?" he demanded.

"I was thinking what a good scientist you'd make."

A puff of laughter escaped him. "You've told me a number of things you see as significant and you may be right. Your recollections are careful and that's always helpful. You think I might need to know anything else? Anything at all?"

He was giving her a chance to spill the beans on Cynthia

Bates. "Not right now." He did not look pleased. "Is there any way we can phone the hospital to find out—"

"My man would call if there were a problem." He studied a slip of paper. "So this Dabrowski. His wife wasn't walking the halls with you two tonight?"

"She doesn't participate in our—<u>my</u> research. I'd just finished for the day and was walking out with Tommy, as I told you."

He led her to the murder room. Colton's body had been removed. Her eyes shunned the fresh chalk outline that indicated his last position. "From what we figure so far," Beaudine said, "Colton was stabbed by somebody standing at his desk. Colton ran over there, ran right into the knife." Clare avoided considering what details gave him this knowledge. "I know you say you haven't been here for some time; I know it could be hard to tell anyway—but does it look like anything's missing?"

They shared a sigh. Colton's office was highly organized but extremely cluttered. Bookcases shelved books in front of books. File trays were stuffed with stacks of papers, neatly laid at cross angles to differentiate the groups within each tray. Most available surfaces—including the floor and the nonstuffed chairs—held similar crossed sheaves of papers. The desk was a study in paper pyramids. Clare looked around, reliving her past. "That empty hook by the door. He kept his keys on it because when he sat down they poked his leg. Have you found any keys?"

"We'll look into it." Beaudine was noncommittal.

Clare looked around some more. Remembered some more. And started to cry. Once she started she couldn't stop. She supposed this was some sort of delayed reaction. Her specialty. She couldn't keep her eyes open—but when she closed them, all she saw was Colton. He'd transformed her from a promising student to a working scientist; from a clever guesser to a relentless investigator. They shared almost nothing but a desire to understand; there were times she'd felt closer to him than she ever would to another human being. She was overwhelmed by an aching regret.

She saw his blood splatter on the carpet, spotlit by his overturned desk lamp. She saw the frozen outrage on his face. She saw his blood splatter, his blood soaked the carpet, the walls. The room turned red, the carpet swam with his blood, the desk the chair her feet sank deep.

She was shaking. She imagined Colton discovering her dead body and she stopped shaking. She forced her breathing into regularity. Tears still swamped her cheeks. She looked to Beaudine. He was studying her, impassively. He handed her a kleenex.

Someone brought him another slip of paper. Apparently nobody was allowed to talk in front of the witness. While he read the note, she looked around the room. Recalled helping Colton with his files: drawers crammed so full, it took two sets of hands to add or extract a folder. Although why he bothered with files when he still had all that floor space under the couch.

His files. Clare looked at his desk. Each side had a file drawer. Both were open. One was as packed as she recalled all his files to be. The other was full but not packed. It looked like a typical, heavily used file drawer. She pointed. Beaudine instantly paid heed. She explained about Colton's files. "Something's missing from that one."

Beaudine looked unconvinced. Nevertheless, "Get forensics back. Everything in there dusted then catalogued," he ordered the nearest homicide squad member. He nodded at Clare, then smiled. "You wouldn't be too bad as a cop."

"Ah. Thanks." Clare glanced at the bloody carpet. Beaudine ushered her out to the folding chairs in the hall, where one uniformed policeman stood guard. Wait here.

One by one, potential witnesses were filed into Beaudine's makeshift office: researchers, professors, students, security guards—a couple dozen, all told, who'd been in the building or on the grounds at the time of the murder. They'd been questioned by underlings, now the boss wanted to meet them. Clare wished the police luck, pinpointing motives and suspects in this bunch. Jealous of success, contemptuous of failure, much quicker to rivalry than friendship, Clare's peers, she imagined, would be delighted to sow a bit of distrust and thus entangle their associates in a murder investigation.

At last a figure in black loped up the hall, tailed by yet another policeman. Tommy didn't look too much the worse for his evening, although his arm was heavily bandaged and suspended in a sling at an unnatural angle. "What did the hospital say?" Clare was acutely aware of his escort's attention.

"A few muscles, a few tendons, another six months I can hold a guitar again."

"Six months. I suppose we should think you're lucky."

"At least I can wave my arm around." A reference to the weeks immediately following his commissurotomy when, as was common, his left side was paralyzed.

"No kibitzing." The cop following Tommy caught up to them. A chair across the hall was indicated. Tommy sat, looked relieved for the rest. A moment later, he was called in to see Beaudine.

When he reemerged, Dr. Sid Stein was swept in. Hmmm. She'd forgotten about the borrowed printout incident. She couldn't picture Sid stabbing anyone, or even arguing with Colton—Stein had always been terrified of the man. Still, she supposed she'd better tell Beaudine, although it seemed ignoble to bring it up, for perhaps Stein had gone snooping in Colton's office, too.

She looked at Tommy, caught him staring. He pantomimed his interrogation, while being tortured; his drugging; his brainwashing. All without letting their nearby guard see the routine. Finally Clare covered her face; laughing would clearly be inappropriate.

At just this moment, Beaudine walked into the hallway with Sid, telling him cordially, "Doctor, I appreciate your sticking around. And your candor."

After Stein departed, Beaudine regarded Tommy and Clare.

Something in his manner suddenly infuriated her. She got to her feet. "Unless you're planning to arrest me, I'd like to go home."

Tommy looked surprised at her tone. Beaudine extended his hand, gesturing inside the office he'd commandeered. "Just a few more questions." Clare stomped inside. She refused to be intimidated.

"A few things you perhaps forgot to mention about your relationship with Dr. Colton—"

"I didn't see it was any of your business." Clare wanted to yell. *Who told you? Was it that scum Stein?*

"The man has been murdered."

"And anything I don't say will be held against me?"

"If it should be."

"Then I'd better tell you about Dr. Stein." Crisply, she detailed Sid's snooping; but of course now the information simply seemed like petty retaliation.

"Back to you and the murder victim," was Beaudine's only response.

"It's true Dr. Colton and I had a falling out. Ten years ago. More. I haven't seen him much since but there were no remaining bad feelings. Are you saying that I killed him?"

"What was this falling out about?"

"I had . . . what in the old days was called a nervous breakdown. Afterwards, well, Dr. Colton still saw me as his perfect little disciple. For a time. I was allowed to collapse, you see, but only on his terms. He thought I'd fallen apart from overwork; he was mostly proud of me for it. But work wasn't the reason, and he—"

"What was the cause of this breakdown?"

"Why is this relevant?"

"It's easier for both of us if you tell me now." Clare closed her eyes. "I'm still here," he acknowledged sympathetically, when she reopened them. "Did you and Stanford Colton ever have relations?"

"Go to hell. And if you want to ask me more questions you're going to have to arrest me or subpoena me or whatever it is you people do."

"That can be arranged, Dr. Austen."

"Then do it. Until then I'm going home." He let her go. She swept past Tommy, past the uniformed sentry, down the hall.

"Clare," Tommy called after her.

"Hold it, guy," their sentry warned.

"It's alright Joe," Beaudine said.

A moment later, Clare heard Tommy lope into place beside her. She couldn't look at him just then. She stared straight ahead and walked as briskly as she could without running. When she and Tommy had turned the corner and were out of Beaudine's sight, she could feel him staring after her still.

Their footsteps reverberated in the courtyard. Tommy couldn't drive so she would take him home, then Bianca would drive Clare back to her car.

Tommy was parked out by the tennis courts, all the way across campus. Tonight, the jacarandas looked like swamp growth. The blue-tiled pool surrounding the sixties monolith library was an abyss. Ordinarily Clare liked strolling the campus at night, enjoying the stillness and the way the occasional weak sconce light transformed Spanish porticos into gothic chasms. Tonight she neither strolled nor enjoyed.

They cut southeast, zigzagging through narrow alleyways between high windowless walls. One of the infrequent dim lights was burned out. Clare felt a crunch underfoot. Was that glass? Oh God it was happening again. No, this was just gravel. Tommy put his good arm around her. "You're trembling." She was aware of the warmth and reassurance in his touch, the darkness and emptiness around them.

"I'm spooked," she agreed softly. And stepped away. "What did the police ask you?"

"What I saw, what I know—what you'd expect them to ask. Although Beaudine seemed pretty interested in how we happened to be walking in the hall on a day we weren't supposed to be doing research. I didn't tell him about . . . you know."

"Neither did I. Apparently the only choices in responding to him are no privacy or no credibility."

"All I could really say is that the killer's as tall as me. Maybe taller. Maybe as tall as six three. I tried to tell them about my head. Didn't go over too hot."

"Why did you want them to know?"

"I touched the guy. The one who stabbed me. And if I touched him again I might be able to identify him."

"But you can't make an identification now?"

"No. It was this arm." Tommy indicated his heavily bandaged left arm. "The arm that can't talk." The arm that sent touch sensations to the nonverbal side of his brain.

"Do you really think you could recognize the murderer?"

"I'm not sure. I feel like I could but I don't know why."

"It may be that your right hemisphere knows something and is using its access to emotions to alert your left hemisphere. Or not."

"That's what I like about science. It's so exact."

They were out of the alleyways now, descending stone stairs to another courtyard, trellised. "How did the police react?"

"How do you think? They took a lot of notes and watched me like I was a homemade bomb."

"Tommy. The murderer doesn't know that you *might* recognize him under the proper circumstances. But you touched him, you fought with him. It was light enough for me to see the knife. He might already believe that you saw him, that you can identify him."

"But I can't. It's like I could if only but I can't."

"The killer could be thinking the same thing about me."

They had reached the steps leading off campus, to California Avenue. Across its four lanes was a parking lot where Tommy's '64 Dart GT sat alone under bright arc lights. It was further away than the moon. Tommy yelled, "Hey bad guys. We don't know anything. Leave us alone." The sound fell flat on the mottled asphalt.

Clare was having trouble putting coherent thoughts together, but was already planning experiments to help Tommy determine what his right brain knew. He might not identify the murderer, but any clues could help the police. Once Tommy told Beaudine what he knew, he would be less vulnerable. Wouldn't he?

They crossed the street against the light. Suddenly Tommy was dragging her across the asphalt, shoving her onto the sidewalk. "Stay down," Tommy yelled and dived alongside her. A car without headlights swerved behind them, speeding over the ground they'd just left. Clare whipped around to stare at the driver. She couldn't see him: he was kissing his girl. He'd never noticed they were there.

"Aw man." Gingerly, Tommy flexed his good wrist. "I landed on the only hand I've got left."

"At least they weren't after us." They helped each other up. Clare wiped dirt and fresh blood from her scraped forearms. "Someday this will all seem funny, I suppose."

The incandescent parking lot lights hummed just above hearing level, setting their teeth on edge. It was like walking through searchlights to reach his car.

Inside the Dart, Tommy explained the push-button transmission. When at last she pulled out of the lot, she turned west on California, then south on El Molino, toward South Pasadena where Tommy lived. No lights lit the winding turns of El Molino; few illuminated the hulking estates lining the road. Pasadena rich fo'ks went to sleep early.

Headlights behind them approached rapidly, then hovered. The brights flashed on and moved to the left in the mirror, as though to pass. But the new car slowed as it pulled alongside. Clare did not believe these were necking teens. "Hold on," she yelled and braked. The other car matched her maneuver. She pushed the Reverse transmission button. Metal screamed.

"My car!" Tommy shrieked to match. The Dart bucked backwards and stopped. The other car made a noise like a backfire as it passed them. "They're shooting at us. Get off this road! Up here. Come on!" Tommy waved frantically toward a stately driveway climbing a steep hill. Clare pushed the Drive button and floored the gas pedal. The motor raced, the car did not move. "The transmission must be fucked. Leave it." Tommy yelled.

Twenty yards ahead, the other car's brake lights ignited, its gears ground, the brake lights raced toward them. Clare clawed at her door, found the latch, threw herself out of the Dart and up the slope to the ten-foot door of a darkened mansion. Tommy pounded on the door while Clare strained to see down to the other car. Flood lights clicked on, blinding her. From the road below, she heard an engine idling. They must make great targets. She constricted in anticipation of another shot.

A suspicious voice boomed behind the mansion door: "My wife has already called the police. What do you want?"

"Tell them to hurry," Tommy yelled back. "And let us in now or you're gonna be mopping us off your porch."

A latch turned and the door opened as if the man inside was too startled not to obey. They pushed inside. A yuppie in a satin bathrobe appraised them. Clare threw her back against the door, slamming it shut.

As she did so, they heard a car pulling away at high speed. "Who the fuck was that?" Tommy whispered at the door. "What is going on?"

"We've got to find out."

PART 2

Kindling

The hallmark of a healthy brain is inhibition—the state in which neurons resist firing. If there is too much excitation—too many neurons reacting—each firing can then activate yet more neurons. This process is called kindling, and can herald an epileptic seizure.

CHAPTER 4

Type One Error

Clare felt a certain fondness for the yuppie mansion owner: after offering them lifts home, he merely added sandals to his bathrobe and they set out; he didn't try to make conversation and he waited to see Tommy safely inside his door.

Tommy lived in a soon-to-be-dilapidated two-story clapboard house, converted to apartments. As he ran up the sagging stairs, the yuppie inched his Jaguar forward to keep Tommy visible in the amber street light. Clare rolled down her window as Tommy hammered on his door. Lights went on in other windows; not his. He kept pounding. The timbre of the car engine changed from idling too long. The yuppie turned the ignition off. At last Tommy's porch light went on and the door opened.

"Why'd you wake me up?" Bianca greeted him groggily. Then she noticed his arm in its sling and got to act concerned in ways Clare wasn't allowed. Tommy put his good arm around his wife and stepped inside. When the car engine reignited, he jumped, then turned to wave good-bye.

Every light in Clare's apartment blazed; the TV and stereo blasted. The floor thudded as the downstairs neighbor thumped his ceiling for quiet. Robert was lying on the floor, Jessie hunched under a chair. "Trying to get us evicted?" Clare stepped over Robert to shut off the multimedia show, then knelt to coax Jessie out.

"Nice of you to stop by. And to phone hours ago, to keep me from worrying. I went over to the campus, but the police wouldn't let anyone in your building."

"You know about Dr. Colton then." She watched Jessie bolt down the hall.

"I got several calls about dear departed Stanford. Everyone's so upset. But you didn't need consoling. Or preferred it from Tommy Dabrowski. Why don't you make some phone calls now so I can find out what happened to you tonight?"

Despicably unfair: Clare started to cry. Robert glanced at her. Colton's final expression had been friendlier. He resumed staring at nothing and in a monotone, lest she trigger new sobs, she began to describe her evening.

He interrupted her almost immediately. "Why was Tommy there on a Friday?"

"He dropped off his journal." At Robert's snort, she added, "I told him I'm terminating research with him." Robert turned to face her, questioning with his eyes. "Why do you think? I'm weak but not that weak. We've been unhappy a long time but—"

"You've been unhappy," he corrected her softly.

She wouldn't have thought it possible: she could feel worse. Returning to more pleasant topics, she resumed telling Robert all that had transpired. At some point his innate empathy forced him to join her on the couch, although he held her tentatively.

Eventually, nearly talked out, she explained that Tommy might have a clue to the murderer's identity locked in his unlanguaged hemisphere. Robert was fascinated, which led to a barrage of questions and speculation. She finally held up her hand. "Stop, stop. I don't know anything at this point and I'm in no condition to brainstorm. Although you are giving me good strategy ideas."

After a long pause, "You're going to keep working with Tommy on this."

"I—have to. I know what his usual responses are, that could be important. I don't see how I could not. I guess I could consult." Coward. She knew she was going to do it.

"You're right, any delay is a problem." They sat in silence, Clare marveling at the depths of his reasonableness. "Let's get some sleep." He kissed her lightly.

"I've got to call Mrs. Bates first." As Robert consulted his watch, "I know, it's after three, but I don't want Beaudine to get to her first." Given Cynthia's current mental state, she'd need quite a pep talk before dealing with the authorities, who were sure to learn that she'd sought out Colton the last two days. "Cynthia Bates is harmless; but Lieutenant Beaudine will think otherwise."

"Based on what you've said about him, meddling is a bad idea." He sighed. "But I'm much too tired to get into it. I've got to make up with Jessie anyway."

"She does hate your moods."

"After seven years with you she should be used to moods."

"I thought we were through fighting for the night."

"Fighting? As usual you've completely evaded any. No. To bed." He disappeared down the hall, behind the closed bedroom door.

Mercifully, Robert was asleep by the time she got off the phone, so she could avoid his unspoken Told You So.

Mrs. Bates had been panicked by Clare's call. "Why are you calling me? I haven't seen Dr. Colton in months. What was that noise—is someone else on the line? Am I a suspect? I didn't do it, surely you believe me. What did you tell the police? Clare, we've got to get our stories straight. They'll take my babies away! Oh God oh God, no William I'm fine, please go back to bed, *please*. I must go Dr. Austen. No, I really can't talk longer. Thank you for calling." With that, the line had gone dead.

How could one person be so wrong so often. *It's not the number of mistakes one makes, Clare, it's what one learns from them.* A voice from the old days, when Stanford Colton provided inspiration, until she'd made mistakes even he couldn't countenance. Of course she'd waited until he was dead to want to make amends. Dead. His blood splattered on the carpet, red spread across the room, too slippery to move, red walls wet floor wet air she was drowning . . .

Stop. Now. She was a goddamned brain scientist. What good was it if she couldn't control her own mind? She wouldn't think about Colton. She wouldn't think about anything. Instead she would breathe. Breathe. Her chest hurt where the killer had shoved her. Her eyes squeezed shut with the pain but the light at the phone table burned red through her eyelids. She knocked the lamp to the floor in her haste to extinguish it. It lay like the lamp in Colton's office, spotlighting the carpet. She unplugged it.

Clare moved to the couch. Sleep was out of the question. She wanted Jessie, but the cat was sure to be curled on Clare's pillow and if Clare went to get her she might wake Robert. Instead she doused the lights and sat waiting: for Jessie to come looking for her, for dawn to edge the blinds.

The deranged surfer stood outside the window—no, it was Mrs. Bates. No! Clare was sure Mrs. Bates only acted guilty but then Clare was always wrong. Stop thinking. She couldn't. Her mind raced with gruesome images. Alright then. She was allowed to flip out until the sun rose. From then on, she would remain in complete control.

"The next time you tamper with a potential witness or any other part of this investigation, plan to spend time in jail."

Clare had finally gone to bed about nine A.M. Twenty minutes later, she'd been summoned to Beaudine's office. He'd talked with Mrs. Bates, who got caught knowing too much and admitted it was Clare who'd told her.

"As I've said, Lieutenant, it was a mistake to call her. I apologize again, for what little that's worth. But I can't stress enough that, however much you dislike and distrust me, Cynthia Bates needs protection."

"She's a little wiggy," Beaudine stared at Clare, "but I've seen worse." They were startled by a loud rumbling—Clare's stomach growling. Beaudine almost smiled. "You want some coffee or something?" She didn't but shrugged in compliance. Beaudine left and returned with Styrofoam cups of a muddy substance that was not for the weak of stomach lining. "So Colton operated on Bates, and you experiment on her. What about Dabrowski, was Colton his surgeon?"

"No. A few neurosurgeons perform commissurotomies and there are several researchers. Very few people have had this operation, you see, so some surgeons also conduct experiments and we all—"

"Who were Colton's other patients? Any idea?"

"With his surgeries yes. Even he couldn't keep those secret." Clare gave him some names. "Beyond that, I'm not sure. But he used to keep patient files in his—desk. Are those the files missing from his drawer? His patient files?"

Beaudine's look turned sourer. "Some of them do seem to be missing." He swigged coffee and pushed away from his desk. Grilling concluded.

"About my staying out of the investigation. I hope that doesn't include working with Tommy to find out what he knows." At Beaudine's smirk: "I see. You don't mind because you think it's an impossible task. Well. I can supply you with data that—"

"Data. Ever been to a trial, Dr. Austen? They got these expert witnesses." He spoke the term as if it signified a rectal disease.

"One expert proves black, the next one proves white with data. Sometimes they all use the same data. And all they care about is looking more expert than the others. Now, I don't mean to insult you."

"Don't you?"

"Not entirely. I kind of liked science in school. The quest for pure knowledge—something noble about that. It's when you people get messed up with the real world that I get irritated. But look. You could be right. So go to it. I should point out that whatever you find won't be admissible in court. And I have two requests for you."

"Requests as in do them or else, you mean."

"Anything you figure out, you tell me immediately. This card's got how to reach me, here and at home. And any investigating you do, you keep in the lab. Period."

That was fine with Clare. She had no desire to work outside her lab. She was all too aware of her limits—and her skills weren't transferable to the world at large.

Beaudine showed her to the door. "You say you can prove who killed Colton, it makes me wonder how you and Dabrowski know—and why you're so eager to get involved. Why you're already so involved." He opened the door, revealing Tommy out in the corridor, awaiting an audience.

"Gee. Maybe you should arrest us right now."

Beaudine made no reply, indicated with a nod that Tommy should come in and Clare keep moving. "I should advise you both." He said it disguised as an afterthought. "Whether or not a clue's stuck in those brains of his, I wouldn't spread it around that either of you think you can identify the killer."

As Beaudine shut the door in Clare's face, Tommy motioned for her to wait.

"I can't believe the stuff you say to that guy," Tommy told her as they headed out to her car a half hour later. "Pretty women and crazy people, they sure get away with shit, you ever notice that?"

"Are you implying a correlation? Actually, my talking back amuses Beaudine."

"Never trust a cop. Never tell him anything you don't have to, always be so polite it makes you sick—and never believe that just because he likes you one minute, he won't turn on you the next."

"Where did you get all this experience with cops?"

Tommy held her car door closed, forcing her to look at him. "Clare. This is serious. Watch out for Beaudine. Are you listening?"

She nodded and looked away, frustrated and embarrassed: she didn't share Tommy's paranoia but could see she'd behaved naively.

She gave Tommy a ride to Hollywood: his band's rehearsal building had been condemned and he had to get his rooms cleared out today, but Bianca was off dealing with their dead car. During the drive, Clare brooded. Tommy was so distant today. "You seem—different today."

"It's driving me nuts, feeling like I could solve this thing but I can't."

"We'll solve it. And we'll start right away—if that's acceptable with you."

"Sooner the better. I know you wanted to stop seeing me. I won't cause you any trouble," he said coolly.

Clare felt queasy. Tommy was shutting her out at her request; worse, she wanted to rescind the request. She caught him staring—then smiling. He'd figured out what she was thinking. "Damn," she hadn't meant to say out loud.

Tommy laughed, then sobered. "I almost got killed this morning. I keep trying to think it was an accident, but I keep not being able to."

Clare veered onto the freeway shoulder; brakes and horns

shrieked around them. A nondescript white sedan slowed as it passed; the driver looked them over, grabbed a car phone, then took the next turnoff. The white car had been behind them since they'd left the Pasadena police station; Clare always watched drivers on car phones, concerned that they weren't watching the road. "You'd better tell me what happened."

He stared at the windshield without speaking, for a time. "Those stairs to my balcony? They've always been squirrelly and the last quake got them all twisted. But they're not dangerous—the boards are sturdy, it's just their angle. Well this morning a whole section breaks and I fall, or I almost do. This thing," he indicated his arm sling, "caught and that gave me time to hold on."

"It's not that far a drop, killed is a little strong for what might have happened." She wasn't ready for melodrama today.

"Usually, no. But there was all this crap under the stairs, stuff I never noticed before. Rusty gardening shears, point in the air; an ax sticking out of a barrel, blade up. All of it like it was just stored there, but arranged so it'd be real bad news to hit from above. My neighbor downstairs says he never saw that stuff before, either."

"Is your neighbor the only one who could have put those tools there?"

"Naw, Caltrans owns the house—it's one of the ones that gets snuffed when they finish the freeway—and they're always doing something."

"Were the stairs sawed or otherwise tampered with?"

"Not that I could tell. I dunno, I guess it was just a coincidence. Bianca pointed out that the killer would've needed time to rig something like that. Bianca's got a lot of common sense, she's really—"

"Did your neighbor hear noises near the stairs last night?"

"He was gone, another one's out of town and the last is this old couple, pretty deaf, I mean my band practices against their living room wall and they don't complain."

"That's pretty deaf. Did Bianca hear anything?"

"No, but she fell asleep before Letterman and you saw what it took to wake her up."

"I think it was an accident and I also think we need to resist paranoia. For example, I was worrying about that white car because it looked like the one following Dr. Colton that night."

"Maybe it was. Maybe it got painted to keep us off track."

"Tommy, stop it."

"Aw shit." A squad car had pulled up behind them. Clare sighed, reached for her registration. "Don't move," Tommy hissed. "In this neighborhood, when you move LAPD calls it 'reaching for a gun'." In the rear view mirror, Clare saw that both patrolmen had emerged from their car. The driver stood frozen, hand poised near holster. His partner assumed an assault position.

Last night, walking down that dark hall with Tommy, she had entered another dimension, a world where everything was threatening and her judgment was useless.

Tommy eased his right hand and his left sling into the air, cursing the pain. Clare raised both hands, fingers splayed. One cop approached, guardedly macho.

"Hello officer. I ran over a piece of metal and I was afraid I had a flat. Fortunately I don't."

Curtly, he advised her to resume driving, then he spotted Tommy. Now he wanted her license and registration, and Tommy's license; he took these back to his car to check against the bad deeds list in the LAPD computer.

"Good lie job," Tommy congratulated her. "See, if you were alone he'd let you go. I get this shit all the time. But don't act mad or he'll cite you for something. They always find something."

When they were allowed to leave, the black-and-white followed them for miles, north onto Western Avenue and then east on Santa Monica Boulevard. Finally, a dented pickup ran a red light and the squad car took off after it. The passenger side cop gave Clare and Tommy a final glare as they roared past.

"Sorry I dragged you into this," Tommy said, then, half a block further along, "This is it. Park anywhere."

The rehearsal building was a five-story brick decorated with deep earthquake damage cracks. Porno theaters flanked it. At the corner, a line of gaunt Latino men waited, watching passing drivers while avoiding eye contact. Next to Clare's parking space, teenage male hustlers also monitored passing cars.

"Nice neighborhood. What are those guys waiting for?"

"Clare, even you haven't led that sheltered a life. Oh, down at the corner? They're illegals. Waiting for work. See?" A van pulled up, the driver said a few words. Two of the latinos got in the van, looking resigned; the remaining men muttered, looking angry—or hopeless. "Must've offered them half a buck an hour."

"You mean they just get in a car with strangers?"

"It's the only way they can get jobs. They've got families to help support." Tommy led her inside the brick building. "You want to really get depressed, ask me about the other guys." He pushed the elevator button and she turned to look at the hustlers, some of whom were old enough to have acne.

The elevator car arrived with a shriek and a clank. It was the old-fashioned kind with two doors, the inner a metal lattice. The interior was paneled wood, with graffiti carved everywhere. There were stains that, judging by the aroma, were urine and vomit. Tommy pressed the fifth-floor button and the elevator dropped five feet, then lurched upward. "The stairs are worse," Tommy reassured her. "Only two trips and we're out of here. I really appreciate your helping. I know this isn't what you're used to and I—"

"I'm fine. The princess and the pea isn't my life story, you know. I—" She cut herself off. To protest was to seem even greener. She'd been in plenty of sleazy places, even dangerous ones. Of course, that was back in the days when she'd believed she could handle anything that might arise.

The elevator shook to a stop. Clare hurried out to a long corridor lit by failing fifteen-watt bulbs.

Tommy's rehearsal room was cheery with fresh multicolored paint and comfortable thrift store furniture. "Feels good in here, huh?" Tommy sighed. "Wish I could keep it. Bianca's the one who fixed it up."

She'd liked it before, she couldn't change her mind now. In silence, she helped Tommy wheel his amp out to the elevator. She watched the floors crawl upward as they descended.

Outside, after much struggle and a rip in her car's headliner, the amp fit in the backseat. "Let's talk about last night," Clare said, but Tommy wasn't listening. He was watching the approach of a tall chubby blond whom Clare found vaguely familiar.

"Hey Harry. Thanks for pissing on my clothes."

"Thanks for kicking me out." Harry sneered at Tommy's arm sling. "What hap, the Lingerie crowd want quality? Do us all a favor and give up, you know?"

"If you mess with her car you're sixed." Tommy advised, then slammed the car door and motioned for Clare to follow him inside, leaving Harry on the sidewalk.

Back in the rehearsal room, they collected miscellaneous cords and small electronic boxes. Tommy's abrupt movements indicated he was steaming about Harry. "Fun day," Tommy noted as they commenced their final elevator descent.

"Look at it this—oh, no."

The elevator shook, free fell ten feet, jerked to another stop. Every muscle in Clare cramped as she awaited the next fall. Tommy commenced a steady stream of swearing, shoved each floor button in turn, slammed his hand against the wall. "Kill you fucker," he started yelling through the lattice.

Clare learned several things: Tommy had a limited vocabulary of four-letter words, but an impressive range of inflection while screaming; their elevator trip was aborted by someone's opening one of the outer doors on any of the five floors; and Tommy believed the culprit was someone stupid who might wise up hearing these yells—or Harry, still after revenge.

It was a deaf stupid person, or Harry. Futilely, Clare tried the emergency phone, right above the official notice that the elevator had had its yearly inspection for 1973. Tommy sank to the floor. Clare joined him, but it smelled so much worse down there, she stood again. "Somebody's got to come by," she hoped.

"Only a couple people rent here and they may have already moved out."

"And the cleaning crew's got the decade off. Does Bianca know where you are?"

Tommy brightened. "At some point she'll figure it out."

"And Robert will get worried. He'll have my car traced to here and—"

"If it's not stolen first."

"Tommy, I'm attempting optimism."

"Oh, I get it. Okay. Hey wait." Tommy slid the inner lattice door open. The bottom of the elevator hung two feet below the top of the fourth floor door. Tommy tried to pry the outer door open—though Clare doubted they could fit through the opening even if the door cooperated. Still he braced his feet and, with his good arm, pulled. His face reddened, his shoulders shook with the effort. The door budged.

The elevator plummeted feet that felt like miles. Tommy yelled, Clare screamed. The car chunged to another halt, sank a few inches, stopped. Clare closed the lattice while Tommy swore at the brick wall outside it. "We're going to be here for fucking days." Tommy stared at the ceiling. "Unless we crash and get it over with. I'm really sorry I got you into this."

If they crashed, she decided suddenly, she wanted to be kissing Tommy on the way down. "We're not going to crash. And if we apply ourselves, we can walk out of here knowing what you know about Colton's murder."

As intended, this distracted him a bit. "The sooner I can return my head to its usual empty state, the better. So yeah, let's—did the light just flash? Oh shit. I'm going to have one." He looked irritated, scared and then blank. His good arm swung at her but not intentionally; his eyelids fluttered, lips murmured, teeth clattered. He was no longer aware of her presence.

Clare put her arms loosely around him, to soften his fall. His right side was quivering, then his left joined in. She kicked his electrical equipment aside to give him what room there was to thrash around. Needlessly; the quivering had lessened, the soundless murmuring abated. His petit mal seizure was ending.

Tommy collapsed in on himself. Despondent, Clare knelt beside him, brushed hair from his face. They'd thought his commissurotomy had beaten the odds: had vanquished his epilepsy. True, this seizure was nothing compared to his previous grand mals, which had hospitalized him a week at a time—the operation had been helpful, then, but not miraculous, after all. Was it better or worse to find out only after all these months?

His pulse and respiration were acceptable. He'd mentioned a flash of light, his personal warning that an attack was imminent. Perhaps that meant his particular electrical misfirings still followed their old pattern, commencing back in his left occipital lobe, where vision is processed, then sweeping the length of his head, through sensory and motor control regions and over to engulf his right frontal lobe.

He was staring blankly, then something altered in his eyes and she knew he recognized her. "Do you know where you are?" she whispered.

"It looks like the elevator where I used to rehearse. I would've liked to take you there sometime but they're tearing the building down." He reached to rub his eyes, stopped as if afraid to touch his head. "Got some short-term memory loss going, don't I? How long was I gone?"

"Fifteen, maybe twenty seconds."

"A mini-mal." After consideration, "Is this elevator not moving?"

"I'm glad you're not more upset. After so much safe time, it's hard for some patients to accept reoccurrences."

Tommy studied his shoes. "There's something I kind of didn't tell you. This isn't the first time I've had a seizure since my operation."

She resisted the impulse to strangle him with a guitar cord. "You didn't tell *any* of your doctors, or just me?" He picked at a shoelace: he'd told no one. "Why in hell did you—"

"Maybe I forgot. Okay, lame time for a joke. Mostly I wanted to forget. Clare—for fifteen years I've seen more experts than friends. I'm not getting another operation and I'm sure the fuck not taking medication again. That stuff made me feel like a rotten vegetable."

"You did all that so you could stay alive."

"So I'm alive. And from now on I'll take my chances. The he-man talks, right? I'm not that brave. If the seizures got bad again I'd probably settle for turnip existence again. But this is only the third one and they only come when I'm stressed out, so if I—"

"Move to Tahiti?"

"They've been easy, that's the main thing. I shake a little, I forget a few things. No big deal. Bianca says so too."

"Since when is Bianca an authority?"

"She's lived with me for ten years, taken care of me every goddamn day. If she says I'm okay and I say I'm okay, I'm okay."

"If she's such a saint, what are you doing with me?" Clare blurted. "No. Don't answer that." Mortified, she couldn't look at him.

"Maybe I'm an asshole. Or maybe—I dunno whether she really cared about me or was just paying dues, to cash in later. She figured someday I'd be a rock star, which obviously I'm not and I don't even want to be. Shit we're doing alright, we're not homeless, we're not illegals, we're not hustlers, the car runs and at least it's old enough to be made of metal!" He stopped yelling. "Why are we in this elevator? Or am I hallucinating?"

The change of subject rescued her from a maelstrom of feeling. Clare explained their advent in the elevator. Interesting to note: Tommy was no longer mad at Harry. His seizure had affected that emotional memory as well. If such a distinction existed. Often Clare felt sheepish, postulating about the brain. Any theory, based on experiment, observation, or gross conjecture, was sure to be contradicted by many of her peers, whose ideas she in turn would dispute. And the truth eluded them all.

"What are you thinking?" Tommy said softly.

"That we've got so much data and so little understanding of it."

"Going scientist on me again." He stood up. "My not telling you about the new seizures—will that mess up your experiments?"

"It's certainly information I'd like to have. But danger to your health is the more critical issue. You absolutely must inform Dick—Dr. Rosenthal." Tommy's chief neurosurgeon.

"I'll tell him. I promise. How did we get here?"

"Is that metaphysics, or does it help to know I drove here from Beaudine's?"

"Beaudine. I forgot about him."

Could his attack have caused more than shortest term memory loss? "Tommy, you remember last night, don't you? What happened?"

"Just think, if somebody only heard that part of the conversation. I love to tease you, you can't decide whether to laugh or snarl. Yeah I remember, old doc Colton lying next to all his blood. There's one I'd like to forget."

"Not until we find out what you know about his killer."

"Last night when I said I knew something but didn't know what it was—I was just freaked out. I'd either know or I wouldn't. I can't believe you don't see that. I don't know anything, so let's drop it." He looked around. "How long have we been here?"

"About an hour. Unless it's tomorrow already." They stared at the elevator door. "Tommy. You've read about how your language hemisphere needs to believe it knows all. Last night, your emotional response to the murder was so strong that your left brain was willing to acknowledge it knew less than your right. But now your left brain's confabulating again." Ordinarily, Clare would never share such monstrous speculations, nor contribute to a patient's fear of warring brain factions; but she had to break through the certainty of his left brain's denial or they'd never get anywhere with their testing.

Her reward was to see devastating conflict on Tommy's face. "Yow. I feel like you put an egg beater in my head. Like you're trying to help me and drive me crazy. Like I've got to get out of this elevator right away."

"You're panicking. Know that and know it will pass. Look at me. Listen to your heart pounding. Try to slow it down. That's right." She held his gaze.

"Honey, you could really fuck with me if you wanted to."

"Likewise, I'm sure."

He smiled wanly and she stepped away from him to sit on the floor. She'd let it go for now. She'd sowed the proper seeds, that was enough.

Time elapsed. Tommy brooded, Clare fought to stay awake. Nostalgically, she recalled what it was like to get lost in dreams. She hadn't remembered a dream in months, but then what was a dream? The most modern scientific discoveries supported the most ancient philosophic mysteries: each brain makes its own subjective world, no two people's alike. Brains, snowflakes, fingerprints. If everyone made their own reality why were they all so grim? Surely she'd live in paradise if she had the choice. Or was heaven as boring as catechism depicted it, with all the—

"Are you asleep?" Tommy's whisper ended her reverie.

"No but I am—very. Tired."

"I wonder if there's enough air in here." Tommy pounded the roof. "I think this panel comes off." His efforts made the car shake. Then fall.

Clare stumbled over her feet in her haste to stand up. The glass of the third-floor door scrolled past them. They weren't falling, they were simply descending. Wait—was that Harry out there? The car clattered, shook and stopped. Hastily, they gathered Tommy's equipment and fled into the first-floor corridor. The stairwell door opened and Harry ran to meet them.

"You okay?" he demanded. "Mark stuck me in that thing once, he thought it was a hot joke, I wanted to maim him." Tommy grabbed Harry's shirt but Clare sensed it was an empty threat. They felt more gratitude for Harry's letting them go than fury for his entrapping them in the first place. The hostage syndrome.

Harry knocked Tommy's hands away. "What, you think I put you in and then got you out? Just cause you're that stupid. I drove back this way, figured you'd be gone and I could get my stuff. But I saw the car still out front with your amp waiting to get ripped off. Then you weren't in the room and the elevator wasn't moving and I found the door open on the third floor and I should have left it that way." He stomped outdoors.

"Hey. HEY." Tommy ran after him. "I thought you did it. I'm sorry."

Harry shrugged. "Later." Walking away, he turned for a parting shot. "Maybe it was Bianca, get it?" He gave Clare an up and down, then hurried off.

"Don't worry, I wasn't going to forget you're an asshole," Tommy called.

Driving home to Pasadena, they discussed who might have trapped them and why, but reached no satisfactory conclusion. They also speculated about why Colton had been murdered; that answer proved even more elusive. Meanwhile, behind them, a VW bus driver on a car phone took much the same route.

When they got to Tommy's, Bianca wasn't home and all his

keys were still with his car, so Clare brought him home with her. A blue Honda kept pace two cars behind them. When they parked on San Pasqual, the Honda driver picked up his car phone. "Either we're imagining all this shit, or it's because of last night," Tommy said after a time. "You want to flip a coin on it?"

"I'm not sure which I less want to be. Crazy or threatened."

"One thing Beaudine's on top of. We've got to pretend we're not trying to find out anything. If there's anything to find out. Which I doubt."

A car swerved toward them: a San Marino richkid chatting on her car phone, applying mascara, and driving, in that order. This struck them very funny. Laughing convulsively, they stumbled away from Clare's car.

Jessie met them on the stairs. As Tommy reached to pet her, Jessie tensed, but allowed him to touch her. Clare was stunned. "Please feel honored. It usually takes months—years—for strangers to get near her."

She and Tommy exchanged smiles, until he said, "Like they say, animals resemble their owners." Clare let them into the apartment without a word. Inside, Jessie shunned Tommy. "Told you," Tommy said cheerfully, and Clare had to laugh.

"Would you like a drink? Coffee, juice? I'm not sure exactly what we've got."

"Is it too early to hit the hard stuff?"

"Is it really only three o'clock? No, under the circumstances, we're entitled." In the kitchen, Clare decided beer was too soporific, and turned to whiskey on ice. Was Tommy on medication that—no he wouldn't be, he'd been lying to his doctors about absence of epilepsy. He'd lied very smoothly. Did he always lie that smoothly?

Out on the living room floor, Tommy was sprawled as Robert had been last night. Fortunately, Tommy was there to drag a pencil, patiently but futilely trying to engage Jessie in play. Clare handed him a tumbler, then he requested a tour of the apartment—which didn't take long. Tour concluded, he wanted to call Bianca to arrange being picked up.

"Uh oh, a dial phone."

"Yes. The wiring here makes a Touch-tone impossible. Does it matter?"

"I always forget numbers and lose those little books so I only know phone numbers by the Touch-tone beeps. There's that look, I feel a new set of experiments coming on."

"I was just recalling what Dr. Colton tells freshmen: in one minute a single brain accomplishes more astonishing feats than decades of neuroscientists. Used to tell, I mean." She swigged her drink, choked; her eyes teared. "I forgot this was whiskey."

He allowed her the lie, busied himself hunting his number in the phone book. While Clare fought her grief, Tommy left messages for Bianca at home and at her gym, then announced, "I'm ready for another drink."

"We'd better hold off until after we discuss—last night."

"Fine. So let's get this brain sleuthing over with," Tommy snapped, joining her on the couch.

"The first step, I think, is to determine what sort of information you have—visual, auditory, et cetera. But I'm not sure that—"

"If you don't know how to do this, we're wasting our time."

"My training has to do with putting information into your head, not pulling it out. We're going to have to go through a certain amount of trial and error." Tommy snorted. "Do you know why you're angry with me?"

"I just want to relax, talk. You always hide behind business, Clare." His glare dissolved into puzzlement. "Sorry. It's not you, it's talking about Colton's killer. Makes me really tense."

"Do you remember what I said in the elevator, about how your left hemisphere needs to know everything and when it doesn't, it confabulates?"

"There's nothing to know. The way you talk, sounds like I'm schizo."

She fought the urge to correct his definition of schizophrenia. "Perhaps you're right. Perhaps you don't know anything. Perhaps—what's wrong?"

Tommy unclenched his left fist. "Hearing that made me feel—sick, almost. Shit, what's the matter with me? It's like I've got two people in one head. That's at least one too many."

"Some of the top neuroscientists in the world think we all have two people—two consciousnesses. One theorist believes we have dozens, each with its own desires, taking its own actions; and the piece that controls language tries to make sense of all the contradictions that arise. Whichever theory turns out to be valid, I can guarantee that you're not crazy. Your brain operates like anyone's, you simply notice the conflicts more because of your operation."

"But my brains wouldn't fight about this. If I knew anything about Colton's killer I wouldn't try to hide it."

"That just seems to be the way your brain—any brain—operates." There could be more to it, but he was looking so much calmer, now was not the time. "I'm going to ask you some questions. But first—can you lift your left arm?" It raised a bit but the pain made him grimace. "Let's use your leg instead. To answer a question yes, raise your left foot. If the answer is no, don't move. Is your name Tommy?" No response. She gently lifted his foot. "Your name is Tommy, the answer is yes, so your leg does this. Okay?" Tommy nodded, his face displaying the particular type of concentration visible during experiments.

"Is your name Clare?" His leg went up. Gently, Clare pushed it down. "The answer is no, so your leg doesn't move." She tried other questions, until she felt confident that his right hemisphere understood the procedure.

Getting his right brain to understand was always tricky. It had a limited vocabulary and primarily knew concrete nouns; the more abstract the concept, the less his right brain grasped of it. *Chair* yes, *liberty* no. A command to smile, yes; to hope, no.

Still, she was lucky she was dealing with Tommy; many split right brains comprehended far less.

New experiments were such a pain. The need to identify Colton's murderer increased her usual impatience. No doubt as a protection against frustration, she hadn't previously considered just how many new tests she might require.

"This is going to be harder than you thought, huh?" Tommy said presciently. "Too bad we can't just hook the old commissure back up for a while."

"Would you mind? It would mean less work for me."

"No prob. I love brain surgery."

Countering the need for speed was the danger of sloppiness: the less rigorous the methodology, the more suspect their results. She really shouldn't be testing him in her living room, with inputs uncontrolled; but preparing new tests was so time-consuming. This effort was a calculated risk to advance their cause speedily. She paused: should they wait? Decided: "I need to prep before we can do much—I'd figured to get ready today for testing tomorrow. But let's try a few questions. Raise your left leg if the answer is yes. Do you understand?"

His left leg lifted. "Great. Okay. Did you touch Dr. Colton's killer?" No response. Yet touch was by far the most likely way his right hemisphere could get exclusive information. "Did your left hand touch the killer?" No. "Did your left hand touch the man in the hall?" His left foot lifted. Perhaps his right brain didn't understand *killer*. Or perhaps it was responding to some other time, another man in another hall. If it understood *hall*.

She posed additional questions. His right brain claimed that all five senses experienced the murderer, and that none of the five sensed anything.

"Just because I smelled the guy or something doesn't mean that's a clue."

"I know. Stand up, if you would."

"I'm not some bribed lab rat this time! Don't order me . . ."

Tommy looked more surprised at his outburst than Clare was. "Man. I don't know which part of my brain keeps getting mad about this, but it's full of shit."

"Try not to worry about it. What I'd like to try now is a walk-through of what happened last night. A reenactment, to help determine what kinds of information you could possibly have received."

"Cool idea. Okay, this is the hall. Hold it, we need more room." Before she could stop him, he tugged at the coffee table, then grabbed his lower back. "What the hell?" He peered through the glass top to the mass-o'-metal base.

"Robert had a motorcycle that was a ninety-horsepower lemon. He was always threatening to turn it into a coffee table. And then one day . . ."

"Alright Roberto! Too bad I'm going to have to sue him. Okay," he limped across the room, "the hallway's over here then. We were walking from back here."

Clare joined him. "The killer ran into me and slugged me out of the way." She touched her sore abdomen gingerly. "He kept running and you jumped out at him. Now. I'll be the killer. I'm running towards you and we intersect—how?"

As he moved forward, Tommy gazed inward, remembering. It gave him a demented look. "You block me—no, you're more in the middle of the hall, I grab at you and then, shit, I wish I could use this arm like I did last night." In slow, then faster, then slowest motion, his injured arm gyrated. He swiveled to his left, his arm moved again, he shifted weight. "Yeah. I was at this angle."

Cross-cuing, Tommy's right hemisphere had positioned its side of the body until he was off balance, forcing the left to shift its side to regain equilibrium—leaving him standing as he had been when facing the murderer.

Clare shivered. She saw the two dark figures as they'd been last night.

"It would help if there were less light in here." Tommy returned her to the task at hand. She closed the blinds; the late afternoon sun illuminated the room weakly.

She saw two dark forms merge, light glint on a knife's blade.

Stop. She must recreate the scene without reliving it or she could miss something important. She pictured a scalpel severing her thoughts from her feelings. "To resume. I'm the killer, I have my arm up like this and you do—what?"

"I grab for you but I miss and then I reach around and— Shit! It's really hard doing this with the wrong arm. And you're so much shorter than the guy last night."

Clare stepped in front of Tommy, her back to his chest; waved her arm like he'd grown an appendage. "Perhaps I can be your arm. Does this help?"

"Swing your arm again? Yeah, that kind of works." He pressed his left shoulder against hers, as though reading her movements through his skin.

Light blinded her. A figure loomed in the entryway. Robert. Excellent; he could play the killer. "You got out early," she greeted him; he'd had a conference today.

"Hey Roberto. How'd your seminar go?"

The expression on Robert's face said he'd misinterpreted the lights-out activities, prompting Clare to explain, "We were just —reenacting last night. I was trying to function as Tommy's arm. Do you have time to help us with the re-creation?" Goddamn it, why did she have to sound so guilty? Her thoughts continued to rage, yet she heard her voice calmly describe their current testing process. Even more dimly, she was aware of Robert stiffly shedding his briefcase, coat; agreeing to play the killer.

Tommy appraised the stand-in. "You're about perfect height. Say. Can you account for your whereabouts last night?"

"I was at home waiting for Clare. Who was with you."

"Me, a knifer, a corpse, and three hundred cops. I didn't know Pasadena had so many." Was Tommy truly oblivious to the room's mood, or was this more of his lying expertise?

"They probably let the San Marino cops help." Robert made a tangible effort to stop glowering.

"And the ones from South Pass. Yeah, none of those guys get enough action."

Tommy and Robert continued to joke about regional police departments. Clare felt annoyed: male bonding rituals. "Can we get started here?" she inquired, her irritation showing, puzzling them both, which irritated her further.

The reenactment went more smoothly with Robert as killer. They determined that, during Tommy's lunging for, grappling with, and stumbling from the assailant, Tommy's left hand had touched the killer in several places: the left hand or lower arm, the left shoulder area, one knee or thigh, and somewhere along the upper back. Were any of these contacts distinctive enough to identify the killer?

Perhaps they didn't need to be! Tommy's senses, even in his split head, transmitted their input to both brains. But the quality of that initial sensory information varied. Most of the sensations to his right brain arrived contralaterally—from the opposite side of his body. But his right brain also received faint, vague information ipsilaterally—from the same side. During Clare's usual experimenting, to ensure testing of each hemisphere separately, she had to exclude ipsilateral sensations. But now she might benefit from them: his right hemisphere could glean additional knowledge that way, and thus might synthesize fragmented knowledge into a stronger whole! For once, a brain attribute might work in a test's favor.

Tommy and Robert were staring at her. To indicate her thoughts were back with theirs, she said, "So we know the killer had a flashlight in his left hand." Sometime during the scuffle, Tommy had touched it and light had flashed briefly. This had given the killer a fix on Tommy, for stabbing. "That's why I could see the knife for a second," Clare realized. "Now I remember that flash of light—I didn't before." She saw the murderer's silhouette, illumined for that instant.

"Clare, turn the lights on," Tommy murmured. "Robert, don't move." When the light went on, it found Robert frozen, poised to 'stab' Tommy, who reeled back, turned his head, eased forward, pulled away, turned his head less severely, turned a bit more: adjusting ever so slightly now.

Between each movement, his eyes shifted. More cross-cuing; his right hemisphere used eye muscles to signal which way to move the head; his left hemisphere analyzed feelings transmitted about each adjustment until "There. That's about right."

Robert was watching Clare study Tommy, then returned attention to Tommy, trying to see him through Clare's eyes.

"Is it possible only my right hemisphere saw him? My head turned towards him like this, right before the light went off. But I mean—Clare, doesn't vision still go to both sides of my head?"

"The left half of each eye's field of vision goes to your right hemisphere and vice versa. You compensate by moving your eyes. But if you saw something peripherally, for a split second so your eyes didn't have time to move . . ."

"Before the light went out and you couldn't see at all!" Robert shouted.

"Yeah." Tommy held his position. His eyes shifted, signaling his head to adjust slightly. "I think my right brain saw something way out here," he moved his hand to indicate the area to the far left of his field of vision. The area occupied by Robert, the stand-in killer.

"I'm not convinced," Clare mused. "In about a hundredth of a second, your eyes could shift enough to let both hemispheres see what was over there. Still, if you moved towards the killer just as the flashlight went out, I suppose it's barely possible that you got a one-hemisphere glimpse."

"What about the other senses? Hearing?" Robert asked, excited.

She dared not give Tommy's left brain more information. It seemed to be cooperating rather than confabulating, but she couldn't be sure. "Did you hear anything, Tommy?"

"You screamed to warn me about the knife. That's why only my arm got nailed. Did I ever thank you for that?"

The way he looked at her made Robert twitch. "Probably. Do you think you heard anything?" She spoke impassively. Robert smiled.

"I'm not sure. I guess not." Tommy shrugged.

Clare filed the possibility for further perusal. Both Tommy's ears sent information to both hemispheres, but the strongest signals went to the opposite, contralateral side. Weak signals going to the ipsilateral hemisphere could be overridden—in effect, drowned out—by strong signals arriving contralaterally. So if Clare's scream predominantly hit Tommy's right ear, at exactly the same time as the murderer spoke into Tommy's left ear, then it was very slightly possible that Clare's scream had drowned out the killer's words in Tommy's left brain, while his right brain had discerned both voices.

"What about smell?" Robert inquired. "Could his right hemisphere—"

"No it couldn't." Both brain halves would have received the same scents.

"You don't even know what I was going to ask."

She supposed she couldn't ask Robert to leave. "Wait a minute. Damn. Damn, why didn't I think of this before? He had a flashlight. He knew it would be dark."

"So he had someone in the basement doing lights!" Tommy added.

"He may have set a timer," Robert advised.

Clare looked at her watch. "I wonder if Beaudine's in his office."

"Stay away from the fucking cops. I keep telling you." Tommy exploded.

Robert agreed. "For all you know, they could be in cahoots with the killer."

Which nonplussed Clare: Robert had always seemed so lawed and ordered. "Lieutenant Beaudine wants to be informed about what we learn." This immediately sounded feeble. What had they learned? Not much. Calling Beaudine with their current findings could only be embarrassing. Still, she didn't like their "ganging up on me."

Now they both stared; she had blurted out this thought. Robert was acting like this to get back at her—but why was Tommy going along? Stop. Persecution complex ahead. "Let's go over everything once more."

Tommy groaned. "Let's have a drink instead. The more I think about this the less I know. It's like trying to remember a dream, putting it into words changes what happened and you can't see it any more the way it really was."

Clare recognized what that whiny tone meant: a testing subject overdue for a break. "You two go ahead and have a drink, I can use the time to plan tomorrow's attack." It would be a relief to distance herself from them. Tommy-and-Robert was clearly not a combination that was good for her.

A bit warily, they let her move to the desk in the bedroom, where Jessie was curled up inside Clare's open briefcase. Clare sat and petted the cat, unable to not eavesdrop on Tommy and Robert making small talk in the living room. The phone rang, Robert answered then hailed Tommy: Bianca was calling. Clare was relieved to hear Robert offer Tommy a ride home. Bianca stopping by and sure she'd love a drink was more than Clare could manage.

Once Clare had the place to herself, she could fully concentrate on petting Jessie, which enabled her to think about new tests.

Robert got home late: Bianca had insisted he come in. Clare wanted details of the encounter but couldn't ask. Robert looked as though he had something to say, but didn't say it. Clare retreated to the bedroom desk, Robert to the one in the alcove off the front room.

She resumed working with Jessie purring in her lap. She woke up to screams. Hers: a black figure hurled her down a dark hall, the deranged surfer lunged, an elevator floor dropped away. Spilled coffee soaked her notes, pain shot through her legs from scratches as Jessie hit the ground running to escape the screams. Her shoulder shook under Robert's hand.

"Nothing's wrong, Clare, it's almost midnight, I woke you up to come to bed." Robert dabbed at the coffee with his pajama sleeve. The wet papers buckled and her barely legible scrawls thickened, giant letters oozing into monstrous words.

Under gentle firm guidance from Robert, she got up, undressed, fell onto her side of the mattress. For a nanosecond she was aware of falling into sleep, which usually woke her. Instead she fell deeper until—

—she was surrounded by blackness. She wanted to wake up, couldn't, struggled, lay immobilized. Robert's steady breathing, the clock's faint clicking—these sounds allowed her head to swivel to see the clock hands glowing an acute angle: 5:35.

She dreamed that she sat up, slipped out from under Robert's arm, tiptoed into a chasm where the hall used to be. A low meow warned her that Jessie was on the floor. Clare knelt, groped, found fur against a baseboard. Clare smiled. She used to kick Jessie sometimes, until the cat seemed to realize that humans couldn't see in the dark, and began to warn of her presence.

Still unsure if she was dreaming, Clare continued into the living room, raised a blind to the predawn sky. She stubbed her toe heading for the kitchen. She hoped the pain proved she was awake, because dreaming about insomnia seemed particularly cruel.

CHAPTER 5

The Fixation Point

The ant climbed out of a valley of grout, crossed a new tile mesa, and disappeared into a crack in the wall. Sitting at her building entry, Clare considered going up to her office and doing . . . something. But the building was locked on weekends and Tommy wouldn't be able to get in. He was ninety-three minutes late. She looked for the ant but this time it stayed in the crack. Relief surged through her at a familiar quick shuffle to her left.

Tommy's cheek was puffy and bruised; his jeans torn, with raw red skin beneath. "Tell me if this sounds like an accident. My car's gonna be out of commission for weeks but the manager of Bianca's gym bought a new one so he loans her the old one so we go do errands, she's driving, everything's cool and since it's automatic with power steering I can drive it with one arm except I become the typical L.A. driver since I can't signal turns but okay this'll do and I drop Bianca off at work, stop at home for an hour, then I'm driving over here and both front tires blow,

I hit a fucking tree, the car turns accordion and P.S., no seat belts: total luck I didn't go through the windshield."

He sank to the step beside her. "I had to slug a bunch of doors before somebody would call Bianca for me but finally the manager brings her, he's driving a new Porsche so maybe I won't have to pay for turning his old Datsun into scrap. He apologized, in fact, said he didn't know the tires were that bad. I don't think they were that bad either. Bianca thinks I'm flipping out, saying everybody's trying to kill me. I had to fight to get dropped off here, she wanted me to go home and rest." He said it like she'd asked him to play guitar in the bathtub. "I told her I rest when I know what's going on."

Clare shivered. "I wish I knew whether to be frightened or not. I wonder if Beaudine could have those tires examined, so we'd know whether someone tampered with them."

They stared at the shrubs lining the walkway. After a time, they held hands, strangers on a jet nose-diving toward the ground. A rotund broad-lipped man in a lab coat bustled past, raising an eyebrow. Clare was unable to care, although she could see the rumors about Dr. Austen and her research subject spreading, like kudzu in time-lapse video. Eventually she said, "In the experimenting biz, there's a situation called Type One error. It's when a researcher thinks the data prove something, but actually the results are due to chance."

"Type One accidents. You're right, these could be. Okay, let's go call Beaudine and ask him to protect and serve us."

Maybe she'd waited outside for so long because she couldn't come back in the building alone. The halls felt empty but not deserted. "Feels like a haunted house," Tommy said. "I lived in one once. Science doesn't know shit, you know. I'll take you there when this is all over and you're up to a good scare."

"That sort of thing doesn't scare me," she lied. It wasn't the existence of ghosts that would disturb her, but the sense that the universe had a rationale so far beyond her comprehension.

"I gotta warn you. I've slept with a light on, ever since."

Was he warning her about the house or his bedroom habits?

When she reached for the knob of her office door, Tommy grabbed her wrist. "Somebody's in there," he whispered. She strained to listen; all she heard was her heartbeat. How do you know, she asked him with her eyes. He nodded to indicate the crack under her door. "Light's on."

"I left the light on." Clare's normal voice sounded like shouting. "I worked up here before I came out to meet you."

Tommy released her wrist, looking sheepish but still suspicious.

She left messages for Beaudine at both numbers he'd given her. Telephone the second was answered by a sleepy androgynous voice. "Do you live with I mean is this his I mean can you make sure he gets my message?" The voice grunted an affirmative.

When she'd hung up, Tommy teased, "Sooo. A little jealousy in the old voice. Clare's got a yen for the dashing lieutenant."

"Like hell. I was only—Stop staring at me."

"Wow. I haven't seen anybody blush in about twenty years."

Betrayed by her own physiology. "I was simply being, well, nosy. I certainly didn't—Wait." Her desk looked different. "I put my stapler on this page to uncurl it—I'd spilled coffee on it last night at home. Now the stapler's over here and everything else looks, I don't know, neater."

Tommy motioned for her to keep talking, then snuck toward the darkened lab. She handed him her heavy tape dispenser. "I must be imagining it. I'm a slob but the law of averages—oh God."

In a flash, Tommy had snapped on the lights and kicked the lab door fully open. Nothing. He knelt to peer under the tables, around the door, into the room's corners. He straightened and handed her the tape dispenser. "Type One error?" She tried to laugh.

He strode over to lock the door to the corridor. "Maybe. Let's get started before we completely freak ourselves. What's first?"

Clare collected her notes and joined him at the tachistoscope table. It was time to bury herself in data and process. "As with any new experiment, I need to lay some ground work."

"Shit, that always takes forever. Fixate on the point?"

"Yes. I'll show you a word then you'll point to the picture that matches." Fortunately, they'd done this experiment with other words and pictures, so she didn't have to train his right brain in the test procedure itself. His right hemisphere even knew to point to a question mark card if it couldn't match word to picture.

The tachistoscope flashed APPLE to his left hemisphere, MURDERER to his right. Then she laid out four pictures from prior experiments—an apple, a house, a dog, a question mark—plus a photo of Dr. Colton clipped from an old annual and an encyclopedia picture of Hitler. "What word did you see?"

" 'Apple.' " Tommy's right hand pointed to the drawing of the fruit. "And—'killer.' So that would be Hitler."

As he reached to point again, Clare held his right arm. "No, point with your left hand." She positioned a yardstick in that hand. The stick waved wildly at first, due to arm sling and injury, but he got it under control. She spread the pictures so that there was no chance of his hitting one unintentionally.

The yardstick snapped onto the question mark. "I can't control this stick. I meant to hit the Hitler picture."

Tommy's left brain knew a few words were crucial to their investigations, *killer* being foremost. Since Friday night, she'd mostly referred to Colton's slayer as his killer. And so, seeing Hitler, the left hemisphere had guessed that she'd tested the right hemisphere on knowledge of that word. Clare suspected his right hemisphere didn't know *murderer* and so pointed to the question mark.

Unfortunately but typically, other interpretations were possible. His right brain may have known *murderer* and transmitted to Tommy's left brain a particular emotion both sides associated with the dark figure in the hallway. And/or, his right hemisphere might know *murderer*, but not Hitler—and thus point to the question mark because no pictures of murderers seemed available.

Now, Tommy's left brain saw HOUSE, his right HITLER. Tommy's left hemisphere indicated the house drawing, his right hemisphere again hit the question mark. At the least, his right hemisphere didn't know Hitler's name in print.

Next, Tommy's right hemisphere saw KILLER. This time, it pointed to Hitler. It could be guessing, although Clare hadn't noticed his right brain guessing in past experiments. Or it could know the word *killer*.

The right hemisphere was again shown KILLER and Clare set out new photos: the question mark, Charles Manson (Robert was going to be furious about their encyclopedias), Jessie in the hallway at home, Dr. Colton again, Clare sitting on a rock squinting in bright sunlight, the exterior of the Neurobiology building at night. She also asked for Tommy's driver's license and served as his second hand while he extracted it from his wallet; then she added this photo to the motley array.

This time, Tommy's right brain indicated Manson—and Jessie. Clare smiled: because she'd confirmed Tommy's right brain did know *killer*; and because she reacted so negatively when Tommy linked the cat with a mass murderer. The cat merely hunted bugs, after all.

"Still working on the concept of killer, I guess," Tommy said disdainfully. The left half of his face grimaced. Terrific. Now she had him insulting himself.

"Let's go on." She continued testing until she was certain his right brain recognized *hallway*, *night*, and *knife*. She then reversed the procedure. Pictures were flashed to Tommy's separate hemispheres, and the words were presented in free vision. His right brain could match the same words to pictures this way, too.

She turned off the tachistoscope and handed Tommy a headset. "We've done this test before too. You'll hear a word or words, then point to the picture that matches."

"I've got bad news for you. I'm getting a cramp in my hand, in fact my arm's throbbing. Can I try pointing with my feet instead?"

When she took the yardstick his fingers remained curled. As his right hand massaged them open, his face twisted with pain. "You should have told me sooner."

"It took me a while to figure out why I felt bad." Clare arranged pictures on the floor so that either foot could reach any of the six. "Do you feel like Mary Magdalene?"

"Excuse me?"

"Washing Christ's feet, you know?"

"Why, do you feel like Christ?"

"Naw I relate more to Judas. He knew he was blowing it big time, but couldn't stop himself."

"A good psychiatrist could purchase a house, unraveling that one with you. It would never occur to me to relate to an apostle."

"Thomas, obviously."

"At least you didn't say Paul. Okay, we're ready to go."

Tommy picked up the photo of Clare, studied it while saying, "Makes you twitch when I get personal, huh? Know why that is? Because I—"

"It makes me twitch when you stall because you hate those earphones." She was usually sympathetic about Tommy's dislike of the dichotic listening tests. Today, she plucked the photo away and went to man the tape player, ignoring his sigh.

Dichotic listening: each ear heard different sounds of the same volume and duration, effectively drowning out half the signals received. It was not known why hearing such simultaneous sounds caused each hemisphere to attend to the input from only one ear, rather than both. Yet the phenomenon provided an extremely effective research tool, enabling her to speak solely to his right hemisphere with the words she played into his left ear—if the inputs were truly identical; she usually had more time to prep tapes.

"**Apple**," Tommy's left brain heard; "**night**," his right brain heard. He pulled the headset off quickly.

"Keep the headset on until I motion to you, some of the phrases will be longer. What did you hear? Put your right foot out first."

"If my left foot's second, what's on third?"

She gave him a look. His right foot tapped the apple picture. "Ap-ple," he said like a first grader. "That's all folks."

"Now your left foot."

"I said there was nothing else. I know you don't trust me but this is ridiculous." Meanwhile, his left foot tapped the photo of Clare's building at night. "Lab. I heard 'lab' too but I forgot. I'm stupider than Robert, is that what you wanted to prove?"

One moment his left brain could be aware that his right brain received different input, then it could forget or refuse to acknowledge that fact. Tommy often registered hostility when this occurred. But he usually didn't get personal.

"Do you know why you're mad?"

"You're fucking with me. Again. I told you I don't know anything about the murder and yet you put me through shit regardless. Forget it," he interjected when she tried to speak. "I know your raps, you know mine. Next test."

Suddenly Clare was an undergrad conducting her first experiment, aware only of how little she knew, wanting to flee because she'd never master neuroscience. Why was Tommy's left brain back to denying—and attacking her? Why didn't she know what to say to break through this? Why was she so unprofessional as to care what he said; so unprofessional as to have let things between them get as far as they had?

His right brain heard "**killer**," then indicated the Hitler picture—and Tommy's driver's license.

"What's wrong?" he demanded. While Clare debated answers, he figured it out. "My right brain heard 'murderer' and pointed to me. Now you think *I* did it."

"No. You were with me when Dr. Colton—I'm not taking it literally."

"I'm only innocent because I've got an alibi? Hey, maybe I offed him <u>before</u> I came to your office."

"Maybe your right hemisphere simply doesn't know the word *killer*."

Tommy's head nodded yes, shook no. He looked uneasy at this, but sounded flip. "I read that dolphins sleep one hemisphere at a time. Maybe at night when my left brain's asleep, my right brain goes out and kills."

Laying out new pictures, Clare knelt beside him. "Based on what I know of you, I haven't seen any evidence that you're a dolphin." This got a short laugh. "If I looked worried, it's because there's a glitch in the results. As Dr. Colton used to tell me, the more you anticipate results, the longer it takes to get any worth having."

"When I was eight I did bad stuff to some tadpoles. I've always felt pretty crummy about it. Maybe that's why."

"As Dr. Colton also said, 'You have enough current mistakes to concern you.' Of course he was exempt from mistakes. But on him all that ego was actually just funny." She felt queasy. She had to stop talking about Stanford Colton.

"You never even mentioned him before, now it's like he was your guru."

"There's a word I haven't heard in a long time."

"I got into the sixties revival. Do you not want to talk about how come?"

"He reminds me of much I'd like to forget." Yet she found herself describing his mentorship, slipped into glowing details until she felt tears coming on. Tommy got up, giving her a moment to compose. He came back with a chair, made her sit, persuaded her to continue.

When she alluded to her breakdown and Dr. Colton's disapproval, "You went way down and dragged yourself back up. That's got Colton's kind of strength beat."

"Actually, at first my cracking up endeared me to him. I'd been spending fifteen hours a day in the lab; he was proud of my dedication. He brought me exotic fruit and *Scientific American* —his idea of light reading—and he lectured me about pacing myself. But you see, I'd been working to avoid my life, and when I told him that he got disgusted. We had a fight—I actually dared to fight with Stanford Colton, if anybody knew I'd either be invited to join the NAS or blacklisted."

"The NAS is some scientists' prestige thing?" After she nodded, "Go on."

"Once I'd recovered, as bad coincidence would have it, I hit a slump, conducted a series of experiments that didn't pan out. I really floundered—I'd never had to face so much . . . failure, before. About that time, Dr. Colton switched me to another advisor. From then on, it was an effort for him to say five words to me at a time."

"What were you working to hide from?"

"He never really forgave me for that breakdown. And even though I told him he was being unfair, deep down I agreed with his assessment. I should have been stronger. I always thought I could be a first-rate researcher, but I found out then, I never will be. I should be further along, you know, for my age, my experience."

"And I oughtta write better songs and see more than fifty people at a gig. C'mon, Clare, giving up guarantees you won't get there."

"No. I've learned my limitations and I've just had to accept them."

"Then again, maybe if I pushed harder and stopped worrying about when I was going to hit the wall, I'd write those breakthrough tunes I want to believe I have in me."

" 'And if everyone who believes in fairies . . .' No. Tinkerbell is a myth. Though in your case I believe you can accomplish whatever you choose." Most epileptics were so stifled by the stigma of their illness, if not the damage to their brains, that Tommy was something of a miracle—though of course that was a nonrigorous concept.

"So what caused your breakdown?" When she didn't respond, he advised, "Like Dr. Colton didn't say to me, if you're that scared to talk about it, you ain't over it yet."

"I fell in love."

"Colton may have been smart about brains but he was stupid about people. That makes a lot more sense to me than working yourself out of control. Was it Robert?"

"God no. This man always kept me on the edge of a cliff."

"He didn't love you back?"

"He loved me for loving him so much. I don't know, I suppose he did love me, as much as he was capable of loving anyone."

"So what happened?"

"He'd just moved here from Chicago. Once he got settled, his wife joined him."

"And that was that."

"Oh no. For months I got to be the other woman; I convinced myself I was satisfied. After all, I was so busy, did I really have time for more? Then I admitted I wanted him to leave his wife. Then I let him know. And then things weren't so nice between us anymore. Looking back now, the strangest part of all that happened is how surprised I was when the affair fell apart. I never believed I wouldn't win. Somehow, it never occurred to me that I wouldn't be the one he chose."

Suddenly she hated Tommy for drawing her out. "We'd better get back to work now." She retreated to her testing station and something in her voice kept Tommy from inquiring further. He put the headset on. She crammed her thoughts and doubts back inside the lead box of her memory.

Finishing the dichotic listening series, Clare established that Tommy's right brain would understand, spoken or written, *killer*, *knife, hall, night.* It didn't know the written form of *Colton*, but did recognize the auditory form. At some point she might try to teach his right brain additional relevant words, but it was far safer to stick with those already known.

She unrolled a large rough outline of a man's body. "Now you'll point to every place on the killer that you touched."

"We figured this out yesterday."

"I know but I didn't write results down until later and I'm not sure I got everything," Clare lied. "Use your left foot."

With cantankerous noisiness, he complied. His right hemisphere pointed to some of the areas named yesterday, but there were also discrepancies, which irritated him further. When his right brain indicated the killer's right hand and lower arm, Tommy said, "No it was the left arm."

"Please don't talk yet," Clare said.

Quivering a bit, his left foot then tapped the drawing's face. That could be quite significant, facial features or skin texture could—

Tommy interrupted her thoughts. "My foot's cramped, I was aiming for the neck that time, not the face."

"You already pointed to the neck!" Clare snapped.

"I touched the killer's neck and throat—but I have to tap the same spot to show that. There's no back or front to this picture you know." He had her there. "I really can't point right sitting down like this, that's why I'm making mistakes. Can I try walking around?"

Was this his left brain making suggestions on its own, or responding to a transmitted frustration from the right brain? "Fine. We'll try it that way."

Walking around and across the drawing, his left foot tapped body areas identical to the points his left brain had named yesterday. "Now this makes sense." He sounded victorious.

However, during his walk, he often teetered off balance: his right leg stopped moving before the left foot could reach a pointing goal. When the left foot did tap a body area, if it was an area the two hemispheres disagreed upon, the movement was jerky; slow. Through ipsilateral connections, Tommy's left brain could affect gross muscle movements on the same side of the body; and in this case it seemed to be fighting for and winning control over the other brain's foot, forcing it to give answers that represented the left brain's version of reality.

Dammit. She shouldn't have let his left hemisphere hear the test instructions. Although it would have figured out the command anyway. The drawing was too obvious. She should have devised ways of questioning the right hemisphere secretly. But it would have taken so much longer to prepare and administer unilateral tests.

"No, Tommy, this doesn't make sense. Your two hands couldn't have touched exactly the same spots."

He stepped back, as though slapped. "You're right. Maybe my right brain forgot everything. Shit."

"Let's try pointing with the yardstick."

He sat down, his left brain preoccupied. Good. Now they might make some progress. No. Shit was right. Again, Tommy's right hemisphere parroted his left hemisphere's claims. "I did forget. This is terrible."

Once, long ago, when Tommy's left hemisphere had been very negative about a conflict in test responses, the right had changed its answers. Was this another such conciliatory ef—

Tommy howled, "I can't stand this. What's happening to me?" Before Clare could reply, the yardstick began moving again. They stared with horrible fascination as it indicated the drawing's feet. "Feet? I know I didn't touch his feet!"

And the right brain hadn't indicated feet previously. Clare fought panic. Nothing was making sense. No wonder Tommy was developing nervous tics. Several times over the last few minutes, he had rubbed his left shoulder against his face, sweeping the cheek from nose to sideburn. "Does your cheek itch? No? You keep rubbing it like this." Clare imitated the motion.

He reflected. "There's a gnat in here, it keeps bothering me."

Was the right brain cross-cuing that it had touched the killer's face? Maybe. She was not in good shape to be drawing conclusions right now. And while Tommy had better stamina than the average split brain testee—his sessions could last three to four hours—today they'd gone nearly four with a lot of discord, which always drained him. "Let's call it quits for today."

"I'd rather keep going, we haven't gotten anywhere."

"There are times to push and times to wait." He didn't look convinced or happy. "There is one thing I'd like to do before the weekend is over. I've been thinking about the killer's either timing the lights to go off, or having an accomplice. Robert gave me some guidelines to determine whether the building control box could be easy to time, or whether it would require a master electrician. The box is in the basement. I'd like to go down there and take a look. It could be helpful to know whether there was an accomplice."

"If Beaudine finds out he'll turn you into Cheez Whiz."

"Therefore, we won't tell him. Do you want to come with me or not?"

"I'll come. This place is too creepy to walk through alone. Maybe not alone, somebody messed with your papers, right?"

Was his reluctance simply caution? Overriding her own caution was the hope their trek would trigger—something, cause some reaction in him. "I think I was wrong about that. It's virtually impossible to get into this building on weekends."

They collected their things and made the descent in silence. As they passed the first-floor landing, echoing down the hall came male voices, laughing. "It sounds like the security guards are taking a break."

"What security guards?" His whisper was even softer than hers.

"There's always one in the building on weekends. I ran into him earlier and he said there were two more guards on duty because of—Friday night."

Tommy tensed. "They carry guns? Shit, urban cowboys. Don't

surprise one around a corner or we're dead." They reached the basement. "It's huge down here. And there's another level below this?" Astonished, he peered down the stairs.

"I was amazed too. There are several buildings like this—all connected by underground walkways. No don't open that door!" He regarded her closely; then frowned at the gray door. "It's probably locked anyway. The building maintenance room is over this way." Her whisper was cracking. Colton's murderer had better have left a framed photo of himself or this wasn't worth the trip.

They passed a metal door sporting a radiation warning emblem. From the other side, weakly, came the sporadic yelping of a dog in pain.

"Animal labs," Tommy figured out. "If you want I can—"

"Here we are." She yanked open a door, exposing a dimly lit room full of pipes, dials, oversized industrial machinery.

"Big Brother slept here," Tommy captioned the view. There was the electrical control panel. They stopped abruptly. The area was cordoned off with yellow police tape and KEEP OUT signs. Gingerly, Clare tugged the tape. They could get under it. But should they? Tommy fumbled with his shirt's long sleeve, retracting his arm so that cloth covered fingers. "We need gloves but this'll do."

Heavy footsteps and a deep voice made them jump. "Help you with something?" While they recovered, a security guard appraised them from the doorway, gnawing the corner of his mustache.

Clare said, "Oh good. I'd given up trying to find you. My office lights keep going out."

The guard flicked open a pocket notebook, snapped a pen authoritatively. "Can't do anything until tomorrow. Room number?"

"In that case I'll just call building maintenance tomorrow morning."

"See some ID?"

"Room two-oh-six," Clare sighed.

"I'm still going to need some ID."

"Listen bud, she's got more right in this building than you do, so don't—" Tommy stopped at Clare's look of entreaty, but met the guard's stare.

"Is Charlie still on duty?" Clare tried to defuse the situation.

"He got off at three." Only her name and badge number were transcribed; Tommy's license got copied in its entirety. "Sorry to keep you, Dr. Austen."

The guard followed them up the basement stairs, then walked a few paces behind them all the way to the building entrance, testing door locks as he went. "When I grow up I want to be a fascist, mommy," Tommy said once they were outside, the guard locking the door behind them.

"You have a problem with authority figures," she scolded as they headed for her car. She returned the nods of three passing students, who may have been in her freshman survey class last spring.

"I'll bet Beaudine hears about our trip to the basement before we get to the parking lot." Tommy brightened: "I do love watching you with those instant alibis, though."

"I think of them with disturbing ease," she may have noted or may have just thought. She was so tired, she wasn't sure. In any event, he didn't respond. Or she didn't register his response.

Giving him a ride home, she unintentionally slowed as they passed the mansion where someone may have taken a shot at them. "I don't suppose there were any bullet holes in your car," she said, then wished she hadn't.

"I suppose I would've told you already if there were. You keep looking in the mirror. Car phones following us, right? When were you planning to mention it to me?" She seemed to have failed some test of trust.

"I didn't want to be an alarmist. It's only been behind us for nine blocks." Silence. As they neared Tommy's house, the car-phoned driver in the Honda turned and drove off. "There. The car's gone. No need to worry, after all."

"Or they figured out where we're going and already know where I live."

Clare's car dragged to a slow halt outside Tommy's apartment. "Look Tommy—"

"Listen Clare—" he said simultaneously.

They shared a brief laugh. "Today was a bad day, tomorrow will be better."

He nodded as though he fervently wished to believe. "Tomorrow morning then?"

"No. I teach in the morning and then I'll need to prep our experiments. Damn, I still need to prep my lectures too. How about—four o'clock? I know that's late, but if I ask someone to sub my classes and then we're in the lab . . . it doesn't seem very discreet."

"Four it is. But you don't need to prep experiments, it worked a lot better when you were just asking me questions, like with Robert yesterday."

Better for your left hemisphere, maybe. "It seems faster the other way but—years of studies prove it's not."

"You're the doctor." Tommy got out without looking at her.

"Tommy," she called before he could slam the door. When he turned, his face was stony. "This is one place you have to trust me."

His eyes softened. "You're right. My left brain just wants to rule the world. Get some sleep." His voice had become a caress. Clare drove home baffled at the shifting awareness of his left hemisphere.

Outside her building, two police cars were parked askew, red lights strobing the dusk air. Neighbors peeked through curtains at her open door. She ran upstairs, fighting conclusions. Jessie did not meet her.

Beaudine stood just inside. Behind him, the living room was a wreck—books off shelves, armchair upended, coffee table glass smashed, stereo components swinging from wires. It looked like the site of a colossal struggle. "Where's Robert? Is he alright?" she pleaded. Her eyes hunted Jessie, too; Beaudine just watched her. She longed for a heavy object—she'd aim for his eyes.

Robert exited the bedroom and spotted her, just as an authoritative voice from the bedroom hailed him to return. He blew her a kiss, then obeyed the voice.

She glared at Beaudine until he started talking. "Seems your —roommate—came home and surprised a burglary, apparently before they took anything but—"

"They?"

"Figure of illiterate speech. One white male went out the door while Dr. di Marchese was taking in the mess."

"You're certain this was a burglary, even though nothing is missing?"

"You got other suggestions?" His voice was excessively bland.

"Perhaps it was Dr. Haffner's killers—of course, you called that a burglary too."

"You got information that says otherwise, Dr. Austen?"

Was that look supposed to intimidate her? "Did you get my messages?"

"I got a lot of messages. What were you doing in that basement tonight with Tommy Dabrowski?"

"The lights in my office kept going off, I was hoping I could throw a switch or something. I didn't realize you had the area secured. That set me to thinking, actually. How did the lights go out on Friday evening?"

"We think the killer had an accomplice. Next time try asking me before you try snooping. And if I can't tell you, still don't try snooping. I'd like to think we're all after the same result, Dr. Austen. I've been very patient but this is as far as that goes."

Robert walked out in time to overhear. "Lieutenant Beaudine, that reminds me. What's a homicide investigator doing at an attempted burglary?"

"Want to make your point?"

"Are we under surveillance?"

"For your own safety, Doctor, from now on I will have someone watching this place. Is that it, Joe?" Beaudine asked one of his men, who nodded.

"Just a minute," Clare insisted. She told him about Tommy's accidents.

Beaudine claimed he'd look into both events.

As soon as the last of the police intruders exited, Clare sagged against Robert. "Where's Jessie?"

"Under the bed. She hissed pretty impressively at the officer looking for culprits beneath it." Clare was already down the hall. "I'm fine, thanks for asking."

"I could see that you were," Clare called back plaintively. She couldn't coax Jessie out, so crawled under the frame to pet her. Jess wouldn't purr but did decide to emerge. Unfortunately, "I'm stuck," Clare yelled into the carpet.

Robert raised the bed frame and she crawled backward; he gave her a hand and she was standing beside him. "What's this white gunk everywhere?"

"Fingerprint dust. They found three sets fresh enough to take seriously. They 'printed' me and got one match, the others matched you and Tommy. How did Lieutenant Beaudine know that? I asked him but he ignored me."

"I don't know. Right now I don't care." As Jessie rubbed against her legs, she put her arms around Robert. "I thought you were dead." They turned at a thud—Jessie had jumped onto the dresser to sniff the police dust. "That's sure to be toxic."

"I'll get the cleanser."

The evening was remarkable for achieving détente if not *glasnost*. They cleaned up after the intruder and the police, attempted dinner but not even Jessie was hungry, compared impressions of Beaudine, discussed Clare's lab efforts with Tommy —about which Robert had excellent suggestions. All in all, she felt closer to him than she had in months.

The intruder had entered via a louvered kitchen window, hidden by foliage as he removed the window slats one by one. After dinner, they bolted the window mechanism so this could not happen again. Then Robert helped Clare rig feline escape routes.

Jessie had stayed inside that morning; she'd not wanted to go out when Robert needed to leave. That was fine, but since there was no place for a cat door in their abode, she'd been trapped with the intruder. They rearranged furniture so that the cat could hide often, and move mostly unseen from room to room. For Robert's help, Clare felt gratitude underlain with irritation: he neither understood nor approved, giving him more than his usual air of condescension.

Remodelling completed, Robert kissed Clare for a while then went to bed. Clare settled in to work. Maybe she'd hit her two classes with a pop quiz. That was it—an essay: *What have you learned from this class?* The answers would tell her what to review most before finals. The quiz would eliminate the need for her to prep lectures tonight.

Rationalization and stall tactics devised, she turned to tomorrow's experiments, sorting lists of existing slides, drawings, and tapes for those that could be applied to their current efforts. Initially she'd presumed they'd know their murder answer within days; if today was indicative, it could take weeks. Did they have that much time?

CHAPTER 6

Neglect

"The doctor will see you now." Clare stood to one side so Tommy could enter her lab. She'd kept him waiting an hour while she readied tests.

He discarded the issue of *Neuropsychologia* he'd been reading upside down and sauntered to his lab chair. "You look great today."

She snorted. "I got three hours of sleep then spent four hours facing students who wished me dead, slowly and after much pain."

"Adversity becomes you."

"Now there's an immortal line."

"I'm really happy you told me that stuff yesterday about your life, it makes—"

She shoved the headset at him, switched the tachistoscope on. "This first test's a double whammy." This was Tommy's name for tests in which he fixed his gaze on the tachistoscope dot while getting additional input from the dichotic listening headset. Today Clare would be certain that only his right brain knew what input it received. Today she would not engage in intimate confessions that she would regret at four the next morning.

Their first experimental goal: to conclusively pinpoint the killer's body areas Tommy's left hand had touched. She flashed pictures of first one then another body part, while asking his right hemisphere which of the two was more like what he had touched. He responded by pulling a toggle switch. When his right brain wasn't sure or couldn't otherwise answer, it tapped the question mark card near his left foot. The method was a variation on an existing experiment so it didn't take her long to get started; and despite Tommy's difficulties maneuvering his injured hand, they made rapid progress. Until light flooded the room.

Steve stood at the switch. "Dr. Austen! I didn't think you'd be here."

"Then why are you here?"

"I mean I didn't know you'd be working with Tommy—anybody—today."

"Hey Steve," Tommy greeted him. "Very fast shirt."

It was a silk bowling shirt, magenta and orange. On Tommy it would look fantastic, on Steve it looked silly. "My girlfriend gave it to me."

"Al-right! So the cold war is over, huh? I told you it would work."

Steve nodded sheepishly. "I don't want to interrupt any further, Dr. Austen. I just wanted to ask if I could cut my hours. I need time to prepare for my orals."

"Yeah, it takes a lot of practice to keep those women happy," Tommy said deadpan. Steve gulped.

Steve had a girlfriend (the mind boggled imagining her). Tommy gave him advice. These data shouldn't disturb her. "Of course. How much extra time will you need?" She'd planned to keep Steve absent while they extricated clues, anyway.

"I—haven't figured that out yet. I—wanted to make sure it was okay first."

"It's okay. But you are interrupting our work right now."

Steve bustled in a circle, not getting any closer to the door. "Thanks for your advice," he muttered to Tommy, who just smiled. Then, spying the variety of color codings in the tachistoscope, indicating slides from several experiments, he said accusingly, "I didn't know you'd be doing a new series this month."

"I had a sudden brainstorm. I'll tell you about it Wednesday." Damn him, now she had to waste time coming up with a plausible smokescreen for their tests.

When Steve had departed, Tommy told her, "He's not really a bad guy."

"He's very nosy, not very bright, and he couldn't keep a secret if his life depended on it—much less yours. You wouldn't believe the confidential information he's told me about his prior projects."

"Maybe he was trying to win you over. Or maybe he realizes scientists get a little carried away with their top secrets."

"Maybe you don't know what you're talking about. Ask me about the time someone broke into my files and stole months of research data and I couldn't prove a thing." And couldn't recover in time to speak at the biannual International Neurological Forum. Her first and last invitation to do so. The whole incident had been her first solid lesson in the value of mistrust.

"Good comeback," Tommy said admiringly. "You can fight rings around anybody I know. Hey—fight, rings. Get it?"

She smiled. "I'm afraid so. Now we really—" But he'd already manned the headset.

Today his right brain did not claim to have touched any part of the killer's face. Had she misinterpreted yesterday's cross-cue or were her testing methods wrong? And, how to interpret when, seconds after tapping the question mark, Tommy's left hand pulled the toggle indicating it *had* touched the killer's eyes and ears?

Heavy footsteps and unrecognized voices sounded in her office. Damn Steve. He must not have locked the office door after him. She stomped to the lab door; just as she grabbed the knob, the door swung inward with much force. Her feet ran backward, striving futilely for purchase on the linoleum. She fell on the base of her spine. Pain shot upward, meeting pain shooting in from her wrenched shoulder. Tommy looked away from the screen in time to see her fall. He leaped to her aid, still wearing the headset, wired to her tape control board, which crashed to the floor.

One man and one woman wearing shocked expressions and the green garb of campus maintenance retreated from Tommy's advance. He thought they'd attacked her. "They're-okay-it-was-an-accident," she yelled and the scene became a tableau.

"You're having trouble with your lights, Dr. Austen?"

The basement alibi. "They seem to be fine now." The maintenance duo insisted on helping lift the control board, which now had a discouraging rattle. Finally, she convinced them they'd helped all they could, and locked the door behind them.

Tommy was examining the board. "Got a Phillips?" She brought him her screwdrivers. "You're not walking so good. How bad are you hurt?"

"A few days of hobbling. Next time I fall, remind me to let go of the door first."

He nodded and shrugged, unbolting the back of the control unit, getting her to act as his second hand. "How stupid can one man feel," he said rhetorically.

"You didn't hear them stomping around out there. If they'd meant trouble, they would have been quieter. You also didn't see my banana peel routine. Which makes you uninformed, not stupid. Do you think you can fix this?" It took forever to requisition equipment repairs and replacements. They did not need more delays.

"Yeah, couple things shook loose, that's all." He continued to tinker. "I had a dream about you last night."

"You remembered a dream? That's fantastic." Many split brainers complained they no longer had dreams. Why this might be was of course a subject of controversy. Clare believed dreams did still occur, but in the right hemisphere, inaccessible to conscious awareness, i.e., language. Tommy had recently started to recall dreams. Had his left hemisphere started to manufacture dreams too? Was her theory wrong? Were new connective routes forming subcortically between the hemispheres?

"Do you want to hear it?"

"Certainly. Any dream you have is noteworthy."

"We were in this factory. Really bright lights, smelled like rancid oil. Automated, except the machines were people, workers welded into equipment. They were building more machine people. The ones on the conveyor belts, they were really scared. It was dangerous for me to be there, so I was disguised as your briefcase or I was in your briefcase and you were trying to act nonchalant. Then all of a sudden I knew we were wrong, they wanted you too, but I couldn't warn you. Then Bianca appeared and motioned for you to get out of that room, but you ignored her because it was Bianca. Then the real Bianca woke me up—I was thrashing around, she thought I was having a seizure so she turned on a light. Afterwards I couldn't sleep any more, I just lay there thinking they're going to come after you too."

"I believe the more—hypervigilant we get, the less we'll be able to function." She told him about her apartment intruder, and about the hours it took her to calm down enough to work again. He looked angry and she guessed why: "I was definitely planning to tell you about it. I wanted to work first because I thought it might—distract you."

"I'm a big boy, Clare. You don't have to decide in advance how I'm going to react, how to handle me. I think this thing's okay now." He screwed the backing in place. She moved away. "What's with you?"

"You have a knack for highlighting aspects of my personality that I hate to see."

"I know it's tough for you, what with everybody else in the world being perfect."

He also had a knack for making her feel defenseless. "Are we ready?"

They resumed testing positions. Unfortunately, despite his denials, manipulating the toggle switch was making his injured arm hurt, hand cramp. She might be willing to let him suffer, if she weren't so afraid it would cause permanent damage.

She terminated the facial features testing; she needed to devise a new tactic there. Next and last up: determining where he had touched the killer's arms, hands, and feet. Such a slow process. Were there really no shortcuts? Or was she just not good enough to see one?

To his right hemisphere, she flashed a lower leg and a foot and asked dichotically, **"Which did you touch?"**

"I don't get it," Tommy said. "'Which did you touch' but you showed me a sled. My ma couldn't afford to take us to the snow, I've never touched a sled in my life."

"Shit," Clare said. Tommy's left hemisphere was supposed to hear **"What do you see?"** The lines were reversed. "Hold on a minute." She switched the tapes.

"Are you still asking my right brain where it touched the murderer? Is that all the further we are? Piss on a stick."

"I'm verifying some results. Do *not* start all that again."

This time she got the proper question to his right hemisphere. It tapped the question mark. "My right brain's a moron!" Tommy exploded. "Ow. Hey!"

Clare laughed and gasped; Tommy just gasped: his left foot had stomped down hard on his right foot. It wasn't funny, it could only delay them further if Tommy developed Mrs. Batesian symp—No, wait. In a flash, she felt stupid and enlightened. "Tommy, I think this is cross-cuing. I think the killer stepped on your left foot."

He looked inward, remembering. "Yeah, I think that's it. I remember my foot hurting, except my arm hurt so much more that I forgot about my foot." Whether the left hemisphere was confabulating, she could determine subsequently. More important was the relief that spread from one side of his face to the other: it caused so much turmoil when he felt his two hemispheres in conflict.

She'd just flashed pictures of a left then right hand, when someone began rapping on her office door. Under the headset, Tommy was oblivious. His left foot tapped the question mark, meaning it didn't touch either hand, didn't get the question, or —damn, take a hint, she wasn't answering the door! She flashed a new pair of photos, left hand then both hands. His right brain indicated it had touched both hands.

Dammit! She angrily waved to Tommy to remove the headset. Puzzled, he obeyed. As much as her throbbing back allowed, she stomped to the office door, threw it open and saw—

Bianca. Flexing her fingers. "Another minute and I'd be a cripple. Going at it hot and heavy I guess." She waltzed past Clare, lazily stretching her perfect torso as she went. "Need a ride home? I'm off work. Don't you know who did it yet? How do you figure that out, anyway?" She looked around the lab, then looked surprised. "You really were experimenting. Work was a drag, this woman comes to class a half hour late, no warm-up then it's my fault she pulls a quadricep. Oh, Trish loaned me her old car but she kind of asked me to not let you drive it after she heard what you did to Glenn's Datsun. Two cops came by to question him. They treated him like a criminal when he said he had it towed to a junkyard but wasn't sure which one. I'll probably get fired."

"Did they find the car?" Tommy asked eagerly. "Did they examine the tires?"

Bianca grew stern. "Remember the last time you got into one of your death-behind-every-corner routines?" He gave a short mortified laugh. She caressed his back and ass then turned to Clare, who had just fallen into her chair with a graceless plunk. "You sit over there? I pictured you right next to him. Don't let me disturb you. Is it alright if I hang out? Then you won't have to drive Tommy home."

"If you want to observe, in principle that's fine; but when I'm working out a new test, an extra presence in the room, however unobtrusive, is distracting."

"Was that a yes or a no?" Bianca asked Tommy.

"Me-ow," he replied and they shared a chuckle.

"Sorry," she told Clare as she at last headed for the door, "Tommy's right. He always is most of the time. Oh, Mark called. Is there practice Wednesday night?"

"We'll talk about it at home." Tommy blew her a kiss goodbye.

"Say hi to Robert for me." Bianca bade farewell to Clare, who somehow managed to not roll her eyes. Seconds after leaving, Bianca was back. "I forgot. They locked the front door for the night. The guard said I'd need a key to get out."

Clare expected each step to send her to China, so heavy did she feel. They had to walk Bianca to her latest borrowed car, a red Fiero. The security guards prowling the campus made it the safest area in the city, but still Bianca needed an escort.

It had seemed an impossible dream but at last she was driving away. "Sorry," Tommy said. "She's bad news when she's jealous."

Clare walked back at a fast clip; Tommy allowed her silence. In retrospect she saw that he had treated Bianca as the beloved kid sister he always claimed she ultimately was. As soon as she realized this, Clare stopped yearning to get home to Robert. Instead, she should go to a circus. Step right up folks, she waffles, she wavers, Dr. Clare Austen, the world's most ambivalent woman.

Reaching her building door, she turned the key so sharply, it broke in the lock. When needed, the guards were nowhere around, despite glass-rattling pounding.

"Clare," Tommy said. She stopped putting fist to pane and the night air became oppressively still. Tommy pulled out a pocket knife, had no luck extricating or turning the broken key. "Can't take you anywhere," he said cheerfully, repocketing the knife.

"Maybe we can get in through one of the other buildings." At Tommy's blank look, she reminded, "The basement walkways?"

"Brilliant. Which way?"

Clare led him around and about to Biochem. This door was wide open. They hurried down a hall, creating fast peripheral shadows on the pebbled glass doors to either side. Suddenly, the movements stopped, their shadows vanished: several lights were out in this section of the hall. Clare stiffened, waiting to feel the grit of shattered glass beneath her shoes; she thanked the god whose existence she'd always doubted when she did not.

"I never used to be scared of the dark," Tommy tried to joke away their haste. They careened around the baluster marking the stairwell. Descending to a landing, they surprised a man ascending. A man with loose flowered shirt and eyes like black holes. He turned and ran back down, away.

"It's him." She clutched Tommy lest she fall toward the fleeing figure. "Attacked me."

"Go get help," Tommy yelled, and descended three steps at a time.

Clare stood immobilized, a lightning debate inside her head: facing those eyes again, letting Tommy's one good arm catch that terrifying man, finding a guard or phone quickly enough. The two pairs of running footsteps were ever less audible. She plummeted down the steps to the lowest basement level.

She found Tommy ascending stairs at the other side of the subterranean maze. "Where's he going, outside?" Tommy yelled. They paused to fix on the distant footfalls.

"This floor—deadends. He has to—go up—then. Five or six —ways out," Clare gasped. They climbed the stairs, paused to listen, took off anew. She turned each corner terrified that she'd find him beyond it.

Her chest ached, her back throbbed. She couldn't run any more. Yet—hallway, corner, hallway, hallway, corner. At times they glimpsed his billowing shirt; or his footfalls were louder. But eventually, they lost him.

"Fucker—knows. Way around—down here." Tommy bent over, sucking in big draughts of air.

Suddenly, Clare thought of something important. As soon as she could speak, she said, "He was. The accomplice. The lights."

Tommy looked at her. "Gotta be. How do. We get out?"

"Not sure. Up a flight. Then I'll know." They climbed stairs slowly, filling the air with their labored breathing. Then another noise began to penetrate.

Screams. Somewhere in this building, a man was screaming in horror. Tapping energy they no longer possessed, Clare and Tommy sprinted forward. Each step jolted pain through Clare's back. Upstairs. Down this hall. The cries were fainter. Backtrack. The cries fainter still. Reverse direction once more. The screams were abating.

They were in Physics. Robert's office was on this floor. She fought panic: Robert had worked late, been surprised by a man with a knife; he cried for assistance until loss of blood and futility—no, that wasn't Robert's voice, it was too high. But then she'd never heard Robert scream.

The cries now had a strange bouncing cadence. Turning a corner, they encountered a figure running their way, mouth open in a rictus worthy of Edvard Munch. From this chasm came the sound they'd sought, now hoarse and hiccuping. The figure stopped when it reached them. The mouth snapped shut. Steve.

"I there's door was no eyes unnh." He sagged sideways. Before they could reach him, he fell on his face, which revived him but bloodied his nose. Through facial hieroglyphs, he communicated that he was alright but someone back that way needed help. They propped him against a wall, shirttail to bleeding nose, and sprinted in the direction he'd indicated.

Some ways down the hall, hearing running steps behind them, they turned to see Steve fleeing toward the stairs. Tommy yelled to him; he simply ran faster.

They exchanged looks then continued. Clare had time to wonder whether the building was really as deserted as it seemed; whether those screams could be heard by researchers deep at work behind thick wooden doors. Then, turning a corner, her vision dimmed. Her shoe slid. Twenty fingernails scraped twenty blackboards. She started trembling: two hall lights were smashed, bits of glass strewn beneath. Further on, a door gaped open. Yellow light sliced into the brown hall.

"Not again," Tommy whispered. They stopped, squinting at the piercing yellow light. Neither took that next step forward.

Eventually: "Steve said somebody down here needed help."

"Asshole said he'd wait, too." They walked forward tentatively yet the tile still shrieked underfoot, gouged by shards of glass.

"Not Lalitha," Clare whimpered at the nameplate on the yawning door. Dr. Lalitha Rao, Associate Professor of Physics and Chemistry. She and Robert had taught a freshman survey course together, three years before. Since then, bit by bit, she and Clare had become confidantes, a role neither was comfortable playing. Clare loved evenings at Lalitha's house: her extravagant Indian meals and intriguing multinational guests, refreshingly few of whom were scientists. But more than that Clare—

"May I help you with something?"

Lalitha's melodic, multiaccented voice came from within, distorted somehow. Against her will, Clare's thoughts returned to the present and her feet moved forward. "What do you want? No! Please!" The voice, fearful now, dragged Clare through the entry room. She became aware of an urgent mechanical howling —a phone long off its hook.

In an instant that passed like an hour and etched itself in her memory forever, Clare surveyed the scene. "May I help you with something? What do you want? No! Please!" Clare hunted the maker of the distorted voice. Over there above the desk: Lalitha's beloved parrot Niels, frenzied, throwing himself against the bars of his small traveling cage.

"May I help you with something?" Clare's gaze crept to the phone, on the floor, overturned, mouthpiece cord stretched taut; slid across red wet tile to Lalitha's red wet hand clutching the receiver, her distinctive diamond ring refracting ruby light. ". . . No! Please!" Long thick black hair floated in a dead sea of blood. Is this when they use dental records maybe it's not Lalitha no she's still got her fingerprints. Her face was featureless, smashed in, Clare supposed, although it looked inside out.

Tommy pulled Clare into the hall. "Got to find a phone," he gulped, heading one way then the other. She giggled. Phone right there, of course, but Lalitha was using it. Tommy ceased stumbling back and forth and shook her. She stopped giggling. Before he could prevent her, she ran back inside to cover Niels in his cage, then ran out and led Tommy across the hallway, threw her weight against the door there.

EMERGENCY EXIT ONLY. DO NOT OPEN. ALARM WILL SOUND. The alarm screeched at maximum decibels, masking the phone's cries, the parrot's frantic mimicry. It prevented talking and thinking. They sat on the fire escape, backs propped against the door, waiting for someone to find them.

If Lieutenant Beaudine was surprised to see them, he didn't show it. After asking all the predictable questions, he grew almost kindly: he agreed to not contact Robert before Clare got home; and allowed Clare to take Niels, after taping the parrot's version of Lalitha's last words. He even solicited Clare's advice: did she think, from the parrot's inflection, that Lalitha had known her visitor? (Clare couldn't tell.)

His impassivity cracked, however, when he inquired about her research with Tommy. He seemed eager for leads, any leads, although he acted like he was consulting a psychic. For an instant, Clare felt insulted. Then she felt nothing again.

Steve was brought in. While he followed his police escort through the small gathered crowd of distracted professors and exhausted grad students, Clare noticed that her assistant had changed his clothes. His hair was wet too—as though he'd showered. His nose was swollen and already bruising from his fall.

After questioning Steve, Beaudine returned to Clare, his manner now curt. He asked her all the same questions over again and finally ordered, "Describe the victim's condition."

"I don't know what my brave and intelligent assistant told you, but I'm not going to let you put me through this. I need to go home."

"When you've finished here." He posted a guard, went downstairs to give a statement to the TV news crews. After an eternity he returned and resumed questions at square one. After an hour of this, he conferred with various associates, then followed her home. Tommy and Steve, it turned out, had been dismissed long before.

Robert was in pajamas on the couch pretending to read, the phone beside him. He looked too worried to be angry—it was nearly three A.M. She stood holding the bird cage; Jessie leaped from nowhere, clung to the cloth cover. Niels squawked once. They must look funny. She was surprised Robert didn't laugh. Instead, he bounded to her side.

Behind her on the step outside, Beaudine appeared. Robert must have figured it all out, for his arms tightened around Clare and he started to weep. She was made of cement. Thus could she stand so steadily, with the already heavy cage swinging under Jessie's added weight. Robert yanked the cat away, helped Clare set the cage down. Jessie went right for it again. Clare removed her ever so gently even though she was being a complete jerk.

"Dr. di Marchese—" Beaudine began. Clare went to shut Jessie into the bedroom, then searched the kitchen for possible parrot food. The front door opened—and Niels squawked. Beaudine's entourage was leaving, with the parrot.

"Wait. You said I could take care of him," she called to Beaudine.

"Can't let you," Beaudine replied. He'd never intended to.

"You and your fucking games, you can't lock him in some goddamned impound. Of all the piece of shit . . ."

Beaudine motioned his men to leave, clicked the door shut behind him without responding to her ravings.

Once the apartment was copless, Clare fell silent. She freed Jessie, settled in at her desk. Robert was on the couch, watching her, his cheeks wet with silent tears for Lalitha. "Come sit with me," he said.

"I can't. I've got to figure out what Tommy knows, it's the only way to stop—this." Jessie jumped onto the desk, Clare touched a tail as Jess jumped off again.

"I know. I agree. But it can wait."

"I can't." Jessie now curled up in Robert's lap. Traitor. Clare busied herself, aware of Robert's attention. Fine. Let him watch her.

Time elapsed. Robert brought Jessie over to Clare's lap. "Don't do this to yourself," he began.

"Stop," Clare said furiously though she didn't feel furious. She didn't feel anything. Jessie fled and for an instant, Clare was swept with an aching loneliness.

Robert went into the bedroom. She didn't know how long she'd been working when he returned to the couch, opened a book, observed her over the open volume. She didn't complain; if anything, she felt comforted. "If I can help," he said.

She nodded without looking up, fearing what would happen if she did.

CHAPTER 7

Symmetry Breaking

"Today, you don't look so hot," Tommy informed her as they prepared for their next session of brain charades.

"Don't tell me you've never felt better."

"Not hardly, especially when our man in Homicide showed up at practically dawn. See, he hoped you'd spill something but—"

"There's nothing to spill, for christ's—"

"Easy. I know that, remember?"

"Beaudine is the single most irritating human being I have ever met."

"He asked me what I do during blackouts. I think he's been reading about seizures where you don't pass out, just make your appointed rounds with no memory of it later. I think he hopes I commit grisly murders during seizures, with you taking notes."

"I don't blame him for getting farfetched. This is making less sense all the time. Although 'data are complicated, theories are sophisticated, simplicity appears only with the truth.' That's something—"

"Dr. Colton used to say."

"No. Lalitha."

"There's another one I never heard you mention."

"I didn't get to see her much. How could anyone—I mean, I can imagine Dr. Colton having enemies. With Dr. Haffner, I wouldn't know. But Lalitha—"

"You sound like a TV anchor. Like other people are gonna take this as a sad story, so your voice better sound appropriate."

"Don't play shrink with me, Tommy. It's worse than when you play Romeo." This sounded much harsher than she'd anticipated, yet it didn't seem to faze him.

"I have these erotic fantasies about you. We go out in the woods, lay down on some pine needles, it's so soft we don't need a blanket, so quiet we can hear the breeze at the top of the trees. We take our clothes off and you cry all over me."

"That is one sick fantasy."

"Shit, now you're laughing like a TV anchor."

More like Humpty Dumpty, being coaxed by well-meaners to climb the wall. "It just doesn't make sense. I don't know why anyone would kill Dr. Colton, much less Lalitha. But why those two together?"

After a moment's deliberation, he sanctioned her changing the subject by adding, "Or why those three?—if Haffner wasn't offed by burglars. Seems like the deranged surfer's got something against scientists. But he's too short to be our guy in the hall."

"Plus. If there is an accomplice—do deranged killers work in teams? Well-organized teams, at that?"

"Cults do. And the Hillside Strangler was two guys. Still doesn't explain why, though. Not in any way I'm smart enough to see."

Clare struggled to erect a dam of words against the wave of hopelessness threatening them. "Certainly, if we understood the motive, we'd have a better chance of naming the killer. But we don't have enough information to know why and trying to obtain it would take so much time. Time better spent working on who."

Tommy nodded vigorously and donned the headset.

That they were desperate to see the murderer caught, and that this was the only way they might help, gave added focus to the day's work. Clare at last completed their oft-interrupted effort to determine which parts of the killer's body Tommy's left hand had touched. Now they could—

Not again. A knock, immediately preceding a key in the lock. "Dr. Austen?"

Steve followed his voice into the lab; a young woman with auburn curls, white skin, and blue eyes accompanied. "You didn't have the sign up again," he chided. The TESTING IN PROGRESS DO NOT DISTURB sign, which Clare had omitted lest someone notice Tommy was being tested so often. "I thought you weren't here. I—was going to leave you a note."

"You needed help writing this note?" Clare looked at the girl, who was examining the lab with undisguised curiosity. Steve looked befuddled.

The girl's clothes might be modern, but her profile, as she turned to smile sweetly at Steve, belonged on a Victorian cameo. "She means me, Steven."

Flustered, Steve introduced them to Deirdre, a senior. "I— I'm really behind. I—can't assist anymore," he explained, "but Deirdre will sub for me."

Deirdre added, "Steve's told me what he does for you and I'm sure I can manage it. If you like my work, I'm available next quarter too."

"Fine." She could help with student records keeping, at least. And not knowing anything might be an asset while Clare tried to keep these experiments secret.

"Thanks," Steve gushed. "And thank you for helping me last night."

"Wish we could say the same, Steve-o," Tommy told him.

"I'm really ashamed about the way I—but I had to get away."

"Anybody would have." The way Deirdre looked at him; the way Steve responded. Marvelous. Clare had just hired Steve's girlfriend.

"What the hell did you tell Lieutenant Beaudine, by the way, Steve?" Clare tried to soften her initial tone, but failed—and caught herself pleased to see that Steve's nose was a mess of red scrapes and purple bruises.

"The lieutenant . . . advised me that you would ask me, and told me not to say anything." For strength, Steve looked to Deirdre, but was still so nervous, he buzzed. He was taller than Clare had realized, tall enough to be—no—Steve? Absurd.

"Next time we let you deal with your own corpses," Tommy informed him, and Steve stiffened. The lovely Deirdre tittered; Tommy appraised her. Steve forced a laugh.

"Was there anything else, Steve?" Clare inquired. Thanks-for-coming-now-go-away.

Deirdre gushed, "I heard you're solving a murder in the lab. I'd love—"

"Where did you hear that?" Clare's voice was amazingly cool.

Steve's whimper revealed Deirdre's source. But where had he heard?

"Isn't it true?" Deirdre pressed.

"Unfortunately, no. I wish there *were* something I could do."

The couple departed, Steve—impossibly—more nervous; Deirdre clearly unconvinced by Clare's denial.

"I was going to fire dear Deirdre," Clare mused, "but now I've got to keep her long enough to convince her she heard wrong."

Tommy nodded. "We've got to explain why I'm here all the time though. With my arm like this, you'd postpone regular testing until it was healed."

"You're right. I suppose I could let it be known I'm pushing you so I can prepare a paper for the conference in January. That's just barely believable."

"I got it. We'll pretend we're experimenting in the biblical sense."

This time Clare was grateful for the knock on her door, although stupefied to find Robert there.

Before following her into the lab he looked both ways, as though crossing a dangerous intersection. "I just stopped by to make sure you were alright. You look a lot better than you did this morning."

"Then she must have been mighty scary this morning. Hey Roberto. Um. Clare. I'm really sorry about the corpses line with Steve."

What did he mean? Oh, of course. He'd been referring to Lalitha. Or, as she now thought of it, Monday Night's Murder.

Tommy described Steve and Deirdre's visit to Robert, then asked his advice about hiding their research purpose. Robert removed his glasses, examined them for smudges, finally put them back on as though he had no choice. "You could always pretend you're having an affair."

Even Tommy sounded awkward as he opted for Clare's impending conference excuse. Robert cut him short. "Must be difficult for that sling to operate these levers." He studied the tachistoscope setup. "Have you talked to Requisitions?" he asked Clare, not looking at her either.

"You know how they are. It will take weeks unless I put a rush on it and then I'll have to explain why I'm in such a hurry."

"And then it'll only take them weeks. I might be able to jury-rig something."

"That would be wonder—" Clare began.

"See what I can do. Let you get back to it." He headed out abruptly.

"Stick around," Tommy said. "Maybe you'll have some input."

"Clare doesn't appreciate meddling. I wouldn't either." She caught up with him at the door. "Promise me something?" She nodded hesitantly. "When you leave, have a guard or three walk you to your car."

She managed a smile. "I'll try to be home early."

"Of course you will." And he was gone.

She returned to Tommy. "Fool. Did you think he doesn't suspect? How could you ask such a question?"

"I was hoping he'd have a real suggestion. Shit. Suspect 'us,' you mean? There's nothing to suspect, except the way you flipped when he mentioned an affair. If you're going to act guilty you should try to be guilty first, Clare."

"This is all a big joke to you but Robert is important to me and—"

"Hold it. You just want to believe I'm joking. And sure, Roberto's important to you, but that doesn't mean you're not wondering whether it's over. Which you are." He put the headset on. She motioned that she wasn't ready for the next test. He left it on. She escaped to her list of test findings.

Tommy's right hemisphere had indicated that it touched the killer's neck, chest, left shoulder, left thigh, right hand, and lower arm; and that the killer had stepped on Tommy's foot. There seemed to be a contradiction about facial data: his right brain had claimed it didn't touch the face, but then indicated the ears and eyes. He hadn't touched the killer's eyes and ears but they were important? How could that be? Aha. Of course. (Maybe.) Tommy had peripherally seen, had fleetingly heard the killer. Yes, that had to be it. (Maybe.) Good. That's where they would begin.

Tommy was staring at nothing. She wadded paper, threw it, but her back was so stiff today, the wad barely cleared her testing station. Still, he removed the headset and asked, "What was Steve doing in the physics building last night?"

"Damn. I should have thought of that before."

Tommy sounded irritated. "So we're thinking of it now."

"I can't imagine why he'd be there. Do you think he's capable of—that?"

" 'He seemed like such a nice boy. So quiet, so polite.' Can't see him with the deranged surfer, though. Who, P.S., Beaudine doesn't believe we even saw last night."

"Or at all. But here's what really bothers me. That man who attacked me doesn't seem like the accomplicing type. He does seem like the horrible murder type." After their latest encounter, even calling him the deranged surfer didn't render him less frightening. But he was several inches too short to be the man who'd knifed Tommy.

"I don't know what that type is. Any type is. I don't know why we're bothering. The more we get into it, the less I understand anything."

A lesson Clare relearned for the umpteenth time: more often than not, rationally discussing murder particulars left Tommy confused/angry/hopeless. "We've got to have faith that if we keep discovering little pieces, eventually they'll all fit into the same puzzle."

"I'll bet you love jigsaw puzzles." His voice said he despised them.

"Absolutely. Those twenty-thousand-piece all white round ones."

He shuddered. "Next you'll tell me you own the complete works of Muzak."

"As a matter of fact."

"I'd rather do experiments than hear this. What's next?"

"I'll ask a question. You'll answer with the levers." Each half of Tommy's brain would see YES, NO, or MAYBE. Each hand would reply by pulling a lever beneath each flashed word. But—the hemispheres would not see the words in the same order, to hinder left brain confabulation.

His left hemisphere saw NO then MAYBE. His right hemisphere saw YES then NO. "Did you see the killer in the hall Friday night?"

MAYBE, the left hemisphere answered. NO, the right hemisphere responded. Both used the second lever to reply.

"Did you see a part of the killer's body or clothes?" His left hemisphere said MAYBE with the second lever. His right answered YES with the first lever.

"Wait a minute." Tommy had observed the discrepancy in levers pulled. "My right brain's saying no but it's wrong."

"You're assuming it saw the same words in the same order. *That's* wrong." His mouth opened, then closed. Ha. She'd outsmarted his left brain, for once.

His left shoulder kept rubbing against his left ear. Cuing her, she believed, that he'd also heard the killer. "Fixate on the dot again. Now. Did you hear the killer's voice?" Tommy's left brain chose MAYBE. His right brain did not respond but the shoulder to ear rubbing resumed.

Ah. Now she understood: "Did you see the killer's ear?" NO.

She hadn't understood after all. "Did you touch the killer's ear?" She asked with a touch of futility, expecting and getting NO.

"This isn't an interrogation, asking me the same fucking questions over and—"

"Stop. I need quiet." As she stared at her notes, searching vainly for new patterns in the responses, Tommy's restlessness and hostility grew. She'd have to come back to this later. "I'll need to double check answers, Tommy. That will happen ongoingly."

He relaxed a bit. "My right brain will screw us, ongoingly," he noted sunnily.

Interestingly, Tommy consistently admitted he had a right brain these days. How would this affect future testing? Now there was a future beyond her powers of belief: a day when the murderer was caught and they were back to business as usual.

"I need to switch to using my foot for a while. My left hand hurts all the way to my shoulder."

She consulted her watch. "We've been here close to nine hours. Let's call it quits until tomorrow."

"I don't want to stop."

"It does us no good if you stress your arm so badly you can't use it for days. And as we get more tired there's a point of diminishing returns."

"I feel like every time we leave here we'll hear more screams."

"I hear them all the time," Clare admitted softly.

The last thing she knew, she was perched on the tachistoscope table, he was slouched in his orange plastic chair. Now they were standing, holding one another. His heart pounded even harder than hers, which somehow calmed her.

She felt an odd scrabbling against her ribs, below one breast. "I'm not getting fresh," Tommy murmured into her hair, "my hand's having spasms." She stepped back and they watched his twitching left fingers freeze into a claw. "These tests are definitely not good for the old hand," Tommy said ruefully. Clare massaged his hand and the muscles loosened. He ran a finger along her palm; she pulled her hand away, finally dared to look up at him. Seeing her sober reflection in his eyes, she grew more sober still. His good hand rubbed her cheek. "My shirt button made a mark," he explained with a loving smile. She took another step back. He interrupted her before she was sure she was going to speak. "I know," he said simply.

She stepped away to turn off the tachistoscope.

"Aren't there any other tests we can do today?"

"Actually there is something we could try with your foot."

"Sounds kinky. Tell me more."

"When the killer stepped on your foot. I can't guarantee it, but we may be able to estimate his weight. We can apply a certain weight to your foot, then you can decide whether it's heavier or lighter than he was."

"How do we know how much stuff weighs, you got a scale?"

"I know where to get one. Come with me." She led him down the hall to the women's bathroom. After a pause, he followed her inside.

It was the kind of scale found in a doctor's office circa 1940, unwieldy and heavy—when she finally got Tommy to help her move it. He had to read the graffiti in every stall first. There wasn't much—it wasn't that kind of school—but it fascinated him. "Listen to these. 'For a good time don't ever call Brian T.' 'All men are islands—post nuclear testing.' Here somebody wants a list: 'What are men good for?' and then there're ten blanks to fill in. One pen crosses out numbers two through ten, another pen says 'At least flies can be used in experiments.' Yow. Some mean females in this place. Do you all think like this?"

She tugged the scale away from the wall. "Only the ones who have cause, I imagine. But I can't really speak for my entire species. Could you please help me lift this?"

"Phew. This one's worse than any men's room ever. I can't even repeat it." He emerged from the last stall with a grim expression. "There was a drawing to go with it." As they dragged the scale doorward, he mused, "You know any happy couples?"

"How about intermittently content?"

"What I don't get is why we all think it's possible. To be happy."

Do we all? Think that? "Stop. I have to set this down. We're probably discalibrating it forever. If that's a word."

"I wonder if anybody ever wrote stuff like that about me."

"I thought Bianca was your high school sweetheart."

"We've had some rocky spells. Even an official separation."

Clare dragged the scale with a vengeance. Back pain flared, a welcome distraction. Tommy and Bianca would fight, he'd cheat, they'd make up, he'd go home.

"But this time it's over," he brooded. "I'm just waiting for her to figure it out. Maybe she already knows."

I'll bet you say that to all the separation girls. "Why is she so jealous then?"

"I get jealous too. Like I hate that guy Andy at her gym—the way she looks when his name comes up. But jealousy's not love. Listen to me, I'm one of those books. *People Who Love to Hate People Who Hate to Love But Wish They Didn't.*"

Clare snorted. They stopped to rest again. "This hall got longer."

"And emptier. Something else bad's going to happen. I can feel it." At last there was her door. Ajar. "Didn't you lock it?" he whispered.

"Maybe the lock didn't catch. I—I can't take any more of—" her whisper broke and "—this!" rang down the corridor.

They backed away, sprinted downstairs, found a guard: their friend who'd caught them snooping around the basement light switches. He was busy with a cheese sandwich and a *Best of Soldier of Fortune* but deigned to accompany them, like a father showing his toddler there was nothing under the bed, right during the last seconds of the big game on TV.

Hand on his gun, he found Clare's office empty with no evidence of intrusion. He watched them drag the scale inside without offering to help. When Clare shut her door, he jiggled the knob and called, "You're locked in now, professor."

As his High Noon footsteps receded, Tommy flipped him off. "Hope he gets to find the next victim," Clare muttered as they dragged the scale to the lab.

"Hope he is the next victim," Tommy said. "But he won't be. Pricks don't seem to be getting offed around here."

What *was* the pattern to the murders? What relevance would that have to their efforts? Would she and Tommy have any relevance to stopping the killings?

Tommy mistook her brooding. "Sorry. Didn't mean to remind you. So now you drop stuff on my foot?"

"First, we'll estimate pounds per square inch of pressure. I have some plywood we'll use to create the same pressure base. Then I'll hold objects of a known weight and step on the plywood. I weigh a hundred thirty so I hope he wasn't much heavier than one eighty; fifty pounds of kitty litter is all I can carry." He was giving her a peculiar look. "I take it you think this isn't going to work."

"Amazing. A woman who tells her real weight. Ever notice that? Women lie about weight. And age. Men just lie about height."

"Don't forget penis size. I can't believe I said that."

He laughed gleefully. "Hope it's my influence."

The experiment proceeded as she'd envisioned it, until, laden with medical tomes, she jumped on plywood duct-taped to his shoe. She teetered and Tommy reached to steady her. "Don't touch me, that could alter the results." They tried again. This time she dropped a book. Next time he lost his balance and they tumbled together, books flying. They howled with pain, frustration—and laughter.

Finally they got it right. Then Clare laid out three stacks of books—the five she had used, a set of two, and a set of seven. Tommy's left foot pointed to the stack of seven. She needed to be heavier. They groaned. Her arms weren't long enough to hold more books, so they anchored a tome to each shoulder. "Do I look as dumb as I feel?"

"Way dumber," he said encouragingly. She took up her armload of books and jumped. They hadn't allowed extra room for the shoulder books, one of which hit Tommy in the chin. The ensuing expletives startled Clare and she missed the plywood. Guffaws broke out.

Eventually, Tommy's right brain found a weight/pressure it thought comparable to the killer's. As a book-laden Clare stepped on the scale she realized, "I could have just weighed myself in the bathroom." This they found uproarious.

The killer's weight was about 195, plus or minus two books, ten pounds. A weight they'd estimated from his shadowy size in the hall. This they also found hilarious. "I think we're losing it," Tommy chortled.

"It's long gone," Clare assured him. They dragged the scale to the hall, away from her door so it wasn't clear where it had been. If maintenance found out she was responsible for moving it, she could forget office servicing for days.

Back in her office, Tommy picked up his backpack. Clare started sorting her notes and slides for work at home. "What are you doing?" he demanded.

"Aren't we leaving? It's late and I've got classes tomorrow morning."

"No, I was getting us dinner." He produced two green apples and two flat sandwiches. "Guess I should've put the apples in first." Using one hand and his teeth, he peeled away wax paper, assessed, proffered the less damaged sandwich. It emitted an odd pungent odor. "Peanut butter, lettuce, mustard and honey. Sounds weird tastes great. I promise."

She forced herself to accept it. Whether she could force her throat to swallow was another matter. "Robert will have waited dinner for me," she explained her hesitation. And Robert was such a wonderful cook.

"Suit yourself. Can never get Bianca to try 'em either." Which of course made her want to down the sandwich in record time. She took a bite of apple. He smiled enigmatically then looked down at his injured arm and wiggled those fingers. "I can use my hand again for a while."

She rigged the tachistoscope for its YES NO MAYBES. "There is one other issue we could clear up tonight. This isn't too bad." She'd sampled the sandwich.

"Give it to me, I'll finish it."

"Why do I have the feeling I'm failing a test?"

"All my life I've searched for a woman with real taste buds."

"I'm afraid you'll have to keep looking." She relinquished the sandwich after one more small bite. She didn't really want to go home. This room tonight was as good as a Baja hideaway. Fluorescent lights provided a full moon; the distant hum of building machinery, waves on a beach; the formica tables stretched like white sand around them.

". . . Jessie in to work, ever?" Tommy was asking.

"I brought her in here once. She went berserk. I think she smelled fear, from the animal labs. It still makes me ill, remembering how scared she—why do you ask?"

"Because then we could stay here forever."

"I know what you mean." She explained about the Baja hideaway.

He smiled cautiously. "Never thought I'd hear you admit something like that."

She was surprised, too. "Have I confused you yet?"

"Keeps it interesting," he said and assumed his testing position. She switched on the tachistoscope, retreated to her testing station. Robert hated her rabid inconsistencies, as he called them. Robert was so calm, reassuring, caring. How then could he so often make her feel something was amiss with her?

Tommy's hemispheres saw YES NO, NO YES. "Do you know the killer?"

"What are you talking about? Why are we here if I don't?" Instant fury.

"There are two possibilities. The first is that you encountered something distinctive on the killer. Touched a wart on his nose, for example. Something that, once we identify it, will be so individual that it will also identify the killer." She paused. "The other possibility is that the killer is someone you know."

"I don't know anybody capable of the stuff we've seen."

"You're certainly getting upset about this."

"Sure. Right. That means I'm lying, hiding something. Maybe I did it. Or Steve, that's who you'd like to nail, yeah, get Beaudine on the phone I think we've got something here."

"Tommy. Listen to yourself."

"I'm not—doing whatever it is you're accusing me of. Come on. I'll prove it to you." He stared at the dot with a vengeance.

Clare sighed, flashed YES NO, NO YES. "Is the killer someone you know?"

Both hemispheres indicated NO. "The. Fucking. Answer. Is. Fucking. No." With each word, Tommy slammed his right hand against the right side of his head.

Clare ran over and grabbed his arm. "Both hemispheres answered no." She kept yelling until at last he heard her.

"Told you." He sounded very tired. "I gotta go home." He continued while she assembled her things. "Of course you don't believe the answers are no. We've been at this for fucking ever and we're getting nowhere. You need some outside consultation, you're on the wrong track."

Clare was silent. He was frightening her. She'd have to ask his right hemisphere the same questions clandestinely, tomorrow. It had been a gross error, trying to save time by not posing questions dichotically. Much more time was lost when his left brain got angry like this.

They walked downstairs without speaking. Clare paused when she saw the unpleasant security guard, remembering her vow to Robert that a guard would walk her to her car. "Maybe he did it," Tommy indicated the guard. "He's the right size too." Clare bared teeth in a simulated smile at the guard, who jotted in his notebook. No, she wouldn't ask him to walk her out; there were enough—probably more competent and surely less obnoxious—guards stationed outside.

There were guards on every walkway, even more attentive to Clare and Tommy's progress than they were to the occasional students straggling back to the dorms. Yet the walk was still unsettling. The night air was heavy, cold and black. The moon had set or not yet risen. Their steps resounded around, before, behind them; until Clare was sure they were being followed, paced and awaited. Tommy muttered to himself as they went. She had to jog to keep pace.

Just before they reached the faculty parking lot, a slight dark figure jumped from behind a tree, grabbed Tommy's bad arm. Tommy howled; Clare swung her briefcase but the figure leaped away before she could connect, and grabbed for a knife sheathed at a hip. "Try it and you're dead," Tommy yelled. The figure backed away, hands raised in a gesture of surrender.

"All I wanted was do you have a smoke," the man whined. Light now illumined the blunt sunken features of a young homeless man who occasionally slept behind the bushes lining the faculty parking lot fence.

Tommy recognized him too. "Larry you stupid fuck. You know I quit."

"How about some coin so's I can get a pack?" Larry smoothed his top, a badly stained lab coat, obviously retrieved from a garbage bin.

"Not tonight man, I have a headache." Tommy must other times be generous, because Larry usually got angry at refusals; now he laughed.

His raucous chicken cackles trailed them across the parking lot, empty except for three cars—Clare's, and two flanking hers. They stopped walking. "There's somebody in that one." Tommy peered into the sedan left of Clare's Nova. She strained to see but it was too dark. They stood uncertainly until headlights passing along the street lit the car's interior. "Shit it's just headrests." Tommy strode forward, then stopped and held out his hand to Clare. After a moment, she took it.

"Now I'm seeing somebody in the other car," she complained. As their scrutiny shifted, so did Clare's perspective. The car, a blue Nissan or Honda, was getting smaller. No, it was driving away. That low hum had been its engine idling. They ran forward. Immediately, the car picked up speed, lights going on only after it was some distance down Wilson Avenue.

They stood in the parking lot for a time, unsure how they should react. Then she took him home. "Making more sense all the time, uh huh," Tommy bid her good night.

CHAPTER 8

Cerebral Dominance

"I don't know what my problem was last night," Tommy concluded his apology. They sat on the couch in her office, their lab work looming: source of all trouble, it seemed this afternoon.

Clare was likewise unsure what his outburst had meant. Either he did know—and liked—the murderer and couldn't face that knowledge, or it terrified him that someone so vicious could be known and seemingly innocuous. It was a crucial point, but irrelevant until she determined which explanation applied— which might be too late.

Larry was dead. Uniformed police had pulled Clare from her first class that morning. (Now there was one way to get her students' attention.) Late for that class, she'd parked near her classroom and thus missed seeing cops and camera crews swarming the faculty lot bushes. Nothing else was being discussed on campus, however, so Clare now knew that they'd only found most of Larry and were combing the environs for the rest of his remains. Tommy had overheard corridor gossip that Larry was slain elsewhere and the pieces strewn under the bushes; but when he stopped to hear more, the gossipers clammed up.

Beaudine had separately summoned Clare and Tommy because they were the last to see Larry alive. Except for his killer, Clare had to remind Beaudine, who just stared. How he knew about their encounter with Larry, he of course wouldn't say.

Once Tommy had reached campus, some lab coat he'd never even fucking seen before had asked how his murder investigation was going with Dr. Austen. Tommy was really sorry but he'd let the guy believe their testing was a cover for extracurricular activities, nudge nudge wink wink.

Clare hardly reacted. That was the least of their problems and was indeed safer gossip to spread. Robert would understand, or not.

Bianca believed it regardless. "When the cops came at crack-o'-dawn we were still going at it. Fighting since I fucking walked in last night and she hit me with, 'I'm sleeping around since you are.' It was crazy. For a while I convinced her you and I really do work by giving her a blow-by-blow—all these tests I don't understand and she gets it even less but I kept 'em coming until her eyes crossed. I think she said she believed me just so I'd stop. But, explaining to her, I realized that of course you know what you're doing—and then I felt shitty about ragging on you. Bianca saw I was feeling bad so she got all talk to mommy and—tell me if this isn't *the* stupidest move—I said I felt bad about you. Kabloom. You know how you can fight for hours without saying anything real and it hurts even more than the true stuff?"

"Yes, I know that syndrome all too well."

"She says she's being followed now, says I'm endangering her life, too. For that, I couldn't blame her for being pissed. I told Beaudine and he said he'd look into it. You betcha." Tommy fell sideways, his head resting millimeters from Clare's shoulder. She did not straighten away.

"Robert and I had a big blowout this morning." Thus was she late for her first class. Then Beaudine hadn't even let her call to alert her second class to go home. "He advised me to get a lawyer but I thought he was bluffing."

"Robert said that? Do you have one of those prenuptial whatevers?"

"No. Beaudine said that. I'm sorry—I switched thoughts on you."

"He told me that too. But I can't afford one."

"Don't they have court-appointed lawyers who are free?"

"Don't you have to be arrested to get one of those?"

"I guess we should find these things out, not assume that since we're innocent we'll be fine." Tommy's hair touched her ear. "I wonder when Jessie's going to get sick. Then everything will be wrong."

"What'd you and Roberto get into?"

"He'd left a note asking me to wake him up when I got home last night. But I just wanted to get my work done and go to bed."

"Bianca called him, I bet she got him all het up the way she was."

"He didn't mention that. But he was furious to awaken this morning and discover he'd had a full night's sleep. We just went on from there. The worst part is, we never really make up anymore. He may say the same conciliatory words he always has, but they no longer seem to apply."

"Sounds like you've changed and he hasn't."

"That does sum it up. I hate it when my life reduces to clichés."

"So I talk in clichés, eh? *Mucho de nada.*"

"Well. That certainly wasn't one." She smiled, briefly. "We should get started. Robert is due to stop by, to rig a new lever for your bad arm."

"Even though he's pissed?"

"Robert's very noble. We can't be sitting like this when he gets here."

"I'm glad Bianca's not noble. Yeah, we should move."

They remained where they were. "Your hair smells like food."

"Bianca tossed our kitchen around last night. The almond extract got me."

"She throws things when you fight?"

"Yeah, it's jive: 'I am furious, I am passionate, I will throw a pan.' Sometimes I tell her what a housewife she is, to make her really mad."

"And then what does she do?"

"She stomps around and puts my pillow on the couch. Last night—haw!—I told her after she'd already got my pillow out. So she just stood there, you could hear the wheels grinding, and then all of a sudden she's out of control, *storms* over to the couch, *rips* my pillow apart."

They managed a brief tired chuckle. "Robert gets robotic. Once I asked him if he needed oiling. It was a low blow, I don't behave any—"

The lock rattled, the door flew open. Tommy jumped into a protective posture. No doubt this looked suspicious for other reasons. "Hey Roberto."

"We were just talking about you." Clare's tone begged confrontation.

"Hear there was another murder," Robert said without inflection. Going directly into the lab, he opened a briefcase full of tools and contraptions and set to work on the indicator levers. He labored wordlessly, until he finally had to motion for Tommy to sit beside him, finally had to ask, "How does that feel?" although it clearly grieved him to do so.

Task completed, he packed up some thirty-one minutes after arriving, seemingly intent on leaving without speaking another word. Clare followed him to the door. He said metallically, "I'll see you at home. Whenever that happens to be." He was now in his mental tantrum mode; Clare could forget reasonable discussion.

"Thanks for your help, it should make testing go much smoother."

"That's what I'm here for," he said in a monotone. Her non-reaction apparently made him angry, for he continued as though spitting through a blow gun; "I know you're under pressure; but then you always are when you want to avoid me. I haven't—"

The door sprang open and a sub-assistant administrator brandished papers and accusations: the bathroom scale was missing and Security had last seen it here; Dr. Austen was expected to pay for replacement. She studied the papers. Bruce Smith was the name of their friend the guard. His signature resembled a backward second grader's. She looked up to discover that Robert was gone. "Three hundred six dollars? Where do you get these scales, the Pentagon?" The sub-assistant didn't know, he was only authorized to inform her of this matter.

Clare thanked and brushed past him to affix the DO NOT DISTURB sign to the door's exterior. He bustled officiously away as she locked the world out, turned, and jumped. Tommy had materialized behind her, reading the paperwork she'd tossed on the desk.

"Bruce Smith, sounds like an alias. So on the home life scale, one being honeymoon, ten being ugly courtroom scenes, I rank you an eight. Was that Roberto being mad? I prefer ripped pillows."

"I prefer Jessie." But Tommy wasn't listening; he was staring at the crack below the door. As silent and swiftly as Jessie herself might have moved, he opened the door.

Outside, Cynthia Bates straightened and twitched, obviously caught at a keyhole. "I thought I heard voices," she said, her faint English accent noticeable. Eager to appear unruffled, she smoothed her hair—but caught her watchband in her diamond stud earring. While struggling with and at last separating the two, she spoke in a fluster. "I mean to say, after that man told you about the scale, you put the sign up but I wasn't sure if you were testing from the way you were talking—out here in your office. I'm just getting in deeper, aren't I? I didn't intend to snoop I simply didn't wish to interrupt."

"We get your drift." Tommy's smile was disarming.

"Come in, we're taking a break," Clare sat on one couch arm. "You look as though you've been feeling better."

Cynthia took the far couch arm. "No, but perhaps if I keep telling myself. It's odd, you two testing today. Have you switched days, Tommy?"

Clare answered, "I'm preparing for a conference in January and he's agreed to come in more often to help me finish this series of tests."

"Which tests are you doing? Would I have been part of the study as well?"

"Probably, but please don't feel obligated."

"Some experiments disturb me less than others. Are these new ones?"

"Here and there." Mrs. Bates had never cared about test particulars before.

Cynthia waited for Clare to elaborate. When she didn't, Cynthia hastily filled the gap with, "I stopped in to assure you that if I do resume testing I'll remain with you."

"I didn't realize that was in question."

"I just assumed he'd—said something." She indicated Tommy, perched on Clare's desk, browsing through a magazine.

Tommy shrugged. He didn't know what Cynthia meant, either. "Said something . . . about?" Clare prompted mildly.

"Earlier he—Tommy—passed me leaving Dr. Stein's office and he seemed so surprised." Tommy indicated he hadn't been. "Yes, the way you said, 'Hey Mrs. Bates, didn't expect to see you here.' Anyway, Clare, I thought he might tell you and I didn't want you to think—"

"I don't understand what I'm not supposed to think."

"Dr. Stein asked me to—'join his team.' To participate in his tests rather than yours. I. Didn't want you to think I'd agreed."

As always, Mrs. Bates was so nervous she seemed to be hiding something. Perhaps a lifetime concealing epilepsy was to blame —unfortunately, their culture, unlike the ancients', did not consider hers "the sacred disease." But—Sid Stein raiding Clare's lab? Implausible. "Did Dr. Stein say why he wanted you to, ah, join his team?"

"He seemed very interested in your research. I couldn't tell him much, which made me realize I ought to take more interest."

She'd now given three reasons for wanting to know what Clare was doing. Clare suspected the real explanation was d, none of the above.

"I believe I'd like to resume our experiments," Cynthia Bates declared.

Oh, no. "I'd rather wait until you're sure." And until Clare had more time.

"The less I do, the more fearful I become. Couldn't we resume our old testing schedule? Tomorrow?"

"Perhaps next week. I'm between assistants and it's put me behind."

"I see. I hear poor Steven found a corpse. There's a new body every day it seems. Inspector Beaudine must be beside himself, his theories no longer apply, do they?"

"He didn't tell us his theories. Guess that makes us suspects," Tommy said, idly flipping magazine pages.

"Oh no, I'm the sort he suspects. No, I'm completely serious. It seems that much of Dr. Colton's funding came from private sources. Older women. Lieutenant Beaudine appears to feel that Dr. Colton wooed these women, oh, overmuch, and that he was killed in a fit of jealousy." When Tommy laughed, Cynthia frowned. "Isn't that the impression he gave you?"

"I just didn't put it together like you did," Tommy said with admiration.

Stanford Colton killed in a crime of passion. Clare's suspicion meter was in the red zone. Would Beaudine really jump to such a bizarre conclusion? And then tell Cynthia Bates? But if Clare hadn't know that Dr. Colton worked the dowager circuit, how would Mrs. Bates know, unless Beaudine had told her?

Tommy laughed once more. When Cynthia looked puzzled, he explained, "I just can't imagine Colton with anybody. Can you?"

Now she looked cautious, perhaps realizing his joviality was meant to draw her out. "I really didn't know the man. Some surgeons follow their patients' progress, but he didn't care about mine." Bitterness laced her words.

Clare hoped this would stir trouble: "Dr. Colton was very happily married when I first knew him. After his wife died, I don't think he wanted to be with anyone else."

"I heard she gave him nothing but trouble and he institutionalized her the first chance he got!" Mrs. Bates had turned huffy.

True, Colton stayed in the lab while his wife succumbed to a dementia akin to Alzheimer's. Most people thought this proved lack of caring; Clare knew he'd altered the course of his research, desperate to find a cure or abatement, furious when there was nothing he could do. But how did Mrs. Bates know so much; and why?

"Maybe he wasn't such a cold fish. Maybe he just hadn't met the right woman." The way Tommy didn't look at Mrs. Bates as he spoke, Clare knew they'd drawn the same conclusion: Mrs. Bates had developed an attraction to her surgeon.

"There is no magical right woman!" Cynthia Bates spoke with unexpected vehemence. "That's an excuse made by men who are incapable of love. I should know. Dear. Now I've embarrassed us all. I do apologize."

Correction? Cynthia's interest in Colton was purely an attempt to compare and contrast her own marital problems? "Why in the world would Lieutenant Beaudine think that you and Dr. Colton were lovers?"

Mrs. Bates registered no reaction to what Clare had hoped was a shockingly blunt question. "He was grasping at straws. He must be grasping quite wildly by now. These other murders have all got such different M.O.s." They looked at her blankly. "Usually a murderer doesn't vary technique so very much. That's what the paper said this morning. This fourth death, the wino, has them particularly stumped. The only connection seems to be his wearing a lab coat."

"He wasn't a wino, just homeless." But wait a minute. "How could Larry's murder be in this morning's paper when he wasn't found until later?"

"I heard it on the news then." She reflected. "Now you don't trust me again. Do you really think I'm capable of such horrible acts?" She sounded like she wasn't sure.

Clare sighed wearily. "So much has happened in the last few days, I'm suspicious of everyone. But no, you're not capable of any horrible acts."

"Thank you for that. May I come in tomorrow? I made a mistake, canceling testing. I thought the experiments were the problem but now I feel so cast adrift."

"Eleven tomorrow," Clare capitulated, exhaustion blasting her. Her body was a city post-neutron bomb; she barely even felt her injured back anymore, she was aware of the pain only theoretically.

"Does the testing ever bother you?" Mrs. Bates was asking Tommy.

"All the time," he replied.

"What type of tests are you doing now? The ones where the screen gives an instruction and my left hand does something inexplicable, those are the worst for me."

"Reaching behind the screen gets me," Tommy replied. "But who can really care about a test, after you've had your brain chopped up? After you've worried for years your own head was going to kill you. Or worse, embarrass you in public."

Cynthia laughed. "Having the operation never frightened me."

"It did me. Mainly because—I hate this suffering artiste shit but—there were reports that you lose creativity. So I waited until I had to decide: would I be an ex-musician or a creative corpse?"

"I haven't a creative molecule in my body. I simply wanted a normal life. Being able to drive, that sounded heavenly. But I still can't. You can? However did you get a license?"

"I lied. If they catch me I'm in deep shit. But I only drive around Pasadena, during the day, in the right lane. I get warnings right before an attack, see, and . . ."

Clare's suspicions faded as she watched Tommy's ebb. All Cynthia's prying was merely done to convince herself she was neither crazy nor unlike other split brainers. Excellent. Let Tommy reassure her further, while Clare prepped the next test.

She went into the lab to ready tachistoscope slides. After searching for fifteen minutes, she concluded the ones she needed were missing, and realized she hadn't heard voices from her office for some time. Yes, she'd heard the door, too.

Her office was empty but there were two voices in the hall. Mrs. Bates had had enough bolstering for one day. Time to get to work, she opened the door to say, but was unable to speak once she regarded the angry faces of Tommy—and Bianca. "Couple minutes here," Tommy said tensely to Clare. She backed away, closing the door too loudly.

Shut into her office, trying not to eavesdrop (and anyway they were talking too softly), Clare decided to call Steve. He'd put those missing slides away. His home phone was answered by a youthful male voice. "May I speak with Steve?" she requested.

"He's—who is this?" The voice sounded like it had swallowed a marble. Clare explained who she was and why she was calling. "If I see him I'll tell him," the voice mumbled.

"Let me give you my home number too."

"Uh—sure."

Clare recited her number but she knew if she had a view phone she'd see the voice owner not writing it down. "It's important Steve get this message."

"I'd give it to him ifwhen I can."

"Has something happened to Steve?"

"He told me to say he's not here." A pleading tone had developed. "I have to get back to studying. Good-bye."

After a moment, Clare hung up too, resolving to stop by Steve's on the way home, however late. He wasn't going to get away with such games. Or perhaps he was: she didn't have his address. The Biology department office might, but its phones were busy. She readied her first experimental setup. Tommy and Bianca's voices were still urgently intermingling outside her door. The Biology office phones were still busy. She decided to walk down there.

Out in the hall, Tommy leaned against a wall, glaring; Bianca waved her arms and yelled softly about how long it'd been since he'd come over to her side of the bed, unasked. Clare made a quick motion that she hoped meant "be right back" and hurried away.

She went the long way around, to avoid walking past Colton's office. At each corner she passed a security guard, but none was Bruce Smith, which was too bad: she was definitely in the right frame of mind to tell him off. Moreso when she reached the Biology office. It was closing—God, it was 6:30 already—and the receptionist greatly resented waiting the seventeen seconds it took for Clare to obtain Steve's address.

Returning, she detoured into the suite of labs occupied by Sid Stein's research team. The good doctor himself sat at an outer desk, stifling a sneer when he saw who had entered. Clare resisted the urge to remove his glasses, poke him in his magnified eyes. "I hear you've made Cynthia Bates quite an offer." As Stein formulated a response, "Explain yourself, Sid. With no bullshit, for once."

"What did she tell you?"

"No. You tell me."

"Happy to. She came here quite upset, demanding whether all tests were as disorienting as yours. I questioned her about your work, to determine what she meant."

In other words, he'd grilled her for possible new research directions. Sid had a reputation for "borrowing" via chats with other labs' assistants and experimentees. For once, it seemed, campus gossip was true. "When you asked her to join your team, did you explain that your work was done postmortem?"

"Oh, that." Stein relaxed, almost imperceptibly. "I simply said that to assuage the woman's fears."

"You're dissembling. I don't know what game you've been playing, Sid, but I suggest you cancel it."

"Clare, you're obviously overwrought. Of course, spending all these long hours with Dabrowski, doing all that 'research,' must be draining."

"My private life is my own business."

He looked stunned when she left his innuendo undenied, but recovered rapidly. "I'm confident you'll realize pharmacology and neuropsychology have little in common. If you are in fact accusing me of stealing ideas or clients. You're not making sense, you see, so I'm not sure."

He resumed reading a journal. She yanked it from his hands. "You have a problem underestimating people, Sid. Oh and by the way, that includes Lieutenant Beaudine." Something flickered behind Stein's face mask. Something very dark. Clare realized he was almost the right size to be the object of their search. No, not Sid Stein: he was a coward, capable only of intellectual attacks. "Just be careful, Sid." She slapped the magazine onto the desk and slammed the door behind her.

Tommy and Bianca were no longer in the hall. Bianca had departed. Correction. Bianca was in Clare's lab watching Tommy demonstrate experiments. He even had the schematic of the killer's body unrolled. "Where does she stand?" Bianca demanded petulantly, failing to notice Clare's arrival.

"She kneels in front and gives me head, what do you think?"

"Don't forget to show her the Little Bo Peep outfit I wear," Clare said.

Bianca looked at Clare nervously, then Tommy told her, "We've got some heavy petting to do so you'd better split."

Bianca grew indignant. "You started this, I only came by to see if you needed a ride."

"And Reagan was our greatest president. Don't wait up." At which Bianca gathered her gym bag and purse and left without another word.

Tommy avoided looking at Clare, tried to roll up the schematic drawing with his one hand. After a moment, Clare went to help him. "I'm an asshole and so's she, we're made for each other." He still refused to look at her.

"When Robert and I started having problems, he insisted on couples therapy, where we learned how to fight fair. But you know, I don't even want to fight fair. I just want him to leave me alone. What I can't decide is whether that's because of Robert, or me." Finished rolling the drawing, they regarded each other briefly. Clare felt as sad as Tommy looked. They retreated to their testing positions.

In her early days with Robert, she'd never felt overwhelmed by his presence, the way she did in Tommy's. But that didn't mean real life with Tommy would be any different. If Tommy used on her the voice he'd applied to Bianca today. If she ever saw Tommy the way she regarded Robert these days.

"Is the sign on the door?" Tommy asked.

"Yes. Not that it seems to help any."

"You don't know, there could be hordes out there raising their hands to knock, seeing DO NOT DISTURB and backing away."

"I've had more people in my office during the last four days than I've seen here all year."

"I know, shit like that makes me believe in astrology. Or conspiracies. What you said to Cynthia. I feel it too. Suspicious of everyone—except you, except when my brain gets its wires crossed. She's definitely not coming clean, you feel it too?"

"I do. But she always gives that impression." Clare told Tommy about her visit with the ever-shifty Sid Stein. "It may be he's got her spying for him. Although I really don't have any research he could use."

"But does he know that?"

"True. I can't see Cynthia agreeing to help him at my expense, though."

"Maybe he told her he could cure weirdness."

"She really is a good person, if she didn't worry so about being odd she wouldn't seem so strange. She'd make a rotten spy. Which would serve Sid just exactly right."

"He's big enough," Tommy mused. "Okay, left foot up if the answer is yes. Is Sid Stein the killer?" Tommy's foot did not move. "That's what I figured. Not him."

"That was one stupid stunt!"

"Stupid? Ten seconds and I finished tests that would've taken days your way."

"The tests are slow because there are so many possible misinterpretations and misdirections. The less rigorous the methodology the more chance for error. We have to test for differentiation among variables that—"

"Uncle. I give. Alright already."

"You know much less than you think, which could hinder our efforts tremendously."

"I get the drift, you can stop now. I already said I was sorry."

"No you didn't."

Tommy thought back. "Hmm. You got me there." He unlightened the mood again: "Don't you see we're running out of time?"

"Maybe the police will solve the case and we can stop trying."

"Ever read their list of unsolved crimes? No one has, it's too long."

"The killer's got to make mistakes at some point."

"I wonder why we're still alive," Tommy said. "Especially since word's around that we think I know something. I guess the killer hasn't heard. Yet."

"I let Sid Stein think we're together—to be together," Clare sighed. "That kind of 'data' spreads like a virus. It may buy us some time."

"Lately I feel so shitty when we leave at night without knowing, I don't even want to keep trying."

"Good attitude."

He put the headset on and they went to work. Tachistoscopically, Tommy's hemispheres saw YES–NO's. Dichotically, his right brain heard, "**Is Colton's killer someone you know?**" And answered YES.

Clare's hands grew sweaty, her insides clammy. Yesterday, the answer had been NO—because the left hemisphere was privy to the question?

She flashed the picture of Hitler. "**Is this killer someone you know?**" YES. Oops, the question was too ambiguous. But she'd anticipated that possibility.

Flashing Hitler again, "**Have you met this killer?**" NO.

Tommy lifted the headset. "You're asking me again if I know the guy, huh? I was testing myself about that this morning." As she reacted, "That was before you said not to. I started thinking, maybe I do know him, you know? P.S., the answer was still no."

Damn him. "What other tests have you performed on yourself?"

"That was it." He donned the headset triumphantly.

Perhaps his self-tests wouldn't matter. When in doubt, carry on. "**Do you know Colton's killer personally?**" YES. Clare missed the adrenaline rush that accompanied the first YES.

They went through every permutation she'd thought to record dichotically: "**Is the killer someone known to you? . . . Do you know the killer's name? . . . Is the killer a man you have met? . . . Before the murder, did you know the killer?**" —twenty-seven questions in all. Clare doublechecked comprehension with pictures of famous but not personally known killers. She dutifully recorded all responses, in case a pattern might emerge during analysis at home. But overall, Tommy's right brain seemed to answer randomly.

Her frustration was all-encompassing. Maybe the whole effort was pointless. A list of known suspects could be endless, incomplete, misguiding in ways she couldn't envision. She liked to think that if she just got enough sleep she'd see a clear path to solution; but perhaps she simply wasn't up to the task.

Now that they'd pinpointed where on the murderer's body Tommy had touched, she needed to determine exactly what he had sensed: at the neck, for example, did he feel skin or a collar, was the skin hairless, what shape and fabric the collar?

For these tests, Clare had adapted slides from her chimeric faces experiment, pictures terrifying to the unsplit brain: two different half people, joined at the visual midline, creating monstrous visages. But neither of Tommy's brains knew the other half had seen a different face. And through a process called completion, each thought it saw a whole picture—somehow each brain filled in the missing half.

She flashed two images to his right brain for comparison: a shirtless man, then a shirted one: **"Was the killer's neck more like this, or this?"** Detail by detail, she would eventually hone particulars. It should be easy to distinguish clothed from naked, but: hirsute from hairless skin? jacket from shirt collar? leather from cotton? These tests would take at least two full lab days; and she wouldn't be able to draw conclusions until they were far along in the slow, cautious process—which couldn't be completed until she found or replaced the missing slides.

Despite their late start, they accomplished quite a bit, much thanks due to Robert's new levers. At midnight, they headed for Clare's car. She was glad she'd parked over by her classroom—they wouldn't pass Larry's last hiding place.

"I am so beat," Tommy informed her, "both of my brains are seeing double."

"At least you can still see." She stopped to squint at the crescent moon oozing light above them. It was misty, that was it. Clare's skin crawled with moisture, that was all. There was nothing to fear tonight: they passed a security guard every five hundred feet as they traversed the deserted campus. Those footfalls trailing them, Clare assumed to be echoes.

Still, without discussion, they ran the last stretch to her car. Her key fumbled in the lock. There. No. Turn the other way—success. She tumbled inside, stretched to unlock Tommy's door. It was unlocked. As, she realized, her door had been. "I'm sure I locked my car this morning, I always do. I think."

"Let's pretend it doesn't mean anything." Tommy fiddled with his seat, reclined himself with a groan. "Don't take me home. Let's pick up a sixer and drive to the mountains. We can sleep in the car."

"That's how I want to spend my night. Isolated."

"Okay, we'll park in the cops' lot. Hey, where are you going?"

"I thought you didn't want to go home." With a snap, Tommy unreclined his seat and rubbed his eyes. "The truth is we're going to Steve's." Clare explained about the missing slides and his gutless effort to duck her call.

Steve's address took them to a four-story brick building called the Stanley, next to an identical abode called the Livingstone. Leave it to Steve to live in a bad pun. His lobby door was locked and there were no buttons to ring individual apartments. They scouted the building's perimeter, looking for another way inside, to Steve's apartment 1B.

The first apartment they passed was dark save for the blue glow of TV light. Silhouetted inhabitants sat erect in arm chairs, blue haloes around their inert heads. Stiff laughter filled the room. Wondering if the sound was a laugh track or the viewers, Clare stumbled against a bush. A dog started yapping and orange light sliced the cement path ahead. They pressed against the building brick. The yapping diminished as a muffled voice called cooingly. Clare saw a small dark form parting a curtain. Following Tommy's lead, she jumped the slice of light. Briefly, she locked stares with the window sentry, a tiny toupee dog baring unconvincing teeth.

At the back of the Stanley, there were no windows. Along the other side, they found a crack between one drape and window molding. Inside, a young man with unruly hair and a not-entirely-formed set of expressions dragged a bulging garbage bag to the front door. As he left the apartment, Clare and Tommy simultaneously spotted 1B on the door, and hurried streetwards.

"How you doing tonight?" At the building's entry, Tommy shouldered past the exiting kid, who stiffened, not wanting to let this stranger into the lobby, but unwilling to make a scene. Clare trailed Tommy down the hall to the apartment.

"Er." Clare paused at its open door, then followed Tommy inside. They did a quick sweep of all five miniature rooms. One bedroom had open empty dresser drawers, boxes packed for shipping: to Steve at a Daly City address, from Steve at this address.

Clare and Tommy jumped at a gutteral howl behind them. The roommate was equally startled; hence his howl. "Take what you want just don't hurt me."

"We're only looking for Steve. I called earlier, about the slides."

"He's—still n-not home."

"Apparently he's not coming back." At the roommate's silence, she said breezily, "I'm Dr. Clare Austen. Steve's my research assistant. Now, two weeks before finals, just as I'm preparing a paper for a conference, he vanishes. How long will he be gone? Can I rely on his help or do I need to find someone else? I'd really appreciate your telling me as much as you can without breaking any confidences."

The roommate's face went from no to full trust, so quickly Clare wanted to warn him about strangers. "He said he found you another assistant."

Clare shook her head. "So he's not coming back, then?"

"No. He didn't even finish the paperwork for dropping out. I'm supposed to."

"Dropping out? He's graduating." The roommate looked wary. Clare backpedaled, "That's such a shame." Over the roommate's shoulder she was aware of Tommy paging through an address book. "Did he go home? Where do his folks live again—near San Francisco—Daly City, isn't it?"

"His parents are dead," the roommate said icily. "His uncle lives in Daly City."

"His uncle who's a researcher at San Francisco State?" Tommy asked, then at the roommate's one sharp nod, "That guy sounds like a total assbite."

"No kidding," the roommate thawed again.

"I feel bad that I worked with Steve for so long and didn't know that." Surely she was laying it on too thick. "Do you think I can reach him at his uncle's?"

"Probably. Yes." But the way the roommate said this, the uncle's was the last place Steve would go.

"Sorry we startled you at first. If you hear from Steve, give him my best." She and Tommy headed out. "And please call if you find any slides."

Out in the hall, they turned at the roommate's urgent, "Dr. Austen." He seemed caught in some inner dilemma. Finally, concern won out. "Do you know why he was so scared?" She didn't and he immediately regretted asking. "If you talk to him, don't say you talked to me, okay? And ask him to call me." Noting the contradiction, he laughed humorlessly, then shut the door on her assurances.

Back in the car, they were silent for some time, until Tommy noted, "Trouble comes to Steveland. You're checking the mirror a lot."

"Suspect everyone." Especially car-phoned drivers taking their route at one A.M. As she turned onto Fremont, Tommy's street, the sedan behind them kept going straight.

"That's right, we're going home now. Nightie night," Tommy told the car. "Bianca's still being followed too."

"I asked Robert if he was, but he doesn't think so. He mostly walks though, so it would be easy for someone to keep track of him without being noticed. What did Steve tell you about his uncle?"

"Not much. His uncle raised him, it was your basic unckie dearest kind of thing. Steve's a little weird but he's not a psycho-killer. He's like Cynthia. He always acts guilty."

"You're awfully protective of him."

"You only think that 'cuz you never liked the guy. Mrs. Bates is a more likely prospect."

"Like hell she is." Arriving at Tommy's, Clare braked excessively.

"You're awfully protective of her." Tommy mimicked her previous tone.

"You're right. We have to stop being protective, we have to stop making assumptions, or we won't stop the killer before somebody else dies."

"Preferably somebody else, if there's gonna be another murder."

Their macabre chuckle turned into a double yawn. Tommy bolted from the car to his stairs, waving to Clare and the plainclothesman parked across the street.

Going home, of course it seemed as though Clare was followed. She parked angrily and hurried up her stairs. There was her own police detective. Whether present to protect or suspect her, she was glad to see him. She considered going over to ask why Beaudine had their homes watched when they were so seldom home. But she could guess the response: if the boss hadn't told her, she didn't need to know.

A collar jingled. Oh, God—Jessie was still out? With all the coyotes and owls that roamed from the arroyo, Jessie was always kept in at night. Had something happened to Robert? Clare grabbed the cat, who seemed tense. She considered hailing the cop but Jessie would be more tense if there were trouble inside. Instead, there was Robert, blanketed on the couch, rubbing his eyes. "Why are you sleeping out here?"

"It was the only way I could be sure you'd wake me up," he said dryly.

Jessie wiggled violently. Released, she sprinted for the bedroom. "How did Jessie get out?"

"She wouldn't settle down, I couldn't sleep."

"You put Jessie out at night."

"She's a cat. Cats take care of themselves."

"If anything had happened to her." She fought recollection of the cat shrieks, two months ago, predawn, blocks away but audible for miles—the neighborhood's biggest toughest tom, fighting for his life, losing to a skeletal coyote.

"You would never forgive me. Nothing new there."

Incapable of response, she began unloading her briefcase at the front alcove desk.

"First Jessie, then Tommy, then your work, then me. I wouldn't mind being second or even third. Or am I flattering myself? Really only tenth place on your list?"

"We've already had this fight. I've already answered these questions."

"I don't understand you any more."

"What makes you think you ever did?"

"Must we delve into clichés? Or would you say you're revealing an archetype."

"You talk like that, I don't."

" 'Hey dude, how's it hanging, like we had a cool gig last night.' Is that better? Perhaps Tommy can give me lessons."

"Why do I get the feeling you're trying to drive me away?"

"That's right, Clare, blame me for your infidelity. All your mistakes are my fault. Now there's a tactic I do understand, you've used it so often."

"It was only because we've been so at odds that I considered —Tommy. Considered and rejected. I want to be with you." It was the hardest sentence Clare ever uttered: hypothetically still true but not much felt at the moment.

"Indeed. And wasn't that convincing." After gathering his

bedding, he shut the bedroom door with the most controlled click possible. She had no choice but to follow, knock, enter. He stood trying not to look hopeful; victorious. Did Tommy play such games? Perhaps his were worse. She plucked Jessie from the bed and was seated at her desk before she heard Robert click the door shut once again.

Jessie was not interested in Clare's lap, desk, or general environs. This did not make Clare feel better, as she began considering substitutes for the slides presumably lost by Steve. Robert had let Jessie out at night. A heinous act, although since nothing had happened, forgivable—save for the intention behind it. She could picture him sitting in bed, pretending to read, listening for her approach. Thus had they ended so many disputes. But not this one.

Framed on the desk were travel photos: the Yucatán three years ago, when they were the happiest, it turned out, they'd ever be together; Egypt last spring, when they were first stunned by serious discord. She'd hated the tombs—surrounding the dead with relics from life only made the mummy's separation more apparent: condemned to view eternally all that mattered but couldn't be reached.

There were therapists who studied family photos for emotional dynamics, but to Clare the smiles and embraces in the two photos were interchangeable. Future photos would be more telling, as she doubted they'd ever vacation together again.

Against her will, Clare recalled brandy one evening at Lalitha's. Lalitha, who had more friends and family, interests and enthusiasms, than anyone Clare had ever met, that night had sobbed about how lonely she was, how she longed to love a man who wasn't threatened or evasive. Robert had assured her she would find such a man; Clare had insisted that the kind of love Lalitha envisioned was a myth (which infuriated Robert, leading to a readying-for-sleep fight that only confirmed Clare's position). Clare wished she'd feigned agreement—her response only added to Lalitha's misery. Clare struggled to banish images of Lalitha's body on that office floor. How brutal her dying must have been.

She had forgotten to lock her office door, she realized as it swung open. She didn't recognize this man. "May I help you with something?" Menace entered the room with him. She took a step backward, toward her lab, but there wasn't time to get inside and lock the door. And the phone was out here on her desk. The phone. "What do you want?" she demanded, lunging for the phone, though she knew she was about to die. "No! Please!" He went for her face. She heard her own bones shattering, choked on her own flesh. When she fell to the floor, he followed her down, each blow sending pain deeper, making thoughts weaker, until the world was black strobed with white pain, until the world was pain.

Clare became aware of Robert, running up the hall from their bedroom, brandishing a heavy glass vase, strewing water and browning flower petals behind him. He clamped his hand over her mouth, his fingers vibrated against her lips. Oh. That loud noise was herself, crying for help. She stopped and he fell against the wall, murky vase water staining the paint.

"Watch out," Clare indicated the stain, wishing he would stop staring at her like that. "Sorry I woke you. I started thinking about Lalitha and it upset me. But I'm fine now." He slammed the vase onto the desk and turned away from her. She watched his back recede, saw the bedroom door shut behind him.

In a flash, she thought of an important new experiment.

In another flash, she recalled that the coming morning would bring Lalitha's memorial service at Lacey Park.

Beaudine was there, studying the mourners, seeing if Kleenex grew damp or only dabbed at crocodile tears. Robert was beside Clare, wet of face but silent, his arm unbearably heavy across her shoulders. She fervently wished that she, too, could cry. As the concluding speaker finished, she stepped out of Robert's reach. Then suddenly, within the general din of grieving, Clare heard absurdity: honks, snorts, sniffles crescendoed; three noses blew in tandem, hiccuping wails provided syncopated accompaniment. She ducked her head and disguised her laughter as sobs.

Naturally, Beaudine chose this moment to study her. She advanced on him. "I'm laughing because we sound like an orchestra," she explained defiantly. He listened, smiled, seemed embarrassed. He was about to speak when Robert joined them.

"I apologize for not getting back to you yesterday," Beaudine told Robert.

"I know how busy you must be."

Clare stared at Robert. Why was he calling the police? He gave her a dismissive wave—he'd explain later.

"I'm late getting to the lab." She walked off abruptly, ignoring Robert's effort to catch her eye.

The mob of mourners filled the center baseball field of the park. Clare took a side path the long way to her car, passing an intermittent jogger but otherwise protected from people by a wall of green. The trees etched vivid lines against the sharp blue sky, suggesting how beautiful Los Angeles must have been before smog. She reached the rose arbor at the far end of the park, stopped to admire one late bloom. Lalitha had loved white roses like this. Clare stooped to inhale, pulled back hastily. A thick spider sat inside the petals. A black widow, no doubt, given the current progress of life.

CHAPTER 9

Acute Disconnection

Syndrome

Mrs. Bates and Deirdre were in Clare's lab, discussing her research with Tommy: murder or romance? Meanwhile, Deirdre rummaged at Clare's work station. When Clare walked in on them, Cynthia had the decency to look ashamed. Deirdre tried to justify herself: "I was trying to see what we'd be working on today."

"From now on, you will discuss nothing with my clients; and about my lab, you will know only what I tell you. Is that clear?" Deirdre nodded. "How did you get in?"

"Steve gave me his key."

"Where the hell is Steve anyway? I thought he would train you."

"He did. He showed me everything."

"Don't tell me you two came in here when I wasn't around."

"Just—once. Last weekend. He thought it would be alright."

Clare held her palm out. "The key. From now on you wait for

me. Was it Sunday afternoon you were here?" Had they rearranged the notes and stapler on her desk?

"I think so. Yes. I apologize, Dr. Austen, we thought—"

"Where is Steve now? I need to reach him."

"I don't know his number but he lives in the Stanley up on Los Robles."

"*Lived* in. He moved out."

Deirdre looked surprised: that Steve was gone, or that Clare knew? "Then I don't know where he is," the girl said evenly, "but he was scared about finding that other body, he needed to get away, that must be why he left."

"There's been another murder?" Cynthia Bates was a study in alarm.

"The one Monday night, that weird physics prof." From Deirdre.

Mrs. Bates snickered. "It's sinful to laugh about the dead, but Deirdre does quite an imitation of the woman's accent. Small wonder the students found her incomprehensible. Deirdre, you must do it for—Clare, whatever is the matter?"

"The woman you're mocking was one of the finest—well. You remember Dr. Rao, don't you Cynthia? You met her in the courtyard and didn't want to shake her hand. I'll borrow some coroner's pictures and show you how she ended up. I'm sure you'll find that hilarious too. Deirdre, put tape in the—"

"Video camera. I already did. And Dr. Austen, I'm very—"

"Get the Kohs blocks out. And pull my notes on Mrs. Bates from the—"

"Files. They're right here. I'll get the blocks now. Which series of cards?"

"Seven." Now why was Steve-the-inept so competent at training?

Through all this, Cynthia Bates sat silently; the woman was terrified of confrontation. It was a first-class irony that her own brains were so often in conflict.

In that regard, she was worse than when last tested. The Kohs blocks made that quickly apparent. The faces of the blocks were painted white, red, or white and red changing at the diagonal. Clare would put a red and white geometric drawing in free vision. Using one hand, Mrs. Bates would align blocks to match the drawing. Both Tommy and Cynthia showed strong left hand preferences in this test—their right hemispheres were far superior in such spatial tasks.

Clare recalled the first time Tommy had done this test: getting his right brain to comprehend the instructions had been a nightmare. Mrs. Bates's right brain understood nearly all test instructions immediately. However, when it came to applying such knowledge, Tommy fared much better. When he did this test, his right hand fumbled, his left hand would creep up and try to assist, which sometimes caused problems. But the competition between his hemispheres was nothing compared to Cynthia's.

Today, as usual, her left hand matched ever-more-complicated patterns, swiftly and surely, yielding a 90% accuracy rate. Her right hand was slow and barely achieved 30% accuracy, struggling over easy designs like the red rectangles, the white triangle with red background.

Initially, Clare had Mrs. Bates sit on her not-tested hand, to prevent interference. During this time, whenever her right hand erred with the designs, the left side of Cynthia's face and body contorted. "I'm doing the best I can, don't criticize me!" her left brain yelled at Clare and Deirdre, neither of whom had said a word.

Uncertainly, Deirdre looked to Clare for guidance. "Get the Series Eight drawings out," Clare instructed gently.

Next, the untested hand was allowed free movement. Cynthia's left hand tested first, tapping its completed correct design in a manner Clare could only interpret as smug. "Wrong," Mrs. Bates muttered and her right hand rearranged blocks, until the left hand knocked it away. The right hand did not try to help with the next design, but the muttering increased. When the left hand gave its smug pat of completion, the right hand viciously swept the blocks off the table.

Deirdre collected the blocks, keeping away from both Mrs. Bates's hands.

When it was the left hemisphere's turn to match the Series Eight drawings, the right hand set to work in its thorough but inept manner. It paused, stymied, and the left hand offered assistance, timidly—then gave bad advice, indicating blocks that were wrong. This was no honest mistake—the right brain had readily completed the same design. However, the drawing was complex enough that the left brain was unaware it was being tricked. Next came an easy drawing. This time, the left hemisphere perceived the trick and once again threw the blocks from the table.

"You see? This is what I must contend with, every day of my miserable life." Cynthia's voice rose from mutter to shriek. "You won't help me, no one even believes me, Stanford laughed, Dr. Madding pats my hand, you goddamned doctors destroying lives. Deirdre, if you like meddling stay on course, if you want to help you're going after the wrong profession." Her face was now so mottled and contorted, she resembled a burn victim.

"Get Mrs. Bates some water," Clare instructed to get her assistant out of the room. Deirdre left gladly. Clare waited for Cynthia to calm down, then said as casually as she could, "I do sympathize with you and I am trying to help. By the way, when did you talk to Dr. Colton about this?"

Mrs. Bates went from calm to guarded. "I know what you're thinking, that my brains were at war and I blamed my doctor and one night I took a knife and—" Her right hand grabbed a sharpened pencil Deirdre had left on the testing table and plunged it toward her chest.

Clare leaped to grab Mrs. Bates's wrist, but the momentum had gone out of the plunge; Cynthia hadn't intended to stab herself. A mechanical beeping sounded under Clare's fingers. Clare released the wrist, revealing a calculator watch, which beeped ever higher and faster as Mrs. Bates pressed various buttons. She held out her wrist helplessly. Clare pushed buttons. The beeps danced through an electronic melody then ceased. They sighed.

"Clare, I did not—hurt Dr. Colton or anyone else. I need you to believe me."

"I do believe you. Yet I also sense you're keeping something—or a lot of somethings—from me. And that disturbs me."

Cynthia's hands wrung, united in distress. "There are things I've done, I don't wish anyone to know. But they don't involve violence of any sort. Do you think Lieutenant Beaudine has reacted as you have?"

"Probably. I suggest you tell him the full story. After all, he even suspects me."

"Really? When you and Tommy are trying to find out who the killer is?"

"I keep hearing that rumor, I don't know where it started."

"Lieutenant Beaudine told me." Cynthia said this so disarmingly, it sounded true.

Clare looked down to hide her confusion. Would he warn Clare and Tommy to keep quiet, then spread the word himself? Was he playing his suspects against one another? She looked up to find Mrs. Bates watching her too closely.

Deirdre returned with water and a large cookie, explaining, "There's a plate of them in the Biology office." Mrs. Bates accepted both eagerly.

"You went all the way over there for water? I should have told you, there's a water cooler in the Xerox room."

"Series Nine next?" Deirdre seemed nervous, standing so close to Mrs. Bates.

"If you don't mind," Cynthia interjected. "That last test took quite a lot out of me. May we stop until next Thursday?"

"Of course." Even while assuring Mrs. Bates that next week's tests would go more smoothly, Clare was already making plans for the extra hour she'd gained before Tommy's arrival.

"What test should I prep for Tommy?" Deirdre complicated matters by asking.

"There's no need for you to stay. I'm trying some mix and matching, it will be easier to compile the tests myself than explain what I need."

"I'll stay, I don't mind. I can help a little and I'll learn a lot." Deirdre was submissive yet defiant; Clare would have to order her out to get her to leave.

"Will you give Tommy this?" Embarrassed, Cynthia handed Clare a lavender envelope then hurried away. A request to join the T. Dabrowski fan club? Now it was good that Deirdre was present: Clare's desire to read the note was that strong.

Clare dispatched Deirdre to learn what testing items were stored in which lab cupboards, while Clare sat at her desk to devise the new test she'd envisioned late last night.

Time passed quickly or Tommy arrived early. He flopped on the couch. "Take my wife, please," he said, Henny Youngman meets Macbeth. "No don't ask." He looked as crummy as Tommy could ever manage to look.

Clare tossed him the envelope. "From Mrs. Bates and I'm dying to know."

"Sure is good to see you," he sighed, then extracted the lavender paper. "That's sweet." He returned it to the envelope, tossed it back to Clare. "I don't blame you for wanting to protect her." Clare read the note. Cynthia couldn't begin to say how their exchanging of fear stories had helped her. She couldn't thank Tommy enough.

"Hi Tommy, how are you?" Deirdre stood in the lab doorway, her voice and manner making it plain she'd like to join him on the couch.

"Doing alright. Denise, right?" Tommy wilted her until he smiled.

Clare was denting the lavender paper. She enveloped the note and stood. Tommy followed her example. "See you around," Tommy told Deirdre.

"Oh, no, this is my day to be here." She stepped into the lab territorially.

"But we're doing behind-the-screen shit today, which gets me real tense. It's a lot easier if nobody's around. Steve always left, I guess he didn't tell you that."

Who could resist that killer grin? Deirdre collected her things.

"That reminds me." At this, Deirdre looked hopeful, until he added, "When you talk to Steve—"

"I doubt I will." Talk about fickle. Although there wasn't much contest: a few smiles from Tommy vs. life with Steve.

"I thought you two were an item," Tommy said.

"Oh, no, not really, no." At his lack of response, the girl added, "Well. Bye. See you tomorrow." She pretended to include Clare.

Clare hung the sign and locked the door. "Quick thinking," she congratulated Tommy. "I thought I was going to have to drag her out. If the world were all women you'd have it made." They seated themselves at their lab stations.

"Or them made, you mean. How's with Robert?"

"Worse than with Bianca. Or no better, anyway."

"At least you've got Jessie."

"To an extent. Although she's been avoiding me lately."

"Can't rely on anybody." He was furious.

"I think it's my rotten moods, she's not sure if they involve her."

"That better be it. Otherwise she'd make a nice pair of slippers."

"If I'm sad, she's around; or suicidal; or happy. But not when I'm angry."

"Okay, she can live. I was kidding about the slippers, you knew that." She nodded and he gave her a sly look. "Maybe a little rug though, with the head attached—but you know what I really love about cats? You look at them and you see, if they were big enough they'd kill us."

Clare laughed. "Not one of the better ways to die. Jessie's

great for getting rid of flies though. I worry one of them will be toxic, but it's hard to stop her."

"Doesn't it seem like there used to be lots more flies? I'm serious."

"Doesn't it seem like we should get to work?" She switched the control unit on.

"Right, I apologize for being the only one digressing."

"Are you still wanting to avoid our tests in case there's no result?"

"Naw. It's just when we finish here I have to go home."

"You have the option of going elsewhere."

"Except that takes cash. I've worked a lot of shit jobs, had some savings. Joint account, yeah? Found out last night, Bianca moved all the money, put it in her name only. Says she was afraid I'd spend it but that's jive, she's just making sure I can't leave."

"Aren't there laws about that?"

"Sure, I'll take her to court. Small claims court, it'd have to be."

"I may be able to get your testing stipend increased, a little."

"I'll figure something out, I don't want you to bail me out."

"You make it sound as though there'd be strings attached."

"You've gotta be making way more money than I do anyway, that's bad enough."

"Does that matter?" She thought it shouldn't but could see how it might.

"How'd the memorial service go this morning?" Tommy replied.

"I got through it. If you want to change the subject, there are kinder methods."

"I did want to change it. I also meant to ask how the service went. I thought a lot about your being there, I'm surprised you aren't more torn up."

"I regret that I don't meet your grief standards."

"You know that's not what I meant. Clare." But she kept her

back to him, putting two pads of paper and two pencils on his table. "Clare." She nodded; he accepted this reply. "So what diabolical treat's in store for me now?"

"An art project." She placed a pencil in each hand, positioned paper on the table for his right hand, held another pad within his left hand's reach. "Draw a cat. Whenever you look at your work, freeze—you should only be drawing when you're looking away."

Both hands set to it, one sketching a cat's head, the other creating a stick figure full body. It was eerie, as always, seeing his hands perform different tasks simultaneously. She had to stop him several times, to prevent him from drawing while watching —to prevent his left brain from controlling his left hand ipsilaterally. Eventually he got the hang of it.

Tommy's left hand was hampered by his injury, the sling and the usual lesser motor control of the right hander. Yet its stick drawing was decidedly a cat. The right hand's cat's head was also a serviceable rendering, but the proportions were off and this drawing showed none of the other's stylization.

Clare presented him with fresh paper. "The killer in the hall, the man who knifed you. You touched him. Draw what you touched."

Tommy looked at her. "Good one," he said, then started drawing. He kept glancing at his right hand's pencilings. Clare allowed this; his left brain was obviously distracted from his right brain's work. His right hand sketched words and body parts, reiterating its claims to have touched the left shoulder, neck, etcetera. When his right hand finished, Clare dared to look at his left hand's work. Tommy stared at it too.

Two vaguely parallel lines, an inch apart, two inches long. Between the lines were tiny jagged circles or awkward squares. It looked like a road on the moon.

"What the fuck is that?" he demanded. Struggling with the pencil, his left hand drew another rough tiny blip. This did not help. Then, with great difficulty, it covered the drawing with a spastic inverted V, slashed a horizontal line over all and dropped the pencil. "Sure, that's better. Mmm *hmm*," Tommy's left brain sneered.

Clare mentally reviewed the list of body areas his right brain had touched. She was distracted by an insistent pounding on her office door. "I'll get rid of them," Tommy was up and out of the room. Clare continued to stare at the drawing, trying to extract meaning from sheer concentration.

She heard the hinges rasp, Deirdre's voice flutter. "Forgot my books," she repeated meekly to Clare as she retrieved her book bag from a cupboard. Irate at the intrusion, Tommy flopped into his chair. When Deirdre passed him, the left side of his body lunged. His left hand grasped her wrist. She laughed nervously, stopped when she saw Clare's face. She tried to pull away, dragging Tommy and his chair.

"Let go," Tommy said weakly. His right hand pried at his left fingers, as tight as a Gila monster's jaw. Deirdre's hand took on the rosy tinge of her sweater.

Was this a seizure? It was beyond Clare's experience. She fought her own fear. Then she glanced at the drawing and realized, "I know why this is happening."

Tommy's fingers slackened and Deirdre pulled away. "Sorry," Tommy said, "but your wrist is irresistible."

"It's okay, you couldn't help it. What happened, Dr. Austen?" The way she tugged at a curl belied the professional detachment in her voice.

"Just some motor control problems. I don't have time to explain more right now, Deirdre. Good night."

Deirdre's face clouded but she didn't protest. Instead, she slammed the door on her way out.

"I hope you have time to explain it to me," Tommy said. "Fuck. That was scary."

Clare's finger traced the drawing's slashed inverted V. "I think this is an A. For 'arm.' We didn't understand, so your right brain grabbed Deirdre to cue us."

"That's it! I feel a *eureka* inside my head. Arm, I touched his arm. Something on his arm. But what?"

"Let's avoid guesswork and find out for sure." Their excitement made the room hum. Clare rapidly sorted slides from her chimerics tests, filling the tachistoscope with arm, hand, and upper body clothing pictures.

Using previously prepared dichotic questions, she determined that the drawing pertained to the killer's right wrist. Then, running out of applicable taped questions and not wanting to lose momentum, she decided to risk letting his left brain hear. "More questions. Don't answer right away; wait until you get a feeling about what the answer is. Did you touch skin?"

"That's not skin." Tommy pointed to the drawing.

"You're not waiting."

He paused huffily. "No. Not skin."

"Did you touch clothing?"

"I can't tell."

"Did you touch a sleeve?"

"I don't think so. What goes on a wrist. A watch. One of those digital calculators with little buttons. Yeah, that's it. That's it!"

"I don't know which side of your head is excited about this answer." Good—he looked chastised. "I need you to rid yourself of your current reaction."

"Get zen. Okay. Wait." His eyes closed; his facial lines smoothed. "Ready."

"Did you touch a wristwatch?"

He waited a long time. Clare clutched a pencil so hard it snapped.

"Yes," he said softly. "A wristwatch. With little knobs that stuck up." He opened his eyes. "But who wears a watch on their right arm?"

Mrs. Bates, Clare recalled. "Cynthia," Tommy said slowly. "Because she can never get her left arm to show her the watch because her right brain doesn't care what time it is. I go through the same stuff, that's why I keep my watch in my pocket."

"Get zen again." When Tommy indicated he was ready, Clare made her voice neutral: "Is Mrs. Bates the killer in the hallway?"

Tommy's eyelids snapped open. "No way, it can't be her."

"Which side of your brain is answering?"

"Both of them! Fuck. It's not her."

"I hope it's not, too, but we have to consider—" He shook his head stubbornly. This subject was closed—forever, he thought; for now, Clare concurred. "Let's move on." She readied the drawing pads. "Answer with another drawing: what else did you touch? Did you touch more?"

His right hand drew a calculator watch. His left hand struggled with lines and curves. Whatever it wanted to express was beyond its (current?) capabilities.

Tommy said, "If we can figure out exactly what kind of watch—"

"I know a way to do that." She consulted her own watch. Almost six. The stores were open until nine. She could leave Tommy and come back or they could start early tomorrow. She didn't want him with her while she gathered watches.

Was that the door again? "Can't you read?" Tommy yelled. The pounding stopped. They grew quiet as a key scraped in the lock.

Robert appeared at the lab threshhold. "Clare, I need to talk to you. It's always a bad time," he snipped, seeing the look Clare and Tommy exchanged.

Clare joined Robert in the office, shutting the adjoining door. "Surely we can do this at home."

"The reason I called Lieutenant Beaudine was to get custody of Niels. He agreed. I locked the cage in the bathroom, Jessie doesn't have access."

"It was good of you to get Niels," Clare admitted, unable to temper her anger. He'd attacked her for hours before this morning's memorial service. Knowing what would really hurt, he'd used that knowledge fully. She had refused to think about it, since, fearing that if she did, she'd be unable to go home to face him tonight.

"It's not enough to apologize but that's where I'll start. I feel terrible about what I said this morning, perhaps worse than you feel."

"Don't count on it." She wandered her office, maintaining a distance he kept trying to close. "Please stay over there," she said finally.

"How did we get to this point? I can't figure it out. But I want to solve this, Clare. You've said you do too and I believe you, despite what I've indicated to the contrary. Tell me what we do now." They were both fighting tears.

When she could speak, she said, "I want to wait. To pretend we're fine, until the murders are solved. If we could just be normal again—I'd give anything for that. I'm not 'sweeping life under the rug,' as you claim. I simply can't face any more right now."

He stared at his hands. "These are more avoidance tactics, yet —let me finish!—I accept them. I'm at a loss to do otherwise. But I want it on record that—"

"Oh for christ's sake, Robert! Alright, you told me so, this time far in advance. I'm telling you, I can't take any more of this shit."

"You even talk like Tommy these days."

She dared not engage. "Frankly it's Jessie I'm striving to emulate."

With an effort visible throughout his body, Robert simulated his old self. He grimaced a smile that, after a time, became genuine—and sad. "I've always wanted to get you to purr," he said, then reflected, "That sounded stranger than I'd intended."

"I got the drift." They used to have contests for the dumbest double entendre. She managed a return smile.

"Your mother called," Robert said. "Wondering about her Thanksgiving invite." They shared a rueful chuckle. Every year they had to explain anew: Christmas they devoted to family; Thanksgiving, they locked themselves at home, devoted to each other. "I assured her we were looking forward to seeing her in December."

"Thanks. Do you think I have to call her?"

"Afraid so. She heard a news report about professors being murdered. All it said was southern California but that set her off. I've got some ideas on what to tell her; my folks called today so I've learned what works and what doesn't."

"Sounds like you had a grim afternoon."

"The good news is my folks are going to Hawaii, won't be available for the holidays." It wasn't that Robert didn't love to see his parents; but it was always a strain for Clare. Somehow he managed to side with her without siding against them. She'd always meant to learn that technique from him. They exchanged a wan smile.

"I've got to get back in there. We seem to be in the midst of a breakthrough." Robert understood. They hugged and she felt—nothing, then relief. It was a start.

They opened the hall door to find Bianca hovering. "Glad to hear you're having a breakthrough, I'm having a breakdown."

For once, Bianca did not sweep past Clare without invitation. Clare felt compassion—and had to admire this suave admission of eavesdropping.

"Is Tommy around I thought I'd—"

"What are you doing here?" Tommy hailed her from the lab doorway.

"Look at us," Bianca indicated the four of them. "So fucking jealous it's shredding us. I came to see if my husband needed a ride but I really came to see what was going on. How about you, looking for dirt?" she asked Robert, who nodded after some hesitation. "I know what you mean about wanting to get normal again," she told Clare.

"Exactly how long were you listening outside?" Clare turned indignant.

"Yeah I know. Totally private conversation but I'm glad I heard because now I know where you two are. Same place we've been fighting to stay in."

"I don't need a ride and you're delaying our work," Tommy replied.

"The fact is, I need to go out for a while to arrange our next test," Clare said.

"You're really having a breakthrough, huh? What's going on?"

"I'll explain later," Tommy said sharply. "At home."

"You'd be able to work longer if you had some dinner first. More energy."

"We're fine," Tommy disagreed.

"Why don't you all come over to our place to eat? Come on, we have to try."

No one really wanted this yet somehow everyone agreed: anyone saying no would be needlessly jealous or harboring designs on another's spouse. And so, Bianca and Tommy headed home to prepare dinner for four; Robert would stop off to feed cat and parrot, then join them there.

On her own, Clare did a department and jewelry store blitz, collecting sixty-three watches—watches with calculators, phone books, video games; watch bands with blips, jewels, 3-D designwork—in two hours. A record the more notable because she had to impress a manager at each stop; and exact a written understanding that these watches were being taken in the interests of science and could be returned for full refund within twenty-four hours.

She might have assembled a few more varieties, but was too disturbed by the last manager, at the Ticq Tocq Boutique, who was following the campus "slayings" closely: hobby of his, he explained expansively. Clare had to feed him a piece of "campus insider info" for each borrowed watch. If she hadn't needed those watches, she would have advised this ghoul to visit the university at night wearing a lab coat, to get first hand knowledge of the slayings.

Her dinner partners were discussing the day's research when she arrived at Tommy's apartment. Her displeasure at this was apparent. "You need a drink," Tommy whispered near her ear. Which made Robert cringe, Bianca tense, and Clare flinch.

The four trooped into the kitchen, where Bianca opened Clare a beer. "Trader Joe's—two-dollar brew for half price," she said proudly. They all agreed Joe's was a fabulous market. Silence fell.

"What a nice toaster. I've never seen one like that before," Clare said finally.

"Hidden under a bunch of crud at a yard sale in Alhambra," Bianca patted its bulbous chrome. They discussed the wonders of yard sales. Silence fell.

They returned to the living room. Clare surveyed the decor. "This place is like a cartoon," she noted and the others laughed. That was exactly what Robert had said.

The small room was crammed with furniture and knickknacks, bright-colored and mismatched, shapes and textures ranging from curious to bizarre. Bianca told Clare the history of finding each item, as though discussing corporate takeovers.

"You should see the bathroom mirror. And our bedroom set." Tommy led a tour. The mirror frame was encrusted with beads and tiny found objects, put together by a folk artist who lived out in Mojave. The bedroom furniture was opalescent lucite etched with black swirls. Clare ran her hand over it as Bianca babbled about how she'd sweet-talked a rival buyer into letting her take the set instead.

"How do you like your futon?" Robert knelt to examine the bedding on the floor. They discussed The Futon, Pro and Con.

"Dinner's going to be a while," Bianca then informed Clare. "I thought the directions said fifteen minutes, but there was a 'two hours' part I didn't notice."

"Maybe you should get started on your testing," Robert said.

"At last I get to see you two in action," Bianca said.

Robert saved Clare from having to reply. "Take it from another scientist," he waggled a finger at Bianca, "we'll only be in the way."

"We can test in here," Tommy said. "There's really nowhere else."

All four helped set up two chairs and a card table between futon and dresser. Then Bianca and Robert retreated to the living room, Bianca half shutting the bedroom door in a show of semi-faith.

"What do you say," Tommy asked as they sat down, "colossal or stupendous?"

"I assume you'll explain what you mean." Alone with him she felt better, despite the glacier of expectations advancing on them from the other room.

"The mistake this dinner was. Is."

"I expected worse. I guess it would be bad form to go get a beer, though."

He gave her a conspiratorial look, vanished into a closet, emerged with a wine bottle. "Buck fifty. I winked at a clerk and he dusted it for me."

"She's better than that, she's just nervous, even I could see that."

"I know. Thanks for reminding me." Holding the bottle between his knees, he demolished the cork with a pocket knife clutched in his good hand. "Hope you don't mind drinking from the bottle."

She didn't. She took a swig and opened her briefcase. "We're going to find out exactly what kind of watch you touched. You'll close your eyes. I'll put something in your hand. If it's a watch like this," she extracted the road-on-the-moon drawing, "hold on to it. If it's not, drop it." It was a variation on an old test but to be sure his right brain understood, she first handed him a hair clip, an eraser, a pen. He palpated each briefly then let go.

Watch after watch got dropped, as fast as Clare could put

them in his left hand. Some watches, his fingers examined more thoroughly; but ultimately, all got dropped. From the living room, meanwhile, came laughter and clinking glasses.

"I'm going to change the rules slightly. I'll give you two watches. Keep the watch that feels more like the one you touched. Drop the other watch."

"Shit. Have we gone through all of them already?" His eyelids twitched but remained closed.

"No," she lied, "only about half of them."

She paired immediately-dropped with longer-considered watches. Each time, he held on to the longer-considered. Then she paired and re-paired the longer-considereds, until his left hand held its final choice. She took it from him: the watch with the most and smallest knobs. Returning it to his hand she said, "If this is what you touched, what you drew, keep it in your hand."

He dropped it immediately. "Pissfuck. Now what?" His eyes opened.

She quickly palmed the watch. "Shut your eyes. We're not done." She tried to voice more hope than she felt.

A tap at the door. Bianca stuck her head in. Her eyes took in the wine bottle, the watches, Tommy's erect back, Clare's notepad in lap. "Dinner's almost ready."

"We'll be a while," Tommy replied without opening his eyes. Clare flashed two sets of splayed fingers: ten minutes. Bianca nodded and her head disappeared.

Clare returned the watch to Tommy's hand. "I'm going to ask questions. Raise your left foot if the answer is yes. Do you understand?" His foot lifted: YES.

"Is this the watch you touched?" NO.

"Is this similar to the watch you touched?" After a long pause, YES.

"Is this very much like the watch you touched?" NO.

"Is this a little bit like the watch you touched?" YES.

"Touch the places that are similar." He dropped the watch.

Nothing was similar, or the question was not understood. She placed his fingers on one part of the watch—"Is this like the watch you touched?"—repeating until they'd traversed every area of watch and band. Only the knobs were relevant, and his right brain didn't seem sure about those.

She quickly bagged all the watches. "Let's go eat."

Tommy opened his eyes, frowning. "What'd we find out?"

"I'd rather not say just yet."

"In other words, el big zippo." His right hand smacked the right side of his head. She grabbed his wrist to keep him from doing it again.

Bianca reappeared to find them nose to nose, Clare's hand guiding Tommy's to the table. "Dinner's getting cold. Bring your wine if there's any more."

They left the wine to sit opposing their mates at a purple dinette table, to eat once-frozen enchiladas that would have taken less time to make from scratch. Robert was drunk, Bianca tipsy, Tommy seething.

Anywhere else. That's where Clare wanted to be.

Three times, Bianca requested the salsa from Tommy, who then more or less threw it at her. As she blotted up the red mess, she inquired icily, "What's your problem, darling?"

"First it says it touched a watch, now it acts like it didn't!" Tommy yelled.

"I didn't get the right kind of watch, that's all," Clare tried to soothe him.

Bianca snorted. "That's the big breakthrough? A watch?"

"Clare sees the world in very small terms," Robert informed his enchilada.

"Try to eat, you'll feel better." Bianca touched Robert's arm. He picked up his fork, turned his still untouched meal clockwise in its red sauce. "How do you identify the murderer from a watch, does it have his name on it or something?"

" 'Alert. I am a murderer.' Like those inshlin bracelets." Now Robert was slurring his words. Bianca tittered, at Robert's joke or Clare's discomfort. "Yeah what's so special about this watch?" Robert demanded.

"I'd prefer that we not discuss the experiments. It could—"

"And whatever Clare wants." Robert turned to Tommy. "Do you know why you're stalled? 'Cause Clare hasn't conducted a test worth doing in years. She prefers to test me." He reached for his beer bottle, reconsidered, grabbed the shot glass beside it.

"Don't forget you have to drive home." Clare's voice cracked, betraying her attempt to seem unfazed. Bianca tittered again.

Robert winked at Tommy. "Slip us a few more drinks. We'll pass out and you two lovebirds will have the night to yourshelves."

"That's enough." Tommy told Robert, then Bianca.

"In our own bedroom! That's what does me in!" On the surface, Bianca was all righteous outrage but underneath, seemed to already be calculating her next display.

"Get off it," Tommy scoffed. Bianca threw her plate against the wall.

"Of course, if it was cats getting killed, she might be more motivated." Robert was talking to his shot glass now.

No one had reacted to Bianca's plate trick. Clare watched the red stain creep across the white paint. The stain moved quickly, engulfing walls, jumping doorways, stalking Clare to the bedroom. Squinting until her vision was narrowed enough to block the red, she gathered her work paraphernalia; reached the front door before anyone seemed aware she was leaving, anyone in that tableau as unreal as the dioramas Clare used to make in grade school. The Pueblo Indians dwelled in caves.

". . . back to the lab?" Tommy caught up with her at the bottom of the stairs outside, saw her face, stopped lobbying for more experiments tonight. "It can wait until tomorrow," he assured her, his voice regretting every wrong ever done her.

"Don't let him drive like that."

"I can't believe you're worrying about him."

"I'm not that Christian. But he's a menace to anyone else on the road."

Footsteps thudded. Bianca and Robert bounced past them. "I'm taking him home," Bianca announced.

"You can't drive like that," he replied.

"I had half a beer. Not that you were around to notice."

"Whatever." Clare and Tommy watched them drive off. "I *was* envying you leaving," Tommy said as he flopped on the stairs. "You can stay here if you want."

"Oh that would help." She joined him, but immediately jumped up and pulled a shard of wood from her rear.

"Maybe it'll get infected," Tommy said consolingly. "Then you can sue the owner and get some bucks. The American way."

"I'm not feeling all that patriotic right now. Thanks anyway." She took a step toward her car.

"You're right, it wouldn't be worth it. There'd be complications, you'd have to get a butt transplant." He stood with a sigh. "Look. When you get home. If you need—anything. I could be there in ten minutes."

"I should be alright. But thanks." She stepped away, turned to say good-bye.

Tommy tried to smile, finally used two fingers to force the corners of his mouth up. She set her bags down, dropped her briefcase, took the two small steps required to reach him. He looked surprised, until their eyes met. "Forget something?" he feigned flippancy.

Feigning certainty, she stretched her arms around his neck. His hand touched her back, his face filled her vision, his eyes were so near she had to look from one to the other to take them both in. They displayed more feeling than could possibly be there. After all, this was only—

Her inner doubts were silenced when their lips met. It wasn't a long kiss or maybe it was. She tasted wine and salsa and a new flavor that was Tommy. She shivered, lost her balance, took a step back to regain equilibrium.

He immediately pulled away, but kept his hand lightly on her waist. "There's no hurry," he assured her softly.

She didn't need reassurance, what she wanted was another kiss. But she'd used up all her nerve.

He brushed his lips against her cheek. "Promise you'll call if you need me." She could only nod, and match his tentative wave as he watched her drive away past the cop watching Tommy's house. When she got home, she parked behind the policeman watching her.

Robert wasn't home. Jessie had scratched decades of paint from the bathroom door in her obsession with the bird inside. Clare hoped none of those chips were lead based. She insisted on washing the cat's paws, which did not ease Jessie's already frenetic behavior. Where the hell was Robert? Did she care, as long as he stayed there? What a coward she was: she was glad he'd behaved so badly.

She'd finished packing and the car was loaded before he staggered in to fall face down on the bed. Clare turned him so he wouldn't suffocate, then returned to the living room. By the time she'd consumed a pot of coffee, she'd devised her next experiments. Meanwhile, Jessie bounced off walls. Great. Now they'd made her cat neurotic.

The final note was brief: *Enough. For Lalitha's sake, take good care of Niels. For my sake—and probably yours, too—leave me alone for a while. I need breathing room. How much and how long I can't say.* She packed the other drafts—the angry, the tear-stained, the long-winded rationales—for disposal elsewhere; struggled Jessie into her carrier case, almost forgot the catbox, then finally drove away, about an hour after dawn. As she pulled out, the plainclothes car was still parked out front, but there was no sign of its occupant.

A drizzling rain was blurring the letters: FURNISHED 1-BEDROOM FOR RENT. She'd first noticed the sign, two weeks ago—so this wasn't unmeditated.

It was a boxy early sixties building, nondescript save for the sunburst sculpted over the courtyard entryway. A radio call-in show blared from behind the door labeled MANAGER, next to the laundry room and Coke machine. The manager, Mrs. Manning, a widow these ten years, was a short woman who seemed to be shrinking inside her loose clothes. She pulled on storm boots worthy of a midwestern blizzard to show Clare the apartment, which was better than expected: the shag carpet was only lime green in the living room, the furnishings were bland more often than confrontational, and there were just enough windows to register daylight. A dusty rental agreement lay on the kitchen table.

Clearly, Clare's desire to move in immediately was highly irregular. Mrs. Manning rolled a number of hmms and oh dears inside her cheeks before letting Clare sign the agreement. It then cost an extra eight hundred dollars deposit to bring the pet in from the car. Worse, the manager had to coo and caw at Jessie, who immediately leaped into hiding under the couch. But Mrs. Manning was going to be fine. She only tried to pry once and it only took her seven minutes to sense Clare's desire to be left alone.

Outside the windows, the drizzle had been supplanted by the raw gray of high clouds and brittle November sun. Clare sat on the floor, unclasped her suitcase, and cried. Jessie meowed briefly but was too afraid to leave her hiding place. Thus, after lining up food, water, and litter box next to the couch, Clare stretched out alongside it, reaching her hand underneath so that Jessie could press against it. They stayed like this as long as Clare could.

She hated leaving Jessie alone in this fearfully unknown place. But—as seemed to be the trend these days—all other options were worse.

PART 3

Synesthesia

In some brains, a phenomenon called synesthesia occurs: a mingling of sensory experiences, in which colors might be tasted, sounds may be felt, odors can take on visual dimensions.

CHAPTER 10

Habituation

Tommy met her outside Neurobiology. She was late and he'd gotten no answer phoning her apartment, so was commencing a search for her. When she explained, "I moved out but I can't talk about it," his expression said he understood—perhaps more than she'd like.

"Bianca got home a couple hours ago. Spent the night with Andy Stuart. 'Two can play your game, Tommy'." His parody of her melodrama was vicious. "I told her I see AIDS tests on her and Andy before she gets near me again."

Clare had tarantulas climbing her throat and violinists practicing in her head.

As they ascended stairs to the second floor, he shuffled and mumbled, "Last night was great though—by the stairs I mean. You know. I just wanted to say—what I just said."

"It seems like you're trying to say something else but I don't know what it is."

"Just. I finally got to the place you've been all along. With all this other shit going down, you're right, now's not the time. For us."

"Ah." Now she was right. Now he was putting her off. The only constant in life was irony. No, there were others: pain, confusion, lack of comprehension. God did exist; unfortunately, he happened to be a vivisectionist.

"It's nothing to do with you, damn. Nothing. It's more I." He cut himself off.

"I do understand. And I know how hard this is for you to say to me."

"I mean, do you really know whether you wanted to kiss me or pay Robert back?"

Clare stabbed her key into her office door, which swung open.

Deirdre looked up from rearranging manila folders in a file cabinet. "There you are. I was beginning to wonder. Some of these files were out of chronological order, I hope you don't mind. You said I should familiarize myself with these drawers." She took notice of Clare's displeasure. "The door was unlocked, I thought you were here already. Otherwise I would never—Honest."

"Deirdre's a woman you only have to tell once," Tommy smiled his most killer smile.

"Somebody knocked for you about a half hour ago, I didn't answer because—I don't know, I'm so new here."

"You mean I could've been in here helping you file?" Another smile. Deirdre responded in kind.

It was a relief to sit down, her back to both of them. Clare unlocked the desk drawer holding the murder tests.

"Did you feel the earthquake this morning? About seven? It was just a little one except to us out-of-state types." Deirdre laughed self-deprecatingly.

Clare heard only part of Tommy's response. Something about how he'd been imagining seeing Deirdre today, thought the trembling was internal. Clare wanted to scream, looking into that drawer: the testing paraphernalia had been moved. And it wasn't a quake that put a different file on top.

She spun around to face Deirdre. "Did Steve give you his key to this drawer?" Clare usually kept her most current testing data in this drawer. She'd given Steve the only other key, which he'd promptly lost.

"No. I didn't know he had one. Is something wrong?"

"Not at all. I'll get you a copy of the key; you can set my notes out for me."

Deirdre looked pleased. "I'd like that. As I've said, anything I can do here."

Perfect timing. Clare could now dispatch Deirdre to return the borrowed watches and her assistant could only accept the chore with a forced smile.

"She should get new watches, too, right?" Tommy prompted.

"I've already taken care of that," Clare snapped. Tommy and Deirdre exchanged a look Clare could only interpret as united against her. After Deirdre assured Tommy that she would indeed hurry back, she left Clare alone with him, loathing all three of them. "Let's get started."

"Yeah, before Mata Hari gets back. I say she's spying for her sweetie Steve. She's good but if we put her off guard she's gonna slip. And fall. But I'm not telling you anything—you figured it out before I did, huh? As usual."

Clare went into the lab. "I see. You were only being so friendly to aid our investigation."

After a time, she heard the couch creak and Tommy appeared in the doorway. "If you think I'd say 'later' to you and then 'yes' to her, you're crazier than I'd be if I did that, which I didn't."

"I believe you," Clare said finally to end the stand-off.

Tommy sat as though his plastic chair were electric. "When did you pick up more watches?"

"I didn't. I think this new test will make them unnecessary."

The dichotic tape she'd made before dawn asked, **"Is this a** watch?" while the tachistoscope flashed Tommy's right brain a picture of a wristwatch. His left foot tapped the question mark card in reply. She repeated variations of the question until she'd confirmed her four A.M. fear: Tommy's right brain didn't know the word *watch*. Trying to identify the road-on-the-moon drawing, his left brain had guessed—wrong. And, not knowing the word being discussed, his right brain couldn't correct the misguess.

"**This is a watch.**" Clare taught his right brain the word. Then she displayed the moon road drawing and asked dichotically, "**Is this a watch?**"

NO. NO. NO. She'd never seen his right brain so adamant. Their seeming breakthrough had been only a misunderstanding, which careless testing methods had perpetuated.

When she explained the misunderstanding, Tommy got so upset he couldn't even swear. "Now what?" he groaned.

"Now we go back to figuring out what this drawing means."

Before she could stop him, he stomped out of the room. "Tommy, be reasonable. We have to keep trying." They collided in the doorway. He now held the oversized green parka he'd left on the couch. "I thought you were leaving," she said lamely.

"I wanted to show you this." He gripped the parka with his teeth and dragged a *Hustler* from an inner pocket. "It's not mine, I hate this trash, I copped it from my doctor this morning when I got my arm checked. Do you know it was a week ago Colton got murdered?"

"I am all too aware of that." But if they succumbed to brooding, they'd be set back further. "Interesting doctor you've got. Mine only provides 1970s *Newsweeks*."

"He's a strange guy. Anyway, I was just sort of going through this and I came to this page and I got filled with this idea that it was important." It was a condom advertisement featuring three barely suited beauties on a beach. "I don't get it but I thought maybe you would. Look, my hand's shaking, that's how important it feels."

"Sit down." Clare took the magazine, held it near his left fingers as she studied the picture. Use our brand and you can have women like these, maybe all of them at once. "Point. Who or what is like the killer?"

Tommy's fingers flailed, indicating various areas, various women. Next they tried pointing with his foot, then with the yardstick in his hand. The answers remained imprecise. "Stop playing games," Tommy yelled at his right brain. At this, his left foot tapped the question mark, which infuriated him.

His face turned crimson and Clare had to shout over his cursing. "Hold it. Hold it. Perhaps this photo is important because the killer is a woman."

Mid-curse, Tommy fell quiet. He looked inward. "That doesn't feel right." He was suddenly very calm. "It really wasn't Mrs. Bates. Anyway, what about the deranged surfer?"

"I don't know how he fits into any of this." Tommy's ultra-calm denial of Cynthia Bates was not credible. But she wouldn't press the issue right now—she'd return to it later, when his left brain wasn't expecting it. One of the few things she felt increasingly sure about: Tommy could not countenance knowing—liking—the murderer.

"This *means* something though." He shook the magazine, an interrogator roughing up a captive.

Tommy's right brain was capable of wordplay. Perhaps the clue was hidden. Hot, heat . . . sun, son—gun? Tan—man? Sand—hand? Beach—teach? Reach? Bodies . . . swimsuits . . . skin . . . It could take days, testing the possibilities. Ocean, water, sea—see? Well, here were two they should investigate: hand, see. Once again tonight she'd have hours of prep work. "We'll figure it out. Let it go for now. This is going to sound silly, but have you ever tried drawing with your foot?"

He hadn't, but he was game for it. They repeated the "What did you touch?" test with his toes gripping pencils, Clare kneeling to hold paper in place.

Each foot's drawing was very crudely similar to each hand's

original drawing. His left hemisphere no longer parrot-claimed it had touched a watch.

Deirdre returned. "That was fast," Clare sighed.

"You promised you'd hurry," Tommy smiled.

But Clare saw a way to get rid of her again. "Did you bring the credit slips? Don't get upset, everyone forgets sometimes. I do need them. However, since we're just about done here, as long as you pick up the slips from the stores today, I can wait until next week to get them from you."

Deirdre's narrowed eyes said she doubted Clare really needed those slips, but the assistant could hardly say so.

"See you next week," Tommy bid Deirdre a sad farewell. As soon as she was gone, he snickered. "A dollar says she's back in two hours."

"You're on. My bet would be ninety minutes."

They shook on it and turned to the adapted chimeric faces tests, which Clare was determined to finish that day, to know precisely what Tommy's left hand had touched, from the killer's clothing to body hair. Additionally, today she asked dichotically, **'Is this what you drew?'** while flashing the moon road drawing beside a photo of clothing; she even juxtaposed it with beard stubble. The drawing's meaning remained elusive.

The chimeric tests were ponderously slow and careful. It was the experimental style that made Clare most comfortable: it had the least error margin. Such precision ordinarily yielded her best results; but her strongest ideas these days came in late night flashes, under the weight of too little sleep and too much conflict. Which made her feel like a musician who played best on heroin.

A knock on the door made her realize how little they'd been interrupted today. It was nearly 8:30. "There's my dollar," Tommy said as Clare went to answer.

He was right. Very belatedly, here was Deirdre, looking stern. "I knew I should have stayed. I could have helped you finish sooner. I don't want to belabor the point, Dr. Austen, but you are doing important work and I would like to—"

Tommy appeared, shirt off, hair tousled—he and Clare had been very busy indeed. "We're done," Clare said weakly. "Just wrapping up."

"Come on in, discuss results with us," Tommy said suggestively.

"I've got to go, I have—plans," Deirdre sounded accusatory.

"Say hi to Steve."

Deirdre started to speak, instead pointed at the door. "You need a new sign," she said curtly and fled down the hall. Clare swung the door wide. TESTING IN PROGRESS had been altered with a heavy black marker. It now read SEXING IN PROGRESS.

There were so damned many cretins on this campus. Clare ripped the sign down, anger abbreviating her movements. "Would you mind putting your clothes back on?"

Tommy was undaunted. "See now she's not sure. If she is spying, she's going to step it up."

"I want her to stop spying, Tommy." She spoke as to a slow child.

"Not before we find out why she's doing it."

"Ah. Of course." She pretended agreement, while seething: so they would only have a mock affair, suffer all those whispers and arch looks without compensation.

Back at her work station, Clare noticed that by this time last week, they had discovered Colton's body. No. Think about the data from the chimeric tests instead.

Since beginning the chimerics two days ago, Clare had determined several things. The killer had worn a long-sleeved bulky upper garment of a softish material; it did not have a high collar. There may have been an underlayer, i.e., a shirt beneath a sweater. At the neck, Tommy had touched curly hair—whether growing from scalp or skin was not known. His right brain also indicated straight hair above the neck, seen or touched: eyebrow, beard, sideburn? The killer's hands wore gloves, under which Tommy had discerned a bulge that suggested a ring—and thin gloves. At the wrist was—something: the top of the glove, the edge of the sleeve, not a watch but possibly a bracelet. On the leg, not denim and not bare skin.

None of this data would Clare tell Tommy, which irked his left brain. She refused to argue the point, instead consulted her watch. "I need to go check Jessie but we can meet back here later, unless you want to stop for the night."

"Definitely not. I can come with you, unless you want to get away for a while."

"It's not that. But I should go alone. Jess is so scared, being in a foreign environment, I want to keep further input to a minimum."

"Yeah, I can see that. Well, guess I'll go to Burger Continental and have a beer."

Tommy had the borrowed car today. They walked to it, then he drove her to her car; he was getting quite adept at driving with one arm. "Meet you at BC in an hour."

In Clare's new living room, Jessie's food was untouched. Spilled water and cat litter all over the lime shag indicated nervous cat activity. Clare peered under the couch. Jessie inched to the edge of the shadow, then leaped to Clare's lap.

Webs of fur wafted around them as Clare petted the cat. After some fifteen minutes of serious comforting, Clare felt bolstered enough to move around and Jessie followed, at last interested in inspecting her surroundings—although when Clare got a room ahead of Jessie, the cat galloped to rejoin her. Still, given that Jess had stayed under the bed, period, for a week when Clare last moved, she was adjusting quickly.

Back in the living room, the cat ate voraciously. For some reason, this made Clare want to cry. Another petting session, then Clare reluctantly collected coat and keys. Jessie returned to her lair under the couch, but now she trotted rather than slunk.

After the dense quiet of her apartment, where Jessie's claws catching in the carpet were unnervingly loud, Friday night at Burger Continental was an assault. As Clare drove by, she saw the al fresco tables were packed—with cheap beer and massive portions of Middle Eastern food, BC was a magnet to academics, slumming yuppies, and artists year-round.

She could find no parking spaces, of course, except at the supermarket around back. A squat bald man watched her park then headed for a pay phone to call a tow truck. There were fifty empty spaces in the lot—but God forbid she disregard the CUSTOMERS ONLY VIOLATORS WILL BE TOWED signs. She had ten minutes before she'd have to fight a tow trucker for her car.

Tommy met her at BC's back entrance, with a take-out bag nestled in his sling. He swiveled her around and walked her out. "Robert's here. He didn't see me."

"Is he alone? I can't believe I asked that." She tried not to sneer at the parking lot monitor's disappointment when she returned to her vehicle so promptly.

"He's with two guys who look just like him. You know how really smart guys have that pasty face and they all wear those glasses."

Clare pulled onto California Avenue, seeing the oncoming headlights yet not registering them until she heard the angry horn blow. "Robert does not have a pasty face. Do I?"

"No way." He chortled and rumpled her hair, just as Bianca often did to his hair.

There were no guards visible on campus as they hurried to Clare's lab. The students they passed were skittish, in a hurry to get indoors. Clare and Tommy took a shortcut up the hillside Japanese garden. This proved a mistake: the stylized greenery at night resembled ghastly limbs. Atop the hill, a figure stepped into their path, brandishing—a sweet roll. Clare smelled coffee. The guard muttered a good evening and kept going. They passed other guards, all carrying coffee and donuts. "Morons all take breaks at the same time," Tommy hissed.

There was a note balanced on Clare's doorknob. Robert had

come by. No. *Please turn off lights when leaving* in Bruce the wonder guard's self-conscious scrawl. Clare crumpled the paper and threw it down the hall. "I was afraid it was from Robert," she said, then ducked Tommy's scrutiny by retrieving the note.

"Did you want it to be?" Following her into the lab, he unpacked the take-out bag, arranging stacks of pita bread and containers of hummus and imtabbal at each of their testing sites.

"Beats the hell out of me." Her thoughts ping-ponged as she shredded pita, dragged it through the eggplant spread. "We'll be doing headset and dot work now." He reached for the headset. "I want to hear from Robert to get it over with—I know he'll have something choice to say and I'd rather hear it now." Tommy, his mouth stuffed with food, nodded slowly. "You'll answer yes or no to dichotic questions. You'll see the answer choices on the screen above the levers. Do you think I'm doing all this as a ploy to get Robert to beg me to come back on my terms?" If she were so plotting, she was despicable.

He considered. "No. Otherwise you would have resisted, even a little, when I dragged you away from BC."

She felt relieved. And no longer angry that Tommy had reneged on his availability to her, at least for now. Only alone could she regain her stability.

This line of thought frightened her though—for it occurred while she proceeded with a test. Could she no longer rely on her work to shut all else out?

"**Is Steve the killer?**" her dichotic tape asked Tommy's right brain, as she watched the levels indicating sound transmissions to each ear. Her vanished assistant seemed a plausible suspect but Tommy's right hemisphere swiftly responded NO.

"**Is the killer Mrs. Bates?**" Damn it to hell. The levels on his left ear fell to zero a moment before those on the right. She hadn't timed the aural distraction correctly.

NO, his right hemisphere indicated, while his right hand

ripped the headset off. "What. Did. You. Ask." He leaped to his feet, towering over her.

"You answered no." Hoping to pacify.

False hope. "Know why we don't know jackshit? Because you won't believe any answers you disagree with." He slammed his fist into his parka sleeve, jerked the zipper closed. "From now on we work separately. You keep making up stories and I'll try to name the killer."

"The fact that you're so inordinately upset makes me wonder—"

"Everything makes you wonder. Then jump to conclusions." He stomped out.

She refused to chase after him. Some time after his footsteps retreated, she went to shut the door—and found him sitting in the hall in an upright fetal position. He raised bleary eyes to hers. "So Cynthia's the one?"

"No. You said she wasn't."

He looked lighter, then bleak. "I don't want to put you through shit but I keep doing it."

"You haven't. You truly haven't." She joined him on the tile floor. "Can I give you a ride to your car?" He'd left it at Burger Continental.

"That's all you had for us to do tonight?" Temper flared again.

"Everything else was based on a yes answer," she admitted.

After a long silence, "Yeah, give me a ride," he said reluctantly.

On the walk to her car, the November air was cold and dark; Tommy's mood, icier and blacker still. Without having discussed it, they now had a new route to the lot, which avoided the bushes where Larry's remains had been found. It took a bit longer, the new way, but also took less out of Clare.

Trekking across the deserted parking lot, she thought her car looked—tilted? As they grew closer, she saw that one tire was flat. Closer, and even in the dim parking lot light, the heavy black markered words were visible on the tire's whitewall. STOP OR YO, followed by a squiggle, as though the message writer had been interrupted.

"What the fuck." Tommy knelt sideways, awkwardly, so that his good hand could inspect the tire. He patted, pushed, and pulled, while Clare's gaze darted everywhere at once, searching the darkness, fervently hoping to see—nothing. No one.

"Let's not stand out here," she murmured; if she spoke louder she might scream.

Tommy's hand opened to reveal a fistful of nails. "This isn't half of 'em. That tire's a goner." Before Clare could reply, he yelled, "Hey! Over here!"

She looked up just as a flashlight beamed their way, blinding her. By the time she could see again, Tommy had explained their predicament to a security guard, who used his walkie-talkie to radio others. Soon they were surrounded by guards, flashlight beams and tinny voice transmissions—the latter confirming that no one had seen any suspicious activity in faculty lot H.

"Looks like somebody wanted you to get the message," said the guard who was exchanging the wrecked tire for Clare's spare.

Clare nodded, then said quietly to Tommy, "It looks like the same printing as that sign on my door. Do you think Deirdre could have done this?"

"You're asking *me?* I'm the last one to know jack about anything."

She said nothing further, except to thank the guards when they'd finished, and agree that it was an excellent idea for Security to keep the vandalized tire and turn it over to Lieutenant Beaudine.

Tommy brooded silently, until she pulled alongside his car, up Lake Street from Burger Continental. He exhibited a much deeper than physical exhaustion. "Sorry I've been such a shitheel. You be okay getting home?"

"Sure." She wished he would look at her. She wished she didn't feel so responsible for their lack of results.

He called over his shoulder as he walked away. "Call me if you—need to."

She didn't have a phone yet, but never mind.

No one followed her to her new abode, which made her feel marginally better, until she discovered that her new street was unlit and parking was scarce within a block of her new home. No wonder Mrs. Manning kept the outside lights blazing all night. Extremely aware of how alone and cut off she was, only Jessie's presence on the other side of the door enabled Clare to reach it. That brief sharp meow enabled her to open it.

There was even more cat litter underfoot. Jessie was very brave now, though, prancing all around to demonstrate. Woodenly, Clare made the bed. Jessie helped, providing a lump under the sheet, a blaze of motion across the blanket. Clare almost laughed.

After a moment's reflection, she unmade the bed and made up the couch: the living room felt less alien and it was nearer the door. Then she unpacked her briefcase and stared at the *Hustler* bikini beauties. But she kept thinking about that message on her tire. When would it be completed? What would it say? And what would the consequences be?

Jessie hissed and ran for the couch as a shadow fell over the picture. The killer had materialized, a dark silhouette against the overhead lights. A knife plunged into Clare's arms, her cheek, she—

She woke up screaming into the carpet. Jessie stood atop a far stack of boxes, legs splayed, fur full, watching Clare intently. Clare flicked litter pellets from her face and arms and looked at the curtains, bright with sun. She'd slept through the night.

For the moment, she was more rested. Long range, she'd wasted valuable time.

Yet she woke up with many new thoughts and ideas. Back in

her school days, she'd often gone to bed if she was stuck, assuming the problem would be solved while she slept, by parts of her brain (probably right hemisphere) not accessible during consciousness except within certain altered states. Frequently—though not always the first morning—she did awaken with a solution. During her breakdown, this ability had been lost. How wonderful to have regained it.

Mmm. Sleeping on the floor had not made her feel sprightly and youthful, but a hot shower revived her. Jessie soon appeared outside the shower curtain, batting at water drops hitting the clear plastic. Alas, she batted a curtain edge and a few drops hit her. She was out of the bathroom in one leap. Clare failed to turn away from the shower stream before she started laughing. She choked on water, yet felt invigorated—and calmer than in recent memory, due to the experiencing of normal life.

Loading her briefcase returned her to the abnormal present. Perhaps Tommy did know the killer's identity, but it was someone met since his commissurotomy and he couldn't link name to face. Or perhaps his right brain knew a lot of information that added up to nothing. Maybe they knew all they'd ever learn.

Somehow the prospect didn't dishearten her. It was simply a reminder to keep her mind open, her conclusions undrawn.

Walking out to her car, she didn't see her police house watcher. Of course not: Lieutenant Beaudine didn't know she'd moved. Should she tell him? She was curious to see how long it would take him to find out on his own. In her new abode she felt safer—cut off from her life. But she wouldn't mind having a cop or three out here after dark.

No one was following her today, if that had ever occurred. Robert hadn't responded to her leaving, if they had ever been together.

Tommy was waiting outside her lab building. He didn't look well. "Bianca stayed out all night. This morning I found a note on the door and after the messages we got last night, I just about lost it. But this note was just from Bianca, saying she's really been staying with Trish, not Andy, to make me feel bad. But I should put the note back on the door if I wanted her to stay away."

Clare busied herself unlocking the glass entry door. "How did you respond?"

"Threw it away. Doesn't change anything either way." Their favorite guard walked their way. "Hey Bruce, caught any scale felons lately?" Tommy sneered.

Bruce stood so straight he arched backward. "Night crew said to inform you, Dr. Austen. They've alerted the lieutenant and they'll keep you posted."

"Thanks, Bruce." She suppressed the urge to salute him. She was grateful she didn't have to contact Beaudine. Perhaps he'd take the security staff more seriously.

Clare assumed she was relieved to still find no message from Robert, in or around her office. "I have a terrible confession to make," she informed Tommy.

"Oh yeah? Spill. I could use some good dirt today. Forget about my own."

"My parents' anniversary is coming up and Monday's the last day I can mail their gifts. I need to go shopping; I was hoping you'd come with me. I'd like to—have a break. Talk things out. Get an overview." Observe Tommy's behavior when he didn't know he was being studied.

"That is one lousy confession."

It was difficult keeping his eyes in view; this would take some practice. "Frankly, I more or less passed out last night and didn't work up any tests for today."

"In that case." He shrugged—he was at her mercy. "I've been thinking about yesterday." His gaze shifted to the right as he spoke.

According to those who researched lateral eye movements, or LEMs, looking to the right indicated primary activity in the left hemisphere. LEMs were a fascinating field of study. Personally,

Clare wasn't convinced the data proved the existence of such telling eye movements. But she hoped she was wrong because then, once she got to know Tommy's LEM patterns, she might use them to determine when his left brain was confabulating. "What exactly were you thinking about yesterday?"

"Maybe I do know the murderer. Maybe it is Cynthia—or Steve."

"Think back to the killer in the hallway." His eyes shifted to the left. A sign that his right hemisphere was envisioning the scene? "Was it Steve?"

His eyes shifted to look at Clare. "It could be."

"New question. Feel certain of your answer before you speak. Is Steve the killer?"

His eyes looked left while he waited for the question, then looked directly at Clare when he replied, "He could be. That's all I can say."

Not having expected any better result, she cheerfully returned to her plan for the day: to study Tommy's LEMs while steering his talk through sites of known confabulation; and while eliciting reactions both emotional and factual. Then she would remember everything that happened and make brilliant deductions about what she had observed. All without Tommy's knowing they were doing other than shopping.

Neither she nor her mother had heard from her father in a decade but never mind. Clare wanted Tommy near men's clothing as well as women's.

As they headed for Clare's car she said, "We've discussed the chance that you heard the killer speak. From now on, when you hear the same word, give me a sign."

"If I hear, you mean. That's really stretching."

"I agree—but it won't hurt to try."

First they went to the big fabric store in Glendale which was always changing owners so Clare never knew its name. "Mom likes to sew," Clare lied as she led him through acres of cloth, some of which must be like the killer's garments. She babbled about her parents as they went. Bored, Tommy fingered occasional bolts. They passed a soft leather and Clare recalled the murderer's gloves. "Can you find a price on that?" Both injured and uninjured hands got involved, as Tommy pulled fabric from the bolt to find the price tag. If his right brain noticed a similarity in texture, however, it gave no indication.

"How long is my office couch, would you say? I've been wanting to slip cover it." His eyes moved to the left, as existing LEM research predicted: such size appraisals were orchestrated by his right hemisphere.

Eyes shifted right, he waited, then replied, "About six and a half feet."

"You thought about that a while."

"I kept running answers through my head—four feet, four and a half, five—until one felt right."

Tommy was known to cross-cue in that way. That could mean his LEMs—

He wasn't beside her anymore. She turned, saw his left hand clenching a thick soft flannel. "Nice material." His right hand reached to pry his left fingers free, but they released the cloth on their own. Clare made note of the bolt's location.

By the time they had walked through the fabric mart, she just wasn't sure she'd seen any fabric her mother would like. However, she would take some samples—including all fabrics in which Tommy's right brain had shown interest.

Meanwhile she'd inspired three incidences of cross-cuing and two confabulations. During cross-cuing, his LEMs were left, then right; during confabulation his eyes moved left, then looked her square on center. It was too small a sampling to really tell her anything. But it was most definitely a start.

Driving back to Pasadena, Tommy brought up the murders and she quickly interrupted, for she couldn't see LEMs while she drove. "Have you had any time to work on your music?" Surely this topic would cover the ten minutes on the road.

"Naw, it's been zerosville. I keep feeling like singing but all that comes out is Lawrence Welk. You know, two A.M. on channel 56?"

"How does one sing Lawrence Welk?"

"An' a one an' a two an' a. He never said it that fast—put him on seventy-eight he's still slow—but that's what it reminds me of. I'll count down that beat but then I forget what I meant to sing. I guess it's because I'm wondering all the time, if my arm'll heal right."

Clare exited the freeway, heading for the sleek modern ship building that housed Bullock's, Pasadena. "However your arm heals, you'll find a way to keep playing."

"Madame Clare predicts." His joking tone failed to hide how much her prediction mattered.

"Most people give up much sooner than you have." He snorted dismissively. "I'm talking about other epileptics, and about patients I see at the clinic. I've told you before, how much I admire you. It's not just because you have such unique hair."

Turning into the Bullock's lot, a quick glance caught the gratitude in his eyes.

"Unique. Shit. That's worse than—" When he said "shit," his left knee snapped up toward his face. "Now what?" he asked with trepidation.

"Shit, I don't know." When she repeated the word, his left arm flapped in its sling. She felt the heat and chill of discovery.

"I get it! That's what the killer said in my ear. Makes sense. Probably what I was saying too. Yeah. I can feel it all through me. That's what he said."

Damn. His left brain was too fast for her. She swerved into a parking space. "Try not to think about it anymore," Clare said noncommittally.

"Sure. Of course," he said in a rare moment of left brain equanimity as they walked toward the store. Reaching the entrance, Tommy held the door for three Pasadena society matrons who blew by without crediting his graciousness. Clare gagged on the three powerful competing perfumes. "Human pollutants," Tommy commented.

Clare led him toward Men's Sportswear. "My parents like to play golf together. I'm hoping I can find matching sweaters."

"They'd really wear them? Jeez." As they traversed Perfume and Makeup, every counter worker but one exchanged smiles with Tommy. He stopped beside that one, a surly middle-ager in a suit, overseeing a maintenance man removing stickers from display case glass. BUYING THESE PRODUCTS PROMOTES CRUELTY. REMEMBER: ALL ANIMALS FEEL PAIN.

"Bad for business, isn't it?" Tommy said sympathetically. "Like you don't have enough to do without cleaning up after crazies."

The manager belatedly acknowledged Tommy's existence. He didn't much like this fellow's wild hair, but at least he understood about those animal rights crazies. "Last week they smashed a window at the mall, threw red paint on two fur coats. Thirty thousand dollars damage."

"Send them to Iraq if they don't like it here." A buxom teenager wearing most of the products she was selling leaned over the counter to get into the conversation.

"Is that what they teach you in school these days?" The manager looked disgusted.

Tommy somehow gave conflicting conspiratorial looks to the girl and the manager. "Hope they leave you alone after this," he bid the manager farewell.

Clare led the way to Men's Sweaters. Tommy got in front of her, walking backward. "Don't be pissed. Just because I talked to that guy doesn't mean I agree with him. I'm on your side about that research stuff."

"You seem to be on everyone's side." She yanked his arm to turn him around; he was about to collide with a mannequin.

"It's a game I play. Pitiful, huh? I used to do it a lot more though." As she examined a rack of pullovers, "I like shopping for your folks. What anniversary's this?"

"Thirty-ninth."

"Woah. That's so great. Bianca and me, we made it to our ninth." His eyes looked right. "See, it's not whether she slept with Andy; I'd take that as a good sign—that she agreed we were history. But she thinks she can fuck him and then come back to me."

"Haven't you done that? During your separations?"

His eyes stayed dead center. "Where'd you get that? Did she tell you that?" His voice was loud enough to attract attention from the scattered menswear shoppers.

"No I . . . just assumed. From things you've said." From conclusions I've jumped to. "What do you think of this one? Is this wool too scratchy?" The fabric was similar to one he'd clutched at the yardage store.

"This one's better colors." She thought she saw his eyes move left, then right, before his head tilted down to examine his choice: a nubby cotton knit. He pulled the sleeve through his left hand, which latched onto the even nubbier cuff. As his right fingers moved to pry the sweater free, his left fingers flicked and released the garment. "I'll sure be glad when I get this thing off my arm," he said.

Which launched him on a murder discussion. It was all rehash, but she questioned and listened as though it were all new. As often as she dared, she jotted in a notebook—notes about gift choices, she claimed. Tommy found this behavior excessive unto anal; but that wasn't what mattered. His LEMs did appear to have patterns; and his left hand seemed preoccupied with cuffs. Had the murderer worn not a watch, but a sweater cuff? Perhaps the—

"For somebody who can't decide what to buy, you sure get excited about shopping." Tommy had been watching her.

"I'm just happy to not be working." As hoped, this got him back to talking about Dr. Colton's murder.

After a time, he paused, then spoke anxiously, looking everywhere but at her. "Remember when we were talking about motives? And teams of killers? Clare—you know. It could be animal rights guys we're after."

He looked surprised when she replied mildly, "I've thought about that. It is remotely possible that some activists could go that far over the edge, try to stop murder with murder. But I don't believe they'd kill randomly—and only Dr. Colton was a valid target. Lalitha was a physicist; Haffner studied human childhood memory deficits."

"And Larry only wore a lab coat to keep warm." Tommy exhaled with relief. "So are you going to buy a sweater, or what?"

No, she hadn't seen any they'd be wild about. Maybe her parents would like matching gloves instead. She led him to Accessories.

A bit defiantly, Tommy befriended the glove clerk, who was going to night school in business administration and disliked all his teachers. While chatting, Tommy also idly examined gloves. At an adjoining counter, Clare studied gloves and LEMs, until Tommy, voice sharp, interrupted the clerk's patter. "S'cuse me, can I see some other colors in these?" Both hands clutched one lightweight beige cloth glove.

"That one comes in sixteen colors. What did you have in mind?" Tommy wanted to see them all? A suppressed groan. "I'll have to go in back."

At Tommy's eager nod, the clerk departed and Tommy hurried to Clare's side. "These gloves. Put them on. Let me feel them. Move your arm. No, like this." He stood as if listening, while his left hand gripped hers. His eyes looked left, right, then met Clare's. "This is what he was wearing. Or something real close to it."

Tommy jogged over to the returned clerk, who was laying out gloves. "Okay, I'll take the black ones." The clerk frowned. The black ones had already been on display. "And these hot pink ones. Oooh la la." The clerk liked Tommy again.

Until Tommy dropped his wallet and muttered "Shit." At this his left arm and leg flailed. He stumbled backward, regained balance while shouting, "We know it's 'shit,' stop doing that." The clerk bagged the gloves rapidly and rang the sale from a remote register. Tommy was too thrilled about their find to care.

Leaving the store, he interrupted his at-last-we're-getting-somewhere exultations to hold the door for what seemed to be the same three matrons, now entering. Only the perfume gusts were different. He winked at Clare and they resumed walking. "Gifts for your parents huh? Sh—damn, are you sneaky."

"I don't know what you mean." But when he started laughing, she joined in.

Once in the car, he used his teeth to unbag the black gloves, pull one onto his good hand and admire it. "Now all we gotta do is track down all the people who own these things and we'll have our killer. So what'd you find out about sweaters?"

"Nothing really."

"Oh yeah. I believe you." But he didn't push.

It was nearly five o'clock, stores would close soon. She ignored speed limits getting to pricey Les Hommes, and then on to a low-budget Target. Tommy cheerfully wandered the stores while, in the interests of science, she borrowed bagfuls of sweaters from each. Then, as they returned to her car, Tommy stopped abruptly and stared at her windshield.

Gingerly, from under a wiper, his fingernails plucked a scrap of white paper, dotted with black ink which had seeped through from the message on the other side.

A message in heavy black printing. STOP OR YOU DIE.

They slammed the car doors and took off, Tommy swearing.

"I didn't even notice anyone following us," Clare said weakly. Now she was doing so much looking into mirrors and over shoulders that she was having problems driving.

Tommy glared at the note. "Coming to *get* you, fucker. We're on to *you* now."

They flew to her office, where Clare prepped experiments using the sweaters and gloves, while Tommy phoned Beaudine. The lieutenant wasn't in. "Tell him we got another threat, same as the tire, and to call us right away at Dr. Austen's lab. Thanks." Tommy also left word that Clare had moved. Then, as soon as Clare was ready, they commenced touch comparison tests similar to those done with the watches.

For three hours they sorted sweaters. The results merely confirmed Clare's shopping observations. Tommy's left hand had touched a nubby cuff the night of Dr. Colton's murder. Nubby, or perhaps ribbed. However, Tommy's right brain couldn't pinpoint a specific cuff; and it alternated answers of NO and ? when asked if the moon road drawing represented a cuff.

Tommy grew contentious. "So now we know that the killer and fifty gazillion other people own sweaters."

She stopped bagging sweaters. "The fact is, these tests have been quite fruitful."

"Bullshit." He paused, looked relieved when his right brain didn't react to The Word, then turned snide. "So who's the killer, then, professor?"

Unperturbed, she set aside the last bag of sweaters: he wasn't really angry with her. "We're closer to knowing that answer. I'm sure of it." She spoke as though she meant it.

"So now we go collect the next note. Or, hey, we might even get to meet the." He clamped his lips shut.

Clare envisioned meeting the killer in the parking lot. "I suggest we wait here until Beaudine calls back."

Tommy relaxed somewhat. "Man, could I use a drink. Know any bars that deliver?"

"That's the best idea I've heard in ages." She led him out to her office, grandly gestured for him to sit on the couch, swept open a file drawer, extracted a nearly full bottle of Bushmills.

Tommy hooted. "You've been holding out on me, Clare."

By unspoken agreement, they pretended they were holed up by choice. By the third slug of whiskey, they no longer snuck glances at the silent phone, the locked door.

Questioningly, Tommy tapped the wall above her couch, indicating a framed note scrawled in red crayon: *Thank you Doctor*

Clare Austen love Janey. "That's from the daughter of one of my patients at the clinic," Clare explained. Her neurological pro bono work. "Ex-patient. He really made great progress."

"Did you mean what you said about how I don't give up like a lot of people do?"

"Absolutely. Although I'm definitely not criticizing them. You all have so much to contend with. What's impressive is how well you've contended."

"So tell me some brain horror stories. Make me glad I've only got epilepsy."

Following his example, Clare curled into a corner of the couch. "Well. I know of a man poisoned by carbon monoxide who was incapable of speaking or moving—he'd lie in one position, overwhelmed by his thoughts. He'd think about acting, talking, but these thoughts became new obsessions. The oddest thing is, if someone talked to him—got his attention—for a time he could function normally."

"Hell, my drummer's like that. Tell me something scarier." He swigged more Bushmills.

"How about neglect? That's fairly common. Neglect sufferers simply ignore half of space, usually the left half. They'll wash half their face. Or draw a clock with all twelve numbers on one side. I've seen patients complain they haven't been fed enough, when half their plate is still full. Rotate the plate and suddenly they notice the food. One man I treated insisted his left arm was somebody else's, was always begging me to get that arm away from him." Tommy was very still, head cocked to watch the left half of space, lest it disappear. "Now don't become a brain hypochondriac. Although during my first year in grad school, I was sure I manifested symptoms of everything from motor apraxia to temporal lobe syndrome."

"What're those?" he asked hesitantly.

"I shouldn't be telling you these." The whiskey made her blunt.

"Come on, just one more story. I can use them at parties."

"Do you go to a lot of parties?"

"No, because I don't have anything to talk about with strangers."

"Now there's one I can't argue with." They exchanged grins. The room's tone had shifted from trapped to cozy. "Temporal lobe syndrome. The three major characteristics are hypergraphia—a compulsion to write; an extremely strong adherence to religious belief—any religious belief, and the beliefs can change minute to minute; and a proclivity for certain—sexual acts."

"I'm warming up to this one. Which acts?"

"Let's just call them—unusual ones."

"How about a demonstration if you can't talk about them?"

"I can only assume you're not expecting an answer to that."

"An answer to what? Look, I have conversation neglect." Tommy sprawled, pondering the acoustic ceiling tile.

"This used to be a dentist's office?"

"No, that's just a classy design feature."

Tommy chuckled. "What I really hate is how I start counting the holes."

She chuckled too. Yet, despite their best efforts, Clare could feel their mood mutating.

"Guess I'll try the Bow-dine again. Should I leave him your home phone number this time?"

"You can't. My phone won't get installed until Tuesday."

By now, Tommy was at her desk. He stopped punching numbers. "I don't like you there without a phone."

His concern made her stomach knot. "Neither do I."

Someone answered at the police station. Tommy quickly ascertained that, yes, the men assigned to watch Dr. Austen's home had been informed of her move. Reaching Beaudine, however, was not so easy. Clare listened for a time, then went into her lab to look for some new line of attack on tomorrow's tests.

"I underSTAND he's out on a case," Tommy yelled. "This is his case too and a goddamn dangerous one."

Clare didn't want to think about their leaving these rooms.

She set to work instead. Did Tommy's LEMs show a pattern? Would it be the same in the lab? Some studies suggested LEMs altered under stress such as testing in a lab. . . . Now if Tommy's right brain heard the killer say "shit," was that enough vocal input for identification? She might at least be able to determine the timbre of the murderer's voice. . . . She felt skeptical that her scream could have drowned out the killer's voice in Tommy's left brain—it took painstaking lab work to create that condition; the chances of its occurring in the real world were remote. Yet only his right brain had recalled hearing "shit." Well, there could be other explanations for that. . . .

Tommy appeared in the lab doorway. "No Beaudine. I phoned Security, we're getting an escort to our cars."

"You what? I thought we'd agreed not to call attention to our working all these extra hours."

"Uh, Clare? I, like, um, think the murderer knows about us already. "You know?"

Her skin grew hot. What an idiot she could be. They shared a laugh that began as a macabre chuckle and quickly exploded. Clare was still breathing convulsively when five security guards materialized in the corridor.

As she and Tommy were walked to their cars, they exchanged promises to neither stop nor leave their vehicles when they arrived home, unless certain of safe arrival to their doors. They pretended such certainty was possible and said good night.

If only Clare had known how dark her new street was at night. And there was no sign of plainclothes cops. The key was barely out of her ignition when she bolted from her car, through the blackness toward her floodlit building. She heard her shoes scuff against asphalt, then clatter on concrete as she ran. STOP OR YOU DIE. Gasping, she dashed up her stairs, fumbled her key into her lock, fell against the door to hasten its opening.

A black and orange streak darted through her legs. Jessie had escaped. Clare ran downstairs after, calling for Jessie as calmly as she could. The cat rocketed into the street as a car careened toward them. A V-12 engine snarled. Jessie froze on the asphalt, eyes glowing in the headlights. The car swerved and its screeching tires sent Jessie bolting back toward Clare, who grabbed a leg and held on despite Jessie's howls. She clutched the cat to her. Jessie's heart thudded as wildly as Clare's. The car sped on.

It took hours for them to regain composure. Jessie kept growling in the direction of the bedroom—but when Clare mustered courage to check, she found the window still locked, the room unchanged. Yet Clare dragged the dresser outside the room, tied the doorknob to it, and spent an uneasy night on the couch, with Jessie beneath it.

Come morning, Jessie was fine, Clare still jittery. With too much ease, she was able to unhinge the bedroom window screen and stick her head outside. She'd intended to rent an upstairs apartment; she hadn't noticed the slope that put her bedroom at ground level. She looked around. The window showed no signs of tampering. The weeds beneath it had been flattened—but when? Surely they'd look less brown and brittle, if trampled last night.

Feeling better, she replaced the screen, locked the window, and went out to her living room. Jessie had pulled tissue wrappings from a box of glassware. Now the paper was everywhere, shredded to molecules.

"Nice work, Jess, you could not have made a bigger mess." Jessie trotted over to bump her head against Clare's shins. Along the way, she paused to bat at a paper shred as though she'd never seen one before. Cats had such convenient memories. Clare stuffed the shreds into the kitchen wastebasket, then glanced outside the window, to a parked car across the street. Inside was a man she recognized as one of Beaudine's.

Later, as Clare headed for her car, she blew a kiss to the cop, who looked at her like she was a drug dealer from Mars.

CHAPTER 11

Completion

"You want to *what?*" Tommy was no longer slouching on her office couch.

"Hypnotize you. It's part of my campaign to turn you into a zombie slave."

"Honey, all you have to do is ask."

Today, they were better able to feign lightheartedness. They had discussed the threatening note and concluded that they were in no greater danger than they'd been all along. The note should serve only as a reminder. But ongoing contemplation of the danger could incapacitate them; or cloud their judgment. Therefore, they would strive to strike it from conscious awareness.

Clare avoided brooding about the future of that note: what would transpire, once it became apparent that they were not going to STOP? Thinking about this made her want to run and hide. But she didn't have the luxury of such reactions. Briefly, she wondered if her resignation counted as bravery. Then she banished all thoughts not germane to the business at hand, and asked, "Have you ever been hypnotized before?"

Tommy shook his head. According to some experts, his ability to concentrate, his imagination, and his level of absorption in novels (back in the premurderous good old days, he was always reading) all argued for hypnotizability. His split brain might argue against; but if data existed on split brain hypnosis, she hadn't been able to find it. Published indications—such as those finding that a preponderance of left LEMs indicated hypnotizability—suggested that a controlling right hemisphere was somehow involved; if that were true, Tommy's split left hemisphere could be affected only if such control was not wielded through the central commissure.

Another big question mark hovered over her ability to hypnotize. She hadn't tried it since grad school. If it did work, though, she might be able to question his right brain openly without interference from his left. "Are you willing to try it?"

"Sure. You're not going to find anything but we can give it a try." If her analysis yesterday was correct, Tommy's LEMs indicated he was confabulating: about minding, or her findings? Sometimes she thought one or both of his brains intentionally tried to impede their investigation.

"Terrific. Close your eyes. Sit comfortably."

She led him through relaxation techniques: lengthening breathing, loosening muscles, until his limbs felt so heavy he was sinking into the couch. She had him imagine strolling woods and corridors, then paused in her monotone stream of instructions. Now to descend Jung's stairs to the unconscious. "At the end of this corridor you open a door and find a long flight of steps going down, it's dark but beautiful, a very comforting place, you walk down the stairs slowly, inhale . . . good . . . exhale . . . you're very heavy yet your—"

Harsh footsteps and a harsher rap on her door. Tommy's eyes jerked open. Sunday, with the building secured, no one should have access. Clare heard a key and sprang to her feet. The door was shoved open—by Bruce the guard, flanked by two big blond men in suits, whose eyes cased the hall in both directions. Her terror turned to rage. "Since when do you let yourself in here?"

One of the men briefly unpocketed a thin wallet. A badge flashed. "Sergeant Campbell from Lieutenant Beaudine's team. There's an intruder in this building, five five, hundred twenty, brown eyes, blond hair, mustache, Hawaiian shirt. I believe you were attacked by this man a week ago Thursday."

Her throat constricted. "Where did you see him?"

"How long have you been here?"

"About a half hour."

The suits exchanged looks. "We lost him forty minutes ago. May we come in?"

"You'd be wasting your time. He's not here." There was nowhere for him to hide except one cabinet she'd opened upon arrival—God, if he'd been in there. "You do know about the route through the basement?"

Campbell glanced at Bruce. The guard nodded surreptitiously. "Yes, we have men down there. If you don't mind, we'll take a look around for your own protection."

Something was wrong here. Clare had limited as in zero experience with such procedures but this one seemed phony. "I can assure you he's not in here."

"If they have to get a search warrant they will," Bruce piped up.

"Smith, stay out of this," Campbell said abruptly, then cocked an ear. "Hear that?" The other suit nodded and the two took off. Campbell yelled, "They've sighted him down below! You take the south stairs." Bruce took off too.

Clare hadn't heard anything. She locked the door and phoned Beaudine, though he had yet to return last night's calls. The police station's lines were busy so she tried his home. "Didn't that seem strange to you?" she asked Tommy as the phone rang and rang.

"Everything's strange to me right now." He looked dazed. She'd taken him somewhere and the interruption had brought him back in a state of disorientation. They'd—

"Who's this?" At last the phone was answered, by Beaudine's housemate, not in a good mood.

"Is Lieutenant Beaudine there?"

"He's at work." Click. She called the station. "He's off today." Click.

She called back. "I just called. Have you got a Sergeant Campbell in Homicide?"

"You got a reason for asking?"

"Someone just tried to search my office claiming he was one of you."

"What'd he look like?" Clare described both suited blonds. "Could be somebody I don't know but I don't know 'em. Stay inside there and I'll get it checked out." This cop must be a rookie—he even offered to call her back with the results.

Tommy still looked groggy. "I didn't know any of that was going on. I mean, I knew but it didn't sink in. I didn't feel suspicious. Just. Tired or something."

"Because they interrupted us, we're going to have to start over." Tommy groaned. "But not right now. There's one further step we need to take now, though. Close your eyes." After she relaxed him again, "Walk back out the door. Now go up the stairs. Inhale . . . exhale . . . walk back the way you came, you're walking slowly but without effort . . . exhale . . . that's right . . . you're moving so easily and the next time we come to this beautiful place you will arrive quickly, your journey will be easy, smooth . . ."

He no longer seemed disarranged, but she was left unsure if she'd accomplished more than deep relaxation.

On a hunch, she called the guard desk downstairs. Bruce Smith's shift was over and the current guard, Lou, was not pleased about it. Bruce hadn't logged out; worse, the station was unmanned when Lou arrived. "I shouldn't have told you that, Clare. You caught me at a bad time. These new guys, they got no respect for detail."

"Lou, it goes no further." She'd known Lou for years. Retired, he worked security to keep out of the wife's hair. He loved to reminisce about his bush pilot days in New Zealand, Alaska, Brazil; and Clare loved to listen. She could trust Lou. She confided her ongoing problems with Bruce. Lou vowed to call his supervisor at home.

"Hates calls on his day off, but he hired this donkey—pardon my French, Clare."

"Damn straight," Clare said as she hung up, smiling at Lou's little chuckle.

Tommy wanted Clare to describe the suits—he'd been too dazed to lean around the door jamb to see them. She was interrupted by a call from the rookie policeman. He was sending someone out: her visitors were not detectives, homicide or otherwise.

"Were either of those guys big enough?" Tommy asked.

"The one who called himself Campbell was only about five nine and his partner was shorter. And they both had stocky builds like farm boys. They looked alike actually; I'd almost say brothers."

Tommy punched a throw pillow. "Just once I wish something would happen that made us know more instead of less." He headed for the door.

"We're supposed to stay here until the real cops come."

"By that time those guys'll be long gone." She followed him down the hall, tugged at the back of his arm sling. "Will you let me the fuck go? If they were going to hurt us they could have done it before."

She kept her fingers lightly on the sling. "They weren't cornered before. Anyway, I'm sure they're gone. They've had quite a head start."

"I'm fucking sick of not knowing what's going on."

"Gee that's funny—*I* really enjoy it."

Tommy whipped around to face her, glaring. After a moment, he fought a smile, shook his head, and offered his in-sling arm to her. With her hand lightly touching his elbow, he walked her back to her office.

Against all campus regulations, Clare phoned a locksmith and put a rush order on locks for both office and lab. This time, only she would have the key. The locksmith would be arriving within the hour; thus she decided to delay further hypnotism attempts. Which was just fine with Tommy.

They adjourned to the lab, to the dichotic tapes she'd made that morning, stalking the library, while frowning students prepared for finals. Despite her reservations about unilateral—single hemisphere—vocal identification, she'd imposed upon thirty-two students, three librarians, and two custodians for an excellent cross section of vocal types and timbres, each reciting strings of one syllable words ending in "-it," in volumes ranging from whisper to shout.

"Is the killer's voice more like this, or this?" It took four hours to find the two most similar voices: one male, one female; lowish tenors notable for heavy aspiration and several other common phonological similarities, with no twangs nor quirks so obvious as to be noticed in one exclamatory syllable. In other words, they had narrowed the field to a general majority of the population. Clare liked to think this put them ahead.

Meanwhile, the locksmith came and went; a pair of uniformed police—one male, one female—stopped by, as cordial as the rookie on the phone. Perhaps Clare and Tommy were no longer under suspicion?

Then again. At last Beaudine arrived, a vision in spandex shorts and a cycling helmet with a little rearview mirror.

"That's some case you're on." Tommy set the tone for the encounter.

Beaudine took last night's note for analysis, after avowing that nothing would be gleaned. He seemed inclined to believe Clare and Tommy had written the note themselves, as they had nailed Clare's tire. Or, given the SEXING IN PROGRESS sign they showed him, he seemed equally comfortable believing that the threat was from Bianca and/or Robert, and had no relation to the murders. He left them stunned, and belatedly outraged.

Some twenty minutes later, Clare grew tired of raving about his stupidity.

But not Tommy. "What a prick! And, he thinks you made up Campbell! Just because I couldn't describe him? No wonder this case is still unsolved."

"As we've discussed some fifteen times now, Beaudine's logic there seems to be that I'm attempting to distract his people from their real work."

"He's so lame." Tommy smacked his open palm against her door. The glass rattled and Clare flinched.

"Okay. When Bushmills crosses my vocal cords I change subjects. Until then," Tommy teased, "how about that Beaudine—"

Clare lunged to get the whiskey and they settled onto the couch. She didn't think it would hinder the work they'd yet to do today. Not any more than preoccupation with Beaudine's attitude would, anyway.

"We don't get offed, we're going to end up in detox." Tommy toasted her with the bottle.

"No shit. As you would say." He grinned and passed her the whiskey. When she took her first swig, she was only distantly aware of that initial burst of flame. His grin hit her harder than liquor, any day.

They swigged in companionable silence, curled up in couch corners, wolfing the chips and dip Tommy had thought to bring with him today. Eventually, he requested, "Tell me more brain stories. You know. People with weirder brains than me."

"Your brain's not weird. Overactive at times, yes; weird, no.

Of course that's a problem all epileptics face: name-calling. Was it difficult for you, growing up?"

"Naw. I just told everybody I was faking to get out of P.E. I like how you're so protective of me. Good thing, too. A brain is kind of like a mother. I can put mine down but nobody else better. What was that other condition you mentioned yesterday? Motor something."

She thought back. "Motor apraxia. I'm always sure I'm developing it but I'm not and neither will you. One variety has to do with an inability to get sets of movements right. I might try to light a cigarette by putting the match in my mouth and drawing the cigarette along the matchbook flint. Or I might put socks on after my shoes, that kind of thing."

"Funny. Unless it's happening to you." He turned envious. "Cynthia says she used to have visions."

"Some epilepsies cause visions, yes. Or an addictive excitement. I had one patient who self-induced seizures." When Tommy shuddered, Clare said quickly, "That reminds me of a really interesting syndrome, the FPP, fantasy-prone personality. For example, there are people who can have orgasms by imagining sex."

"This is my kind of syndrome." He stuffed the last few chips in his mouth.

"If I were an FPP, I might vividly experience a trek up the Amazon—the smell of moss, branches touching my body, monkeys shrieking—while we're here talking. Based on studies of brain stimulation levels, it seems that for some people, those imaginary friends are just as real as anything in the 'real' world. Anyway, our notion of reality is spurious; it *is* an individual experience. That old bit about whether Chuang-tzu was a man dreaming he was a butterfly or vice versa may not be just some philosopher's tract after all. For that matter . . ." Tommy was staring so intently.

"I wish you could watch yourself when you talk about this stuff. Your eyes get this glow, you start talking so fast but it all makes sense. It's how I feel sometimes when I'm playing, like I'm plugged into my amp. Bianca doesn't—" He stopped talking and smiled; conspiratorial, sad, admiring, loving.

The break was clearly over. Clare refiled the whiskey bottle, Tommy tossed the food remains, and they sat down to attempt hypnosis a second time.

She got him down Jung's stairs, through the door. "Let your arm float in the air, there's a slight breeze." His good arm lifted and remained poised, undulating a bit. With previous subjects, this had indicated that consciousness had indeed shifted. "I'm going to ask questions to be answered yes or no. If the answer is yes, lift your left foot."

"I'll . . . fall . . . over." Tommy's speech was very slow.

"You're right. Find a chair, a comfortable chair. Let me know when you find it."

"I'm sitting now. You should have a chair like this at your lab."

"I'll try to get one. When you answer a question, use only your left foot. Do not speak. You will not notice what your left foot is doing. This will not upset you in any way. Now, from your comfortable chair, you can see the hallway the night of Dr. Colton's murder, you can see everything that happened, but watching cannot hurt you and does not affect you. The killer who attacked you with a knife: is the killer a man?"

"Told you that before," he said, as his left foot lifted.

Hmm. Was his left brain aware of his left foot's movements? She tried an issue in hemispheric dispute. "Did you touch the killer's right hand?"

His left foot lifted. "No that's wrong," he said, slowly, with a trace of ire.

Clare tried a few more unimportant questions. His left brain remained aware of his right brain's answers.

"Stand up, Tommy, we're walking back the way we came now. When you get to the top of the stairs, you will be back in this room. Now or later, you might remember my questions or your answers. If you do, you will feel relaxed and pleased. You are climbing the stairs, it's an easy climb, you have four more stairs, three . . . two . . . one. . . . Open your eyes when you feel like it, there's no hurry."

By the time he met her gaze, she'd stifled her disappointment. "How do you feel?"

"Decent. Good. That was weird though." It took him a few moments to talk up to speed. "I didn't feel any different, but now that my eyes are open I realize I did feel different and your voice sounded different. So what'd we find out?"

"At this point I'm primarily perfecting technique."

"We don't have a lot of time Clare." But he remained calm.

"I know." If only there were someone she could trust who knew hypnosis.

"What's the matter? All of a sudden you looked really nervous."

All of a sudden she'd realized there was someone. If she could face Norelle right now. "I just remembered I have to prep for two classes tomorrow."

"That means we're splitting up."

"It will be easier for me to concentrate." He grinned: he liked being a distraction. She smiled back. He was her favorite distraction, there was no question about it.

His grin faded. "Bianca and I agreed we'd get straightened out tonight. No broken dishes, no rude names. Just, where do we go from here and how do we get there." He sneered—at himself. "Maybe once I know what she's thinking I won't feel like such a scumbag. Like those guys who let wifie put 'em through med school then say bye-bye. She took care of me during all those bad years, now I don't almost die from a seizure once a month and I want to tell her, hey, yeah, thanks for stopping by."

"That isn't how it happened. You're not just walking out." He clucked like a chicken. "No, I don't believe it's because you're scared. I think you want this talk to truly help. And it might."

She couldn't decide which she hated more about herself—hoping the talk would fail, or hiding that hope to give him marriage counseling.

"You really think it will help?"

"On the other hand, Robert and I had one of those talks. On the same day as—Dinner."

"Dinner the infamous. Talk to Robert yet?"

She called for a security guard escort before she replied. "No, I haven't spoken with Robert. And it bothers me that I keep thinking about it, when I don't even know if I want to hear from him. I've got terminal indecision about him."

Tommy helped her shut off lights. "Just because you've decided doesn't mean you won't fight the decision for a while."

"Are you talking to me or to yourself?"

"Whoever's listening, I guess." Just then, someone knocked and announced himself as "security." "Hope *he* wasn't listening," Tommy whispered.

Clare's smile dwindled as she unlocked her door and mustered her strength. She needed all her reserves to cross the threshhold. She felt that weighted down by all she didn't understand. Her work with Tommy was giving her such a strong sense of failure, she almost preferred the vague paranoia that preoccupied her on the drive home.

It was a relief to be away from the lab. Yet before she knew it, her night's respite was over and they were back in her office for a new day of tests, sitting on couch and edge of desk, while Tommy attempted to describe his Big Talk with Bianca.

"She can't go from point A to point B, logically, without taking a trip to the ozone in between. Am I making any sense? My head feels like it's stuffed with Twinkies." He buried it between two couch cushions.

"Now there's a hideous prospect." She almost got him to smile. "Overall, I've got the gist: whatever you said, she twisted it to prove the opposite, meanwhile contradicting what she'd complained about a minute before."

"That's it. Mindfuck style 27A. First she says you've convinced me she's stupid, that's why I won't confide in her anymore. I say all I'm doing is testing, which I've never talked about much. These days, there's especially nothing to say. So then she uses that to prove we're not trying to figure out the murderer, we're fucking our big smart brains out. Now I could almost give her that one, you-'n'-me, touchy subject, right? But then she gets into her sister, I'm a dirtbag because I'm not nice to her sister. P.S., she hates her sister. Got to a point, I started talking about moving out—my drummer's got a second bedroom out in Highland Park. Then all of a sudden she's reasonable. We work some stuff through, sort of, and THEN she says I only threatened to move to manipulate her into giving in. At that point I—wish somebody had done that." He referred to the knock on the door.

Enervated, Clare stood. Whoever it was, she wasn't ready for them.

It was Deirdre, with two strangers. Their overly direct gazes and studiedly folksy manners implied Jehovah's Witnesses, but the woman's dress-for-success suit was too pricey, the man's jacket too natty. "This is Dr. Austen," Deirdre informed the couple, then slipped past Clare into the office, where she squeezed fingers and crinkled eyes to greet Tommy, who winked at her. Fleetingly, Clare considered asking Deirdre if she owned a thick black marker.

The strangers took turns talking. "I'm Matt Woods and this is Yvonne Hankoff."

"What a pleasure to meet you, Dr. Austen, I've long admired your work."

"We represent the International Foundation for the Study of Neuropsychological Trauma." A notepad was consulted. "Are you still conducting investigations into the effects of commissurotomy on patients Tom Q, C.B., Wm. H., and N.S.?"

"I no longer work with Wm. H. He moved to Montreal."

A note was jotted. "May we come in?" But they were already

past her. "You're a candidate for one of our one hundred twenty-five thousand dollar grants."

"I don't recall applying for one."

"We prefer to approach worthy aspirants—unexpectedly."

"As we have today. We get a truer reading of the work being done."

"And how do you happen to know my assistant?"

Deirdre looked up quickly from her whispers into Tommy's ear. "I ran into them downstairs, they were looking for your office."

That was plausible. Nothing else was. Clare regretted to admit it, but her work these days was not distinguished enough to warrant attention from a foundation she'd by the way never known existed. "Naturally, I'm flattered and can always use funding. If you'd send me information about your foundation I'd be interested in applying."

"Of course. Before that happens, we'd like to tour your facilities, discuss your current objectives, and observe your work. We'll be in Los Angeles through Thursday."

"If today is inconvenient, Dr. Austen, we can set up another time."

"Wednesday might be possible. May I have a number where you can be reached?"

"We're at the Bonaventure downtown. Here's the phone and room number. In fact, that reminds me. May I use your telephone?"

Clare overheard a request for the reception desk and inquiry about messages for room 717, while the other one asked, "Is this one of your subjects?"

Tommy offered his hand. "Tom Q. Split brain number 27A." The message inquirer got off the phone in time to share in the polite laughter.

Cordial leave-takings got rid of the duo and their guide. Clare returned to her desk perch. "What did Deirdre have to say?"

"She wants my body. But the way she put it was could I work

on you to let her help more. So what was that about? If those two are for real, I'm Richard Nixon."

"I'm going to do some checking." She called the Bonaventure. Yes, her would-be patrons were current guests. She called the Biology office for listings of grant sources. Yes, the Foundation did exist, headquartered in Maryland. No one answered its phone—it was after East Coast business hours—but the phone machine both solicited messages and revealed Mr. Woods and Ms. Hankoff would be back Friday.

"I still don't buy it," Tommy said. "You giving them a demonstration?"

"Perhaps. If only to see what they might reveal. I hate to waste the time, though."

They went into the lab, where within an hour they were interrupted four times: by Mrs. Bates—might she come at twelve instead of eleven on Thursday?; by the chief of Security—they were the last to see Bruce, who hadn't completed his shift yesterday and whose phone was now disconnected; by Deirdre—her afternoon class got canceled, she had free time if Clare needed her; and by Robert's T.A., delivering a note.

> Clare, I hope this doesn't intrude on your request for breathing room and time. I've debated long and hard but finally couldn't just not respond to your exit. I respect your wishes and understand the need for them. I want to see you but will make no effort to do so. I love you. Robert.

She wasn't sure how long she sat at her desk, staring at Robert's impossibly legible printing. Knowing him, this was a first draft, besides.

The way Tommy studied her when she returned to the lab, she'd been gone for some time. "How you feeling?"

"I'm not."

"You want some time to yourself?"

"Not you too. I'm sick of being treated like an invalid. I'm sick of everybody being so damned understanding."

"Are you on the rag or what you stupid bitch?" When Clare blinked: "I'm trying to not be understanding," Tommy smiled; his eyes encouraged her to do likewise.

She tried to oblige. "I'm exhausted. I need to go home. Do you mind?"

"Not if you let me walk you to your door."

"Gladly," Clare admitted. She dreaded climbing her stairs: they took a turn at the top to a perfect place for someone to be waiting, out of range of Mrs. Manning's floodlights. "Maybe we can do some work there. Let me think a minute." Her notes swam with Robert's printing. "Yes, we could do a few tests, anyway, though—"

"The tests can wait until tomorrow. Far as I can see, you could use some rest. I've been watching you today." His concern made her queasy. He was right: sleeping on the couch with the lights on was hardly a restorative experience.

It seemed an incredible waste of manpower for Beaudine's man to apparently remain parked in place when she wasn't home, but she'd be the last to complain about seeing him there. Her street offered no parking within a hundred yards of her apartment building; and Mrs. Manning's floods made Clare's walk that much blinder, as she negotiated the unlit street.

"The fuck you move to such a dark street for?" Tommy huffed, jogging behind her.

"It was daylight when I rented." Their jogs became sprints. With some shame, Clare realized she felt much safer when she wasn't with Tommy.

They reached the courtyard without incident. As they passed the laundry room near Clare's stairs, Mrs. Manning pounced on them, her housecoat flapping like wings. "Your fiancé came by." Her tone was accusing.

"I'm not engaged."

"Just as I suspected. He insisted—demanded—I let him into

your home, said he was missing important papers and you had them. I told him no way, Mister José, unless I got a call from you first."

"I appreciate your protecting me. What did he look like?"

"He was a tall young fellow, dark hair, stubble. Why don't men these days shave? Mr. Manning always had a cheek smooth as—never mind that."

"Did he wear glasses?"

"Yes, trifocals towards the end."

Tommy rescued them from confusion. "No, she means the guy today."

"Oh. I don't recall." An air raid siren blared from her abode. "Gracious. Already time to call my niece."

"Thanks again," Clare called above Mrs. Manning's slamming door.

"Robert tried to push in here," Tommy stated speculatively. Out in the air, the possibility sounded weak. "Nope." They ascended her stairs, slowing as they neared the turn, behind which could lurk. Anything. Tommy stopped. "She-it. I thought you said this place was safe. C'mon. Back to my car."

He dragged her out again, insisting she'd be glad he did. From his trunk he grabbed a bulging grocery bag. He wouldn't let her see what was inside. Back on the stairs, he unbagged a flashlight, dropped to a crouch and snuck up the steps, his head at knee level. He shone the flashlight into the alcove. "All clear." He handed her the flashlight, then unbagged a hammer and nails. "Shine the light up here in this corner," he instructed, as from the bag he pulled the pièce de surprise: four rearview car mirrors. "I was gonna put these outside my place, but you need them more."

After some consideration, and with Clare serving as his left hand, he nailed three mirrors above her door, angled toward the alcove. The fourth he nailed beside her door bell. Descending a few steps, he directed her as she beamed the flashlight into each mirror. After some adjustment of angles, Clare could see into the alcove while still at fleeing distance. "If you come home and find somebody messed with the mirrors, then you jam. Natch. Shine the light. I want to check for blind spots." He jumped into the alcove, hunkered down, flattened against walls. After more adjustments, she could see everywhere in the alcove.

Feeling safe and warm inside, Clare led the way indoors.

"Uh. Nice place." Tommy took in the gold plaid couch, the cottage cheese ceiling, the debris covering the lime shag carpet.

"Dammit Jessie!" The room was even more of a shambles than it had been this morning. No wonder the cat was hiding.

Tommy gave a low whistle. "Time for the kitty shrink?"

No. Jessie hadn't overturned that crate of iron cookware—Clare herself could barely lift it. "Oh God. Jessie? Jessie?" Trying not to panic, Clare ran from room to room. In the bedroom, curtains flapped. Open window. Correction. Broken window. Clare fought visions of Jessie running on pure terror, anywhere to get away; running two blocks to Colorado Boulevard, where high speeds and heavy traffic—

"She's in here." Tommy sounded like an echo. He was in the bathroom, smiling into the black plastic wastebasket. Huddled inside: a mass of dark fur, pink tongue. And white teeth, as the cat hissed at Tommy. Two glowing eyes ascended when Jessie saw Clare. Clare scooped her up. Jessie purred briefly—she was still scared.

"Did the same person do this who pretended to be Robert to Mrs. Manning?"

"It could really be Robert, people get crazy during breakups," Tommy warned.

"It wasn't Robert." Her insistence was muffled; her face buried in fur.

They debated asking the cop outside if he'd seen anything, but didn't much feel like exposing themselves to do so. Instead, they nailed closet shelves over the broken window, after Krazy-Gluing broken glass to the outside shelf surfaces. Next, they barricaded the bedroom door with the dresser, then added iron pots to the drawers. It would do until tomorrow, when Clare would convince Mrs. Manning to let her new tenant put bars on this too-easy entry.

Every unstocked closet and cupboard was open, every drawer overturned, every box dumped and rifled; but as far as she could tell, much was broken, all else was scattered—yet nothing was missing. Including the easily robbed set of silver that had been her great-grandmother's.

Clare sat with Jessie on the couch while Tommy began straightening. He wasn't really helping but he needed an outlet. "Nine days trying and we still don't know jackshit!" he yelled. A water glass broke in his hand.

Clare silenced apologies: they were cheap glasses and she broke one a month. His hand was bleeding a little but she was incapable of releasing Jessie. She directed him to soap and towels. He returned with a finger bundled in Kleenex.

"We know a lot," she disagreed. "Approximate height and weight, voice, and a good amount of clothing. If someone else saw the killer on campus, Beaudine could use our information to do a matchup. I sent him a list of our results this morning."

While Tommy raved about her contacting the cops without his approval, she brooded: she suspected that they could know quite a bit more, but weren't looking at the data correctly; that his right brain had given them many clues, if only she could piece them into a less fragmented picture.

Tommy flopped on the other end of the sofa. "Maybe you could trank half my head, like they did before my operation, and ask the other half questions."

He was talking about the Wada test, during which sodium amobarbital, a barbiturate, was injected through an artery into each brain half in turn, putting it to sleep for a few minutes, while tests determined which side of the brain controlled language.

"I've thought about that. It's very risky, as you know."

"So's not knowing what I know."

"Beyond that, there's no one I could convince to administer it, or trust to do so discreetly."

"So let's try acupuncture. Hypnosis again. Something."

"I'm just not good enough with hypnosis. But we have an appointment tomorrow with someone who is." Telephoning Norelle after all this time had been rough; seeing her tomorrow would be more so. "What we can do tonight is clear up some important loose ends. I'm going to ask you questions. I want you to sing the answers."

In unsplit brains, certain speech disorders were circumvented when patients sang rather than talked: singing was controlled by other brain regions, often in the right hemisphere. This might be true for Tommy, too, although many musicians processed music differently than nonmusicians—musicians used their left hemispheres more. At the least, however, his right brain might cross-cue more easily while he sang.

This hypothesis Clare had made after reviewing his journal entries that morning. Since his operation, it was more difficult for him to learn lyrics—and to sing with emotion. He had to devise a technique he called automatic tune pilot: he sang the words by rote, paying no attention to them, and the emotional content somehow surfaced. To the listener, he sounded the same as he always had, but the inner process was far different. What Clare thought this meant: his left brain was relinquishing control to the right.

What Clare hoped: Tommy's left hemisphere would more readily relay his right hemisphere's reactions when singing, as it was already used to yielding control.

Clare reminded Tommy of those journal entries. "Answer on automatic tune pilot. If you can't answer, at least sing what you're feeling at that moment."

"Next we'll be using tarot cards. Or a Ouija board."

Clare started to defend her experiment then stopped. Ouija board. Hmm. "Thanks for the suggestion." She made a note. Tommy muttered like Donald Duck. From her briefcase, she pulled the girlie mag, opened to the semibikinied beach beauties. "What is important about this picture; what does this picture tell us?"

"I can't find the words," Tommy's voice was a singsong.

Clare pointed to one of the women. "Is it her?"

"No no no no no-oh," Tommy sang. It sounded vaguely familiar. " 'Not a Second Time.' That Beatles song? We did a thrash cover of it." At her blank response: "Thrash. Makes punk sound philharmonic." She cringed and he chortled.

"Why don't you sing all the lyrics—not in thrash, if you can help it. It could be that the other words are important."

He sang them rapidly, shook his head. "I don't feel anything."

Clare returned to the photo. 'Is this important?' She inquired about every item on that glossy page. Each time Tommy sang his no-no-no refrain. Was this because it was the only lyrical negation his right brain knew? She hadn't expected actual lyrics to comprise his answers. Jessie bit Clare's hand gently and Clare realized she'd been petting the cat increasingly rapidly.

"Everything I ever wanted," Tommy sang, then looked puzzled. "Does that mean it's the whole picture?"

Clare made him sing the whole song. She interrupted the repeating chorus. "Let me guess, this one's called 'Unsatisfied'."

"Watch it. Don't say anything sounds like you're poking fun at that song. Paul Westerberg's the greatest fucking songwriter you'll ever hope to criticize."

She convinced him to accept her apology and continue. But no other lyrics resonated in him. Yet how could the whole picture be relevant? She pointed to the sky. No-no-no. He clamped his mouth shut before the final no-oh. He was getting tired of that one. Then he crooned, " 'Moooon river . . .' "

No moon, no river. Swell. "The sun!" Clare cried. "Sunny.

Somebody's son?" She asked every question she could think of about the sun, the light. She had him sing the words to "Moon River." He didn't know many of them.

"This isn't working," Tommy was morose and furious simultaneously.

She put away the ad. "The other day you kept thinking about Lawrence Welk. That 'an a one an a two an a.' Sing that and see what happens."

Today he sang onetwothreefour at supersonic speed. "The Ramones. They were like the first punk band."

"Which song was that from?"

"I saw 'em once when I was a kid. All their songs started that way."

They didn't get far with the "one an a two" either. And monitoring his LEMs wasn't helping today. But again she knew she'd gotten useful raw material for later analysis. If only she could determine its import. "Some of the tests we've done suggest you saw the killer. Did you see the killer? Did you see any part of the killer?"

" 'Eyes like diamonds, heart like coal,' " Tommy sang, mortified. "First song I ever wrote. I was twelve. Really a turkey. Don't make me sing the rest of it."

But she did. As before, only the initially sung line had impact on him. "I liked parts of that; rhyming coal with soul was good," Clare said.

"Let's just be amazed at how much I've improved."

Did his right brain mean it had seen the killer, or had specifically seen the killer's eyes? Diamonds might also be significant, although she thought they'd ruled out jewelry. Of coal and heart she could make nothing but perhaps they were homonyms. Or synonyms. They posed more work for her later, that was clear.

"I can't do any more right now." Tommy rubbed his head, eyes, ears.

"I'd offer you dinner but I still haven't gone shopping."

"Call for a pizza—oh. No phone until tomorrow."

They found snacks: the fortune cookies from the Chinese take-out; and a big tin of gift crackers she'd been mailed, an early Christmas gift from a former patient. As they sat down to eat, she said, "After this you might as well go home, I've got a lot to figure out. For tomorrow."

"No way am I leaving you alone here tonight. What if that guy comes back? I'm going to call Bianca and—you don't have a phone. Well, she'll figure it out. Well. How about if you go to a hotel?"

"I—I'm probably more protected here. And I can't move Jessie again." Perhaps she could invite a friend over—except then she'd have to explain where Robert was. "I—don't really know what to do. But I do know that Bianca won't forgive or forget if you don't come home."

"I won't exactly forgive myself if this is your last night alive."

She was silent a moment. "I think whoever broke in here wants information, not me. The fact is, if he'd come here to kill either of us, we'd be dead by now." Tommy nodded, reluctantly. "Anyway, my cop is outside. Let's ask him to get someone else out here, to watch the back of my building. I should be fine then."

They went out armed with the flashlight, an iron skillet, and a knife, heading for Beaudine's watcher and then Tommy's car. They hadn't been outside a minute when Tommy stopped and swore. "I left my keys on your couch. What an asshole."

Halfway back up Clare's stairs, Tommy stopped again, shone the flashlight into the mirrors. There was no one in the alcove, yet he blocked Clare from continuing. "Listen? How quiet it is? There were birds chirping when we went out. Even a couple crickets. Now there's—"

"Now there's only me," whispered a deep, accented voice behind them. Before the man knocked the flashlight from Tommy's hand, it revealed he had a gun. "Be perfectly still and do just as I say. I'll shoot you both if I must. It would be for such a good cause. You know about killing for a good cause, don't you? This gun has a silencer, isn't that clever? No, don't speak: 'Who are you, what do you want,' don't bother. Is that a knife hilt, Mr. Dabrowski? Please drop the knife, very carefully, thank you. And that—is that an iron pan? How quaint. Put it down."

English accent, Clare decided. But far more pronounced than Mrs. Bates'.

"We're all going inside. Now. Please unlock the door, there we go."

He sat them on the carpet, back to back; then he took the couch. Clare's neck crinked as she took him in: short, flabby, balding; once sharp features now softened by wrinkles. His eyes drooped in permanent sorrow, the pupils too dilated for Clare to determine their color. He regarded her with purest hatred.

Worst of all, Jessie chose this time to emerge from safety under the couch. She hopped up beside the man, whose gaze mellowed until he looked back to Clare. "Please don't hurt her," Clare begged.

The man sneered. "What a ridiculous thing for you to say."

"Jessie! Go!" Clare screeched, startling all four of them. Jessie fled the room. Back to the bathroom trash basket, Clare prayed.

"Whatever you're here for, assface, let's get it over with," Tommy said. Clare was horrified: he was trying to draw the hatred away from her.

"Please. Call me Hugo. All my dearest enemies do. And you're so right. Let's do move on. I want to know who you're working for." He raised the gun.

"I don't know what you mean." Clare was amazed at how calm her voice sounded.

"Your research, it's expensive, surely you realize that. Who funds it?"

Clare rattled off her grants. "But my research is bare bones, less than—"

"I know why you killed Haffner but Colton? Was it arrogance or orders?"

The room filled with swimming dots. Clare was going to pass out. "I swear I don't know what you're talking about."

"I know about the rivalries, the jealousies, the ambitions. Who planned the betrayal?" If possible, he became more hate-filled. Clare was certain he would shoot her.

From Tommy's voice, he thought so too. He croaked, "You have to listen to us. We didn't kill anyone. We've been trying to find out who did."

"Now there's a brilliant ruse. And aren't we making progress. Your little list of killer's attributes. What? Clare? You thought the police were on your side? How very naive."

"I don't know what you're—none of this is making any sense."

Hugo sighed and stood. "Must I give your memory a nudge?" He headed toward her. She felt Tommy's weight shift.

He sprang at Hugo, who smashed him across the chest with the gun. Tommy fell sideways, Hugo hefted the gun and advanced. Tommy had fallen on his injured arm and was having trouble righting himself. Clare leaped to her feet, grabbed books and threw them. One grazed Hugo's back. He fumbled but recovered before she could jump him.

He cocked the gun at Tommy. "Do nothing further, Dr. Austen. Now. Over here where I can see you. Behind him. Quickly."

Gasping, she tried to talk reasonably. "Listen—to me. We don't know—what you want. And we can't—answer your questions."

Without looking away from Tommy, Hugo said musingly, "I almost believe you. What's the matter with him?"

Tommy was quivering, eyes rolled back, lips fluttering. Clare reached for him; Hugo waved the gun to keep her away. "He's having a seizure, a small one, which could grow much larger if you continue this. You might not even need to shoot him. Think of the bullets you'll save."

Their eyes met. "If you are telling the truth about these matters."

"*What* matters!?"

"If you do not know, at the risk of sounding like a refugee from a B-movie, you must cease and desist. You could not be in deeper, further over your heads, and so forth. Is he going to be alright?"

Clare took this as an okay to kneel to check Tommy. His vital signs were returning to normal. She heard the front door click shut. Hugo was gone.

By the time Tommy had revived and been reminded of what had occurred—he remembered Hugo, alright, but not details of the encounter—many minutes had elapsed. Neither had any desire to chase Hugo anyway; but they should call Beaudine. "Maybe Hugo will call him, he has better connections with the cops than we do."

Moving in strange small circles so that no one could surprise them from behind, they ran outside. The unmarked police car was gone.

Cursing Beaudine, his underlings, and his ancestors, Clare and Tommy ran back to pound on Mrs. Manning's door. She wouldn't let them in, but did call 911 for them. Afraid that if they went inside the police might not know where to stop, they paced the courtyard until two patrol cars, complete with revolving lights, cruised by. They darted into the street to flag the cars to a stop. Only now did Beaudine's watcher appear; just as Mrs. Manning came out, to mutter repeatedly, "Not acceptable. Not acceptable." It was all sorts of fun introducing the landlady to the boarded window and the plan for bars. Clare's insistence on paying for everything did not quell the muttering.

The detective outside had not noticed Hugo; nor signs of trouble, before answering a burglary call a few minutes before. All the cops took notes and exchanged insults: dueling departments.

At long last Tommy and Clare were left alone in her apartment. Still in shock, pretending they weren't shaking, they coaxed Jessie out of the wastebasket and retired to the couch, side by side. Jessie sniffed around then perched on Hugo's spot, observing them with the benign enlightenment of a cat falling asleep.

"I feel an eviction coming on."

"This is a dive anyway. Nothing pers—what was that?" Tommy jumped.

"The refrigerator shutting off."

He knocked his head against the wall. "I'm perfectly calm, why do you ask?"

The jump had moved him closer. Of all the stupid timing, Clare felt electrified by his nearness; when he shifted his leg, the air between was so charged, she felt the changes in pressure on her own skin. They used to sit like this in her office, going over his journal entries. Having only one copy had been a great excuse.

"Remember back when we used to read my journal and the most we had to worry about was if Steve would put the right slides in?"

"I was just thinking about that." And Tommy would tease her and she would resist her attraction to him because. "These lights are giving me a headache." Which was true, but after she doused the overheads and set her desk lamp nearby on the floor, she returned to sit some distance further from him. Terminal ambivalence, she noted with self-disgust. Or perhaps simply fear.

"Tell me some more stories," he said, curling to face her, head resting on arm stretched along couch back. Occasionally he stroked her shoulder while she spoke.

"That seizure you had tonight. It's a particular type named after an early brain scientist, a fellow named John Hughlings Jackson. He was born in the nineteenth century, well before neuroscience was anywhere, and he didn't have much formal schooling. A farmer, I believe he was. But he was also a fantastic observer and his theories still get quoted, his findings still hold up. He was an incredible man."

"So he went around staring at all the epileptics in his neighborhood?"

"No. It was his wife. She had epilepsy."

"His personal human guinea pig."

"That's not how I see it. Oh sure, he found it fascinating, he studied her in detail, he definitely had the research mentality. But Jackson watched her, loving her, feeling helpless, wanting to learn everything because then perhaps he might cure her." She turned, mirroring Tommy's position. His fingers stroked her cheek.

"Should have just let her writhe around. Maybe he felt helpless but she was useless." He sat up, pulling his hand away. "Shit. Guy comes after you with a gun and Tommy to the rescue, falls on the floor and loses it. I could never protect you no matter how much I wanted to. No matter how much you take care of me."

"As it turns out I can take care of myself. Just as you can."

"I'm not talking about equal rights. Sure you can take care of yourself. I don't want you always to have to do it by yourself."

"I'd say your seizure was a pretty effective way of clearing the room."

Tommy chuckled. "Scared him, huh? Yeah, even Bianca's still scared of me."

She touched his knee to get him to look at her. "I'm not."

Their kiss lasted a very long time; of this Clare was dimly aware when she pulled away for an instant's air. He continued kissing her cheeks her chin her throat. A faint growth of beard scratched her, smoothed by the softness of his lips his tongue pressing so hard she felt her pulse pound against his mouth, her breath stick in her lungs. She didn't care, she couldn't be close enough to him. Her lips found his once more and she lost all awareness of everything but that kiss.

Eventually they tried stretching out on the couch, but slapstick ensued. Jessie refused to relinquish her spot, despite or because of the indignity of being tapped by a foot, bumped by a leg. Then Tommy's sling caught on a cushion. They relocated to the floor, first clearing an area amidst the debris of her ravaged belongings.

By the time they were next to each other on the carpet, they were laughing, giddily. Looking into each other's eyes, the laughs softened to smiles. Clare closed her eyes for their kiss, realized that Tommy's remained open. She opened hers and was swept inside him, seeing herself through his eyes, feeling so much love, so much warmth, she squeezed her eyes shut before she passed out.

The instant her eyes were closed, she could see Robert, asleep on his side of their bed, as though at any moment she might return. Her eyes snapped open.

"What's the matter?" Tommy asked, brushing hair from her face; a commonplace gesture that now made her shiver.

"Absolutely nothing." She banished all knowledge more than an hour old, and smiled. His fingers clutched her hair and pulled her back to meet him, making the banishing much easier.

They took turns undressing each other, which led to more comedy. They had to sit up—Tommy couldn't remove garments while balancing on his injured arm. His expression got studious as he concentrated on dismantling her outfit. She watched him, smiling, reveling in the feel of his fingers on the cloth, on her skin. "Whoever invents these things is a celibate asshole," Tommy muttered, grappling unsuccessfully with her bra clasp. "Ingenious," he sneered when Clare showed him how it worked. His jeans, determined to stay buttoned, had been contrived by the same individual.

The closer they got to being naked, the slower the process became, what with times out to kiss and caress, to savor every moment of these first-time events. At last, with their clothes in heaps around them, they regarded each other, embarrassed yet thrilled. They embraced, skin to skin, touching at every possible point.

In Clare's dreams she relived the moment he first entered her, legs entwined, eyes locked, his weight slowly building against her, until she was engulfed, surrounded, the universe filled with him.

The next morning, when they awoke still intertwined, the air chilling skin that wasn't touching, muscles stiff and bones aching from the barely padded floor, Tommy smiled and kissed her cheek. Clare decided she could not possibly feel better. "Good morning," she smiled back.

"No kidding," he replied.

CHAPTER 12

Reductionism

A sharp cry beyond their heads made them jump. "Morning, Jess." Tommy reached to pet the cat, who wasn't due to eat for another hour but what the hell, the humans were awake, give it a try. As Tommy's hand touched Jessie, she braced and hissed, then ran for the bathroom. "Nice to see—" Tommy stopped and tightened his hold on Clare as someone knocked at the door with wood-rattling force.

"Who—is it?" Clare forced her voice not to quaver.

"Pac Bell. Installation," a muffled female voice replied.

Of all times for the phone company to be prompt. They scrambled for clothes. Tommy whispered, "What if it's not. The phone company."

Clare sighed. "Can you prove you're from the phone company?" she called through the door. "We've had a few break-ins here," she explained sheepishly to the silence outside. Meanwhile, Tommy raised an iron pot and flattened himself behind the door, preparing to brain any intruder.

Sounding more wary than Clare had, the female voice replied, "Down here." A corner of paper slid under the door, catching on the carpet. Clare unfolded an official looking Pacific Bell document. "Need that back, though," the voice added. "Work orders for the day." Clare showed it to Tommy. He shrugged and Clare unbolted the lock, handed the paper to a petite chubby blonde whose waistful of equipment jangled as she waved off Clare's apologies. "Life in the big city." She returned the paper to a clipboard. "New jack, right? Where you want it?" Clare led her to the kitchen and the installer set to work.

Uncomfortable now, Clare sat in a chair, facing Tommy on the couch, fighting images of Robert breakfasting alone.

The installer reappeared. "Out to my van." She opened the door briskly. "In and out a lot. Want me to do a special knock?" She demonstrated a syncopated series of raps.

"Nice rhythm." Tommy smiled at her and thereafter, she was on their side. Before she left, she even told them which purchases at what hardware store would be required to put a fish-eye peephole in the front door.

It took two hours and uncountable trips in and out for the jack to become operational. As soon as the installer departed for the final time, Clare phoned to arrange for the bedroom window to be replaced and barred, and for a locked iron grill door to be added to the bottom of her stairs. Tommy insisted on staying until these rush-order security measures were completed. Clare was particularly happy for his presence when Mrs. Manning appeared, her mouth set in a narrow eviction line. After chatting with Tommy over coffee at the kitchen table, she left with brow furrowed, seriously considering a rent reduction for the improvements Clare was funding.

Immediately, Tommy set to washing Mrs. Manning's coffee cup at the sink. "I can get that later. Come sit with me." Clare dragged his chair closer to her own, marveling at her comparatively brazen assurance, today.

"Guess it's been a long time since I lived in a place that

didn't come with ants and roaches. I'm automatically Mr. Clean." Plunking down at the table, he kissed Clare, scratched Jessie's chin. The cat lounged on the table, shifting occasionally to stay in a swatch of morning sun. Tommy frowned into his coffee cup, extracted a multicolored cat hair. "You let her hang anywhere she wants, huh?"

"Except the stove." A house guest had once expressed shock, so Clare knew disapproval was possible. "It's not that she's a discipline problem. It never occurred to me that she ought to stay on the floor. Does—it bother you?"

He dropped the fur back into his cup. "I'll get used to it." He took a swig of coffee, grew very serious.

"If it bothers you I—I'm not sure what I'll do." Her stomach cramped. Could such an issue really drive a wedge between them?

He remained sober. "Clare. What happens if we get fur balls?" He smiled a smile as loving as his kisses. "Your face when you laugh. It makes me pray I never go blind."

Outside, one of the iron workmen smashed metal against metal. They started; Jessie twitched. "Wish we had more to laugh about." He stared into his coffee cup. "You know what gets me? The more I think about Hugo, the less scared of him I feel. Maybe because I don't remember everything. But look how Jessie—shit, she isn't as friendly with me as she was with him."

"I know. I'm not sure I remember much more than you do—the whole encounter's a blur to me. But by the time he left, I didn't feel threatened by him, either. Perhaps we're suffering a shock reaction of some kind."

"Stop me if I sound like I should be locked up. But. The way he knew about cop stuff? Maybe he was a cop. Maybe Beaudine was trying to scare us into confirming some crazy theory of his."

"I'm afraid we should both be locked up—that doesn't sound unlikely. I've been thinking about Hugo's questions. Didn't he make it sound as though Colton and Haffner were doing research together? I'm sure that can't be true. Dr. Colton would never have allowed it, even if their research fields weren't so different. And even then, if research *was* their connection, that still wouldn't explain the other murders."

"Some psycho's out to get lab coats. That's the only possibility that ties all four murders together."

Clare nodded. A serial killer preying on research scientists was the unthinkable yet most credible explanation for the murders. Yet, she didn't mention that a psychotic killer might seem just as harmless as Hugo had; she didn't want to taint her efforts to ask Tommy's right brain what it thought of Hugo, later. "Do I what?" She wasn't sure she'd heard Tommy's next question correctly.

"Know how to use a gun."

"You pull a trigger and bullets come out the barrel."

"Yeah, that's about what I know, but we've got to learn more. Pronto." His voice made her shiver. "By the way." He slung his arm around her, nuzzled her cheek, provoking a different sort of shivering. "No more lab coats. You don't even stand near somebody wearing one. Yes?" He licked her ear lobe. She nodded, turned to face him.

Their kiss froze, lips infinitesimally still apart. "All through, lady," an iron workman called as he pounded the door, seemingly with a mallet. "One hour, fifty one minutes." She'd promised a bonus if the work was completed within two hours.

After she tested the new iron entry door and learned to emergency-release the window bars, Clare praised and paid the workmen, dropped the extra key in Mrs. Manning's mailbox, as promised, then ran upstairs to call the bank: to empty her savings into her checking account, to cover the hefty payment.

Tommy took the phone and punched a number repeatedly, listening intently. When he came to find Clare in the living room, she kept her voice light. "No answer? Maybe she's at the gym."

He looked briefly befuddled. "Oh. No, I was calling this number, to learn the tones. You thought I was calling home?" He lunged and landed beside her on the couch. "What? And waste time I could spend with—Jessie?"

The cat had hopped up to perch between their heads. They reached to pet her simultaneously, clasped fingers and stroked her with one large hand. When they strained to kiss over her back, she leaped away with a little puff meow, to perch on a box, facing a wall, rump fur and tail twitching at them. She had never been jealous of Robert, if this was jealousy. Perhaps she sensed that—

Tommy interrupted Clare's pondering. "What time do I get hypnotized today?"

"Damn! That's today! Our appointment is at three in Encino so we'll need to leave at two. Thank God, it's just noon. I completely forgot that today is today. Doesn't it seem like it should be tomorrow already?"

"Time crawls when the phone company knocks at dawn." Tommy crumpled Clare's installation receipt and tossed it to Jessie, who regarded the paper ball, rose, and walked stiffly out of the room.

"You do have time to check in at home before we leave."

"I know." He wrapped his legs around hers. They kissed for a while, then Tommy pulled away and slapped hand against thigh, signaling his leave-taking.

They descended the stairs as slowly as they could without losing balance. "We forgot something," Clare realized as she unlocked the grill. "How will I know you're down here when you get back? Wait. I know." She ran upstairs, tossed and dug through her ravaged belongings, at last found the rape whistle her mother had sent for her Christmas stocking. Mother's gifts. Always early and invariably bizarre.

Standing outside the grill, Tommy puckered lips against iron mesh for a final kiss, then tooted the whistle lightly, creating a brief soft shriek. "Two toots means it's me, three toots means it's not."

"That makes a lot of sense." Clare smiled. One final final kiss and he receded from view. Clare waited for his got-to-the-car honks then plodded upstairs.

She spent their separation attempting to straighten her living room and to not think about Robert. Instead she alternated hopes of Bianca moved out with Bianca simply not home. What she feared was a lengthy confrontation occurring—she and Tommy had to leave on time or they'd get caught in early rush hour and miss the whole appointment. Why had she encouraged his heading for home? It had been a test, perhaps. A test with no right answers.

Two muffled shrill toots cut through her quandary. She dashed downstairs to welcome Tommy back.

"Jesus." Bianca had made him that pale and shaken. "What did she say to you?"

Tommy walked past her, up the stairs. "She was totally cool. I told her about the break-in and Hugo and no phone and she could see how you couldn't spend the night alone." He sank onto the couch. "Don't we have to go or something?"

"Not just yet. If you don't want to talk about it . . ." She retreated to a couch corner.

He gave her the world's weakest smile. "I drove home, nobody followed me. Bianca wasn't mad at all—she figured I'd be sneakier if I was cheating so she was just relieved I was okay. Then she started asking me what Hugo looked like. It took a while for this to sink in—all I could think about was getting back here to you." He said this like he'd just confessed to embezzling from children's charities. "Finally, Mr. Sensitive notices something's real wrong. Turns out she was getting ready for bed last night, heard the doorknob rattle, then the window tap—which is what I do when I forget my house key. She opened the door and a guy blew in. The room was dark and she was scared, but she thinks it was Hugo. Whoever it was, he shoved her against a wall and said, 'Tell him to stop or you're next.' Then he blew out again."

"Hugo? She's sure it was Hugo?"

"No of course she's not fucking sure. He didn't leave her his card."

Clare forced herself to remain seated beside him.

"Sorry. I'm sorry. It's just. I was over here with. While." His face twisted with self-loathing. "It never occurred to me he'd go after Bianca."

Ah. It was allowable that Clare be threatened, so long as Bianca—No! She had no right to think this way.

"Bianca was so quiet after that. When she's truly scared there's no emoting. I tried to comfort her and I guess I succeeded."

"Beaudine should be informed about this, right away."

"Bianca called him last night."

"And she reached him?"

"Yeah. Said he was real nice. Guess it's just us he goes rude on."

"How is she feeling now?"

"Okay. She went to work. She's going to hit them up for a loan so we can turn our place into an iron cage, too. And she's going to have people bring her home—in case I'm not there."

"So you think Hugo has been around often enough to know your signal to Bianca and—"

"I don't know what I think, I don't know what I know, my fucking brains are such assholes. If this hypnotism doesn't work, maybe I should go for a lobotomy."

"I know it's not the same class of damage at this point, but if it's any help, I spent the time away from you brooding about what I've done to Robert."

He looked at her as though she were too contemptible to consider. "No way is it the same thing."

"I simply meant—if we'd been in the lab all night, you wouldn't feel nearly as bad." She forced herself to meet his gaze.

After a time he conceded, "I guess you're right." He studied the air. "I don't mean to take this out on you."

"Of course not." She studied her watch. "We should go."

He kissed her like a brother would and they headed out, exchanging nods with Beaudine's current watcher as they walked past his car.

They drove west from the San Gabriel Valley, across the San Fernando; their route required merging or branching onto five freeways and traffic was slow, so Clare could study the branching patterns of drivers behind them. She could not detect anyone following them, which disturbed her: were the car phones no longer interested or was the killer getting more adept, while she continued to fumble? She forced herself to stop thinking of this, and further refused to recall her last exchange with Tommy, lest she then not be able to face Norelle.

Tommy seemed equally preoccupied with interior conflicts, until he at last inquired, "So who's going to hypnotize me? We're not going to a psychic, are we?"

"Norelle Westin is a psychologist. She—used to be my therapist."

"During your breakdown?"

"Primarily." Revealing experience with therapy generally provoked one of two reactions: excited rhetoric about the listener's own experiences; or defensive discourse about the uselessness of all such efforts. Whenever possible, Clare avoided the whole subject.

"Is it weird, going back again?"

"I'm expecting her to look at me with deep disappointment. Or shriek and hide her eyes. Otherwise, no."

As could have been predicted, these things did not occur. Norelle seemed the same as ever; though perhaps her sensuous eyebrows were a bit darker, making the contrast with her white hair that much more pronounced. She still leaned forward when listening, intent on every syllable. And she still transmitted her unique blend of assurance, ease, and anticipation: she hadn't seen it all, never would, and didn't want to; however, she did expect to manage whatever might arise.

Perhaps it was Norelle's ability to transmit acceptance, even of the just-met; perhaps it was Tommy's residual reaction to Bianca's night without him. But for the first time, Clare watched him meet someone and not pour on the charm.

Or perhaps it was Norelle's lack of facility with chitchat. Irrelevant conversation always died an early death in her vicinity. "Come in," she said after introductions, guiding them from waiting cubicle to office. "I've got to leave right at four."

"I'm sorry we were late," Clare began.

"You were always eight minutes late," Norelle patted Clare's back and chuckled. "It forced me to do work on my billing. That's eight minutes a week I now don't spend on it."

Clare forced a smile, distressed that she had missed such an obvious personal pattern.

Perhaps it was residual reaction to Bianca's night; perhaps Tommy simply could not be hypnotized. But fifteen minutes later, Norelle informed Clare, "We're not getting anywhere." She turned to Tommy, who had compressed a foam pillow to fit in his hand. "You seem to be having trouble relaxing."

Tommy released the pillow. It flew across the room. "What makes you say that?"

Norelle laughed, her broad shoulders bobbing with each deep rasping exhale, wheezing a bit from the lungs she'd developed before she quit smoking and the weight she'd acquired since. "Try less hard this time. Follow my instructions but don't think about what they mean. Imagine you're from another planet and you only know a few words of English and you have to concentrate on each one completely. Now, sit comfortably. Oh, and another thing. You don't breathe the same air, you're wearing a portable alien air supply system, but it jams unless you inhale very, very carefully. That's it. Now close your eyes," Norelle added quietly.

Over the next few minutes, Norelle coaxed him through relaxation exercises. Clare felt envious and protective as she watched the gradual transformation—to the way he used to look. The last week had added years of strain and trouble. What had it done to her—and how much could Norelle see?

On the phone with Norelle yesterday, Clare had explained what hypnotism efforts she had made, with what results. Norelle tried some other avenues, but wound up in the same place; whenever Clare started to question Tommy, she could not get to his right brain without interference, albeit muted, from his left. Finally, Norelle and Clare exchanged a look, and shook their heads.

"Anything?" Tommy asked eagerly as soon as Norelle told him to open his eyes. He found his answer in Clare's expression. "Now what?" He sounded hopeless.

"Now we go back to the lab and try something else." Clare looked at her watch, warned Norelle, "You're going to be late."

Norelle shrugged. "I understand your disappointment, Tommy, but I have tremendous confidence in Clare. This didn't work but something else will. Doesn't seem like it at the moment, though, does it?"

Clare looked away to get her briefcase.

Norelle saw them out to the cubicle, then asked to speak with Clare alone. Here it comes, Clare decided, as Norelle shut the adjoining door. *You look worse than I've ever seen you, Clare, I'd like you to come in five times a week until—* "I wanted you to hear this from me, before you learned it elsewhere," Norelle began. "Robert called me a few days ago. He said he was worried about you and asked me to get in touch, see what I could do. I suggested he tell you that; and I would be happy to talk to you if you called me."

"Thanks for telling me." Clare wondered if she was going to faint. "There, um, seems to be a pattern in the men I pick, doesn't there?" She tried to laugh, it came out strangled. She pretended not to mind Norelle's scrutiny. "I was expecting you to recommend I get committed or something." The next attempt to laugh was aborted lest it turn to sob.

"Would you like to come back later and talk about any of this?"

"There's—really no time. Until the murders are solved."

Norelle enfolded Clare in her arms. How hokey, how California nouvelle neurosis, Clare had sneered the first times Norelle had hugged her. Apparently Clare had finally been brainwashed, for Norelle's hugs were now an incredible source of nourishment.

Nothing further was said, until Norelle had ushered them across the waiting cubicle. "I'll be away for three weeks—beginning tonight. But I'll call you if I come up with any new ideas for your hypnotism; and my service can reach me for the next week, if you think I can help in any other way."

Clare nodded thanks and simulated amusement. "Where to this time? White water rafting on the Amazon? Norelle's vacations are always either brave or risky, depending on who you ask," she explained to Tommy. Norelle loved jumping cliffs into the unknown. It was a quality Clare had always wished was contagious.

"Africa," Norelle replied. "We'll be hiking into some game preserves. I hope I'm ready for it physically."

"Hey. Take care of yourself," Tommy bid Norelle good-bye. "And thanks for trying with my brains."

Once they were in the car, he demanded, "What the fuck did she say to you? You look like she's making you get rid of Jessie."

Clare zoomed up the freeway onramp, hit the brakes. Traffic edged forward from their entrance to beyond the horizon. She pounded the steering wheel and cursed, then spat the news of Robert's phone call to Norelle.

"I can see getting a little irritated but you're approaching frenzy."

"There's more to it. Bernie did the same thing and when—"

"Hold it. Who's Bernie? The married man?"

"No. During my breakdown, there was someone else."

"Man." Tommy massaged his forehead. "The rush I just got. It does really bad stuff to me, hearing about men who knew you before I did. I didn't mean to interrupt though. In fact I gotta know everything."

Clare's internal raging eased. Tommy's feeling rather than provoking jealousy proved a curious tonic. "Bernie. He said he was destined to save me—he liked to talk like that and at the time I needed big statements to hear at all. He loved taking care of me. But it seems he didn't want me to get better. And he didn't want me to lean on anyone but him. Not that I understood any of this at the time, of course. God, was it confusing."

"Two slimeballs in a row. Or were there others I don't know about?"

"Not really." Clare shifted up to second gear. Traffic had sped to a crawl.

"Seems like it's a good thing Robert happened along, or you wouldn't even be able to trust me as much as you have."

"Yes. Robert was good for me. Or better, anyway. What's so upsetting now is that he knows about Bernie's tactics. I'll skip the gory details but Bernie had devised a whole campaign. He'd call Norelle secretly, then bit by bit try to convince me that she was conspiring against me. And this was at a time when Norelle was my one link to sanity. It was terrible. Robert knows all that. Yet he did the same thing."

"Not necessarily."

At last she could shift into third, then fourth gear, accelerating past the problem—a car shouldered with a flat, causing massive spectator slowing by rubberneckers yearning for an accident.

Tommy groaned. "I love L.A., don't you?"

"You're certainly promoting Robert today."

"I just want you to see him clearly. Because then I'll be sure you don't just like me because I'm not Robert."

It was a charming sentiment; but after his earlier displays regarding Bianca, she couldn't trust this response.

Tail lights suddenly flashed red all around them. Screeching tires, crunching bumpers echoed in her ears. The victim cars limped to the shoulder, the other tail lights inched past the scene. For some miles, Clare concentrated on the road—twilight was a dangerous time to drive: too dark to see detail, too bright for night lights to really be visible. And they needed to hurry; she wanted to be in her lab before the campus developed its echoing nighttime emptiness.

"I hope you can see better than I can," Tommy said finally. "Although everything looks like this, these days. It's getting dark, doc, it's going black, this is the end, eunnhh." He finished his death scene and leaned over to swipe her cheek with a kiss, then left his head resting on her shoulder.

Ignoring her wiser impulses, she laughed and kissed at him. "If you keep distracting the driver you're going to have to move to the rear of the bus."

"So pull over," he said. "We can both get in back."

"I'd consider it if the back seat wasn't designed for midgets."

"Hah. Some excuse. Well, we haven't tried that couch in your office yet."

When they reached her office, an hour and fifty minutes after commencing the thirty-minute drive, they did indeed try the couch. For a short time, they pretended their biggest problem was fear of being discovered in a clinch. But the lab door gaped beside them. They disembraced and stood with a mutual sigh.

Clare's was partly a sigh of relief: it was too easy for her to forget to be wary of him. But she stopped short of entering the lab. "The fact is, I need to make a tape and pull some slides. I'd been planning to do it last night but I forgot, after Hugo."

Tommy pivoted her to face him. "Clare. I hope Hugo wasn't the only man who made you forget about work last night."

She looked around the office. "His visit was the point when I forgot, yes. I did remember again later, but by then we were—on the floor."

"On the floor. I like the sound of that." He started nuzzling her neck. She stiffened, then could no longer resist, once he got her laughing, with: "We can talk dirty anywhere and no one will know. 'I'm sorry, Dr. Hyde, I can't attend your symposium, as I'll be doing floor work at that time.' So how long is this tape business going to take?"

"At least an hour, I'm sorry to say. Do you mind waiting out here?"

"Naw, I can handle it. I'll just be thinking about all the floors we've still got to try." He pulled her in for a good-bye kiss. After some time, he stepped away. "This isn't making it easier to let you go. Better make some tapes for tomorrow, too, you're going to get forgetful again tonight."

She continued smiling at the closed door, while rapidly and efficiently planning words and phrasings for the new tape. It was impossible to remain wary of him. Interesting, also, was his jovial acceptance of a testing delay; and lack of irritation that she was composing a tape to hide questions from his left brain. Gee, they should have hit the floor a long time ago. Speaking purely from a research viewpoint, of course.

Tommy knocked, opened the door, caught her laughing. "Don't ask," she advised.

"Stop having fun in here and get to work." Then he turned serious. "Listen. I should call Bianca, make sure she's okay. I just —wanted you to know so you wouldn't. You know." She nodded, tried to keep smiling. He blew her a kiss, shut the door.

She heard him cross to her desk, pick up the phone; refused to hear the ensuing half-conversation or analyze his voice tone. Instead she switched on the tape machine, with such force it shut itself off, as during a power surge. And here she was waiting for another marriage to fail. No, this one *had* failed. Tommy would not otherwise have approached her.

One hundred minutes later, having prepped as many tests as she could envision for today and tomorrow, then steeled herself to hear how Bianca was, she at last could reunite with Tommy. The door stuck, she yanked and rattled it noisily until it popped open—revealing Tommy asleep on the couch, exhaustion evident in the jagged arrangement of his limbs; he'd passed out before he could fully stretch out. He twitched occasionally, as Jessie did when dreaming. Hmm, dreams. That gave her another testing idea. She returned to her lab table to jot notes, looked up to find him stumbling into the room.

"What year is it?" He swooped down to kiss her; missed; corrected.

"Two thousand forty-nine. It took a little longer than I expected to finish the tape. How's Bianca?"

"Fine. She's fine. The cage is installed, Trish and Andy are staying with her tonight. I told her we'd be working pretty late, she said good luck." He flopped into his chair. "This morning when I was comforting her, way back inside I kept thinking, shit, too bad she got attacked, now I have to wait longer to move out on her." He brooded a moment. "I didn't want to talk about that. How long was I asleep?"

"I don't know. Do you feel awake enough to get started? Are you sure? We'll start with headset and tachistoscope then. I'm going to ask questions about this." She spread the bikini beautied ad page, now somewhat tattered, on the table in front of him. "You'll see possible answers on the screen. Pull the toggle switch to answer yes or no, tap the question mark card if you can't answer."

"Roger wilco. Why do they say that, anyway? Never mind, wasting time." He manned his headset and stared fiercely at the dot, a fighter pilot on a mission.

Clare asked about every possibly important word or phrase she'd been able to imagine, based on their previous efforts with the photo: homonyms, synonyms, antonyms; puns, adages, slogans, rhymes. She started with sand/hand; finished with the song lyrics he'd sung in her apartment. Two hours later, she'd run through all her ideas and still hadn't a clue to the picture's import.

Tommy read the results on her face; tried and failed to look optimistic. "We're not done, though, right?"

"Certainly not." She brought a box over to his table. They kissed halfheartedly and she dumped the contents of the box before him.

"Scrabble letters? Are we taking a break? I hate board games."

"This is going to be rough on your arm, I suspect. We can try using your toes if need be. I want you to use your left hand to spell what's important about this picture. If you don't know how to spell the whole word, that's fine. Any letters will help. Let's try a dry run. What is your name? Spell your name."

He had to sort of stand and kind of twist to maneuver the letters. Eventually, he extricated a T and an M, fell back onto his chair for a rest, and whistled a cheer. Clare didn't feel quite so elated. His right hemisphere's ability to recognize certain vocabulary words didn't guarantee ability to spell them; his own name might be the only word his right brain knew.

"Now spell my name. Clare." He stood and twisted but his arm didn't move. After a time, he lost his balance and she leaped to help him regain his chair. He lost his balance because his left foot was tapping; she hadn't placed the question mark card underfoot for this test but the message was unmistakable.

"Shit, a fucking first grader's smarter than my—"

"No, Tommy. First graders don't fuck." This silenced his left brain's tirade. He snorted. "And it's much too early to get discouraged." She tapped the photo. "What is important about this picture? Tell me in any way you can."

He stood, twisted. His left hand, shaking, grabbed one letter, knocked others to the floor. Clare retrieved them, checked his progress. He was lining up a series of vowels. Rather, one vowel, over and over. "Eeeeee? The fuck does that mean?"

"Let's try to find out." She went over every portion of the picture, testing homonyms, rhymes, puns. The only time his right brain responded was when she indicated the stretch of beach. Then it juggled the eeee's again.

" 'Sand,' 'beach,' 'shoreline'—what? What's with those goddamned eeee's?" Tommy demanded, sinking into his chair. "Is it still too early to get discouraged?"

"We'll figure out what this means. We're definitely closer to an answer, I just don't know how." This sounded so absurd, they almost smiled. "Don't you agree that 'e' must mean something?" She studied his LEMs, as she had throughout this experiment. He looked left then center, then shook his head.

"I don't know. I fucking don't know."

From her previous LEMs observations, he might be confabulating. Why his left brain would evade that question, she hadn't the faintest idea. Why she tried to draw conclusions from such a pitifully skimpy sampling of LEMs was easier to explain: it gave an illusion of progress. She gathered Scrabble letters hastily, not wanting him to sense her despair.

He attempted some stretches; the twisting and reaching had kept him in pretzel postures. She helped him massage his cramped thighs and back, until he touched her arm. "Better wait on that, unless it's next stop the couch."

"Oh." She cleared her throat. He looked embarrassed too, so she said quickly, "Have you ever heard of a process called lucid dreaming? The whole field of research is controversial, and there are those who believe it's bunk."

"You sound like you agree with 'those.' "

"I admit the existing data hasn't convinced me. Still, it is intriguing. In lucid dreaming, the dreamer controls the dreams, first by knowing a dream is occurring; by maintaining and honing a consciousness that's usually absent in the dream state. Some researchers discount the evidence that such awareness is possible; others question the methods used to prove that a particular dreamer is in a lucid state. None of that should hurt our efforts, though."

"Especially since I hardly ever dream at all anymore."

"That will slow us down, but—what's wrong?"

"Nothing. The opposite. I like your telling me this stuff. You usually want me to know as little as possible. No, don't defend yourself, you're probably right to keep me stupid. But still. This makes me feel like a partner, instead of a test tube."

"Which makes me feel like a bacterium. No, don't defend me. It was good for me to hear that." She led him out to her office, where she fished through a stack of neurological journals as she explained, "There's a series of things you'll tell yourself prior to sleep. I've had you prime yourself to remember dreams, yes? This priming is similar. Although now you'll want to awaken during a dream. Then you'll stay awake for about a half hour—once I find the article I can give you exact times. Here it is . . . no, false alarm. Anyway, once you're awake you'll do more priming. The goal is to return to sleep and that same dream, then alter its course. Eventually, supposedly, you'll be adept enough to skip the waking up step. . . . Here it is." She flipped through the article. "I'll have to translate this from scientese to English for you."

While she found a pen and annotated margins, Tommy joined her on the couch. "What makes you think we're going to be getting any sleep? There's a lot of floor in the world, you know."

"Oh, eventually you'll get tired for a few minutes here and there. And when you do, I want you to dream about being in the hallway, fighting with Colton's killer. But in your dream, you're going to shine the flashlight on the killer's face."

Tommy stopped tickling her ear. "Man. That sounds so easy. Damn. If only it works." He studied the annotated article pensively.

"Now we can't get discouraged if it doesn't work right away. Please note that this lecture is for my benefit, too. You have to keep at it."

"Agreed. But I didn't see his face. Why will I see it now?"

"I'm hoping that your right brain can synthesize what it knows and produce an image."

"You still think I know a psycho-killer. Did you ask my right brain again today if Mrs. Bates is the one?"

"Yes I did. Once again the answer was no."

"What about Hugo?"

She didn't have to answer. Her face told him she'd had no luck with that, either. "But I repeat: it could be someone you know; we have to explore that angle."

Tommy moved to her desk. "I need to make a phone call." He punched a number, waited. "Ilsa? . . . Yeah, it's me. . . . I know, I know, too long, but you're the one who moved to fucking West Covina. . . . Miss you, too. . . . Tonight, if you're going to be home. . . . Cool. See you then." He made a kissing noise and hung up.

He returned to sit pressed beside Clare on the couch. She got up to straighten the journals. "You're going all the way to West Covina tonight? Isn't it dangerous for you to drive after dark?" She stopped talking, the only way to prevent demanding explanations: who the hell was Ilsa and how dare he call her now?

"I was figuring you'd drive. You're right, I shouldn't have assumed you would. But. When we were talking about guns? Ilsa can get them, fast. And teach us what we need to know about using them. She's great, you'll love her too."

"Tommy, I don't want a gun." And she didn't want to meet any Ilsa, age under 85 or IQ over 85.

"Every time we walk out of here I feel more scared and I think you do too. It drives me nuts knowing I can't be with you every minute and even when I am I'm no guarantee of protection. At least with guns we could pretend we were safer."

They got their security escort to her car, then headed east over some twenty miles of especially tacky mini-malls, chain stores, and fast food kiosks, to exit the freeway into a brand new housing development where people paid voluminously to live in huge pseudo-Spanish tract homes along wide avenues with tiny trees. From what Clare could determine, no one followed them on this trip, either.

Suddenly, after crossing a boulevard, they were driving through a poorly lit but discernibly run-down neighborhood. Here were small, aging wood frame homes with falling porches and sagging chain link fences. Hieroglyphic gang graffiti marked territory on every garage wall Clare's headlights hit.

They parked under a scrawny tree dying a slow death from smog; walked across crab grass, past a Chevy speckled with primer paint, over thick plywood laid where cement steps had once been; stopped under a yellow porch light caked with bug corpses. Tommy reached through bars to knock on the door. A voice hailed them from inside. Clare couldn't understand it but Tommy yelled back, "Yeah it's Dabrowski."

A buzzer sounded. Tommy pulled the bars and held them open with his shoulder, put his hand on the doorknob. A different buzzer sounded and he pushed the door open, stepping inside and motioning his head for Clare to follow. By the time she was in the dim room, Tommy was across it, hugging the occupant of a wheelchair, then introducing Clare to Ilsa.

"Glad to know you." Ilsa's rousing bellow smothered Tommy's words. "Now to see you." She pointed an object in her hand. Click. The TV went off; the room went black. Click. Overhead lights went on and Clare regarded a frail redhead with ultrapale, freckled skin. Her legs were cocooned in a down sleeping bag. In a holder affixed to her wheelchair was a rifle. "Dick, he's here," she bellowed over her shoulder.

Elsewhere in the house, water stopped rushing through pipes and floorboards creaked the approach of a tall balding youngish man with khaki pants buckled under his belly and a towel around his neck. He embraced Tommy heartily then wiped shaving cream from his ears. "Getting ready for work?" Tommy inquired.

" 'Fraid so, they got me back on graveyard. Just for this month though, 'til they replace the turkey who fell asleep, woke up to find every single mother dripping spray paint."

Tommy introduced Ilsa's husband to Clare, then explained, "While we sleep tonight, Dick will be keeping our city buses safe from graffiti."

Dick snorted, tossed the towel onto a couch covered by a red blanket, and slipped his arms into a transit cop's sleeves. He strapped on a holster, checked his watch, hurried into an overcoat. Ilsa frenched him farewell and he was out the door. The bars clanged shut behind him, making the house shake.

Ilsa waved them toward the couch and an orange floral chair. "Sit down, you're giving me a neck ache."

Clare sank into the chair and got a surprise. "This is the most comfortable chair I've ever sat in."

"That's why it's still here, homely as it is. I used to love it, but now I stay in this thing. Too much trouble getting out any more than I have to. There was a shooting down the street about five years back. I was getting out of our car. Bullet hit me in the spine. Easier to get the story out of the way so you're not wondering all night how I got this way. Does Da-browski want a brewski?"

"Yow. That was terrible, Ilsa."

"I've been practicing. Whatever you want, help yourself, kitchen's that way." Ilsa waved to a door for Clare's benefit.

"I could use something. I'm not sure what." Clare followed the wave. "Beer, Tommy?" He nodded and began explaining to Ilsa that they needed guns.

The kitchen linoleum was faded blue and mangled by wheelchair wheels. Opening drawers until she found a bottle opener for their beers, she found an entire drawerful of medication for Ilsa. Clare felt ill at ease, not in the surroundings or Ilsa's lively company, but at the indication of such a vast gap in her knowledge of Tommy's life. For some time she stared at a wall calendar filled with reminders of doctor appointments, birthdays, and bills due; and, in bold red letters twice a month, DICK GETS PAID. She was incapable of formulating reactions to Ilsa and Dick's life that weren't sappy or superficial. She instead allowed herself to simply like them, to savor the love that swept like a wind between them, and regret the anxiousness flickering over them as Dick left for the night. Meanwhile, she flipped through the calendar pages until she found a T.D. #27 in March that must be Tommy's birthday; then hated to admit her satisfaction when she found no birthday listing for B.D.

By the time she returned to the living room, Tommy had explained their predicament and Ilsa was shaking her head. "You can't help us?" Tommy took a beer from Clare, spilled it in his anxiousness.

Ilsa handed him the towel Dick had tossed on the couch, and he mopped up while she mused, "Can I get you a piece? Sure. I could do that tonight. Tomorrow's Dick's night off, he could give you a crash course in using it. But if you're dealing with somebody who's got one too, and who's better with it, you'll be wishing you were unarmed. If you're the only one with a gun, you don't need it anyway. Besides which, that cop's suspicious enough of you already. Dick had an encounter with him a few years back. Beaudine's a very bad man to let see your unregistered firearm."

"How do you know it's Beaudine? I didn't tell you his name."

"I figured, Pasadena homicide case. Aw, shit. Betsi came out here, few nights back. She made me promise I wouldn't tell you. Bianca, I mean. When is that woman going to decide on a name? Each one's worse than the last."

Clare sat very still, lest she laugh; and fervently hoped Tommy would ask all the questions she wanted to ask.

"Why was Bianca out here?" When Ilsa didn't answer, Tommy counseled, "You can't stand her and we all know that. If she made you promise to keep quiet—to lie to one of your oldest friends—and you break that promise, she's in the wrong, not you."

"Goddamn us, every one." Ilsa gulped from the tumbler of whiskey and ice tucked alongside her legs. "She said she missed seeing us. Wants to get together, have us out for dinner, like that. Said she wishes you'd stay home more—and that I believed, though as you know, I gotta take her with so much salt, it fucks with my blood pressure. Main impression I got, is that she's jealous as all hell."

"How did Beaudine come up in the conversation?"

After a brief inner debate, Ilsa asked Clare sheepishly, "You're the doctor, right?" then matched Clare's nod. "Betsianca was ragging about you. She thinks Beaudine's suspicious of Tommy because of you. And thinks Beaudine should suspect you. And thinks if Tommy keeps trusting you he's in trouble. I don't know, my first impressions of people aren't always right but I still listen to them and they say you're okay."

"Thanks." Immediately, Clare feared she'd sounded stupid or condescending, but Ilsa smiled and returned her gaze to Tommy, leaving Clare to wonder whether Bianca had fabricated her encounter with a threatening man who looked like Hugo.

"Don't let on I told you. It'll just make you both crazy. She'll have to prove it wasn't like it was and—shit, I don't need to tell you, you know better than anybody."

"Oh yeah, I know." Tommy tugged his sling. "That's why you didn't ask me about my arm. Bianca already told you. See, it's just as well you spilled, I would've wondered about that later. You're no good at being sneaky, Ilsa, Bianca should've known."

Ilsa smiled—and yawned. "Past my bedtime, kids. Next time come earlier? For a real visit? And goddamn it, take care." She hugged Tommy, then shook Clare's hand firmly. "If you wouldn't mind, Clare, could you come help me get into my PJs? I can do it myself but it's easier with help and I can't ask the wolf, he'd take advantage of me."

Tommy growled and nipped her neck, then took the beer bottles into the kitchen. Clare followed Ilsa down the hall.

Once in the bedroom, Ilsa whispered, "Shut the door. Guess

I'd really better change, too." From the bed, Clare took the neatly folded nightgown Ilsa indicated, while Ilsa quickly stripped off her sweatshirt. "I'll talk fast so he doesn't get suspicious; if he still wants a gun, if you think he's going to try to get one, then bring him back here. I can't tell him that, just give him ideas. But above all make sure he's careful. I didn't want to tell him, because he gets so twisted up about what he owes that woman, and that's the last thing he needs now. But Bianca was scared—real scared. For him as well as herself. And I can't recall another time I caught her thinking about anybody besides herself. She said something about getting warnings. She didn't want Tommy to know, thought he had enough to worry about, trying to name that killer. Which sounds like the case."

"Warnings? Plural? And she was out here several nights ago?"

Ilsa nodded after each question, leaving Clare feeling sympathy for Bianca; and respect. She really was looking out for Tommy first.

Much louder, Ilsa said, "Yeah, I love flannel, don't you?"

Clare mimed agreement and compliance with Ilsa's requests, then led the way back to the living room, saying over her shoulder, "The only problem is, it's so comfortable, the temptation to wear pajamas in to work is overwhelming."

Ilsa tittered, bid them good-bye once more, then stage-whispered to Tommy, "She's a keeper. Don't screw up."

"Hey, thanks for the vote of confidence," Tommy laughed and shut the door behind them. Clare was glad it was dark, she had to be blushing. As she pulled her car out from under the dying tree, Tommy laughed and ruffled her hair. "The Ilsa seal of approval. Good to know that when society ostracizes me for abandoning my lovely and devoted wife, we'll have one friend left."

"I like her. I like both of them." Clare said neutrally, fearing the hope and warmth surging through her.

"So what was it she had to tell you in private?"

"Should I turn left or right to get back to the freeway?"
"Left. Was there more about Bianca she didn't tell me?"
"Why would you think that?"
"Clare. Okay, maybe you're allowed to answer this one. From what Ilsa said, do you think Bianca lied about a guy threatening her last night? To keep me home and away from you?"

Clare fought conflicting desires, loyalties. "No. She didn't make that up. Or, if she did, it was because she's worried. She thinks you're both—we're all—in a lot of danger. Ilsa believes that if that possibility got through to Bianca, it must really be true."

Tommy's voice was heavy. "I wonder if other stuff's been happening to Bianca, like last night."

"Perhaps you should ask her if it was."

He was silent a time. "If I thought I could get a straight answer . . . Nah. It's like you said. We're all targets. We all have to—pay attention. I just gotta make sure I watch out for her, too." He studied mini-malls for several miles. "By the way, Ilsa hardly ever likes anybody, so feel honored."

"I do. Where do you know them from?"

"Dick and I were pals in grade school. After high school we didn't see each other much—he got wrapped up in Ilsa which was fine, but she and Bianca were instant enemies and it got to be too much, always having to side against somebody you loved. I didn't see them for years, then Bianca heard about Ilsa getting shot and started sending me to visit them. Eventually that got weird, so she and Ilsa tried to tolerate each other, and now they usually almost manage it." He lapsed into silence. The ticking of tires on rough asphalt clocked away minutes. Then he noted, "You seem upset."

"I'm not. I have reached my limit on Bianca stories for the night, though."

"I get that. I keep dragging you further into my mess. What's really a bitch is that I can't make myself feel completely sorry about it. Which I guess proves what a selfish prick I am. Don't respond to that. I don't want you to defend me. And I definitely don't want to hear if you agree."

They grew quiet until Clare turned onto her street; as she angled into a space, her headlights caught Beaudine's watcher sipping from Styrofoam. He vanished when the headlights went off. They ran for her building. As Clare unlocked the new grill door, Tommy kept his back to her, watching for approaching Hugos. Just before the grill clicked locked behind them, Tommy beamed his flashlight into the mirrors atop the stairs. No one was waiting in the hidden alcove. "This is great. I actually feel safe." Clare ran ahead to unlock the door.

Inside, Jessie strolled lazily to greet them. The cat was putting on weight; unsure when she'd be home, Clare left a bowl of dry food out at all times, these days, and Jess took full advantage.

They stood in the kitchen while Jessie picked at her dinner. She'd eaten so much all day she wasn't hungry now—and she was always hungry. "There are starving cats in Africa, Jessie," Tommy warned. She looked up at her name, then strolled from the room, twitching her tail. Clare continued to watch Jessie, lest she notice the strain building around Tommy.

He went out to flop on the couch. From out of nowhere sprang Jessie, over him then away.

"Aaaahhhgg," Tommy yelled.

"It was just Jessie," Clare said between laughs. "She does that once in a while when she's been cooped up." She joined him on the couch.

"Somebody should tell her, *I* don't have nine lives." He clutched his heart, then got down on his knees, stalked Jessie into the kitchen, tried to corner her. "Sooo. Kitty's feeling frisky, eh?" Jessie leaped over him and bounced into the living room, onto the couch, eyes glowing, then bounded back onto the kitchen table. Tommy sat on the floor, panting. Clare came to the door. "It's not easy crawling with three paws." He stood, dusted his knees, watched Jessie with exaggerated mistrust.

Why did it seem as though he was intentionally focusing on the cat?

"Any more tests for us to do tonight?" Tommy's voice was all business.

Clare stiffened. "I don't know what to do next. Everything I've tried lately has fizzled. I need some time to just stare at the results we've got—there must be a pattern I'm missing—but it's been a long day, I'm too groggy to find patterns tonight."

Tommy took the news of deadlock remarkably well. "You'll figure something out. I'm pretty beat, too. C'mon." At last he looked at her, reached for her.

She took his hand and he led her into the bedroom, which for the first time felt safe to Clare. He helped her make the bed; smiled into inconsequence her explanations as to why she'd been sleeping on the couch. He kissed her tenderly, then might as well have kicked her in the gut: "I can't stay tonight. You're safe in here but Bianca."

"In that case, I'll see you out."

"Clare." She waited for more, only heard Jessie shredding paper in the living room. He stepped in front of her, compelling her to look at him. When she at last did, he regarded her with an odd mixture of sorrow, longing, and lust. "I want to stay here," he said. "I have to go." He pulled her to him, awkwardly, buried his face at her throat, her hair. "I sure hope you think more of me than I do, right now." He straightened and stepped away. "Don't answer that."

She walked him to the front door. "It's okay, your leaving. Well. It's not okay, but I accept it. I won't forever but right now it's the way things have to be. Were Trish and Andy going to stay until you got home?"

"I don't know, see, that's part of it. Maybe they'll all be there. Or maybe I'll walk in on Bianca and Andy, in some ways I'm hoping for that." He looked frustrated and regretful. "We should've waited until I straightened out all this shit. I shouldn't have made you go slog through it with me."

"Yes, we probably should have waited. But I can't say I wish we did and I'm not at all sure it would have been any easier if we had." She unlatched the door and added quickly, "Don't forget your lucid dreaming exercises."

"I won't. What time tomorrow?"

"Let's see . . . Mrs. Bates is coming in, and I've got my classes, so let's meet at two. No, I forgot. Those grant givers are coming to observe me testing Cynthia. I'd like you to observe them—can you be there at noon?"

Tommy nodded. "Damn, do I not want to leave you."

"Three honks then one when you get to your car?"

Tommy nodded, gave her a swift kiss good-bye, then hurried out. As soon as she heard the grill clicked shut, Clare ran to get the phone and raced back to the open door, poised to call for help if . . . There were the honks and the engine revving.

She replaced the phone and locked the door, made coffee. While it was brewing, she wandered the apartment, briefcase in hand. The kitchen proved to be the only room in which Tommy's absence was not palpable. She sat at the kitchen table anxious and confused. How casual they were getting about arranging murder investigation time. Granted, they could only experiment fruitfully for a limited number of hours each day. But that wasn't it. They were losing their purpose, their belief they could reach a solution. It was up to her to break through to a new direction. She scoured her notes for clues. But they made no more sense than anything else in her life.

CHAPTER 13

Fight or Flight

If Clare got murdered, the deed would not be done by Dr. Colton and Lalitha's killer, but by her students; and no jury would convict them. She had no recollection of the lecture she gave either class that next morning; and from her students' reactions, she'd said nothing worth remembering despite the obligation she felt to get them ready for finals.

Her lectures, such as they were, completed, Clare hurried to her office, hoping to find Tommy. Instead, there were the grant givers, Matt Woods and Yvonne Hankoff, chatting with Deirdre in the hall. When they saw Clare, they abruptly stopped talking. Deirdre looked particularly evasive.

Clare spoke carefully. "Hello Deirdre, I forgot you'd be helping out today. Mr. Woods, Ms. Hankoff, I'm glad we could accommodate your schedule, I believe you'll find Cynthia Bates an interesting subject. Can Deirdre get coffee or tea for either of you?" When they declined, she led them into the lab. They seemed nervous. Yvonne continually arched her long neck and smoothed her bobbed golden hair; Matt repeatedly removed his crooked horn-rims to massage the bridge of his crooked nose.

"Series Four B, Deirdre, please." Clare set up chairs for the observers while giving them an overview of her work with Cynthia and today's tests. "If you have any questions, please ask now or much later; there are very few experiments I'll discuss while the subject is present."

"Of course," one of them replied. As they had during their initial visit, they took turns speaking.

"Over what period of time do you examine each subject?" the other inquired.

"The record so far has been six years. There are so few commissurotomy patients, I try to hold on to them as long as they let me."

Polite laughter and brief note-taking. "Two of our grant recipients on the East Coast work closely with the surgeons performing the commissurotomy, and requested that those doctors be included in grant allocations. Would that be the case with you?"

"No. Dick—Dr. Rosenthal—is semi-retired these days. And Dr. Stanford Colton is—was—the other neurosurgeon who operated on my subjects."

"Ah. Yes. We were shocked to learn of his . . . death. You worked quite closely with him at one time, we understand. We hope his work will be carried on, he was truly a great contributor to the field."

"I also hope his work will continue."

"Do you have any plans to step in?"

"No, I'm very busy here. And ultimately more interested in the current work I'm doing." Something in their professionally cordial questioning style had altered after Dr. Colton's name was introduced. If she steered to a new topic, would they steer it back? Damn Tommy for being late, she needed a second opinion here. "By the way, let me give you a copy of my latest paper, due to be published in April. It contains a preliminary study of Cynthia Bates."

"Please do, we'd like to see that." They seemed cautious now.

She imagined them exchanging glances as she turned her back to extract copies of her paper from a cupboard.

They skimmed through it. "Your work seems rather similar to Dr. Colton's in some basic ways."

"Does it? I haven't kept up—he rarely publishes. The last I knew, he was creating memory deficits in feline and primate brains, which is not at all related." She struggled to remain casual. "If you're interested in Stanford Colton's research—"

They abandoned their customary politeness to interrupt and quickly deny any such interest.

"I misunderstood. Most people are interested, around here, anyway. Dr. Colton was always so damn secretive, it inspired undue curiosity." When they relaxed, so did she. "As I was going to say, Cynthia Bates was commissurotomized by him." Did they seem disappointed that this was her tidbit about Dr. Colton's research?

Belatedly, she realized that Deirdre had completed the series 4B setup long ago and was scrutinizing every word exchanged. Spies spying on spies. In a way, it was funny. Clare didn't feel like laughing.

"Look who I ran into outside! He's early with nowhere to go so I invited him to watch me." Mrs. Bates bustled into the lab, so cheery that Clare could only expect to see Tommy accompanying her.

"Hey everybody." Tommy greeted each with a nod, saving Clare for last. Their eyes locked, briefly; they smiled, for an instant, and Clare needed several moments to recover. Meanwhile, Mrs. Bates introduced herself and Tommy to the grant givers.

Surprisingly, Cynthia had jumped at the opportunity to test for these observers. Clare suspected it was because she'd promised the experiments would be gentle easy ones. Still, she was grateful that Mrs. Bates had agreed; it was certainly a better use of time than manufacturing fake tests for Tommy to take.

Clare pretended to busy herself at her testing station, letting the conversation go where the grant givers wanted to lead it. Either they weren't fishing for Colton information after all, or Clare had made them craftier about extracting same, but the topics now were more general: commissurotomies and operations, epilepsy and its treatments.

Gradually, she became aware of Cynthia's contributions to the discussion, and found them disturbing. Greatly. Clare wandered over to the counter where Mrs. Bates had deposited her purse; when she was sure no one was looking, she pocketed Cynthia's wallet, turned—and met Deirdre's eyes. The girl shook her head once, discreetly, as though to indicate she would say nothing—yet. Clare kept turning and found Tommy watching this exchange. Damn. Had they all seen? No, she hadn't been that obvious.

"We'd better get started," Clare said, voice clipped. The alleged grant givers and Cynthia Bates stopped talking mid-word and looked at her, puzzled by something she'd failed to keep out of her voice.

Tommy dragged a chair in from the office, sat down with visible satisfaction, and said, "Yeah, let's go, it's great not being the victim for a change." This lightened the mood and Mrs. Bates took her place at the tachistoscope screen.

First, Clare flashed phrases on the tachistoscope; she gave Woods and Hankoff a typed list of the phrases being flashed. Afterward, Clare paused to explain, "Cynthia has just been tested on her ability to recognize palindromes—strings of letters that read the same left to right, right to left. She was to press a button when she recognized a palindrome—such as items one, three, four, and seven on your list, 'Otto,' 'nurses run,' 'Anna,' and 'bombard a drab mob.'" Woods and Hankoff tittered. "Yes, they are funny. Some of my favorites are too long to be used in this test: 'May a moody baby doom a yam.' Or: 'Sit on a potato pan, Otis.'" As intended, the palindromes loosened up her guests; but not enough to slip and reveal anything substantive about the purpose of their visit.

Over the next ninety minutes, Mrs. Bates kept her hands behind the screen, performing tasks that caused little conflict between her hemispheres. First, her left hand retrieved marbles from a box of objects, while her right hand retrieved dice. Then Clare put a simple geometric drawing in free vision and Cynthia's hands took turns: one drew the object, the other found the 3-D equivalent in a box of carved wooden forms.

As always, it was troubling and marvelous to watch her hands accomplish such separate functions with such ease. But only Woods and Hankoff displayed suitable alarm and awe. Tommy kept glancing at Clare as though he had something to ask or tell her. Deirdre studied them all. Clare registered these behaviors through an anxious fog: all she wanted was to end the session and get Mrs. Bates alone for interrogation.

At last the tests were over. In case the observers really were grant givers, Clare gave them copies of a brief statistical analysis of the brain functions they'd observed, of the variance in performance levels between Cynthia's and other subjects' hemispheres. Woods and Hankoff seemed satisfied and impressed. They moved into Clare's office, chatting with Tommy, Deirdre, and Cynthia, while Clare pretended to log Cynthia's test results but actually stayed in the lab to give the guests a chance to reveal themselves to Tommy. Clare joined them after hearing Hankoff remind Woods of their next appointment. Not long after, Mrs. Bates and Clare small-talked the two guests down the hall; Cynthia continued outside with them.

Back in her office, Clare studied her watch, estimating how long it would take the trio to exit the building. Then she unpocketed Cynthia's wallet while Tommy and Deirdre stared. "Deirdre, Mrs. Bates forgot her wallet. Can you run out and catch her? Ask her to come back to pick it up."

Deirdre replied, "The problem is, I could just bring the wallet to her. Except you want her back so you can talk to her alone, without her knowing that's what you want. I suggest that I say

I'm late for my tutorial and didn't think of bringing it to her until I was already outside."

"Thank you. That will work perfectly." Clare was pleasantly surprised.

"I am on your side, Dr. Austen. And—I'd better go catch Mrs. Bates." She grabbed her things. "Did you want me to come back later?"

"Best not, I don't know how long I'll need with Mrs. Bates."

"See you tomorrow then. 'Bye Tommy."

"I'm counting the minutes." He winked at her and she was gone. Tommy shut the door and took Clare into one of his lopsided, one arm embraces. "What's with the wallet bit?"

It was hard to talk with his lips pressing against her throat. "Cynthia knows too much—far more than she used to know. I don't think I have time to explain, though. We shouldn't be talking about her when she gets here. Jesus, I feel like Cynthia's hands during tests—trying to think when you're making me do nothing but feel."

"Want me to stop? Didn't think so. Do I stay while you talk to Cynthia?"

"Please. Yes. I'd like you to observe her."

Tommy kissed her one last time, then fell back onto the couch. "I better cool out for a minute. So what about your visitors? Think they're for real? They seemed kinda too interested in Colton but not so much that I was sure of it."

"I had the same impression." Clare sat at her desk, rearranged clutter so that her phone held center stage. "I wish we—"

A knock sounded on her door. Clare closed her eyes briefly, then called, "Come in." Tommy blew her a good luck kiss then greeted Cynthia with maximum charm.

"That dear Deirdre—listen to me, isn't that a mouthful—I mean to say, Deirdre ran after me, my wallet somehow escaped from my purse. Clare, I don't wish to meddle but please don't be so rough on the girl. She said she would have brought it to me, but you didn't trust her with it."

And thank you, Deirdre. The girl obviously had an excellent future in this academic community. Only Clare, it seemed, had never learned to play by the rules. "Actually, I wanted you to come back here. We need to talk. Please sit down."

Cynthia's gay mood swiftly dissipated. She joined Tommy on the couch, got no comfort from his steady evaluation. "Let's have it," she said with a steeliness Clare had not before seen in her.

"When you were talking with Mr. Woods and Ms. Hankoff—"

"Oh, I do hope I said nothing to hurt your chances of winning the grant. You should have signaled to me, kicked me, I'm such a blabbermouth."

"Cynthia. Overhearing your conversation, I noticed that you've recently acquired considerable knowledge about the condition of your brain. You even mentioned the corpus callosum, a term I've never given you."

"What the hell is that?" Tommy demanded.

"It's the more precise term for the central commissure. I thought you might have come across it in your reading."

"Tommy didn't, but I did." Cynthia's tone was defensive. "I recently decided I should learn more about my . . . situation. I believe I told you that."

"I don't believe you learned that much that quickly. Furthermore, you made comparative references to two other split brain patients. Yes, you've met them, but I doubt you all exchanged medical file information. I think you read their medical files instead. I think you're the one who stole Dr. Colton's files, and I want to know when and how, and I want to know right now, or I'm calling Lieutenant Beaudine." She gripped her phone. "Start talking, Cynthia."

"You believe I killed him, don't you?"

"I *know* you're stalling." Clare picked up the receiver. At Cynthia's strangled "Wait!" she slowly replaced it.

Mrs. Bates spoke in a rush, as though fearful that a pause

would lead to Beaudine's involvement. "Yes, I took them. I'd tried to speak with Stanford, but he shunned me. My hands were in such a state, I craved information, I thought it would help me comprehend what was happening to me. The day he was murdered, I went to beg him for his time. As I reached his hall I saw him enter the bathroom down the way. I ran to his door, it was open, I'd seen him consult my file once long ago, so I knew where it was. I opened his desk drawer, found my name, grabbed my file but the drawer was so full, I had to pull the ones on either side, too. I stuffed them into my coat and shut the drawer, jumped away from his desk just as he came back. He was furious I'd invaded his sanctuary."

For a moment, she was too angry to continue. "Again, he refused to speak with me, after all that we'd been through together. Well, I don't suppose he saw it that way." She fought tears. "I stopped begging him and left. As I returned outdoors, the lights went out. Which I've heard preceded his murder. I just missed the killer, it seems, and being killed myself. Or—if I'd been there Stanford would still be alive." She began sobbing. "I didn't kill him. That you must believe. I swear I didn't, I couldn't."

Tommy moved over to her other side so that he could put his good arm around her, pulling her back from a plunge into hysterics.

Clare had to keep attacking while Cynthia was vulnerable to further confessions. "Why did you feel you and Colton had been through so much together?" Again, she rested her hand on the phone, the conduit to Beaudine. "What was your relationship with Stanford? As you so intimately call him." Tommy looked at Clare with sympathy; he understood why she was attacking.

Unfortunately, it seemed Mrs. Bates also recognized the bluff. "An aging schoolgirl's fantasy, that's all. I. Did. Not. Kill. Him." Her eyes pleaded with Clare to let her be; and warned that she could not be pressed further.

"Where are the files now?" Clare asked gently.

"At home. I considered burning them, or at least burning the others. I know they could damn me. But I couldn't destroy any of them, I couldn't do that to—any of us." She turned to Tommy for understanding; received it and turned back to Clare. "Reading the files did help. It was a comfort to see myself in such scientific terms, as a medical case, no worse than at least a few others. But now—what should I do with the files, Clare? I've thought of giving them to Lieutenant Beaudine, but I'm terrified he won't believe I'm merely a thief, not a killer."

"For now, give them to me." Clare ignored Tommy's double take, to worry: did Mrs. Bates exhibit gratitude or relief? "Is your husband picking you up today?"

"No, I took the bus." Now Cynthia was puzzled.

"Perfect. We'll drive you home and get the files. Immediately."

"Cynthia," Tommy said coolly. "Would you wait in the lab a minute? I need to talk to Clare."

"Of—course." She looked at the telephone as though Beaudine were sitting on it. "But Tommy, please—"

He shushed her and, murmuring assurances that he wouldn't let her be hurt, he led her, shaking, into the lab.

After pulling Clare out into the hall and slamming the office door behind them, he seemed briefly at a loss for words. Then, "Clare, do not take those files. Call Beaudine or let her burn them. We're going to get screwed here, I can feel it."

"She will destroy them, if we let her go home alone. They're evidence, Tommy, they could be important. But if we call Beaudine—we can't trust him not to overreact, or misreact. All I can say for certain right now is that we've got to save those files. I'm terrified about getting involved but I don't know what else to do."

"Oh, maaaaannn." They stared at each other a long time. "The real pisser is, we both know they won't let us share the same prison cell. But you're right. Beaudine'll lock up Cynthia and close the case if we tell him now. And if she goes home alone, they're gone. Shit. Shit. Shit. Let's go get 'em."

Just as Tommy was letting Cynthia out, the phone rang. All three froze. Expecting to hear Beaudine's sarcastic "Dr. Austen?" Clare answered hesitantly. But the caller was Matt Woods, thanking her for a fascinating demonstration; they'd let her know about her grant within six months. She hung up, the three exchanged looks, and they set out.

Cynthia lived in San Marino, haven of the stolidly wealthy, a few blocks from the John Birch Society Book Store, on a tree-shrouded cul-de-sac in a modest mock Tudor home sure to have a resale value close to a million dollars. The entrance hallway was a clutter of expensively framed photos of her children and other relatives; none were photos of Cynthia or her husband save their professionally painted wedding day pose.

Cynthia led them upstairs to her bedroom, pointed to the middle drawer in the reproduction Louis Quinze dresser. "In there, under my—brassieres."

Clare found three bulging files. She picked them up with her scarf, wrapped them in it. She would not, at least, get her fingerprints on them. "Where are the others?"

"That's all, I took mine and two others, those are all I have." Cynthia's voice rose with each word, until it was shrill to the limit of human hearing.

"I believe you," Clare said hastily. Mrs. Bates stood still and mortified, until Clare added softly, "Thank you for trusting me with these."

"You can trust me as well, Clare. I know what sort of limb you've climbed onto for me now, and I know it's not the first." Leading them back downstairs, she added steadily, "If you do find that you must tell Lieutenant Beaudine about the files, could you warn me? If at all possible?"

"If I do, and if I can, yes. Certainly."

Cynthia nodded and shut them outside.

Once in the car, Clare leafed through the files, using the scarf like a glove. Tommy watched eagerly. Finally, she reported glumly, "They're typical medical files—treatments, dates, symptoms. And they seem to be complete. This far, at least, Cynthia has been telling us the truth."

"Hey, we didn't expect to find clues in them. We just wanted to save them, remember?"

"I know. I just hoped that—I just hoped." She put her car in gear. As they pulled away from the Bates home, a curtain swayed at an upstairs window, as though someone had been watching them.

"Do you think Cynthia was lying when she said these were the only files?"

Tommy grew circumspect. "No, I believed her then. Why?"

"The gap in Colton's file drawer—these folders aren't thick enough to fill it."

When Tommy finished swearing, he demanded, "Are you sure? How can you be sure? Fuck. You're sure. Then where are the other files?"

Clare parked at a stop sign. "Should we go to Beaudine?" Behind them, a honk.

Tommy waved for the honker to go around. And waved anew when another car pulled up, several minutes later. Finally he whimpered. "Oh, man. No, not yet."

Clare put the car into gear, clumsily. The engine died. She tried again. "We could go back to Cynthia and demand the other files."

"She'll point to the fireplace. If she ever had them. You know what bugs me? Even if she did kill Colton—she's not in this alone. Who would be crazy enough to have her as an accomplice? Sure, the killer's psycho but that's different. And how come Hugo and Mrs. Bates both have English accents?"

"To cover the simplest of the points you just raised: their accents may be significant but they're from different regions of England and there are so many expatriate Brits in L.A. I hear those accents all the time. Beyond that—whenever we talk about motives and accomplices, I feel lost, and I'd like to avoid those discussions, though I admit the issues dovetail: if we knew why it would be easier to figure who."

"Yeah, you're right again. We get nowhere talking it through. It's my fucking right brain that's got to do the talking. Fast."

Clare pulled into the faculty parking lot that wasn't near Larry's bushes. There were enough people around that Clare felt safe walking the extra distance to Neurobiology. Another daylight advantage: the campus snack bar was open; they stopped to collect food that could pass for dinner, then continued to the lab. "Once again, I saw no indication that we were being followed."

"I know. It gives me the willies." When they reached her office, he pulled her in for a kiss. "First time we've had to ourselves and the day's almost over," he groused.

Clare broke away and led him into the lab. "How was it at home last night?"

"Total waste. Bianca wasn't there, I had to do some calling around to make sure she was okay. Finally woke her up at Trish's. She expected me to not come home; said she'd rather have us working around the clock to solve this thing, even if she has to spend the night alone. Or at Trish's, which is where she stayed. I saw her for like five minutes this morning when she came home to change. It's so weird. Now that it really happened —you and me, I mean—she's blocking that it's even a possibility."

"Which makes you feel like a heel."

"The heel of a bum wearing the wrong size shoe. Hey. We're back," Tommy greeted his lab table. "Like we never left, huh?"

They kissed once for luck and set to work. Clare dragged out a toy store bag; a purchase made that morning.

"Tell me you didn't. Tell me we're not." Irritation flared when he saw the Ouija box. "Scrabble letters I could handle but consulting the oracle?"

"With Scrabble letters, I suspect I demanded too much:

spelling words is more difficult than recognizing them. Today, I'll put words at different points around the board. You'll have more choices than I can give you with the tachistoscope and your right brain will only need to recognize words and guide the pointer."

Tommy reflected for a nanosecond, then vexation turned to admiration. "You're right, for the gazillionth time. See, I told you you'd come up with some new angles."

If he only knew how close to stalemated they were. All their new angles were scant degrees separate from those previously tried. If she didn't soon get an answer that launched her on a completely new path, she wouldn't know what to try further. But she could hardly tell him that.

"Before we get started, did you have any dreams last night?"

"Nope. But you said it could take a while."

"That's right. You just have to keep at it." She spoke to reassure herself as well. And yet, despite her growing hopelessness, she felt excited, today—by the unorthodoxy of using a Ouija board in a clinical setting. Studying LEMs during a shopping trip, or asking Tommy to sing his responses, had been similarly inappropriate. Clare was only breaking the "rules" out of desperation; those rules existed to ensure that researchers obtained results worth having. Nevertheless, the act uplifted her. She'd once had a reputation for eccentricity; how she had reveled in her detractors' sniffs and huffs when one of her "wild" hunches paid off. Of course, when her hunches failed her, then the result was simply poor science, and the sniffers had their revenge. She no longer advocated taking such chances; thus she was surprised to discover how satisfying she still found the surge of adrenaline accompanying such recklessness.

She didn't dare tell Tommy any of this, either. He was counting on her to know what she was doing; not to dabble in neurological alchemy.

First, she tested his right brain's ability to guide the Ouija pointer; a slow, awkward task with his arm sling, despite the stick extension she devised. "Is your name Tommy?" Bit by bit, the pointer crept toward YES. "Is my name Robert?" The pointer hobbled across the board to NO. "Do you remember the night in the hall, the killer with the knife?" YES. "These are tests to learn where you touched the killer, which parts of the body, what clothes. Do you understand?" Even more hesitantly, the marker moved to YES.

She printed words on scraps of paper above certain letters on the board—ARM above A, FACE above F, SWEATER CUFF above C—until each bit of their acquired knowledge was represented. Then she put EVERYTHING above E, ? above Q; and went around the board reading each scrap in turn. After several such circuits, she tested his right brain's comprehension. "Point to *arm* . . . point to *neck* . . ." until she was sure it understood each word. "Now, I'll ask one question several ways. Please be patient and don't move the pointer until I'm done.

"How do you know the killer? What did you touch that tells you who the killer is? Which touch is important?" She continued to ad-lib variations; Tommy's expression indicated intense concentration. She paused. "Now. Show your answer."

She engaged his left brain in idle conversation, hoping to distract it, to prevent any effort to ipsilaterally control the muscles in Tommy's left hand. Meanwhile, the pointer jumped and quivered around the board to EVERYTHING, then to ?. Either his right hemisphere was confused, or it could not explain how it knew the killer's identity. She ad-libbed another string of questions, all of which had succeeded in dichotic listening tests. The pointer responses were identical.

Did his right brain want to be asked additional questions, did it know more? YES, it replied. But it was unable to use the pointer to give her a clue as to what else she should ask, or what sort of information it had yet to divulge.

Wordlessly, Tommy watched her remove the slips of paper, although not speaking critically and uncooperatively was obviously a strain. Clare set new scraps around the Ouija board. This test had so many choices, it would take several rounds to lay them all out. She unfolded the *Hustler* condom ad. "Man, am I sick of those three babes," Tommy said at sight of the bikinied beauties.

"I know what you—wait a minute, wait a minute," Clare was suddenly excited, looking at the trio. "Yesterday with the Scrabble letters. Were all those eeee's because there are threeee women, threeee people in the photo?"

Tommy got excited too, until the pointer limped toward NO. Clare's shoulders and spirits sagged. Tommy said, "Ever wanted to kill half of yourself?" The pointer headed for YES and they laughed, with some discomfort.

Subdued, Tommy made no complaints during the next two hours of futile efforts to determine the bikini picture's relevance. Finally, she ran out of ideas and stared at the Ouija board. Would it be worth the fleeting satisfaction to hurl it across the room? It had turned out to be a new route to the same dead ends. Studying his LEMs during the Ouija testing had likewise been unenlightening.

His left hand was having spasms. She massaged his shoulder, arm, and fingers. "Is that all we can do today?" he asked between consolation kisses.

"With the Ouija board, yes. I couldn't figure out a way to use it for this next test," she lied. Her next questions were sure to infuriate his left brain. "You'll need to put on the headset and fixate on the dot." He complied, eagerly, thrilled that there was more they could try, while Clare moved to her testing station.

She'd made this tape before yesterday's testing session but hadn't used it, hoping to first acquire more information by other means. But this tape was all she had left, so that was that. As might be called the theme of today's testing, the next experiment used methods of questionable value or effectiveness to attempt to circumvent a dead end. On the tachistoscope screen flashed names—CLARE, THE BEATLES, HUGO, and others—while the same names were heard dichotically. As soon as his right brain learned to recognize these names, she used them to teach the concepts *friend, stranger, not a friend, not a stranger*. Then she posed a variety of questions, once again striving to determine if the killer was someone Tommy had met before the encounter in that dark hall.

She was so tired and discouraged, it took some time for the import of the final, tested and retested result to hit her. The killer was *not a stranger, not a friend*. Either she and his right brain were miscommunicating, or he really was acquainted with the murderer. What she could do with this information, she needed a break before she could decide. She and Tommy were both worn out, and had been fumbling their efforts for the last hour. When she might dare to tell Tommy the results of this test, she would also decide later.

She removed the headset and kissed his ear. "Dinnertime. We're in the middle of a test but we're going so slowly right now, I think we need a break." He agreed and they kissed on it, with so little energy it made them chuckle, weakly.

Out in her office they collapsed on the couch, fortunately indifferent to the taste, freshness, and texture of their foil-packed burritos.

Clare sank against Tommy's shoulder. He put his arm around her and a few minutes later, she jerked upright, yanked back from semiconsciousness by his voice, inquiring, "Are we on to anything with this test? That we couldn't leave for tomorrow? 'Cuz I'm past the point of no return, and if my right brain's as tired as the rest of me, it's gonna start making mistakes soon."

"In that case, we're stopping for the night." Clare felt relieved, until Tommy pulled her closer with a last-chance determination. "You're planning on going home now, I take it."

"Pretty soon. Bianca wasn't sure whether Trish could stay with her, or what. Maybe she just said that to get me to show up. I told her I would. I guess I could just call her."

"No, you should go home. Everything will be much more difficult for all of us if Bianca stops accepting your absences."

Feeling ill, perhaps only from dinner, Clare studied his profile. Her yearning to kiss him became an impulse to scream and throw him out, not to return until he'd left Bianca! Calm down now: as soon as the murder was solved, she could kick him out. Yes, and didn't she have a lot to look forward to; including a numbing suspicion that once the confusion of the murder was settled, he'd patch up his marital problems as well.

His profile turned to face her. "I know what you're thinking. Or what I'd be thinking. But I give you my word, Clare, I'm not going to jerk you around." He kissed her lightly. "If you want to not—do this anymore, until Beaudine's got the killer locked up and I've cleaned up my act, I understand."

She turned away too hastily. The room strobed with bursting white lights and swimming black dots. Fighting her dizziness, she replied, "I can't decide that right now." They curled up together until the gloom of separation had dispersed.

Clare reviewed their conversation. "I'm having a delayed reaction to the way you said, 'once Beaudine's got the killer.' Do you really believe he's going to solve this before we do?"

"Don't you?"

"I'd like to think otherwise. And I've got a good feeling about the experiment we're doing now." She couldn't tell him why, unfortunately. There were enough opened cans of worms in the room tonight.

"What was that noise? It sounded like you were gargling with yogurt."

"I was imagining the room full of worms. It's a long story."

"And I don't want to hear it." Tommy's chuckle became a yawn.

And the next thing she knew, metal clattered outside and she recognized the cleaning crew's wash bucket hitting the tile. They were awfully early tonight, or—

"Tommy! Wake up." When he opened his eyes, he beamed, sleepy and loving, until she said, "It's morning. We fell asleep."

"Aw shit." He bolted to his feet, his sling catching on Clare's elbow with a rip. He was out of her office instantly and stumbling into the hall, tripping over a large brown envelope, an interdepartmental mailer. Odd time for a mail delivery. She turned back to toss the piece on her desk, then joined Tommy in a dash to her car.

His car was parked back at her place; he'd left it prior to their appointment with Norelle. He did nothing but swear on the trip.

"There's a good chance Bianca will still be understanding," Clare interjected as she turned onto her street.

"Yeah. Maybe. Man, if anything happened to her last night—"

Clare loosened her stranglehold on the steering wheel. "Your apartment is fortified and she's had Trish and Andy looking out for her." Tommy snorted in reply.

Heading up Clare's street, they passed Beaudine's watcher, who observed their approach in his outside mirror. Tommy unsnapped his seat belt. Clare braked, a bit too forcefully, alongside Tommy's loaner car. He jerked forward, bumping his crown against the windshield. "Sorry," she said coolly.

"Told you I was an asshole." He opened the door.

"As if your saying that makes a difference."

"I wouldn't feel so bad if it wasn't that I'd rather be with you. You can see that, can't you, Clare?"

"I can't even see that as a sentence in English," she said, to suggest she was no longer angry with him.

He took the suggestion at face value, smiled, and ran to his car, calling back to her, "I can be in the lab by ten."

"I'll be there." Waiting. Looking forward to solving the murders, so that she would no longer be forced to wait for him.

CHAPTER 14

Strange Attractors

She opened her door to Jessie howling and the telephone jangling. Her number was unlisted, so this had to be a wrong number. Or. She hurried into the kitchen, ignoring the phone, and fed Jessie, who continued her staccato indignant meows between gulps of breakfast, though it was only 6:30—earlier than the cat ordinarily ate. The phone ceased, mid-ring. Clare relaxed momentarily, until Jessie abandoned her bowl to wind around Clare's ankles. Clare's being gone all night had clearly disturbed Jessie greatly.

The phone started again.

"What is it?" she snarled into the receiver in as tough a voice as she could muster.

"Clare? It's Cynthia. I'm terribly sorry to ring you so early."

"How did you get this number?"

"Why—I called Information, they found it in new listings. I didn't know you'd moved, what a lot of extra stress at a time like this." Clare said nothing, trying to decide how much truth

Cynthia was telling; she tuned back in to hear ". . . thought I should try to reach you right away. My husband attended a charity dinner last night. A group of them got to talking about the murders and someone of high rank in the police department revealed that Lieutenant Beaudine is about to make an arrest for Dr. Colton's killing; that the culprit had known him for years and they had been feuding, professionally. My husband said it all sounded quite definite, and was told to friends; this official had no need to pretend the case was any further along than it actually is."

Tommy had been right. Beaudine had beat them after all. Clare felt a twinge of competitiveness, then vast relief. Now she could get on with her life. But—"What about the other murders? Surely the same man wasn't feuding with all four."

"I'm afraid I don't know any more. Although it does seem as though, if you haven't given those files to Lieutenant Beaudine, there is no longer a need to do so. After all, it would land us both in trouble."

Perhaps it was the limitations of the telephone, but Clare did not detect shiftiness or dissembling in Cynthia's manner. "I see what you mean," she replied noncommittally. "And I appreciate your calling, for both our sakes."

Mrs. Bates sounded a titch mistrusting. "I'll let you go, then. I hope I didn't wake you. But I thought you'd want to know—that."

"I'm glad you called."

"Will you let me know if you hear anything further?"

"Of course. Good-bye, Cynthia." As soon as she hung up, Clare called Information. Sure enough, her number was in new listings. Incompetent bastards.

She put water on for coffee and called the phone company to demand a new number. A recording told her to call between nine and five. Instead, she called 611 and vented so much frustration and anger that the poor repair order taker assured her a new number by noon. Feeling marginally better, Clare poured water into the drip coffee filter with one hand, petted Jessie with the other. The cat undulated on the kitchen counter, butting her head into Clare's arm.

Besides the obvious problems believing Cynthia, could Beaudine really be hunting four separate felons? Or was he planning to charge the suspect with one death at a time? Dare she call him and ask? Or should she wait until his next move became clear? If only she could discuss this with Tommy. But he was at home with his wife.

She sat down with coffee and briefcase at the kitchen table. Jessie immediately hopped in her lap. If this was a trick on Cynthia's part—to keep Clare quiet about the files—it had worked.

Was there something in those files Cynthia wanted to keep hidden? Clare opened her briefcase to stare at the scarf-bound folders, then hurried into the living room to paw through boxes and returned with a pair of thin rubber gloves. Now she examined and compared the three files exactingly. Each folder contained the expected records of exams and medications, surgical procedures and repercussions; descriptions of current treatments and extrapolations about future avenues to explore. She came to the same conclusion she'd reached after yesterday's quick perusal: there was nothing unusual in nor obviously missing from any of the three.

Another dead end. She rewrapped the files in the scarf, hid them in the back corner of her bedroom closet, then rushed around to get ready to return to the lab: she had time to make another tape before Tommy joined her.

She tried not to notice Jessie sitting in the hallway, watching her exit. The cat's life had narrowed considerably: no one home except to sleep and not always then; no way to go outside; and now that she was waddling, no mountain of dry food to flatten. Clare dropped her briefcase and plopped down on the floor, waving a length of packing string to invite Jessie to come and play. Ten minutes later, Jessie was curling up on the couch to sleep and Clare could head out with a clearer conscience.

On the street, Beaudine's current watcher regarded her with terminal boredom. Would the poor man still be stuck out here if an arrest were imminent?

Walking across campus, the sun was so low and the light so golden, Clare checked her watch: 7:30. She'd never been here quite so early, except long ago, departing after working all night. Amazing, the number of early risers on the grounds. She also thought she recognized several night shift security guards, though they looked quite different in sunlight.

As she opened her office door and hit the light switch in one rote maneuver, it registered that a faint light came from inside her lab. Her locked desk drawer yawned open, exposing data on her current murder tests with Tommy; files from her cabinet were piled on her chair. On her desk was a drawer key she recognized as the one she'd given Steve—the key Deirdre had sworn she didn't have. Deirdre.

There was Clare's assistant, standing frozen in the lab doorway, holding a flashlight and a box of tachistoscope slides.

"Dr. Austen. I know you said I shouldn't come in here alone and I'm sure you're mad and I don't blame you. But please hear me out. I only wanted to understand what we're doing here in the lab and I—"

Clare slammed the exit door behind her. "Cut the crap, Deirdre. You're spying for him and now you're going to tell me why. Talk fast."

"I—he—we're just interested in what research you're doing. You don't like to discuss it so . . ."

Deirdre's voice faded as Clare examined the files piled on her chair. "You're especially interested in my current tests with Tommy. Steve knew I mistrusted him so he figured you'd have a better chance. Don't give me that confused look, I know about you and Steve. Or do you really expect me to believe it was just a coincidence he brought his girlfriend in to replace him, right before he disappeared? Stop insulting my intelligence and tell me why he's so interested in my work." Clare leaned against the door, pretending to block the exit in case Deirdre tried to flee, but really to regain equilibrium. The balance of power had just shifted, she could feel it. Deirdre had momentarily looked confused, then unburdened, and now poised.

Still, when Deirdre spoke, she sounded shaken and tentative. "I don't really know what Steve wants to find out. He told me to learn everything I could, and he wouldn't let me question him about it. He just said I had to trust him, that he was in a bind and I was the only one who could help him. It was like I didn't care about him if I didn't operate on blind faith. So—I did. Unfortunately, because I don't know what I'm looking for, I haven't been able to tell him anything he was satisfied to hear."

Clare sensed factual elements in the story, but there were definitely fictions as well. "Get Steve on the phone. Right now!" she shouted when Deirdre hesitated.

"I can't! I can't!" Was Deirdre buying time as she paced the room, turmoil evident? "I don't know where he is. He calls me around eight at night. Not always, but I stay home then just in case. Sometimes the connection is bad like long distance and sometimes it's not. He hasn't called in three days, I don't even know what that means."

Clare moved toward her desk, but Deirdre's attention shifted to the door. "If you run now, you'll have to keep running." Deirdre threw herself onto the couch like a teenager who'd just been grounded.

Clare picked up her phone and found Beaudine still at home. Hearing the urgency in her voice, he simply said, "I'm on my way." Twenty minutes later, he arrived and, after Clare explained why she'd called, he took Deirdre into the hall for questioning.

Stuck in her office, Clare first put away the files Deirdre had gotten out: they included all records on Tommy, murder related or no; several folders on Mrs. Bates; and a few previous, now closed, subjects—no pattern was obvious in Deirdre's choices. Then, sitting at her desk, Clare struggled to plan the tape she had come in to make, but couldn't concentrate with Beaudine and Deirdre's voices rising and falling beyond the door.

She picked up the interdepartmental transit envelope that had tripped Tommy outside her door earlier. She began to imagine his homecoming, forcibly detoured her attention: this side of the large square transit envelope was blank; the other side would have fifty "deliver to" lines. It was reusable up to fifty times: you crossed out your name, wrote a new recipient's name, and campus mail did the rest. Clare enjoyed reading the names preceeding hers, studying the patterns: who sent to whom and how often. It was mindless, but entertaining. She flipped the envelope over.

All previous names had been obliterated by a heavy black felt marker. She dropped the envelope. Too late. Her fingerprints had to be all over it. She should let Beaudine open it—but Deirdre's voice sounded tearful; it sounded like a bad time to interrupt. Clare went to get the cotton gloves she used when handling tachistoscope slides. She felt far more curiosity than fear. At times Lieutenant Beaudine might seem inept, but it certainly helped to have him just outside her door.

Within the interdepartmental envelope was a layer of Bubble Pak, wrapped around another envelope: bright green and orange; it was a junk mailer that showed up periodically. *Uncover the secrets of the universe and receive a free beach blanket*, embossed letters promised. It was a come-on for a video science series. She and Robert used to laugh about it, envisioning a related T-shirt: I UNCOVERED THE SECRETS OF THE UNIVERSE AND ALL I GOT WAS THIS CRUMMY T-SHIRT.

Oh, God, had Robert left those black markered notes? No,

this mailer showing up now could easily be a coincidence. Everyone on campus received them, periodically—students, faculty, and staff. Come to think of it, she'd seen them in the trash bin at her old apartment complex, too.

By now she had the Bubble Pak unwrapped and the envelope flap lifted. She could feel a bulge inside, hard as metal or wood. Perhaps it wasn't a horrible note, but a gift from Robert, trying to make amends.

She extracted a folded piece of paper with black spots where the heavy ink had bled through. She unfolded it, already knowing what it said. This one was a little different: STOP OR YOU DIE TWO. Robert couldn't be the author, he wasn't semiliterate like this jerk. She jammed her fingers into the mailer envelope to extract the bulge.

In her palm was a delicate antique silver and marcasite hair clip in the shape of a parrot. The clip held a thick hank of black hair, with a brownish red, leathery patch at one end. Even before she was fully aware of what she held, she began screaming.

In retrospect, she could recall how Beaudine smashed into the room; how Deirdre followed, hesitantly; how curious faces soon appeared in the doorway. A hand gripped her shoulder, shook it; she continued to scream. Another hand made her drop the object and covered it, but she could nonetheless see it, feel it. It was the hair clip she'd given Lalitha, with the murdered woman's hair still in place, and a section of her scalp, clotted with blood, at one end.

Clare clutched at the hand gripping her shoulder. Beaudine drew her to her feet and vised his arms around her. Eventually, she stopped shaking. He sat her on the couch and shut the door on the faces peering at her.

Deirdre had her own fit when she learned what Clare had received. Beaudine took her into the lab until she stopped flailing and shrieking. Clare heard him questioning the girl for a time, then he escorted a quivering, pink-cheeked Deirdre back through the office and out, warning her not to speak with any of those still congregating in the corridor.

He slipped on Clare's gloves, though they barely covered his thick fingers; and gathered the components of the package to take in for analysis. While he did this, he questioned Clare. Between gulps for air, she explained what the hair clip was and how she had received it that morning. She couldn't speak for a time, realizing the murderer had been less than five feet away at some point last night, while she and Tommy slept on this couch. Would they have awakened in time, if the killer had come in?

"You've thought of something."

Clare began an explanation, but after a time, noticed that Beaudine was lost in thought, staring at the grisly package. "Are you even listening to me?"

"Outside envelope's addressed to 'Dr. Clare,' inside one says 'Mr. Dabrowski.' Who calls you Dr. Clare?"

"No one. I didn't notice that, frankly."

He unfolded the note. "Stop or you die, t-w-o. This a misspelling of the 'too' that means 'also,' or's it supposed to mean the two of you will die?"

"How the hell should I know?" His tone, his attitude, were suggesting something incomprehensible. "You think Tommy and I wrote these notes, don't you?"

He regarded her blankly. "Do I?"

"Which means you must also think we're the killer. Killers. Of all the hideous, moronic. Aaahh!" she yelled, then began to cry. Beaudine remained impassive. "I loved Lalitha. I could never have. Oh God. Lalitha." She choked.

"Dr. Austen." His voice was soft. She looked up and found traces of sympathy in his eyes. "You have to understand. Anybody who's not dead is a suspect."

Clare recovered enough to feel her skin crawl. "Did the murder victims receive threats?"

"Not that we've been able to determine." He revealed information as if each word cost a year of his life.

"Why are we being warned instead of killed?"

He relaxed back into her chair. "Now there's one I was hoping you could tell me."

"Were you able to find out anything about the other notes we received—or the nails in my tire?" His shrug infuriated her. "Or about the man who held us at gunpoint? What about the man who threatened Tommy's wife? The accidents Tommy's been having, that may not be accidents? Don't you know anything?"

With this, she went too far. His expression caused her to appreciate Tommy's fear of the police. "I mean," she amended, "anything that you can tell me? Did you get any information from Deirdre?" He shook his head. "How did she get in here? Did Steve give her that key after telling me he'd lost it?" Beaudine shrugged. "Steve has an uncle in Daly City who might help you find him."

Beaudine watched her minutely. "Steve is in the middle of a murder investigation and he's not stupid. He knows he'd be in deep hot substance if he left town without my approval." His tone made him sound like a doting older brother.

"Oh." Nonplussed, she became captious. "Where is he? I need to talk to him."

"Why?"

"Because he's spying on me, dammit. I want to know why."

"How's your investigation of Dabrowski's brain going?"

His condescension was galling. "I sent you a list of what we've learned so far. I'd hoped to get some response from you about that. Instead, I heard a rumor that you're close to arresting Dr. Colton's killer. What about the other murders? Or is one out of four the best that can be hoped for?"

"Where did you hear this rumor?"

"Around. Is it true?"

"Why would I want to tell you police business?" he mused.

"Because if it's true, Tommy and I can stop trying to name the killer."

"You got a point. No, you go ahead and keep trying." His manner was so offhand it was unreadable.

"If the rumor were true," she pressed, "would that suspect be wanted for all four killings?"

"We're not in danger of leaving an extra psycho on the streets once we wrap this up, no," Beaudine said affably. The phone rang. On the second ring, he answered. "Austen's office. . . . Yeah this is Beaudine. . . . Yeah she's here but she's busy right now. . . . Are you alright?" he asked Clare, then replied before she could react, "Seems to be hanging in there. . . . Sure I'll tell her. . . . Same to you." He hung up. "That was Dabrowski. He's going to be late."

"Since when do you screen my calls?"

"Only trying to help. Seemed like you weren't in a condition to answer it." He stretched and collected his new evidence. "Who has access to these intercampus envelopes?"

"Just about anyone." She relived opening the mailer and moaned. "Tell me when you find out anything about this. *Please*."

"I can almost promise, you'll be the first to know."

With that he was gone, leaving Clare shaking, and trying to pinpoint what about his exiting manner had seemed so very ominous. Perhaps it was simply that he was gone, that Clare was alone, with no distractions.

She stumbled into the lab, fumbled through making a tape, but each minute alone was more oppressive. The package and its import smothered her, as though the air had turned to Bubble Pak plastic. She had to get outside, had to be around people. Anyone, so long as she wasn't alone.

It was nearly ten. How late was Tommy going to be? What could she do in the meantime? She could try to locate Steve, she concluded, then ask him why he'd gotten Deirdre to act as a spy. Clare locked up, left a note for Tommy, and set out on a Steve hunt. She would check back now and again to see if Tommy had arrived.

She started at the Biology office, going the long way around to avoid Dr. Colton's hall. She copied Steve's schedule of classes; then visited his professors and questioned three separate yet identical administrators. Where he was, no one could—or would—say to her. She was in such a state, trying to not think about the morning's events, that at first she didn't notice how she was received. But finally, as she sat on a courtyard bench watching passersby and wondering what to try next, she began to recall fragments of conversations, reactions, expressions.

Of course it was all innuendo, *sotto voce*, double entendre. But she'd been part of this so-called intellectual community long enough to read between their lines: among her peers, she had become an object of suspicion, aversion, and contempt. Much of it was gleeful, for in the past, she had competed with the most ambitious of them, spoken out against the most pompous of them, retaliated against the most vicious of them. And once having engaged, she would always be considered a part of the game. Which in turn made her fair game.

She thought of that transit envelope. Anyone could obtain one, affiliated with the university or no. But could it be that the murderer was not just preying on lab coats—as Tommy called them—but used one, too? So many of Clare's peers were willing to destroy with subtle words, refined sabotage. Had someone taken it further?

No longer did she feel safer, surrounded by people. Most of those in the courtyard were just students; but then, baby rattlers have the most venomous bites.

Still, she couldn't bring herself to return to the isolation of her office. So, envisioning herself as a moving target, she bustled around campus, aimlessly—until, passing the monolithic library building, she recalled that she'd once seen Steve chatting familiarly with a library clerk. Perhaps the clerk would know Steve's current whereabouts.

Perhaps. However, the clerk was not at work today, she soon

learned. Exiting the library, she walked up the cement ramp across the moat, turned a corner—and there was Robert.

At some point they realized they were stock still and staring, which led to feigned smiles. Clare thought about walking on. As she concentrated on trying to get her feet to move, Robert said, "This is both easier and harder than I'd expected. Seeing you for the first time, that is. How—have you been?"

If she told him she would cry; or scream. "Not terrible. Busy. And yourself?"

"Making sense of it all. And worrying about you. It's odd, suddenly being on the outside of your life—people have been speaking to me differently. And disturbing me, with the amount of hostility that exists towards you at present. I can't win: if I defend you, I'm carrying a torch; if I prove they're misinformed, I'm still blinded by love." He seemed to wish he'd answered "fine thanks," instead. "I take it you and Tommy haven't solved this thing yet."

She shook her head. "And I've been so immersed—in that effort, I've only just discovered the hostility you're talking about." She explained her Steve hunt, and the disturbing reactions she'd encountered. "What are they saying about me, Robert? Do you have any idea why? No, please tell me. I need to know."

They were blocking the library exit, it became belatedly apparent to them. Three students with freshman timidity hovered across the ramp, waiting for these professors to move. "Let's walk," Robert suggested, and they made a partial circuit of the library, eventually sitting on the cement edging the library's shallow tiled moat. Meanwhile, Robert reviewed the anti-Clare sentiment. "I believe it has several origins. Fear about the murders makes everyone think—crookedly. You're in the limelight closer to the center of the investigation and thus a more convenient lightning rod for discontent about quick publicity and slow results. This has gotten mixed up with rumors that you and Tommy know something or are advising the police or withholding information—here the stories get confused, you see. Further, there's gossip that you and a research subject are . . . involved. Fueled by the news that we're no longer living together."

Even with such subject matter, his deft, precise analysis of facts could calm her.

He reflected a moment. "I've defended you, and not blindly. We both made mistakes; I behaved in a particularly ugly manner towards the last." He seemed to want her to deny this. When she didn't, he sighed. "You were—still are—under great pressure and what did I do? I reacted viciously. I see now that you would never be so flighty or fickle as to move right on to Tommy—whether or not there's any hope of our getting back together. I also see that it wasn't an easy or unmeasured decision for you to move out. This has been a time of revelations for me, I hope it's been as fruitful for you. However, I'm not fishing for any kind of response. I didn't intend to get into any of this, but I've been doing so much thinking about it; you know how I get."

Incapable of moving, much less speaking, Clare stared at the turquoise moat tiles. Finally she said, "I haven't been privy to any revelations. I can see we have a lot left to talk about, to sort out, but I can't do that yet. I appreciate your defending me; at the same time I wish you wouldn't. I'll go back in my shell until the killer's caught, then campus opinion won't matter until I'm able to face it. God I hate them, haven't they got anything better to do than . . ." She stopped short. It was of course herself she hated. Flighty, fickle, a coward, and a liar.

"The worst part of all is how we used to love a good rumor, ourselves." They shared a sort of chuckle. "There is something you should be aware of. Bob Lantz was playing handball with Julie Robitaille and Sid Stein. And Sid mentioned, as though it were common knowledge, that because of some supposed longstanding hatred of Colton, and jealousy of Lalitha, if the police didn't initially think you were such a frightened mousy type, they'd already have you locked up for those murders."

"Oh. My. God."

"Neither Bob nor Julie understood why Sid would spread such garbage. That's one rumor you can ignore—no one will believe it. But you seem to have quite an enemy in Sid Stein. Do you have any idea why? I've rarely heard you mention him."

Clare's fingers scraped raw as she clutched the concrete, trying to stop the world from gyrating, her thoughts from flailing. How vindictive was Sid Stein? And why? Could it be Sid who had sent the black-markered notes? Or was he simply privy to Beaudine's plans? Had Mrs. Bates told the truth? Would Clare be taken into custody soon? Would she then be safer than she was out here, where all she knew was how little she understood?

Robert was watching her with some alarm. "I shouldn't have told you. It's really nothing for you to concern yourself with right now, Clare."

She had to make Robert stop staring. "I'm glad you told me. Well, 'glad' is the wrong word. I've got to get back, though. I'm —late meeting Tommy for testing. Thank you for being so honest with me." Each new word sounded lamer than the last.

"I miss—" Robert cut himself off, with chagrin.

Clare touched his arm, then stood. "So do I," she said softly, and realized it was true. She did miss his presence in her life. A new source of confusion, as though she needed any others. She waited for him to stand, too.

"I'll just sit here for a while, I think. Good-bye, Clare."

She headed off abruptly, feeling him watching her departure. She nearly ran to her office.

Tommy was standing outside her door, frowning. "Oh thank Christ," she moaned, embracing him in full view of a group of lab coats down the hall. She nearly fell into her office. Tommy locked the door and joined her on the couch.

She told him what had transpired since they'd separated that morning. It took over an hour for her to relay the information, and for both of them to recover from it. Tommy's distress about Bianca's suffering threats while alone was nothing compared to his reaction now. Clare filed away this knowledge for some future time when she was capable of pleasure.

Eventually, they noted that the murderer could keep them from progressing without killing them: they could readily envision reaching a point where they so feared the next communiqué that they would be incapacitated. But for now, the package made them more determined to catch the bastard. And so they analyzed every aspect of Clare's morning, concluding with Robert's warnings. Clare suggested, "Mrs. Bates may have been telling the truth after all. It's so insane. But it could be that Beaudine *is* about to arrest someone—me."

"Or us. Since you're the scared mousy type, I have to help you kill them." Tommy was able to find this amusing, for a second.

"Somehow that's strangely comforting." She studied her hands. "Why were you so late? Bianca?"

He stopped petting her hair. "That's putting it mildly."

"About us?" She could feel his nod but couldn't stop staring at her hands. "Do you want to tell me about it?"

He lay down with his head in her lap; perhaps this wasn't intended to force her to look at him. "When I walked in she was on the phone, in real bad shape. She said, 'Here he is now,' hung up, and then blammo. She started hysterical and took off from there. I've told you how she gets, you've seen little versions of it. Multiply that by the deficit, that's how much worse this was. I didn't have a lot to say in my own defense—nothing, to be exact —so I just listened. Watched. Ducked. I thought I was going to lose my mind when I called here to say I'd be late and Beaudine answered. Even though he said you were okay, all I wanted was to get over here right away, but at that point I couldn't leave. I seriously believed she might kill herself—and Bianca has never been big on pain." He squeezed his eyes shut.

Clare waited, then prompted, "I take it the situation improved."

He kissed her stomach, sat up, entwined around her. "After I called here, everything changed. She talked real rationally about why I'd taken up with you, what was wrong with our marriage. Have to give her credit, she's noticed more than I thought. But after I agreed with her and added a couple more points, she must've bawled for an hour. She wasn't the only one watering the rug, either. Then she decided she needed to get away for a while and called her gym to get in on a trip they're taking, some aerobics weekend sabbatical thing. At which point I got extremely pissed."

"Because Andy's going to be there?"

"No, no, because I couldn't put my finger on how but I was sure she was faking, sure she'd decided to go way before now. I don't know why she'd bother to pretend but it turned everything we'd just gone through into a game."

"Not necessarily. I'd guess that she's frightened, and wants to protect herself, but doesn't want to admit that to you."

"I can see that," he said at length. "Guess she couldn't play any scene totally straight. She's always got to have that little edge. So. How was it seeing Robert?"

Clare heard his voice stiffen. She allowed herself a second's clandestine pleasure that Tommy was unsure of her response. "It was like running into somebody I used to sort of know but hadn't seen in ages. Which made it strange that—" She stopped but not soon enough.

Tommy examined her face, searching for the whole truth as he waited for her to continue.

She hated Bianca for being a dissembler. It forced her to be otherwise. "I realized that, in some ways, I miss him, too."

Before he looked away, his eyes displayed empathy. And injury. "There'd be something wrong with you if you didn't. If you could just walk away, not look back."

They kissed, tentatively, then held one another, fiercely. There was a knock at the door. "Who is it?" Clare called, unable to keep her voice from quavering.

"I'm looking for Dr. Maxwell," an unidentifiable voice announced.

"Two doors down." The footsteps receded but Clare felt no less exposed. "I haven't seen anyone following us—not since the night Hugo questioned us. Do you think there could be a connection?"

"Probably, but don't ask me. My brains don't make connections. Think Beaudine will let us keep testing after he arrests us?"

"He won't—he can't arrest us. He couldn't be that stupid."

"He doesn't have to be stupid. Hopeless and pressured would do it."

"I still can't believe he could convince himself we're guilty."

"Yeah. Me neither," Tommy agreed slowly. "Course, if he did bust us we wouldn't have to go in there anymore." He grimaced toward the lab. "Or out there." He waved the world away.

"I appreciate your helping me look on the bright side."

"There is one piece of good news. Bianca's gone. Until Tuesday morning. So I don't even have to go home to check in. Unless you want me to."

"What do you think?"

He leaned over to his jacket, folded on the floor alongside the couch. He fished in a pocket, extracted a toothbrush, displayed it with equal parts swagger and shyness. Then he pulled out a bottle that had been wrapped in the jacket. Champagne. "We're going to solve the murders tonight so we can celebrate this weekend."

"Or if not, at least we'll have a consolation prize."

"Hold on there, Clare, I'm the one who's supposed to say stuff like that."

"I'm just a little disappointed that Beaudine may intend to arrest us, that's all."

"We'll prove him wrong. Or you will." Tommy led her into the lab, after checking the deadbolt on the outside door. "I know I've ragged on you in the past but that was because I was afraid I'd let you down. We've been hitting the wall lately but you'll break through it. We just can't give up, that's all." He kissed her and sat her down at her testing station. "I was thinking about how you ask my right brain which body parts are more important. Maybe you should ask it which experiments to go further with, you know? Maybe you can get it to say, 'getting warmer, getting colder.'"

"That's definitely worth a try. Let's finish up the test we started yesterday and I'll think about how to do that." A week ago, Clare would have been thrilled by yesterday's results—by Tommy's right brain decreeing that the killer was *not a stranger, not a friend*. But at this point she expected to dead end when she tried to determine who that not a stranger was.

Nevertheless, she dichotically ran through the short list of possibilities: **"Is the killer in the hallway Mrs. Bates? . . . Is Steve the killer? . . . Is the killer Hugo?"** rephrasing each question several times. Meanwhile, on the screen flashed YES or NO and Tommy pulled the levers to indicate his responses. NO every time, as he'd answered previously. Why had she even asked the questions again? Probably to avoid the results when she made a few weak grasps at new straws.

From their nighttime security escorts, she'd learned that Bruce the security guard had disappeared, right after he'd brought the fake cops to Clare's office. **"Bruce the security guard. Is he the killer?"** NO.

Deirdre was spying on Clare and many of the papers she'd had out that morning involved the murder experiments. She wasn't tall enough to be the one they'd encountered in the hall —but who knew if any of their data were correct? Therefore: **"Did Deirdre have the knife in the hall?"** NO.

"Is Sid Stein the killer?" NO. Clare felt a pang of disappointment with that last negative response, but no surprise. Sid's going out of his way to spread nasty rumors about her was not much evidence for murder.

Yesterday when she'd tested right brain comprehension of *not a stranger*, she'd overlooked one possible wrinkle. Tommy's right hemisphere classified people never met nor seen as strangers.

But what about people he'd encountered but didn't know? She motioned for him to remove the headset, while laying out YES and NO cards in reach of his left foot.

"I don't want to take the time to make a tape to ask you these questions," she said. "This new test has to do with the possibility that you are acquainted with the killer. I'm telling you this because I don't want to waste time waiting for you to get mad, once the line of questioning becomes clear."

As hoped, he reacted with chagrin. The goal was to shame his left brain into remaining cooperative.

"Ready? Good. You'll touch a card to answer each question. Is the man who attacked me in the parking lot a stranger?" NO. "So that man is not a stranger?" YES. "Is Lalitha not a stranger?" After a pause, his left foot tapped YES.

She asked a few more questions, confirming the wrinkle she'd previously overlooked: anyone that Tommy's right brain had encountered, dead or alive, was no longer considered a stranger. "Put the headset back on, please, Tommy."

For a long moment he seemed about to speak, but ultimately complied without a word. She queued the tape for her final prepared set of questions, variations on one theme: **"Is the surfer attacker the killer?"** These questions had been the toughest to prepare, because his right brain didn't comprehend *deranged*, and long descriptive phrases like "the man who attacked Clare in the parking lot" caused technical problems, dichotically. However, she did believe she'd formulated at least three successful ways to ask the question. But each time, the answer was NO.

Clare fought an internal war: if she weren't so ready to admit defeat, she'd be able to see new avenues to take; no, the answer would elude her no matter what. Meanwhile, operating via rote memory of clinical techniques, she asked Tommy's right brain which lines of testing should be pursued further. She showed his right brain examples of each test they had done, then asked question after question, phrased and rephrased, about the usefulness of continuing each test. The YES and NO answers appeared on the tachistoscope. Dutifully, she recorded the hesitant, unenlightening and seemingly random responses his right brain gave by pulling the levers. Why she hid these answers from his left brain, she couldn't say. Both his hemispheres were cooperative today. It was her brain that was causing the problems.

The fact was, she was giving up. She had given up yesterday, when even the Ouija board came to naught; but she was admitting it only now. At least the killer would be happy: no more threatening notes would be needed to get them to stop.

Tommy disrupted her brooding. "Uh, Clare. What's going on with you?"

"Roadblock, stalemate, impasse. I've tried everything I know how to try. I don't know what else to do. Most frustrating of all, I feel like the answer's in here, somewhere." She slapped her notebook. "But I can't find it. I just can't see it."

"Maybe it's not there. Maybe that's why. Maybe my right brain doesn't really know enough to give us a name, after all."

According to her studies of his LEMs, he was confabulating. Which should she distrust, her admittedly shaky LEMs data or Tommy? In lieu of screaming, she started to cry.

From across the room he reached for her and without drawing nearer she felt his touch. "Would it help if we went through your notes together?"

It hadn't done any good to hide them from his left brain. "I don't see that it could hurt, anyway." She dragged her chair and notes over to his table.

For the next few hours, they went through them all, line by line by page by page. So much data; how could it add up to so little? Here and there Tommy would find an interpretation she hadn't considered; she would formulate a few more questions; his right brain would make a few more inscrutable replies. By the time they reached the last page, Tommy was astonished she'd discovered so much without his awareness; and impressed with her ingenuity. She was glad he still thought well of her, but it didn't mitigate the reality: her cleverness had gotten them nowhere.

She closed the notebook. He took her hand and they stared at the back cover. "I might come up with something else to try, later. But this is definitely it for now. As Dr. Colton told me when my first big research project fell apart, sometimes straight lines lead to labyrinths, and sometimes those mazes have no exit but your starting point, and sometimes you're lucky to even make it back to that point."

"Terminate." Tommy went around the lab shutting off equipment. "Sometimes you can build your own mazes, too. We're taking the weekend off. Pack your bags, woman, we're moving on."

Getting away from the lab lost some appeal when they called for a guard escort. A water main had burst over in Engineering and all available guards were involved. It would be at least ninety minutes before an escort could be freed.

It was only five o'clock—just turning dark. And the guards were congregated halfway between Clare's lab and her car. So they opted against waiting for an escort.

For Clare, the journey to the parking lot was a tour of murder and failure. No longer feeling she had purpose in Neurobiology, with every step she felt Colton's bloody carpet tugging at her shoes. Once outside, over there in that courtyard was where she'd last spoken with Lalitha, along with Mrs. Bates. It was the penultimate time Clare had seen the hair clip. Just up there were the koi ponds where pieces of Larry's corpse had been scattered. Ah, there was her Nova. She hadn't thought she could make it this far. Her strength was eroding, her nerve had failed her. Even her fear was no longer accessible. As they had walked, she had sensed Tommy's alertness to that echoing step behind them; his awareness of each long shadow shifting beside them. But she had been incapable of paying heed, herself.

"We made it," Tommy announced to the parking lot.

"Now what?" Clare asked, as Tommy waited for her to unlock her car. She was having trouble finding her keys. He took her purse, shook it, gave it back to her to hold while he dug his good hand in and extracted her keys. When she continued to stand there, he unlocked her door and helped her get inside. "Now you drive me to my car," he said softly, touching her cheek.

They drove separately to her apartment. Tommy gestured for her to park behind Beaudine's watcher, then drove her to a supermarket to buy supplies: groceries, wine, condoms, coffee; and a catnip mouse for Jessie. Back at Clare's, he instructed her to put away the supplies while he fed Jess and started dinner. Then he reluctantly assigned her food preparation chores—he couldn't chop and dice with one hand.

Clare gladly put herself on automatic and obeyed Tommy's commands. Not thinking yet keeping busy was exactly what she needed; by the time they were sitting down to a dinner of wine and pasta, she was refreshed emotionally and had regrouped mentally. Most restorative of all was the realization that Tommy had figured out what she needed; and also sensed when to stop playing commander. By the time she was restored, he'd resumed being a partner, not a boss.

They did the dishes then adjourned to the couch, to sip wine, kiss, and watch Jessie harass the catnip mouse. To convince themselves that no other reality existed.

The phone rang. Tommy flipped a coin and it came up heads, meaning Clare did have to answer. It was Mrs. Manning, who chastised Clare for making her call 411 to get her new tenant's number. (How nice. The phone company had now listed Clare's *new* unlisted phone number.) But that wasn't why Mrs. Manning was calling. There was a Lieutenant Beaudine downstairs, wanting to see Clare but unable to reach her, due to the iron gate, which he wouldn't allow Mrs. Manning to unlock for him.

"Are you here to arrest us?" Clare greeted Beaudine, reassured to see his obligatory sidekick look briefly amused.

"Should I be?"

Clare responded, "Would either of you like some wine? Coffee? Here, at least let me clear you a seat." Seeing the room through Beaudine's eyes, she was humiliated. It was messier now than it had been the night of the break-in and Hugo's advent.

"What can we do for you?" Tommy inquired once the cops were off their feet. Beaudine's eyebrow raised at the "we." Clare took a quick gulp of wine.

"From whom did you hear the rumors of your impending arrest?" Beaudine kept shifting his gaze from Clare's eyes to hands to jaw to eyes, until Jessie sprinted across his shoes. He glanced at the cat and this gave Clare private time to formulate her answer.

"I pieced them together, actually. I'd heard bits of information from Deirdre; from Robert—Dr. di Marchese; for that matter, from a variety of people around campus. First I heard you were close to making an arrest, then that the motive was an old grudge, then that people were claiming, falsely, that I'd been feuding with Dr. Colton for years. It all seemed to add up to your targeting me."

Beaudine grunted and scrutinized Tommy. "Any new accidents?"

Tommy shook his head. "We're not being followed anymore, either. Or they're getting a lot sneakier at it."

"How's the research going?"

"Moving along," Tommy said, at the same time Clare replied, "Dead ended."

Beaudine looked from one to the other, sagely. "How's the police investigation going?" Tommy inquired politely.

"The same," he admitted, then smiled inscrutably as he noted the look of surprise they exchanged at his apparent forthrightness. He and the sidekick stood.

"That's it? That's all you wanted to ask? Why did you come

here?" Clare kept revising—trying to sound chummy, not suspicious—with poor results.

"We were in the neighborhood." He opened the front door.

"What have you found out about the latest note?"

"We never know anything this soon." He shut the door behind him.

The iron grill snapped shut downstairs. "What the hell was that about?" Clare demanded of the room at large.

Jessie batted the fraying mouse back into view, pounced, found a weak point and ripped it open. Catnip flew. She alternated wallowing in the crumbled twigs and shredding the gray fabric casing. "I know exactly how that mouse feels," Tommy said.

Clare got the wine bottle from the kitchen and refilled their glasses. "Let's pretend he didn't happen." She looked around the room and sighed. Somehow the shredded cat toy made the whole mess unbearable.

"Tomorrow we're moving you in," Tommy vowed. "Tonight, we're forgetting everything happened. Except this." He gave her a long deep kiss, guaranteed to produce amnesia. Then she took his hand and led him into the bedroom.

Undressing one another, they set a slowness record. Although now more adept at removing each other's clothing, they also took more time to kiss and caress each inch of flesh exposed. Sensation built upon sensation until Clare was no longer aware whether they were standing or prone, whether Tommy was licking her wrist or kissing her breast. She could taste his voice, feel his scent enveloping her, see her own love and pleasure mirrored in his eyes. Gradually, eventually, the sensations began to recede and separate, until she was aware of him lying beside her, fingers stroking her arm, exhalations tickling her ear.

He whispered her name as though it were a secret they shared. She shifted to look at him, a laugh or sob catching in her throat. "I'm going to nod off any second," he said apologetically.

"So am I," she assured him. He rolled onto his back; she helped him straighten his sling, then shut off the light and lay beside him. He found her hand, entwined his fingers, threw one leg over hers. "Lucid dreaming exercises," she reminded him.

"I thought you were giving up on our investigation," he teased.

"Oh. I forgot." She considered. "Well do them anyway."

"Yes, massah. Although there's no way I'm going to be dreaming about murder tonight. I'm going to dream I'm the size of an ant, spending my life wandering around on . . ." She waited for him to finish, instead heard his breathing grow more shallow and regular. He was asleep. And she had lied—she was nowhere near joining him.

Without Tommy to distract her, she started thinking: about their failed investigation, her encounter with Robert, Beaudine's visit, Bianca's weekend away. With each new topic, restlessness grew, for looming behind each of these unpleasant thoughts were other, unthinkable ones. She wanted to get up and pace, but if she did she'd awaken Tommy. Damn, she was going to be awake all night. Panicky, she cut off new thoughts as they began to sprout, but newer ones kept replacing them. She tried to mimic Tommy's breathing. That helped a bit. She reviewed their activities before he'd fallen asleep, and that helped a little more. Jessie jumped onto the bed and settled purring alongside Clare's ear. The rhythmic rumbling filled her head and at last she drifted off, counting kisses.

Come morning, she awakened feeling delirious, realized Tommy was kissing her knees, working his way up from her toes. Jessie sat on Clare's other side, watching somberly. "Good morning," Tommy greeted her and went back to work, then stopped, meeting Jessie's gaze. "Jessie do you mind? It's really rude to stare."

A few more halfhearted kisses and he looked at Jessie again. "We have two options," Clare informed him. "Get used to it or get up and feed her. It won't do any good to shoo her away, she'll come back. If we shut her out, she'll scratch at the door."

Tommy jumped out of bed, took Clare's hand, drew her up to stand beside him. "So let's go feed the little assbite."

They escorted each other to the kitchen. Clare poured food and Tommy set it down, then petted Jessie with sarcasm and affection. On their way back to the bedroom, Clare remembered she had to change Jessie's water. Reluctantly, Tommy let her go, then upon her return, ambushed and tackled her onto the couch, to make love while laughing—and shivering in the unheated room.

Afterward, they lay smiling and shivering. "Why are you staring at my leg?" Clare inquired.

"Thousands of goosebumps on this thigh alone." Tommy jumped up to turn on the heat, returned to announce, "I have to kiss you for every bump. One." Kiss. "Two." Kiss. They were in the twenties when, "Uh oh I lost count. Guess I'll have to start over."

"Don't bother counting—every time you kiss me I get more bumps anyway. We'll never catch up."

"Cool," Tommy started kissing her again frantically, until she was laughing so hard she was gasping. Then they lay quietly, inhaling the other's exhales.

When he started humming, she asked eagerly, "What are you singing?"

" 'Got me a lady doctor, she cures the pain for free, mm mmm mm lady doctor, no there ain't nothing wrong with me,' " he sang suggestively.

Clare was mortified. "Oh. I thought it would be a clue."

"Ha! The will to investigate returns."

"I wouldn't say that, but—oh. Did you have any dreams?" He shook his head and darkened until she kissed him lightly. "Let's not think about it. Any of it. Let's just pretend this weekend will last forever." Which got her thinking about Bianca. She turned away from him. "I could use some coffee."

After caffeine and food, they commenced housecleaning and unpacking. Clare hadn't brought much with her but it took hours to put it away—Tommy had to examine every item as though it contained the key to her soul. At some points she cringed at his discovery of her secret banalities, at other points she relished his interest in such discoveries.

During these enterprises they remained naked, with which Clare gradually grew comfortable, for it was obvious that Tommy was embarrassed too; and despite such discomforts, it made even housekeeping erotic.

In fact they didn't get dressed again for three days, Clare realized in retrospect, although during that period she lost all track of time. They kept the curtains closed and the lights on while they made love and lay around together; cooked and ate; played with Jessie. Clare hadn't noticed how nervous the cat had been these last few weeks, until she realized that now Jessie was behaving like the old Jess.

"Know what this feels like?" Tommy asked at one point, as they sprawled on the living room floor going through Clare's childhood photo album, exchanging questions and answers about their pasts. "When I was a kid there was this orchard behind our house where I'd build tent forts and hide out. Cardboard and sheets over branches, a little breeze and the fort blew down, but me 'n' Dick would lie in there and tell everything we knew. I never felt so close to anybody—until now."

Tuesday a big wind would hit their tent. "I didn't realize you and Dick had been friends all your lives."

He looked disappointed at this response but replied, "Not so much these days, like I explained before. Although a few months ago when Ilsa kicked him out, Bianca was away and we stayed up talking all night and that was great."

"Ilsa kicked Dick out? I can't even imagine them fighting." This news upset her inordinately. Once again, she'd been completely wrong in an assessment.

"Man they've separated so many times. They keep going back

and trying some more though. Gotta hand it to them, they don't give up."

This made them both very quiet. "I hate thinking of them fighting," Clare said at last. "I hardly know them but somehow I was setting them up as—a goal, in some way."

"I get that. When it's working between them it really works." He touched her chin, forcing her to look at him. "I've got different goals though." He kissed her hard, as though to suffocate all her doubts.

They returned to Clare's baby pictures, with Tommy delivering a running commentary. "Here she is, queen of the first grade. I've got to have a copy of that one. Uh oh, storm warnings. 'Give me another new toy or else!' Hey, I like the shorts here. You could fit three kids in each leg. Look at those eyes; you were hot stuff before you could walk. I'll need a print of that one, too." They moved into more recent albums and he got progressively quieter. The last page of photos, he studied a long time: Clare decorating last year's Christmas tree, herself festooned with strings of lights to keep them above Jessie's reach as she looped them around the tree.

She sensed something was wrong but couldn't imagine what. "Don't tell me you want copies of those, too. They're not even in focus."

"I missed out on so much of your life." He shut the album, stared at the back cover.

"I understand why that bothers you. I guess I'm not as affected because I'm so much older than you are, I've seen so many more years."

He yelled and pinned her to the carpet, using both legs and his one arm. "Give. Me. A. Break. Next you'll be telling me you count wrinkles every morning when you get up. Then I break every mirror in the house. With your head," he concluded with mock violence.

"No I don't. Really." He released her, looking satisfied. "I can't count that high," she added with a giggle that turned to a shriek as he tickled her ferociously. "Stop. Stop. When I laugh I get more wrinkles. No! Please please stop I was joking!"

He unpinned her and they lay panting and laughing, eyes locked. His expression changed and she had to look away. When she looked back, he was still watching. "What?" she demanded, feeling exposed.

He stretched out beside her, still staring. "You're the best thing I ever laid eyes on," he whispered. "You don't believe me—I can see it in your face. But I'll make you see it too, Clare. I will."

She was incapable of response. They lay side by side for an indeterminate time, eventually slipping into sleep.

The phone rang. "What time is it?" Clare jumped upright.

"What day is it?" Tommy responded.

"I think it's Sunday morning because Jessie's had four meals since we got here."

Lacking a coin, Tommy flipped a book. Once again they lost the toss and Clare answered.

"Dr. Austen? It's Steve. Your old assistant?"

"Yes Steve, I remember you. Where the hell are you? I'm sorry, I didn't mean it like that." She supposed she couldn't hope he'd confess he'd left town because he'd committed a few murders; but in any event, she'd get less information out of him if she attacked. "You disappeared so quickly, I was concerned."

"Once I decided to leave school I had to avoid my uncle—I knew he'd be very, very angry. He wants me to go to medical school but I really don't want to. In my typical fuck up fashion I didn't admit it until two weeks before graduation."

Both his self-hatred and his fear sounded genuine. "I think I understand. May I ask why you're calling?"

"I heard how you were looking for some slides, I'm really sorry about that. I know the ones you mean. I dropped their box so I brought them home to put them back in order, then gave them to my girlfriend but I guess she hasn't had a chance to bring them to you yet. I want to give you her phone number in case you need to ask me anything else but that's not why I'm calling. I didn't want to bother you at home but I can never reach you at school. I'm calling to ask you a favor but—"

He sounded like he needed permission to continue. "I'll help if I can," she said.

"Could you ask Deirdre not to call me anymore? She's been calling my uncle too, the last couple days, all the time. I don't know what she wants but it's really causing problems. He doesn't know yet that I left school."

"Is that why you want to give me her number? I think this is something the two of you should sort out, Steve. It's not good to have your teacher try to fix a lover's quarrel."

Steve spluttered, first in confusion, then in disgust. "You think *Deirdre's* my girlfriend?"

It was Clare's turn to be confused. "You mean she's not?"

"No, my girlfriend's name is Sally. She's a lit major at PCC." He said this as though science majors were a lower life form; and Pasadena City College was far more honorable than his own privately endowed, world-renowned university.

"Has Deirdre tried to reach you prior to the last few days?"

"No. Do you know what she wants?"

"I caught her going through my files and she told me you'd asked her to spy on me." Steve's shock and outrage sounded even more genuine than his previous self-hatred and fear. "I suspect she's been calling to ask you to confirm her story, in case I talked to you." After a few moments, Clare interrupted his protestations of innocence. "I believe you. Steve! I believe you!"

"I knew I should've never let her sub for me but she was so insistent and I needed to get away but no one else could do it and I didn't want to leave you without—"

"Stop right there. She was insistent about getting your job? Why?"

"I—I didn't ask. I'm sorry, Dr. Austen, but I didn't know she'd cause problems. I'm sorry for everything." He babbled on.

"Steve. It's okay, Steve. Truly. Why don't you give me Sally's phone number and I'll see what I can do with Deirdre. Although I can't promise anything. She may avoid me now that I've caught her in the act." Steve recited his girlfriend's number. "You might try calling Deirdre back, you know."

"She won't leave a number. I tried the number she left you for emergencies but it's not in service. I don't know her last name but—"

"Steve. This may be important. Did Deirdre start pressuring you for your job before or after Dr. Colton was murdered? Which was two weeks ago Friday."

He thought a minute. "It was that same weekend. I remember because I was watching a TV news crew standing on Hill Street reporting about the murder with the school as a background. She came up to me then." Clare was silent, trying to discern the import of this. "Dr. Austen? If you don't have any more questions—I'm calling long distance and—"

"Of course, Steve. I'll let you go. Don't let your uncle push you around, med school's definitely the wrong place to be if you don't want to be a doctor."

Tommy was on the couch, waiting for details. Hearing them, he whistled and shook his head; and agreed they'd have to find out more about Deirdre. "Should we call Beaudine?" she wondered.

"I want to say yes but if we do, it's that much weirder that we're always finking about Deirdre but hiding the files Mrs. Bates stole."

"On the other hand, there's a two-wrongs-don't-make-a-right argument to be made."

They debated it a bit longer, then Clare put in calls to Beaudine. The police station and his home both asked if her call was urgent. "I—don't think so but I can't say; he might want to talk to me sooner rather than later," Clare replied. The message takers took this down verbatim and warned that she probably wouldn't hear from him before tomorrow afternoon.

Thanks to Steve's intrusion, Clare and Tommy discussed the murders a bit—and even tried a few tests. All were variations on old themes: "Is Deirdre the killer?" NO. "Is the killer in the hall Steve?" NO. The tests led nowhere.

Without further discussion, they resumed enjoying their idyll —although unable to enjoy it as fully, now that the end loomed near.

PART 4

Chaotic Dynamics

From astrophysics to neurobiology, studies of the universe strive to find order and define patterns, even though, under and behind those patterns lies unpredictability, randomness. Or so it's been thought until recently. Order has been discovered within that disorder, linking otherwise disparate fields: there may exist deep kinship between the firings of neurons and the drought cycle of the Nile and the behavior of subatomic particles and the swirls of a cigarette's smoke. Investigating the rules of randomness is a new science called chaotic dynamics, which may some day predict the unpredictable, once it understands the pull of "strange attractors" and the other laws of chaos.

PART 4

Chaotic Dynamics

CHAPTER 15

The Falling Sickness

Monday morning, reality intruded severely: Clare's alarm jarred them awake and she could only afford two lingering kisses before she was late for her two classes. Since the discovery of the grisly note, the campus now felt like the killer's domain, and neither looked forward to her venturing there alone. But Clare didn't want Tommy to accompany her to class; and she was sure she'd be safe: she'd park in the loading zone just outside the lecture hall, and come right back.

When she returned in the early afternoon, they had a day and a half idyll time left if they didn't sleep—Bianca wouldn't return before ten tomorrow morning—but it seemed like only seconds remained. She ran from her car, provoking the usual apathetic stare from Beaudine's watcher. Upstairs, she found Tommy reading with a frown. He'd gotten dressed so she remained clothed too; and tried not to read meaning into his frown.

"How'd the teaching go? Anyone follow you?"

"No one. And I spent both classes watching all my students

wondering whether I'm capable of four murders. Well. 'All' might be an exaggeration. But when I referred to subject Tom Q, the whispering got pretty thick. One of my aides told me he'd heard a discussion about what tools I'd needed to cut Larry into pieces. If I thought it would teach those little snakes anything, I'd take it out in their grades." After he laughed unconvincingly, she was forced to note, "You look awfully glum."

"Beaudine returned your calls. I didn't want to answer your phone so I just picked up, didn't say anything until I heard his voice. Made him bitchier than usual. When I told him what Steve said he acted like we're trying to fuck with him. Pissed me off so bad, I told him maybe he ought to start hanging out in a lab coat to get closer to the killer."

"Oh dear."

"He thanked me for my continuing interest in the investigation. Fucker jacks off so much his head is full of. Ah, forget it." He pulled her closer but remained separate.

"Something else is bothering you."

"I dozed off. I think. It was like I dreamed I was dreaming. And I woke up feeling really shitty, maximum nightmare feeling."

"Do you remember the dream?"

"I was playing a gig. Robert was in the audience, dancing, totally in a groove, man was he hot. Then he looked through this telescope and I could see through his eyes. I wasn't playing some dive club stage anymore, but an arena—smoke machines, light show, the works. The telescope turned into a cannon, he started firing these balls that hit the stage and splattered. The balls weren't balls though, they were heads, still alive, howling: Colton, Lalitha, Larry. Then I knew your head was next and I must have screamed because Jessie hasn't let me near her, since."

"It sounds terrifying. How do you interpret it?"

"Shit, I dunno. Robert's the right height but—"

"Robert can't be a killer! Robert is not the killer!"

"Don't yell at me, I know that. Lately I've been hating him because he got to spend four years with you, that's got to be where it came from. But it makes me sick that my dream machinery turns jealousy into—that."

Could there be another interpretation? If so, it eluded her too.

They resumed pretending the world didn't exist; although for Clare, it now took effort to pretend—more so because she sensed Tommy making similar effort at times. Late that night, when they retired to the bedroom, she was unable to get lost during their lovemaking. Whenever she glanced beyond Tommy at a wall, the ceiling, a pillow, she started extrapolating to other walls, more ceilings—the world outside.

"What's wrong?"

She'd always yearned for a man who sensed her every mood, but it proved to be a liability at times: some moods, she wanted to hide. "The light's a little bright, once it's off I'll be fine."

"Here, swap places, it won't be in your eyes then."

"No, then you'll be lying on your bad arm. I'll just turn this off." She reached for the lamp's switch.

"No!" He spoke so roughly he frightened her. "Ah shit. I don't like to talk about it because it makes me feel like a freak. But sex in the dark—it's too disorienting. Each half of my body's getting these rushes of feelings but I'm not quite sure what they are, sometimes not even where they're coming from. If I can look around, I can keep it from getting too extreme."

"I had no idea. Let's move the lamp further away then." Embarrassed, Tommy got up to do so. "Everyone should be such a freak, you know. Your paying such close attention, concentrating every second, explains why this has been so—intense."

Tommy sat on the bed's edge, pulled her up to join him. "That is not why our being together is 'intense,' you moron." After a time, he stopped kissing her. "Where'd you go?"

"Now I feel like a freak. I was just wondering if any of my

other split brainers have the same experience; and how to test it in the lab."

He feigned a bow and said gleefully, "It's a privilege to inspire new experiments. Just remember this moment the first time you catch me thinking about new lyrics."

"As if I'd forget this." She drew him down to join her.

They'd intended to stay up all night, yet the alarm caught them intertwined and asleep. Groggily, Clare stumbled out of bed, hunting her small clock, which had fallen under the bed frame. Tommy fumbled to the window and pulled the curtain. Harsh sunlight emphasized the thickness of the window bars, the cracks in the walls, the stains on the sheets, the puffiness around his eyes. (No doubt hers looked even worse.) Tuesday morning had arrived.

There was time for coffee, kisses, and separate showers before they had to walk each other outside—where Beaudine's watcher was nowhere to be seen.

"Maybe he went to get coffee."

"Perhaps the lieutenant has made an arrest."

"Whatever it means, I don't like it."

They couldn't sustain a good-bye kiss. And Tommy slammed his fingers in his car door. "Welcome to Tuesday," he grimaced. They promised each other they'd be alert and careful. And then they drove off in opposite directions.

Once at school, Clare couldn't bear pacing her lab alone, not thinking about the killer, not imagining Tommy welcoming Bianca home. So she busied herself trying to locate Deirdre instead. Fortunately, Clare hadn't had time to turn in Deirdre's new-hire paperwork. Even if some information in it was false, she should find enough that was true to locate the girl.

It took fifteen minutes of going through the files to convince herself. The paperwork was missing. And without it, Clare didn't even know her too-clever assistant's last name.

Trying to seem casual about it all, Clare strolled into the Biology office. Fortunately, the secretary had no curiosity regarding this professor's recent recurring interest in the department records. She didn't care who did what, as long as they let her punch out on time. Unfortunately, the secretary was at a loss to find a student by first name only. True, it was an unusual first name, but the secretary didn't know how to get the computer to do a first-name sort. Yes, Clare could obtain a roster of all enrolled biology students, but not right away: fill out these forms, then check back tomorrow.

Next, from Administration, Clare determined that no Deirdre was an honor student; nor an award, grant, nor scholarship recipient. Then she gave up. She didn't have the stamina to make further forays around the campus today. The balance of tension was shifting; locking herself in her office now appealed.

She was at her desk staring at her notes, searching for a reason to continue their testing, when someone walked up to her door. She waited for a knock. Or for the someone to keep walking. At last she called, "Who's there?"

"It's—me."

"Robert. Um. Come in." Holding tightly to the doorframe, she was loath to relinquish its support. Robert mistook her hesitation before widening the doorway; or perhaps he didn't.

He remained in the hall. "At the risk of pushing my luck—or pushing you—is there a chance we could get together and talk?"

"Please. Don't stand out there." She retreated to her desk chair. He shut the door behind him, waited an awkward moment, sat on a few inches of couch. Today seeing him lacked the shock of the first time; in fact, she felt angry. "Why the hell did you call Norelle?" she demanded, with instant regrets—she wanted no confrontation.

"I was genuinely concerned, but not thinking clearly. It was a stupid decision. As soon as I hung up, I remembered what you'd gone through before with Bernie. Although my intentions were quite different—or I believe them to be." When this seemed to assuage her, he sighed. They studied the floor for a moment. "How's Jessie?"

"Fine. Adjusting to the move." Against her will, Tommy's dream flickered through her thoughts. "Oh, I meant to mention this before—you know that T-shirt we used to joke about, 'I uncovered the mysteries of the universe and all I got was this crummy shirt'?" His look was blank. "Don't you remember, we'd periodically get that junk mail offer for the video series?"

His puzzlement continued to seem genuine. Not for a nanosecond did Clare observe even the slightest indication that the mailer provoked a recent memory. Surely if he had left that note, he—

She was suspecting Robert of four brutal murders. And he had no idea, as he sat there looking wistful and sad; and thoroughly ill at ease. "It's good to see you," she tried to make amends.

"I suspect it's Thanksgiving coming up that made me stop by here."

She nodded. They'd first met preceding a Thanksgiving and had always made that anniversary a special time. "I know. I've been aware of it, too. But to make a special effort to sort things out this week—that's not a commemoration I want." And of course, she was hoping to spend at least part of the holiday with Tommy.

"I don't want a wrap-up, a final chapter, but that would be preferable to being a loose end, wafting around. Give me a minute, I'll see if I can mix any more metaphors."

"It is time to talk." Her forcefulness surprised them both. It was time to tell him about Tommy, to stop his harboring false hopes that—

The door swung open. "Hey Robert," Tommy said woodenly; Robert returned the greeting even more stiffly. Tommy looked from Robert to Clare. "I can come back later."

Robert stood hastily. "I'm on my way out."

"How've you been?" Tommy edged around him, sat on the far end of the couch.

"This time of year, my main concern is dread about grading the finals my students are feeling dread about taking."

They continued their effort at social repartee while Clare fought a desire to flee. To keep running, forever. Because Tommy had entered her office, even before seeing Robert, as though heading for an execution; and there was more than politeness in Tommy's grasps at conversation, at keeping Robert in the room.

"Robert," Clare interrupted. He looked at her, Tommy looked everywhere but. "Why don't we meet for coffee at the Bar later? Say about four?"

"I'd like that. Very much. I'll see you then. Good luck, Tommy."

"Say what?"

"With your testing today."

"Okay. Yeah. Watch out for those finals." But Robert was already gone.

She rearranged papers on her desk. "Clare. If you keep sitting over there I'm gonna go out of both my minds. Coming up the hall and hearing his voice in here. Ow!" He'd thrown his head back to rest on the couch, overshot and hit the wall.

What a fool she was. Nothing had changed. She went to join him, pausing to lock the door en route. "Robert needs to talk to me and it's not fair to keep putting him off."

"Sure. I get that. It's cool."

"I take it Bianca got home safely."

"She's home anyway. Had a great time this weekend, Andy was there too and he's so much fun to be around, she spent all her time with him, blah blah blah. She got real disappointed when I didn't react."

"If you can't come over tonight I understand. I could postpone with Robert so we can see each other longer this afternoon."

"No don't do that." His haste to say this filled her once more with fear. "I have to leave by three. Holiday's coming up, you know, and we're supposed to drive to her folks' place in Phoenix. We're leaving today."

"Ah. You didn't mention that. Before."

"I thought I could get out of it. Put her on a plane—her folks would spring for the ticket. But she went nuts when I mentioned not going, making her face the questions about why I'm not there. Add that to my not caring that she's fucking Andy Stuart and—I have to go, I owe it to her. You see that, don't you?" He let her draw away from him, followed her with his eyes.

"Does her fucking Andy Stuart have anything to do with the decision?"

He sounded surprised. "No. Not at all."

"Are you going to. Sleep with your wife? On this trip?"

"I'm going to be missing you on this trip. The whole time."

"That's not an ans—"

"No! Is my answer."

"What if she goes nuts again when you refuse her? Surely you owe her that much, too."

"Don't do this, Clare."

She nodded as though "this" were her doing. She nodded because now she could see their last few glorious days together were not enough. He preferred discomfort, fights, and misunderstandings with Bianca.

He exhaled as though the matter were resolved. "I don't want you by yourself when I'm gone. Can you and Jessie go somewhere? Where do your folks live?"

"My mother lives back East, she can't fly and neither can Jessie. I don't know where my father is."

Tommy looked confused, no doubt recalling her alleged shopping quest for matching parental presents. "Can you get a friend to stay with you?"

"Lalitha's dead. My other true friend is on sabbatical in the

South Pacific. Anyone else I might know is strictly a career acquaintance."

"There must be someone who—"

"I'll find a solution. Don't worry about it."

"But you won't stay by yourself?"

"No. Stop pestering me."

"I don't believe you, that's why I'm. Aw shit. Maybe Bianca should call her folks, call the whole trip off."

"I suppose I could stay with Robert." Clare lost all hope when Tommy nodded as though this wasn't the worst idea he'd ever heard. To hide her despair, she made a point of checking her watch. "It's nearly two-thirty. I'm late for an appointment at Administration. I had to be so pushy to get it, I really must go."

They stood. "I'll be back Monday morning. Let me give you her parents' number."

How fascinating: he'd written it down for her before arriving, now produced it from the same jacket pocket in which he'd stored his toothbrush while Bianca was out of town.

He walked her over to the Administration building. When she was sure he was gone, she returned to her office, gathered her things and sleepwalked to her car.

Without any memory of the drive, she found herself parking on Raymond Street and heading around back through the alley to the Espresso Bar, a seedy relic of the beat era, dimly lit with baroque Chinese lanterns, heated only by the smoky fireplace and the patrons' noisy discussions of art, politics, and romantic prospects.

She was forty minutes early but Robert was already there. She ordered a double cappuccino and brought the glass mug to his table beside the stolid upright piano.

In case she looked like she felt, she opened with an excuse. "We've reached such an impasse with our work. I'm so discouraged." A lot of time got killed answering his questions about the murder investigation. She even dragged out her notebook, though it was uncomfortable, sitting close together to review the pages.

As soon as the notes were perused, their chairs scraped farther apart again, and he allowed, "I don't know what else you might try. But maybe I'll think of something later."

"If anyone can find a new angle, it will be you."

"I had a slew of serious topics to discuss—one of my mental checklists, you know those. But now I don't feel like tackling point one."

"I could use some good random conversation."

After some clumsy beginnings, they were able to talk about this and about that, nothing personal yet rarely superficial. They talked through a second round of coffee, then ran out of steam as they warmed their hands on glass mugs number three. Clare stirred the cinnamon into the milk froth, stirred, stirred.

"How've you been?" Robert asked softly.

"Adjusting to the move. Not as quickly as Jessie, but. I think I made the right decision." When he blinked then looked away, "I don't want you to disappear from my life though. Which I didn't acknowledge until I ran into you the other day."

"All you've said applies equally to me. Except I—acknowledged before that day. But I'm primarily thankful that we can already do this." His wave indicated their afternoon at the Bar. "I was afraid it wouldn't be possible until much later."

"I know," Clare murmured into her coffee, took too big a swallow, coughed.

"I could use some dinner. How about you?"

"I'm really not hungry. Whereas Jessie is sure to be."

"Some other time then." He wanted to finish his coffee fast but it was still too hot.

"Would you like to see where Jessie and I live?"

He considered as though assessing the risks in a dangerous enterprise. Finally, "Yes. Yes I would."

He was stunned by the outside security features, speechless when she explained the need for them. The mirrors by her door amused him, until she said, "Tommy installed those so I could see if anyone was hiding up here."

"Ingenious." He didn't voice reaction to the news that Tommy had visited her new abode.

Jessie was skittish at first, then refused to leave Robert's lap for the evening's duration. He petted her as though the world would end if he stopped.

To Clare, Tommy's presence in the apartment was palpable. But each glass of wine better enabled her to cope, and sip by sip she was more aware of the present than the past. Robert's reasons for refilling his own glass each time would have to be his own business.

Despite such tensions, it was so easy talking with Robert, that ultimately she nearly almost enjoyed herself. He seemed pleased, as well, until he realized simultaneously that it was well past midnight and he could barely walk, much less drive.

Coffee rendered them alert drunks. Robert kept gulping more and looking worse. "This is stupid," Clare finally decreed. "We're so scared of giving each other the wrong idea. When the obvious solution is for you to sleep on the couch."

"I couldn't stand to." He shook his head violently. "No. You're right. I'll stay."

What are we trying to prove? Clare could dimly wonder, in her alcoholic haze. And even more dimly feel disdain. What adults we are. How rational. How thick-skinned.

She brought Robert two blankets then retreated to her bedroom, quickly shutting the door. The room still reeked of sex and this was not the time nor the way for him to learn she'd betrayed by omission, in failing to mention her fling with Tommy.

She lay in the dark clutching Jessie, aching to be with Tommy, aching in a much different way to keep Robert from being hurt further. Her head throbbed, her heart thudded. So moronic to drink so much. If she lay very still the room tilted; but if she kept moving Jessie would leave—and the cat's warmth and softness were all that kept reality from spinning out of control, away from Clare. So she let the room tilt, fought against retching, and gradually passed into unconsciousness.

Searing pain yanked her back from dreams. Fingers touched her shoulder, felt wetness. Blood. Ears heard noise under the bed: scrabbling then silence.

Something had startled Jessie, Clare realized dazedly, causing her to scratch Clare's shoulder inadvertently as she darted away, to scrabble for safety under the bed. But what? Clare lay very still, listening, but heard only her own galloping heartbeat. The shoulder pain was a welcome localization of discomfort. Her body was stuffed with greasy cotton. She was moving from drunk to hung over, so some hours had elapsed, though the air was still dark.

There—outside. Faint then fainter rustling. Something was climbing the brief weedy incline that connected the back of the apartment complex to the street. She held her breath, strained her ears but divined nothing more. Robert was out sleeping on the Hide-A-Bed so they'd had another fight and he'd even gone out to buy cigs—they must have had a major blowout. No. This wasn't their apartment, she was in a different life now. Robert never smoked anymore, anyway, even when maximumly upset. And no brand of tobacco produced that acrid afterscent growing ever stronger.

Smoke. The room was filling with smoke. Fire! She leaped out of bed onto the floor, which hours later she would recall as being almost too hot to touch. She groped, found Jessie, tried to drag the cat out from under the bed. "Damn it Jessie, come *on!*" Clare yelled, which did not make the cat more willing to release claws from carpet.

Clare tugged harder, fell backward with Jessie in her arms. Rising, she pressed the wriggling terrified animal close, used precious seconds to stand still, murmuring soothingly, until Jessie was no longer tensed to spring away.

Clare clenched the cat with one arm; somehow with the other

arm she unlatched and raised the window. Smoke poured in the room. Clare coughed and groped wildly, futilely, for the mechanism that released the window bars.

Gagging so violently she could barely hold Jessie, Clare fell away from the window, gulped relatively fresh air against the floor. Yes, stay near the floor, that was what they said to do. Head near her knees, she waddled toward the door, remembered after opening it that she was supposed to touch it first to see if it was hot. Like the floor. So hot. The air scorched her throat, her skin.

She waddled down the hall. Hot tile stung her feet. Wrong turn: the bathroom. As she backed out, clutching Jessie like a talisman, the darkness bulged with searing lights, streaks of fire shooting only behind her eyes. She was going to pass out. No! Keep going. Got to. Got to. Robert fell asleep with a cigarette no he didn't live here.

The hall walls fell away—she'd reached the living room. Robert. Wasn't it tonight that she'd dumped blankets on the couch for him? Right where Tommy used to sit. "Robert," she croaked, but the word barely rumbled in her throat. She groped for the couch, dragged herself along the couch arm. Jessie no longer wiggled against Clare. Was the cat still conscious? Was Clare still conscious? She found Robert's foot, which temporarily invigorated her. She'd invited him over, forced him to face their separation. He'd drunk so much he couldn't regain consciousness, all three of them were going to die. She shook his leg and mouthed his name, but could not interrupt those drunken snores ending in gasps.

She fell back onto the carpet. It smelled singed. The floor was so hot. She wished Jessie would stop running through that newspaper. No. Jessie was limp in her arms. That crackling wasn't paper it was fire, tearing the building out from under them. She could only breathe between coughs now, little huffs of air, air so hot blisters bubbled inside her throat. What luck to remain conscious while dying. What luck what . . .

Tonight her street was not forbiddingly dark but bright and warm in the blaze of the fire. She was sitting on a curb, Robert choking beside her, Jessie shivering and pressing deep into Clare's arms: trying to hide from the growling fire trucks, the yelling firemen and police and news crew, the gawking neighbors and the dazed no-longer tenants. Nearby stood Mrs. Manning, her thin cotton nightgown billowing in the wind from the rushing flames.

Warning shouts preceded the collapse of Clare's roof, down through her floor, down to the laundry room below. Mrs. Manning's roof caved in a moment later. With a triumphant roar, the newly released flames shoved into the night sky. "My whole life. My whole life," Mrs. Manning echoed over and over. When Clare at last dared look at the buildingless landlady, she saw her lips no longer moving but still heard the words.

At some point Beaudine appeared with a lidded cardboard box cut with jagged air holes. He held it while Clare got Jessie inside. Clare realized he'd been around earlier: a flash mental picture showed him standing in the same spot with flames shape-shifting behind him. But now the fire was vanquished, the flames were gone and behind the lieutenant, yellow smoke roiled. He pulled her blanket tighter—the blanket someone's hands had draped over her—and led her across the street to a shelter né living room. There, paramedics kept checking Clare, Robert, Mrs. Manning.

Another memory flash: the emergency team's oxygen mask forced against her face, repeated orders that she breathe. And an oxygen mask fully shrouding Jessie's small head, a paramedic rhythmically kneading the cat's stomach until Jessie regained enough life to flail and hiss.

Beaudine must have been questioning Clare because she remembered his mouth moving, his eyes probing, and next he was behaving the same way in front of Robert and now Mrs. Manning. She couldn't hear questions or answers. Had her lips moved in responses as theirs were doing? She couldn't recall.

She was naked under the blanket. That's right, she hadn't worn her pajamas tonight because they smelled like Tommy who had liked them and worn them during that previous century called yesterday.

The fire was back and now it was winning, sweeping across the street engulfing their refuge. No, no that was the sun. It was morning. Mrs. Manning was no longer visible. Robert sat with head in hands. The box lid was off—oh God! where was Jessie! —oh here she was, asleep in Clare's arms, hunched up in case she had to awaken instantly and bolt away.

A man and a woman who thought they were experts were telling Beaudine it looked like an electrical fire, just last month the complex had been cited for overextended faulty wiring—

"No. They were trying to kill Tommy. And maybe me too. They didn't know he wasn't here anymore," Clare said in a low monotone that stopped the conversation and halted Robert's rasping breathing.

One of the duo told Beaudine in a smooth expert's voice, "We've got no evidence of arson at this time but of course we'll keep looking."

Clare didn't have the energy to argue with them, nor to resist as Beaudine delivered Clare, Robert, and Jessie to Robert's apartment. She could barely listen as Beaudine advised her to sleep here until further notice: with its freestanding pairs of upper and lower apartments, this was an easier building for his people to observe and much harder for anyone to sabotage—if arson had indeed been the fire's cause, which they wouldn't discount despite the lack of evidence.

As soon as the strangers were gone, Jessie hopped out of the box, immediately comfortable in this place that had once been home. Clare looked around like a psychic in a trance, regressed to a past life. It was so quiet she was sure her eardrums had burst in a great explosion.

No explosion. That was Robert slamming the front door— he'd gone out, she hadn't noticed that. He sidestepped her to enter the bedroom. She trance-walked behind him, stopped when she heard two gunshots. No: Robert snapping his suitcase latches shut.

"What are you doing? Beaudine told us to stay put."

"He told you to stay put. You'll be safe here. I went down and spoke with Mary and Bill." The downstairs neighbors. "They'll be home pretty much all weekend. Stomp on the floor if you need—anything. I also talked to Sandy and Dean. Pound on the bedroom wall for them. I left a note for Sam and Manny. I'm sure they'll be here in a flash if you hit the kitchen wall."

"Where are you going?"

"Anywhere you're not." He pushed past her, she trailed after. He took Niels's cage from the bathroom then looked at her for the first time since Beaudine had dumped them. His face said he was exhausted, in shock, and filled with hate for her. "You suspect someone was trying to kill Tommy. In the middle of the night at your apartment. You had several opportunities to tell me, Clare."

"But I—" No use. No point. He was gone.

She stood facing the door, maybe seconds maybe hours. Then Jessie bumped repeatedly against her shins, ran to the kitchen when Clare noticed the bumps. Breakfast time. Clare found the extra bag of cat food she'd forgotten to take, fed Jess, converted newspaper shreds and Beaudine's carrier box into a litter box.

Gee, it was after seven. She'd have to hurry or she'd be late for her classes. She showered, pulled clothes from the to-be-donated-to-the-homeless bag she'd left in a closet, promised Jessie she'd be back soon, grabbed the keys Robert had tossed on the carpet, searched for her briefcase until she remembered: it was burned up, notes on the murder investigation inside it. Luckily, her car had a Hide-A-Key. Thankfully, Beaudine had thought to have her car driven over here. And today, his men actually followed her to the faculty parking lot.

Her students found Clare fascinating, her lectures ignorable.

At last this ordeal was over and she got help from Security to get into her office. Since Lou was on duty in her building, she didn't have to apply in triplicate and wait a week to get a locksmith out to make her new keys.

She was standing in her lab, remembering why each piece of equipment was there, when the phone rang. It was the Biology office secretary; she had the printouts Clare had requested. Pretending she knew what the secretary meant, Clare went to pick them up. Fortunately, the secretary had affixed a Post-it that said DEIRDRE so Clare remembered: she was trying to find her assistant. Only one of the three Deirdres on the student roster was a biology major, so Clare requested phone number and transcripts for Deirdre Costello, which the secretary readily accessed on her computer.

Clare had only to study Deirdre's list of classes to know that Steve had told the truth, Deirdre wasn't spying for him. All those pharmacology classes and labs proved it.

Ironically but typically, when Clare returned to her office, she found Deirdre waiting in the hall. "I didn't expect to see you here."

"I work for you on Wednesdays. I know you have every reason to fire me but I was hoping—praying—we could start over. I was wrong to trust Steve so blindly. I can't blame you if you don't trust me, Dr. Austen, but please give me one more chance. I won't be a spy. I'll be the best assistant you've ever had."

"Come in, Deirdre. Sit down. I have been thinking about our situation and I've been of two minds about what to do. But overall, my strongest impulse has been to forgive you." Deirdre looked surprised and suspicious. "After all, there's been no harm done. I'm not being completely honest, here, though. T-ommy" —his name caught in her throat—"put in several good words for you. And he finally convinced me that I've been one of those researchers who pretends their work is full of earthshaking secrets, when it's not. So you have him to thank."

This Deirdre was willing to believe. "That's terrific, Dr. Austen, I can't tell you how much I appreciate it." She jumped to her feet. "Which tests should I prep today?"

"None. I won't be testing again until after the holiday. Today, though, if you want to help, I need copies of some files. Feel free to refuse—you're not an office clerk! I was going to spend the morning at the Xerox machine myself, until I agreed to hold an extra discussion section for one of my classes. I've got to go to that soon and I'm catching a plane out of town this afternoon so I'm terribly pressed for time."

"I'd be happy to help."

Clare gave her a handful of folders, including Tommy's nonmurder file. "I need one copy of the last six months' data—the top three or four pages per file. I'll be back in an hour. If you finish before then, just shove everything under my door. I'd give you a key but . . ."

"I understand and agree. I need to win your trust back step by step."

They walked out together, Clare leaving Deirdre at the Xerox room and continuing out, downstairs, through the first floor hall, back up the stairs on the other side of the building. She sat in the stairwell, out of view of the second floor, a journal open as though she'd just had to stop and read. No one passed her. And not long after Clare estimated that Deirdre should have finished two copies of each file, she heard a brisk walk much like Deirdre's up on the second floor.

Clare snuck upstairs, down the hall to Sid Stein's door, threw it open and caught Deirdre handing a sheaf of Xeroxes to Sid. Deirdre stepped back and looked fearful. Sid grew taller and more arrogant.

"I hope your protégée is giving you the kind of research directions you need, Sid. Now I understand how you always seem to know when to offer your services on the hottest projects around here."

Sid smiled the smile of a used car dealer facing a customer

who'd bought his sourest lemon. "Neither your envy, nor your accusations nor your work is of any interest to me, Clare."

She pretended to be insulted, snatched the pages from him, turned to Deirdre. "Needless to say, you're fired and your school record will reflect this incident."

When Deirdre started to speak, Sid tapped her arm, very slightly shook his head, as though to reassure that he'd save Deirdre's reputation later, after poor second-rate Dr. Austen calmed down.

Clare stormed away, shaking. She feared that Sid would see through her, see that she wasn't really upset about his stealing research ideas or insinuating himself onto big, successful projects. Rather, she was concerned with his being the right height, correct weight, and perfect temperament.

Minutely observed by Beaudine's men, she fled the campus, hoping Deirdre would pass on the lie that Clare was going out of town for the holiday—protecting Clare until she could convince Beaudine that Stein was the killer. She was probably safe so long as Sid believed that she merely suspected him of spying. But she dared not take chances. Poor Deirdre, stupid Deirdre. No doubt ambition drove her. No doubt Sid had promised her a cushy position, postgraduation. Had their encounter *à trois* shortened or lengthened the girl's life span?

What was she thinking? Sid Stein was an idea thief, not a murderer. Wasn't he? Clare didn't know, she couldn't tell what the truth was, nor what she truly thought. She had to get inside, away. Of that she was certain. She hadn't been thinking clearly this morning, running all around campus, exposing herself to all sorts of danger. She had to hide. From precisely whom she couldn't say, from exactly what she wasn't sure.

She parked a block from Robert's apartment, in the carport of a unit she knew to be for rent, with a note claiming car trouble and giving Robert's phone number in case someone needed the Nova moved. Walking briskly to the apartment, she was trailed by a car with two of Beaudine's watchers inside, turned the corner, spied a parked car holding another pair of men she'd seen with Beaudine. All four watched her ascend the stairs.

The morning paper was still on Robert's doorstep. She stepped over it and left yesterday's mail in the box, locked the door, shut the blinds. Two candles in the hallway, far from all windows, would provide her only light. She sat between them, chin on knees, Jessie in the tent under her legs.

She considered calling Beaudine. If she told him about Sid's spying, Beaudine might even pay Stein a visit. That would only tip Stein that Clare was on to him. If he was the killer. Tommy's right brain had said Sid wasn't. Perhaps she should call Tommy in Phoenix. No. For whatever reason, his left brain had balked at knowing the killer's identity. She might ruin everything with that phone call.

No that wasn't why she shouldn't call. She wasn't thinking right or her thoughts weren't making sense to her. Smoke! Another fi— Oh the candles. She blew them out, holding her breath until the singed extinguished wick scent dissipated. Tommy would be back in less than four days; Jessie had enough food; they could wait.

By the time the sun set, she could maneuver quite well in the glow of a clock face here, the VCR digits flashing there, the wall heaters' pilot lights flickering in every room but the kitchen. She opened the broiler door to shed the oven pilot's light on that room. Then, walking from room to room to room to room, she was aware of Jessie following, several paces behind. Now her cat was afraid of her. She sat on the couch, eventually coaxing Jessie to join her.

In another few hours it would be okay to sleep. That would eat up a lot of time; when she woke up it would be less than three days until Tommy returned and they could do tests that gave Beaudine his proof. Until Tommy and Bianca returned, rather. "And Bianca," always "and Bianca," Clare mustn't forget that again. Why, right now in Phoenix they were probably rolling out pie crust dough, boiling cranberries, cubing stale bread into croutons.

Anyway that was how Clare and Robert spent the night before Thanksgiving. The holiday when they locked themselves away, curtains closed, phone disconnected. Tomorrow would be the frantic cooking—Tommy and Bianca would fix turkey, that would be even more work—and the leisurely feasting, culminating in the toast to their having found one another. A toast always initiated by Robert but of course never again. He finally saw who he was really toasting, just this morning he found that out.

Jessie had saved Clare's life last night. All their lives. If the cat hadn't been scared, hadn't scratched Clare's arm. You don't smell smoke when you're asleep. You don't feel fire burning through the floor, the bed, the sheets. Jessie hadn't smelled smoke though. Or had she? Wasn't she frightened by someone walking outside? Clare had forgotten to tell Beaudine about those rustling noises up the slope. She should call him but she couldn't—she was supposed to be out of town for the holiday, it was her only protection. What if the killer was being routinely questioned by Beaudine when she called? No. She had to protect herself. If only she knew from whom.

It wasn't as dark as it had been. That was a big relief to Clare, until she realized the reason: it was morning again, she had sat cowering on the couch all night. Time flies when you're all alone. Jessie was just waking up, hungry again. But it was correct for the cat to be hungry, it was breakfast time.

Clare wasn't hungry. If she swallowed even a bite she'd vomit. It would be nice to sleep but she couldn't fall asleep or there'd be another fire.

Insane! There existed no cause and effect between fire and sleep. She was thinking crazy thoughts. There existed no cause and effect whatsoever. In a flash of lucidity, Clare realized: of course, crazy thoughts. She'd had them before, years before, without Jessie's warmth alongside her leg to remind her of reality. She was having another breakdown, that's what this was. Silly not to have seen it before. She'd been having one for weeks, that's why logic had deserted her. How else to take wrong turn after wrong turn in their research. Wrong turn after wrong turn with Tommy. She'd really thought their union could last—she should've seen right off, such delusions were the product of an unhinged mind. But of course if she could have seen that, she wouldn't be suffering from a breakdown, would she?

The phone rang. Jessie jumped, her claws catching Clare's leg slightly. The cat was trying to warn her again. "Don't worry Jess, I won't answer it," Clare may have said aloud. At some later time, the phone rang again. When the jarring noise ceased, Clare unplugged the cord from the wall.

Time for Jessie's dinner. Clare swayed when she stood, weak and dizzy. Oh good, she was tired. She fed Jessie and went to fall onto the bed. But she couldn't sleep, even after covering her ears to shelter them from Robert's phantom breathing beside her.

Out to the living room she groped her way—the sun must have set once again. Ever so slowly, to guard against squeaks, she opened the Hide-A-Bed. But this held just as many memories. The floor was no better: floors equaled Tommy. The bathtub was too short and from inside the bathroom she couldn't hear if someone was trying to break in. Finally, she camped on the kitchen table; when she inserted the extra leaves, it was more than long enough to accommodate her. It wasn't comfortable but it would do. Thank Christ, I'm falling asleep, she thought. The realization woke her again.

At some point she did fall asleep, though, because she awoke silently crying, a puddle of tears on the table. She dabbed these away with her blanket, lest they mar the recently refinished wood. She was crying because she'd been dreaming that she and Tommy were making love. Even in her dream, she knew it was a lie.

She lay on her back, clasped hands on stomach and chuckled. All she needed was a lily. She saw her love life flash before her eyes, ending with Tommy, all her thoughts ended with Tommy.

Good thing Robert wasn't telepathic—it would hurt him so to know this. Too bad he wasn't telepathic. Everyone had to face up at some point. After all, certain research indicated that emotions were separated in the brain halves: the right hemisphere primarily dealt with negative emotions, the left hemisphere was more prone to positive. Now, if she dared posit that "normal" brains behaved like Tommy's split brain, then all left hemispheres confabulated like his did. Therefore, positive emotions were bogus, negative emotions more clearly interpreted reality. QED.

Despite the bad dream at the end, sleeping had helped. Calmer, she could look around her dark universe with newfound acuity. She had some testing ideas for surmounting Tommy's resistance to naming the known killer; and she no longer feared unduly for her life. Whatever arose, she would handle. Somehow.

What was the time? The day? She dared a peek outside, saw three papers piled on the front step. That meant today was Friday. Was it twilight or dawn? A half hour later it was darker outside, that made it Friday night. Monday morning, Tommy would return and they could finish their experiments, hand their proof over to Beaudine.

Outside, a red red sunset. Fire red, blood red. The carpet was warmer than it had been. She could hear she could see the fire advancing on her, flames jumping up to touch the ceiling that was her floor, jumping then reaching then stretching farther still, ever bigger, ever stronger, pushing with all their might, smashing through the floor supporting her, tossing her against the roof. She was floating near her ceiling, bounded by her walls, abandoned even by gravity. The air was so hot each inhale scorched her lungs, the whole building exploded with the heat and she tumbled into the night sky. Freezing air forced the flames to retreat, the heat that had held her aloft quickly dissipated, she froze from the inside out, plummeting to earth, shattering on impact with the black charred ground. Her body was decorated with an intricate lace of cracks and lines, wrinkles and whorls. Workmen arrived, quickly rebuilt the complex exactly as it had been before, though no greenery could now grow in the burned earth. Mistaking her for a statue, they built around her, trapping her inside, for this house was not a home, no one would live here and so the doors did not open, the windows were painted illusions, the walls were the latest technological marvel, stronger than steel, denser than concrete. It would stand until the whole world disintegrated. Only then would she be released.

She would stay inside until the world disintegrated. That was the wiser choice. Look what happened when she ventured outside, fancied herself brave. She spent one whole weekend with Tommy. Ironic, wasn't it: she was so drawn to his spirit, his boldness, to the way he plunged in and carried on. Now she'd left her old life and he'd skipped out of town with his wife, leaving Clare to face a killer she couldn't name. Couldn't, because she'd failed the most important experiments she would ever conduct. The only killer's identity test Dr. Clare Austen could complete would be to go over to the campus and wait until the killer came for her. That wouldn't be standard methodology, though. She couldn't get such sloppy work published, unless they slackened the rules, posthumously.

She was delirious. There was a gas leak, that was it. Carbon monoxide: colorless, odorless, quickly deadly in her hermetically sealed situation. Carbon, the building block of life; oxygen, the giver of breath—but not when it was mono, solo, alone.

She cracked open a window, closed the gas line. Now the guiding pilot lights were off and the heater wouldn't function, it would get very dark and cold but she could adapt, she'd rather turn blue than red and anyway Jessie would help her stay warm. Of course. Jessie was here too. She'd forgotten. Where was that cat?

Jessie was asleep on the bed, coiled to flee, mistrusting Clare's exploratory pats of the mattress. "Almost dinnertime, Jess," Clare assured the cat, then realized she should eat too.

She stumbled through blackness to the kitchen, opened the refrigerator, slammed it shut. The light was too bright—a beacon proclaiming her existence to all those spying outside. She reopened the door, just enough to reach in and unscrew the bulb. There. It took a long time to identify food items by touch. An orange, bread, cheese. She carried this cache to the bedroom with a heaping bowl of cat food so she wouldn't have to stumble back to the kitchen when Jessie became hungry.

The darkness was getting to her. She opened a curtain, lay in faint moonglow trying to absorb the light through her pores, squeezing her eyes shut so she couldn't see who that was, silhouetted outside.

A bit later, feeling calmer (of course no one was out there or she'd be dead by now) she opened her eyes—and squeezed them shut again, blinded. It was daytime now. That must mean she'd fallen asleep. Jessie's food bowl was empty and the cat was staring at her, twitching her tail. When Clare met her gaze, Jessie flopped down beside her, purring mightily. Clare wondered if Jessie sensed how crucially comforting her presence was right now.

She left the curtain open, feeling daring to do so. The light slowly eased; Clare heard gentle taps on the window and realized it was raining. She loved lying in bed listening to rain, feeling kinship with ancestors all the way back to cave days in the pleasure she derived from shelter.

Her stomach rumbled and she went out to the kitchen, getting breakfast—or was it lunch?—for Jessie and herself. Then she peeked out a living room window to watch the rain on the grass and was shocked to see five papers on the step. It was Sunday now. She'd slept through an entire day. No wonder she felt refreshed.

In fact, she even had new ideas about how to construct experiments to give Beaudine proof that Sid Stein was the killer. Although Tommy's left brain resisted acknowledging that the murderer was someone he knew—no, wait. These weren't new ideas, she'd come up with them days before. Thursday or Friday. Damn. She'd better write them down.

She didn't take her forgetting as a sign of mental confusion. She always forgot, that's why she took notes. If only she could forget on command, though. No, that wasn't really necessary. She didn't need to obliterate her memories of, say, Tommy, now that she understood him.

And she did understand. And bore no ill feelings. He'd meant it when he said he didn't want to hurt her. He wasn't lying when he claimed to be leaving Bianca. But those were separate issues from whether he loved Clare. He didn't. Not the kind of love she craved, anyway. Her presence and availability, her sympathy and support might enable him to make the break, end his marriage. However, she was a means to that end—the very timing of their involvement made it temporary.

Maybe that wouldn't be true. Still, it was wiser to prepare and protect herself.

But if she closed herself off, kept her distance, if there *were* a chance, they'd miss it.

God, it was so complicated. And she lacked all clarity.

CHAPTER 16

The Dichotomy

Damn it, she was better now, why was she imagining, seeing things again? As she stared out at the rain, she saw a car pull up, brakes hit so hard it swerved on the newly wet street. The car took a faint stab at parallel parking, then with its nose still in the street, the driver's door opened and the driver dashed across the street up the stairs to her door.

The building block of the universe was surely irony. Today was the first time in recorded memory that she felt alone yet not synonymous with incomplete. She had barely begun to appreciate the change and now, immediately, it was being threatened.

Her eyes were pretending the visitor was Tommy. But it couldn't be: he wouldn't be back until another newspaper hit the welcome mat. She retreated from the window. Now her mind was creating auditory hallucinations, as well. A voice like Tommy's was calling her name, while someone slammed fist against door.

Jessie had bolted from the room when the hallucination arrived, now returned and waited near the door. Hmm. Clare stood uncertainly for seven more knocks, two more callings of her name.

She opened the door. "You're back early. I didn't answer right away because I wasn't sure it was you."

"Jesus fucking christ." He swept her into a clinch so tight she giggled.

"If you hold me any closer I'm going to end up behind you."

He eased his grip infinitesimally. "Have you been here the whole time? Why the fuck didn't you answer the phone? I tried to fly back but the only flight that was open had engine trouble so it got canceled after we sat on the runway for years. I would have been here sooner but Bianca refused to let us drive over ninety."

"There was really no need to rush. Although I have come up with some new tests I think will work."

"Clare." He pulled away to study her. What he saw disturbed him.

"I'm fine. Now. The last few days have been a little rocky, though."

"Why the fu—I could kill you for not calling me. Thank God for Ilsa."

"What do you mean?"

"She thought she saw you go by in the background, wrapped in a blanket, during a news report about an apartment building that burned down. She called the TV station for information, then tracked me to Phoenix, told me what she'd found out: everything except where you were now. I called anybody I could think of. Beaudine told me he'd brought you here. With Robert."

"Robert found out you'd spent the night with me so I've had the place to myself," she explained as Tommy led her over to the couch to collapse.

He insisted on knowing what had transpired. It was a short story: there wasn't much to say about the last few days, except that she'd been doing a lot of thinking. Once this was said, it penetrated that she wasn't responding to his efforts to kiss her. The efforts instantly ceased and he studied her anew, but remained unenlightened. He sank deep into a corner of the couch and moaned. "From the minute Ilsa called, it was like a grenade went off inside me. I kept thinking, 'No matter what happens Clare can't get hurt.' I kept thinking that over and over, like my hearing it was gonna change anything! But man. If anything had happened to you."

This was exactly the kind of statement she had to stay on guard against.

"But something has happened, something you're not telling me. What were you doing all that thinking about?"

"Just. Our experiments. What went wrong with Robert and me. Trying to put everything in perspective. When can we go back to the lab? I'm excited about the new direction I mentioned earlier."

"We can go over there right away. As soon as we're done here."

"Aren't we done? Are you hungry, by the way? There's some really good cheese for sandwiches."

"Did you do some thinking about me, too?"

"Here and there, but now isn't the time to get into that."

"Look, Clare. You can kick me out if you want. Bianca and I aren't speaking since I was so anxious to get back to you, but she's moving in with Trish, so I've got a place to stay. If you want me out of your life, though, you'll have to say it, straight out. Because I love you and no way am I leaving otherwise."

His eyes were black, dilated, intense. He was confusing her but she managed to regain her newfound clarity. At the moment, he did love her, for the reasons she'd determined previously; she'd helped him through a difficult time, of course he—

Suddenly, with a new sort of clarity, she saw her certainty of failure as an excuse for avoiding risk.

But which clarity was the real clarity? She started to cry, could not stop no matter how she tried. And that effort was so great, she had no strength to resist when he put his arm around her and pressed her close. He was crying, too; this confused her further. She lost all semblance of clarity, then stopped fighting to regain it. She couldn't muster the power to keep her distance when the murders kept pushing them together. So, for now, here they were and that was that.

No plainclothes cars were visible outside. Could Beaudine really have such a short attention span? It was lucky she didn't notice the absence of cops earlier. Without that sense of distant protection, she would not have survived her long weekend as well as she had.

They headed for the lab in Tommy's borrowed car. Fortunately, he didn't ask where hers was. She didn't want to reveal how frightened she'd been.

Behind the drizzling rain, the campus appeared to be deserted except for the recurrent security guards. As they trotted up the stairs to Clare's floor, Neurobiology felt as hollow as a skeleton's bones. Tommy contrived a light tone and said, "I'm insulted you didn't ask if I kept up my lucid dreaming exercises, which I did, every night."

"And you had a dream about the murders?"

"Nope. But I was real good about doing the exercises."

They forced a chuckle as Clare hastily unlocked her office door. Once inside, she slipped the deadbolt as soon as he finished checking for intruders, then advised him, "I'm afraid you'll have to wait out here while I make a new tape."

"Yeah, I figured. I was thinking I'd go through your old notes again until you're ready for me."

"They're gone. In the fire. Though I've read them so often I should be able to recreate most of them from memory. The beach picture is gone, too. The files Mrs. Bates stole. Everything."

Tommy kissed her eyelids, kissed away the tears that had begun to form. "Everything except you, me, and Jessie."

"Somehow I have to make this up to Mrs. Manning. She kept repeating that her whole life was gone."

He groaned in sympathy, kissed her once more. "We can't think about that right now."

Once Clare had shut herself into her lab, she clutched the doorknob until she regained equilibrium lost during those kisses, that caring.

Her mental state kept ricocheting between opposites—certainty and terror, love and doubt, hope and realism. Yet when she could control her fear of this oscillation, her perceptions seemed enhanced. She saw things—differently, now. If neuroscience were capable of drawing a neuronal wiring diagram, she suspected a schematic done of her a few weeks ago would diverge from one done today. Consequently, the testing data—and how to proceed with it—looked subtly yet profoundly different.

She made a brief tape and compiled a long list of questions. When she brought Tommy into the lab, she posed one set of dichotic questions, all variations on the theme raised by Deirdre's spying: **"Is Sid Stein the killer? . . . Is the killer Deirdre?"** To each question, Tommy's right brain answered NO.

Then she unplugged and stored the headset—a bit of ceremony not lost on him. He watched with much curiosity as she laid out YES, NO and ? cards in reach of his left foot, then sat at his table with her list of questions.

"I'm going to follow a line of questioning that usually infuriates you. If you get upset in any way, don't try to hide or change that reaction—because today we're going to figure out how you're really reacting. And why. As always, I'll restate each question several times, since I can't be sure which words and phrasings your right brain understands. That's not because it's stupid, but because neuroscience doesn't know enough yet. Ready?"

He nodded vigorously. In every way she could devise, she asked whether the surfer attacker was the killer. NO. Whether Mrs. Bates was the killer. NO. Whether Hugo was the killer. NO.

Whether Steve was the killer. NO. Whether Bruce the vanished security guard was the killer. NO. Whether Deirdre was the killer. NO. Whether Sid Stein was the killer. NO.

"You definitely found out stuff while I was gone. About Deirdre and Stein."

"I did and I'll tell you about it as soon as we examine your reactions. Did these questions upset you?" She knew this answer: with each new phrase, he'd constricted further, until now he seemed in danger of fusion.

"No shit. And like usual, I wanted to yell 'Come *on*, we've been through this already.' But. The way you put it to me before we started this time, makes me see how getting mad that way is an excuse—it's hiding what's really bugging me. But. Trying to look behind the excuse, my thinking goes mush."

"Did you feel equally upset about each suspect I mentioned?"

He took a moment to consider. "I felt way worse about Steve, Stein, and Deirdre than about Mrs. Bates, Hugo, Bruce, and the deranged surfer. Maybe I feel worse the better I know somebody —like you've been saying all along. Although I had more dealings with Cynthia than with Sid."

"I have theorized that you can't tolerate the killer's being someone you know or like. But that's just a guess, based on very limited knowledge. A pattern seems to exist but what causes that pattern, I really don't know. It may be syntactical—something about my questions may create a confusion that's more apparent when your right brain actually knows the subject of my question. As I said, I can only guess; but we can't blame your hemispheres for the reaction. When a brain's functions seem arbitrary, it's our understanding that's out of whack."

Tommy visibly relaxed at this. "So how did Deirdre and Stein make it to your lineup?"

She explained how she'd caught Deirdre spying for Sid. "That doesn't implicate either of them in the killings. But it does get them added to the list of suspects—although Sid seems interested in much more than just our murder research."

Tommy's frown had deepened with each new revelation. "Maybe you shouldn't have told me," he concluded. "Now I feel even worse when I think about them."

"That may or may not cause problems," she admitted. Damn. Well, no time for self-recriminations. She would forge ahead, continue to discover her mistakes during these tests instead of trying to avoid errors by advance planning. She suspected the quantity of mistakes would be the same, anyway.

"Our next test involves comparisons. You've done these before, back last summer." She set cards near his left foot: MORE, LESS, SAME, ?. "To make sure you remember the test, we'll do a few run-throughs. Is Clare more or less tall than Tommy?" LESS.

After a few such comparisons, she believed his right brain knew the meaning of each card. "Now. When I ask you a question, answer with your left foot first, then with words. More importantly, I need you to carefully study each response over time. When I pose a question, you might have an impulse to answer one way initially, then reconsider. Be sure to alert me when this happens." She wanted to hear from both sides of his brain; and in particular, she wanted to know if his left brain changed any answers after receiving emotional input from his right brain. "Let's begin. Think about something that makes you very happy. Would that be playing music?"

"Definitely. Or you."

"Those feelings are 'good.' Now think about the killer in the hall. Those feelings are 'bad.'" She set new cards next to those already down, yielding MORE BAD, LESS BAD, SAME BAD, ?. (Fortunately, they'd done similar work in the past; it had been horrendous, getting Tommy's right brain to understand these concepts.) "Compare 'playing music' and 'the killer.' Your feeling about the killer is . . ." MORE BAD, his left foot responded.

"More bad," Tommy said, his left brain agreeing with his right.

She took a few more trial runs, one of which made her feel sheepish and ashamed—she had him compare his reactions to

Trish and Andy. Both brains felt MORE BAD about Andy, causing her much distress: first, because she'd been hoping he'd feel no worse about Bianca's friend than her possible lover; second, because Clare wasn't supposed to be testing Tommy's feelings about his wife, anyway. Lest Tommy start wondering why she'd asked, she quickly had him compare his reactions when he thought about Robert, then Jessie.

Tommy felt MORE BAD about Robert. "But at least Robert doesn't shed."

"If you hate the shedding now, wait until spring," she advised ominously.

"I'm glad you warned me."

She went through the previous list of possible suspects, comparing one to another. His hemispheres agreed on each answer and ultimately she determined Tommy felt worst about Steve and Sid Stein. "Clare, you wanted me to say if my reactions to anybody have changed. In the last tests, I felt better about Cynthia than I do now. But you know what else? You should ask me about those grant people too."

"You're right." And so she used today's tests to assess his hemispheric reactions to "Matt Woods," "Yvonne Hankoff," and "the grant people." Curiously, his left brain responded negatively but his right brain transmitted only positive reactions. Could it be that his left hemisphere was rounding up suspects that his right hemisphere knew to be in the clear?

She picked up the cards near his left foot. "This time, answer only with words; wait before your answer and tell me if your reaction changes as you wait. Think about the killer in the hallway. Notice how that makes you feel. Now think about Steve. Notice how *that* makes you feel. Now try to compare the two reactions."

Tommy waited a long time. "At first it seems like they're similar, but comparing like this, makes me realize I'm basically just ticked off at Steve."

Next she asked about Sid Stein. Close to a minute elapsed

before Tommy apologized, "I feel so bad about him, I can't concentrate enough to compare. I just keep thinking about what you found out."

Double damn. If only she hadn't told Tommy about Deirdre's spying for Stein. Perhaps she should work up another dichotic tape; but she didn't know how to conduct this experiment dichotically.

One by one, they went through their suspects. When they got to Cynthia Bates, Tommy responded as he had with Stein: indescribably negative. "I have to admit something. I felt real bad about her every time she's been mentioned today, right from the start. I tried to overlook it at first, because if she's the killer, we've really fucked up in how we've handled her."

"Shit." Were any of these test results going to be valid?

"This is going to make you feel worse. I keep going through names, over and over in my head, it's like I can't stop myself. And when you were testing me about whether I understood this test? You gave me two names that swamp me the same way as thinking about Cynthia and Sid Stein. One of 'em's Andy Stuart. That reaction's all tied up with Bianca, you know, but it's so powerful I had to mention it. Also. The same thing happens. When I think about. Robert."

He was right to fear her response. She forced her fury into check. "Are you saying Robert is the killer? You could not make a more ridiculous choice."

"Sure I could. Andy's the one who makes no sense. Which probably means it's him, huh?" His effort to lighten her mood did not succeed.

"What you have concluded, then, is that we have four suspects. Cynthia Bates, Sid Stein, Andy Suart. And Robert di Marchese."

"Based on how bad their names make me feel, yeah. None of them really make sense, because we know zip about motives. But take Andy. Who's to say he's not a psycho with a grudge against lab coats? Or—now don't scream—let me pretend I'm

Beaudine and I'm considering Robert. He knew Lalitha, they worked on the same kinds of stuff. Maybe he saw her as competition. Maybe she got funding he wanted or glory he thought he deserved. Maybe that set him off, thinking about murder. Then, once he figured out you were gonna leave him, maybe he went nuts, started killing lab coats, then tried to frame you for his crimes. After all, he's been helping spread these rumors about you feuding with Colton and so forth, even if he claims he's been defending you."

She was too stunned to respond. Of all the insane—

"I didn't come up with that scenario. Beaudine did. Last time he questioned me. His attitude is, he'd turn his back on a homeboy with an Uzi before he'd go near an academic with a grudge. I didn't tell you because I thought it was bull jive and I knew you'd react like you're reacting. But maybe it's not bull. Don't forget that nightmare I had about Robert."

"I have not spent the last four years of my life unknowingly living with a serial killer."

"Funny you put it like that. The day Larry got killed and Beaudine called me in, I was waiting outside his office and I could heard him yelling, 'This is no serial killer, this is no serial killer.' Even when all his partners were yelling that it had to be."

"What the hell is your point? Is this supposed to prove Robert's guilt?"

Tommy spent some minutes gazing inward. "I think what's really going down today is that I hate Robert 'cause of you and I hate Andy 'cause I can't cop to how mad I am at Bianca, so I hate him instead. That leaves us with Bates and Stein. Now how do we figure which one is the killer?"

Silently, Clare reviewed today's lab events. She jumped when Tommy touched her hand, realized she'd been quiet for quite a while. "No," she ruled on her inner debate. "This is the wrong time to rationalize away—anything. We have four suspects. We'll investigate each of them."

"I'm sorry," Tommy whispered, "I should've left it alone. But

I couldn't. Since Ilsa called me and I found out you almost died. I haven't been able to pretend anymore. About anything."

To narrow the field of suspects, she tried every test that made even dim sense, then tried some that didn't. Tommy made suggestions and they acted on those too. Around midnight, they admitted defeat. It was proving impossible to sort out Tommy's extremely negative feelings about the four suspects. Thus the starting point became their conclusion: hearing any of these four names, Tommy reacted with a visceral distress much like that engendered when he considered the killer.

"Let's take a break," Tommy suggested, and they went out in her office to pace, stretch, and sip cautiously from the Bushmills —they wanted no dulling of their perceptions now.

Without the distraction of testing, Clare's emotional ricocheting resumed; fighting to maintain stability, she felt like a gull in an oil slick. And Tommy's efforts to converse made them both twitchy. Taking a break was not working out.

Almost eagerly, they sat at Clare's desk and went over today's notes, then recreated as many of her old notes as they could recall. They were still poring over these when they heard the hall washer's bucket clatter outside, circa five A.M.

Tommy said what Clare had just been thinking. "We've still got four suspects. Maybe we should—confront them, one at a time. If I was around them with you asking some questions— nothing real direct but in the right direction—that might help me weed some of them out, at least."

STOP OR YOU DIE. "But if, while talking to a suspect, we realize we're talking to the killer—what if the killer realizes that we know?"

"You're right, forget it, it's too risky."

Reluctantly, Clare informed him, "That's not what I meant. In fact, I'd been thinking along similar lines—it's time for us to do field research. With both of us observing your reactions, along with each suspect's reactions, we might learn as much in twenty minutes' conversation as in another month in the lab."

"Then why didn't we do this a long time ago?"

"This is the first time you've named anyone consistently enough to be considered a genuine suspect. And—" After a time, she noticed Tommy was waiting for her to finish. "It's dangerous. But we have to try," she concluded lamely, not knowing how to explain; and not wanting to, anyway.

The last few days had changed her. Distorted or cleared her perceptions, she didn't know which. Her despair had strengthened her—or destroyed her concern with consequences. She didn't feel capable of returning to Bullock's to test Tommy with sweater fabrics. But stalking the killer felt no more impossible. For she could no longer retreat to her lab. It wasn't a refuge after all. No matter what she did, how she tried, she would be hurt the same amount. Hiding in her lab, buried in her work, it would simply happen more slowly.

They took turns with the Bushmills, then held hands as they discussed potential lines of questioning. With each prospect, she would start a conversation that touched on other possible reasons for Tommy's negative reactions—Sid's spying, Cynthia's shiftiness, Andy's affair with Bianca, Robert's history with Clare —and Tommy would assess whether those were the sole sources of his negativity. Tommy also felt it might help if he could witness each suspect's reaction when Clare just happened to mention that their murder investigation was hopelessly blocked. Beyond that, they couldn't plan. Clare's ensuing questions would be dictated by each suspect's prior responses.

Then they discussed ways of protecting themselves during these field experiments, but there wasn't much they could plan there, either. As they contemplated possible futures, a smothering silence fell.

Gradually, Clare's shaking subsided and Tommy's cheeks regained color. They returned to the apartment in hopes of a few hours of sleep. Once there, sharing Robert and Clare's bed was impossible, so they clung together on the couch, with Jessie sprawling across their hips. Clare lay immobile so as not to disturb Tommy, wondering if time was passing as slowly as it seemed.

"You ever gonna fall asleep?" Tommy whispered.

"I doubt it. How about you?"

"No way." And so they held each other for a time, then got up and got started.

Clare phoned her teaching aides to say she would not be attending her classes. Yes, she realized she was to begin reviewing for finals. The aides should take questions and compile lists of problem areas for her to tackle when she returned on Wednesday.

Meanwhile, Tommy composed a note to Beaudine, explaining about the four suspects. If anything happened to Clare and Tommy, the note could lead the police to their killer—although it was clearly information Beaudine would dismiss if they presented it to him now. When Tommy went to drop the note in the corner mailbox, Clare phoned Dean and Sandy in the adjoining apartment: she might have to go out of town suddenly; could they check on Jessie and care for her if Clare didn't get home?

Petting Jess goodbye nearly overwhelmed Clare and she had to run outside before she lost the ability to leave at all.

CHAPTER 17

Chimeric Faces

Tommy was so preoccupied with events to come, he didn't notice anything odd about her car being parked a block away, in someone else's carport. Beaudine's watcher was back, but indifferent to their departure. They headed for campus, where on this sunlit weekday morning, they would be least vulnerable during their confrontations. From Clare's lab, Tommy called the Physics office, pretending to be a student. He learned that Dr. di Marchese would be hearing thesis orals all morning, but was scheduled for drop-in student appointments between 1:30 and 3:00 this afternoon.

Last night they had decided they could not confront Andy at home without immediately provoking excessive suspicion. A much safer alternative was to approach him while he was at work. Thus Clare now phoned Le Gym to inquire when that hunky Andy Stuart would be teaching aerobics today. Starting at noon? She'd be there.

They kept trying to devise an excuse to get Cynthia Bates to come to Clare's office. But they feared such efforts would put Cynthia on guard, with too much time to fortify defenses. They could see no way around it: they would have to pay her a surprise visit at home.

But first they went down the hall to Sid Stein's suite of labs. Sid's secretary had just splattered Diet Pepsi on her new blouse when they arrived; she was less than cordial. "You can't see him. There's no point waiting. Excuse me, I have to get this out before it stains."

She hurried out and down the hall. To the bathroom, or to warn Sid? Tommy and Clare sat stiffly, only slightly less so as the secretary's pumps snapped their way back up the hall.

The splatters were gone and so was her surliness. "Dr. Stein was called away on a family emergency. He left last Wednesday afternoon. We just don't know when he'll be back, but I am expecting him to check in. Is there a message?"

"Darn, I need that information today. Can you give me a phone number?"

"I'm afraid not. He left strict instructions. Confidentially, his parents always worry that he puts work before family; now that his father's in the hospital, Sid—Dr. Stein wants to prove otherwise." The secretary was thrilled to be privy to this personal information about the great doctor.

"Of course I understand" that they'd have to get the number some other way. Clare led Tommy to the Biology office, turned him loose on the sweet young thing at the computer. Ten minutes later, they were back in Clare's office studying a printout suitable for an FBI file on Dr. Sidney Stein.

Parents Martin and Louise lived in Freeborough, New Jersey. From long distance Information, Clare obtained numbers for three Martin Steins in Freeborough vicinity. Two were not the proud forebearers of the great doctor. At the third number, there was no answer.

"Bates next?" Tommy suggested.

Clare felt the murderer's presence all around as they returned to her car. Today was sunny with just the right faint breeze, as perfect as a day in early spring. Yet she might as well be lost in strange alleys at three A.M. Stalking the killer was far more ominous out in the world than from within the lab. Everything was safer in the lab. Still, the further they got from those rooms, the greater was her sense of release, contradicting yet coexisting with her fear.

As they drove to Cynthia's, they reviewed their planned line of attack. They had come to question her about the arrest rumor, they would say. If she didn't believe this, they would "admit" they were looking for more files she had stolen from Colton. If she didn't believe that. Well.

They pulled into Cynthia's cul-de-sac. Clare shivered—and was grateful to see activity in the Bates driveway: the maid, apparently. A plump woman with Latin coloring wearing a butcher's apron was loading a vacuum cleaner into an old but well-kept station wagon. She flashed Tommy and Clare a polite stranger's smile as their car rounded the street's curve and braked in front of the house. The maid returned inside. Clare and Tommy exchanged a glance and strode up the flagstone walkway.

Once standing on the porch, Clare resumed shivering—but she had plenty of time to regain control. It took several minutes for the doorbell to be answered. The maid now strained to smile and opened the door only a crack. *"No está aquí, lo siento, nadie está aquí,"* she kept repeating. She shook her head to indicate she didn't understand their questions, then shut the door with a firm click.

Sitting in the car contemplating this turn of events, Clare saw a second story window curtain sway in the breeze. Not in a breeze—that window was shut.

"Did you see that?" Tommy demanded. "Cynthia's up there, isn't she?"

"And not terribly eager to see us today."

"I say we pretend we didn't notice, come back later when the maid's gone and Cynthia's not expecting us."

They went back to the porch. This time the maid simply called through the door. "I understand no one is home except you," Clare called loudly. Not just the second story but the whole neighborhood would hear. "Please tell Mrs. Bates I'll try phoning her tonight about seven." As they departed, the maid came out to the porch and watched them drive from sight.

"Wait before you reply, to assess all your reactions. How do you feel about Cynthia now?"

"No differently. Shit."

"Try not to think about anything that just happened. We'll come back to this later."

They returned to campus. From Clare's office they called the New Jersey Stein number again. At last, some semblance of success: on the fourth ring, an elderly male, immediately likable voice answered. "Sure I know Dr. Sid," he cackled.

"Are you his father?"

"That's me. Retired, that's why I'm home during work hours. Worked my whole damned life away."

"How are you feeling? Sid—said you weren't well."

"No complaints besides this damn rheumatism. He talks about me?" The elder Stein sounded so pleased, Clare could only murmur assent. "You say you work with him?"

"Yes and I've been told I might reach him with you."

"Sid? Here?" Martin Stein was an actor to rival Olivier or he was astonished by the suggestion. "He hasn't been home in six years." The voice relayed a nonjudgmental sorrow.

"I know. He's told me how much he misses you." She knew parents were often sweeter when talking about their kids than when talking to them; it still seemed a shame that this lovely old man had that rotten son.

"We miss him, too," Sid's father confided. "Will you look at the time? I've got to pick up mother from the hairdresser. It's been very nice meeting you, miss."

Clare assured him the pleasure was mutual, hung up and told Tommy what he already knew. "Sid did not go home for a family emergency."

"Wonder if he even left L.A.?"

Clare's thoughts iced over. She preferred believing him out of town. "I wonder how we can find out where he is."

"Deirdre," they said simultaneously. They studied the data Clare had obtained during her previous search for Deirdre. The departmental records listed the same bogus phone number Deirdre had given Steve. But Clare realized that she knew Nicky Julen, the graduate teacher's aide in one of Deirdre's classes. Nicky was that rare type who couldn't be swayed by campus gossip. Therefore, if he knew how to contact Deirdre, he'd be willing to tell Clare, this month's pariah.

He was in his office when she called. Yes, he might have a number for Deirdre Costello, "but there's no point in calling it. She left a note for me over Thanksgiving, asking that her final be postponed. She had to fly home for a family emergency. Her father's in the hospital."

"Ah. I should have checked my message box. No doubt she left me a note, too. She's very reliable." Clare exchanged brief chitchat with Nicky then slammed the phone down, suddenly feeling as though Sid Stein could hear the conversation.

Before she'd finished telling Tommy about the call, he jumped up from her couch and declared, "Sid's it."

"Is that what you're sensing? Wait and assess reactions that aren't immediate, too. But stop for a moment and consider—it's human nature to jump to conclusions. It's all part of the same need for answers that makes your left brain confabulate. Realize that, and separate such explanations from your reactions when I ask you: Is Sid Stein the killer?"

He stopped pacing, looked inward. "No. Fuck. I can't tell. Maybe yes, maybe no. But why else would he and Deirdre split with the same jive excuse after you caught them spying?"

"I don't know. But it is possible that Sid is simply a snoop. Even though we work in different fields, spying could help him to follow up or branch off from my work; or give him advance wind of any breakthroughs—which could mean a head start, insinuating himself into position to catch some of the extra money that always gets thrown around once a breakthrough is publicized." Tommy grunted. "Yes, he is slimy, but not necessarily murderous. Does what I've just said alter your reactions to him?"

He stopped pacing, closed his eyes, at length replied. "I'm not sure. Check again later when it's not so fresh in my thoughts. So which suspect do we miss next?"

Clare consulted her watch. "It's a little past eleven. If we go to the gym now, we can talk to Andy before his first class."

Le Gym was on the western outskirts of Pasadena. The drive was excruciating: every street they took had construction equipment and workers blocking lanes. As they idled in one gridlock or another, they discussed other ways of confronting Sid Stein. Which might just have to wait until he and Deirdre returned to town. If they did. If they had ever left.

"I'm starting to appreciate Beaudine more," Clare said.

"No shit. Next to us, even he's a good detective. You been watching for anybody following us? Not that either of us would know anyway." Tommy slid down in the seat, leaped up to straighten, slouched anew. Since they'd left the apartment this morning, he'd vibrated with tension and the vibrating was getting worse.

"If you don't try to maintain a bit more calm, you're not going to make it through this." And he was going to push her right over the edge she'd been teetering on, these past several days.

"Sorry. Sorry. When I get scared, I get hyper."

She darted a glance his way. "Scared. I don't dare even admit to that."

"That's kind of what I mean. All this time it's taking to get to our suspects, is giving me too much chance to think about what could happen once we do. Get to them."

"This is absolutely the wrong time to be discussing this," Clare stated emphatically, as she pulled into Le Gym's parking lot.

It was 12:18. Yet the parking space marked ANDY was empty. Clare parked an overview's distance from the old warehouse converted to muscle palace. Tommy studied the staff parking area. "I don't see Bianca or Trish's cars either, so he didn't ride in with them."

As they sat, a man pulled his Mercedes into a red zone and walked briskly inside. Clare mused, "He looks familiar but I can't say why. I didn't know I knew anyone who drove a Mercedes."

After ten minutes that felt like months, Tommy sighed with relief and irritation. "Let's split. I've heard Bianca bitch about what a flake Andy is. About how late he can be. Anyway, if he drives in and sees us just sitting here, he's gonna wonder. We can come back later. Once Andy shows up, his shift'll go at least seven hours." As Clare started the car he added, "Shit. This is a lot to go through to still have four suspects."

"I know. I'm trying not to feel discouraged, but this is too much like being in the lab—we may be learning something, but I don't know what."

They returned to San Marino. This time they parked around the corner from Mrs. Bates's home, inviting phone calls to 911 about prowlers: they ran low beside fences and shrubbery down the cul-de-sac to her house, up the driveway to her garage. The maid's station wagon was gone. The side door was unlocked. Would this constitute breaking and entering?

Clare fought terror, would have fled if Tommy had not already entered the service porch. The instant she stepped inside the house, she felt claustrophobic, trapped. The sky was hazing, the windows glowed an eerie dull gray, foreshadowing rain. Had she rolled up the car window? Why was she thinking such pettinesses?

They walked softly and the kitchen linoleum, then the dining room carpet, absorbed the sound of their progress. Still, Clare had a strong sense of being observed. Stepping from dining room to hall, she heard a creak and ducked backward, expecting to find Mrs. Bates wielding a hatchet. But the area was empty. Tommy was a room ahead now; Clare entered the hallway as he left it for the den. She dove to tug at his sling, her throat pulsing with fear. Her expression alarmed him; his eyes darted, searching for the source of threat.

"We're going too far." Clare said softly. "We—"

"What are you doing in my house?" At such close range, the low-pitched demand sounded like a growl. They swung around, found Cynthia at the arched entry to the living room. Upon eye contact, all three took a step back.

"We need to, um, speak with you." Clare fumbled the simple phrase.

"So you've come for me," Cynthia whimpered.

An admission of guilt? Clare dared a glance at Tommy, who watched Cynthia intently. "We came to talk to you earlier, but you wouldn't let us in."

"Let's sit here by the fire." With feigned hospitality and without turning her back, Cynthia led them into the living room. As Clare and Tommy moved to arm chairs flanking the fireplace, Cynthia lunged toward the mantle. She grabbed a brass poker in one hand, brass shovel in the other, wildly throwing her head from side to side to keep them both in view. Between and behind her legs, orange flame rolled liquidly over presto logs, a tiny phony fire in the vast austere stone hearth. In other circumstances, it would have been laughable. Fireplace poker, that was how Dr. Haffner had died.

As Cynthia swung the weapons up and ready for use, Clare was able to ponder the possibilities: this chair could be tilted in Cynthia's path, that marble sculpture on the coffee table used against her. Haffner had been taken by surprise. Cynthia might injure one or both of them today, but she didn't have the advantage—unless she was in a particular psychotic state that gave her extraordinary strength. Tommy reached toward his neck and Cynthia shrieked, "Don't move! Stay where you are!"

Tommy kept his hand behind his head. "Got some hair caught under my sling, that's all," he said casually. Peripherally, Clare saw him pull the sling in such a way that its tension slacked around his left arm. He eased his elbow out of the fabric—freeing his arm for use, if necessary, however painful that might be.

Clare tried to distract Mrs. Bates. "If we could just talk about this."

"You won't be successful," Cynthia pleaded. "I'll leave such a mark. You might get away for now but they'll find out you were here, they'll know you did it."

Her words tumbled around Clare, who fell against a chair before she completely lost equilibrium. Cynthia squinted, suspecting a trick; resumed that wild head turning to keep both in view. "You think we came to kill you," Clare marveled.

Cynthia's head stopped swiveling, although her eyes kept flickering. "It's not necessary, I assure you, Clare. I won't say a word to anyone. Look how quiet I've kept about those files."

"This is nuts," Tommy said carefully. "We thought you were going to kill us."

Cynthia peered at him, searching for the meaning behind this new deception. "I'd hide you here but I'm sure they'll return. The police, that is. Money! I can give you money, you'll get away, by the time the warrant becomes official you can be across the border. I shouldn't fly though, that might be traceable."

"What warrant?"

Cynthia's nervousness evaporated. With a sly camaraderie, she explained, "The warrant for your arrests. As soon as Lieutenant Beaudine found out about the funding problem, he had his motive. You didn't get that stipend last summer because Stanford recommended you be denied. So you avenged yourself. With the help of your lover." She raised a knowing eyebrow at Tommy.

"I don't recall being turned down for money last summer, and I certainly never knew of any sabotage by Dr. Colton. If I did, it wouldn't drive me to murder. I lose grants all the time, just like everyone else. And I don't believe Lieutenant Beaudine is foolish enough to call that a motive." Clare moved closer to Tommy.

Cynthia waved the poker, muttering, "Stop, don't, stay where you are." Clare ignored her. Tommy had inched around so that he had a chair between Cynthia and himself. They had a direct line out of the room; Cynthia had an obstacle course to run. But they wouldn't bolt—yet. She hoped Tommy had been able to assess—something, already; but she would keep provoking until he gave a signal to leave.

"Stop pretending to be threatened, Cynthia. We're here because we have reason to believe *you* killed Colton; and—"

Cynthia sagged against the mantle, dropping the poker, chipping the hearthstone. "Do what you like with me. God knows I deserve it. Do what you like," she intoned.

"Let's get out of here," Tommy said decisively. Baffled, Clare followed Tommy down the hall and out the front door, then jogged along the sidewalk after him. Dimly, she was aware of tree-root-cracked concrete beneath her feet, a rush of clipped greenery at her sides. Still vividly in view was the image of Cynthia Bates sagging against her fireplace, the now blue and green liquid flames rolling behind her. *Do what you like with me, God knows I deserve it.*

Once in the car, Tommy used his arm sling to mop his face. Clare touched his cheek. It was clammy cold, yet he was sweating. "That was the fucking weirdest scene I've ever played," he said. "She still thinks we're going to kill her. And toward the end it seemed like she wished we would."

"I know. I'd convinced myself it was all an act—that she was trying to confuse us. And succeeding. But the way she looked as we were leaving . . ."

"Maybe it was an act. That makes it even weirder." He leaned his head against her shoulder. "I feel like I'm going down a water slide, belly up and head first."

"I'm going to make a statement. Try to assess your reactions when you hear it. But first, breathe more slowly; and deeply." He was still in that cold sweat state. As he lengthened his breathing, she used his sling to wipe his face dry. He worried her, but that would have to wait. "Here's the statement: Cynthia Bates is the killer."

His breath caught then released. "No."

"You can't sort out your reactions?"

"I think I can. I think it's not her. But it's like when you asked me about Sid Stein. I may need some time for all this to settle." She touched his forehead; he was warming up. Sensing her concern, he said, "I dunno why I got like this. When she grabbed that poker—no, this came on later. When I started feeling like she wasn't the one. I mean, if dealing with her was so rough. What's it going to be like if I'm squared off with somebody and all of a sudden I know. This is the killer." He shuddered.

"Maybe it's time to turn this over to Beaudine."

"And tell him—what? That I don't get the feeling Cynthia Bates is the killer? Or that Sid and Deirdre both claim they have family emergencies? Forget it. It takes a corpse to get his attention."

"Could he really be putting a warrant out for us? How can he be that stupid? On the other hand, he does assign men to watch our homes whether we're there or not."

"And then they miss minor details like Hugo. Well, if there is a warrant, we've got to hustle before the fucking cops arrest us." They pulled into the gym parking lot. "Shit, there's Bianca's car." There was a car in Andy's parking slot, too. "Man, I am not up for this one."

"Then let's wait."

He considered waiting, with the yearning of an emphysemic craving a cigarette, then shook his head. "We can't."

"Then let's review one more time: we go in, I hover in the background while you say you want to talk to Andy—and Bianca, if we can't avoid her."

"Then I make a few remarks about them fucking, try to get them going so they're talking and I'm figuring out whether that's the only reason I hate Andy."

"Now what if he suggests going somewhere private to talk? Considering how things went with Cynthia, we definitely want a crowd within screaming distance."

"No shit. If that happens I insist that talking in public is the only way I can guarantee not losing it and punching him or something."

However disturbed he'd been leaving Cynthia's, he was already more upset about being here. Clare waited for him to make a move inside. He would know when he was ready.

There was that man again. The Mercedes driver she knew from somewhere. Exiting with him was another familiar-looking man, younger, pudgy and unfit, yet wearing the gym staff's distinctive black sweatshirt emblazoned with a hot pink LE GYM. ASK ME. "Taylor something," she said in the first man's direction. "Now I remember. I know them from Tekassist. The one with the Mercedes is a chief executive. The one in the sweatshirt was in middle management, although I'd heard he'd been fired. His name was—Ron."

"The guy in the sweatshirt calls himself Glenn here. He's the daytime manager. Which is weird because Le Gym never hires anybody who's not a perfect specimen. He's the one who loaned me the Datsun with the bum tires. The other guy, Taylor? I see him here a lot, bossing the employees around. What's Tekassist?"

"Part of a conglomerate, I don't know which one. They supply lab animals to researchers who don't raise their own. It's very big business, especially with this new genetic engineering of mutant creatures designed to suit specific experiments. Perhaps 'Glenn' was transferred, not fired. Although I can't imagine why Tekassist would operate Le Gym."

They watched Taylor walk his alleged ex-employee to a BMW. He seemed to be giving orders before he got in his Mercedes and sped away. The BMW pulled up to the gym entrance, stopped with brake lights glowing. Ron alias Glenn ran inside, ran back out wearing a plain gray sweatshirt, jumped in the car, and sat fidgeting at the wheel.

Clare started to speak, then the gym door opened and Andy Stuart, dressed in civvies, ran out and around to jump in the beemer. But the passenger door was locked and while waiting for "Glenn" to unlock it, Andy dropped a thick manila folder. Papers scattered. "Glenn" ran to help collect every last one.

"There he is," Tommy whispered.

"Damn, we've missed this chance to talk to him. Before they drive away, take a good look at him. As you did with Sid Stein, recognize your preconceptions about Andy. And sort out any changes in your reactions over time, when I ask: Is Andy Stuart the killer?" During this, she had kept her eyes on Andy, as though she could will him to remain in view. Now she regarded Tommy with alarm. His face was contorting in pain.

"I don't—I can't—" he cut himself off with a guttural sob. Tears poured down his face. His left arm was shaking. Clare hurried to rearrange the sling; he must have loosened it too much, at Cynthia's. His fingers gnarled and strained, and his elbow straightened, causing him to cry out and wrench his face. A twisted finger pointed at Andy and Clare belatedly understood.

Andy Stuart was the killer.

The BMW was driving out of the lot. Clare started her car and followed. Now that she could at last see the killer, it seemed essential to keep him in view.

"God, Bianca," Tommy said.

"We should warn her." Clare braked.

Tommy waved her on. "We will. But she's safe until Andy finds out we're on to him. And right now, I want to know why that fucker's not at work."

Clare sped up to keep the beemer in view. "I wonder if he's been seeing Bianca so much in order to keep tabs on you."

Tommy nodded then shouted, "Sweatband! GodDAMNit! Watch out, don't drive too close. If you stay in the other lane you can see them from further away."

"But what if they turn suddenly?"

"Shit, you're right. Don't ask me, I couldn't even figure out a simple fucking." He paused, then continued less explosively, "It wasn't a sweater cuff I touched. It was a sweatband. Like Andy has on his wrists today."

"Shit is right. Well at least you figured it out—it might help Beaudine. Damn. I've never wanted a car phone before. We should call Beaudine."

"And tell him my arm twitched and I felt real bad just like in our lab tests, so that's his man? Fuck, even I don't believe it. How could Andy be the killer? What did he have against all those people?"

"Perhaps nothing, if he's psychotic. Or perhaps Tekassist is behind the murders. Andy used to work there too, don't forget. Not that Tekassist makes sense, either. None of the victims used Tekassist services. And the company is so huge, so powerful. They wouldn't need to resort to murder. They'd just phone their lawyers and congressmen."

"Some kind of coincidence though, if nothing's going down. Two ex-Tekassist guys taking orders from their ex-boss. All three of 'em looking worried. And one of 'em, my brain says is a killer." Tommy tried to peer into the BMW's smoked glass windows. "I bet they're going to the freeway."

A few minutes later, as they passed the last stoplight on Arroyo Parkway before it became the Pasadena Freeway, Tommy won his bet. "Downtown?" Tommy wondered next, but this time guessed wrong. They did take the Santa Ana Freeway west, passing near downtown L.A.; and at this point, the BMW indeed took an offramp—but then headed northeasterly, away from those few aging skyscrapers and rapidly spreading highrises, that skyline that seemed to double in volume each year. Clare lagged farther back, feeling too noticeable as they trailed the BMW along empty boulevards beside rusty railroad tracks and smog-pitted metal warehouses.

After that brief bit of industrial badlands, they were in a barrio. Here she pulled closer: there were many cars and, amazingly, much foot traffic as well. The pedestrians were all Latino; a few looked hostile about the passing Anglos; a few looked fearful: was Immigration about to sweep the area? The BMW turned right at a red light. When Clare reached the intersection, the light was green and a thick surge of pedestrians blocked her turn. Finally the last stragglers were through the crosswalk.

Tommy informed her, "He turned right again, two lights down. I think. Shit."

She screeched up the side street and around the corner he'd indicated, spotted brake lights some blocks away, turning left. Yes, there was the BMW, driving through residential streets now, an area clearly impoverished but strongly a community, unlike most sections of L.A. Kids played in yards and around parked cars. A man stopped his pickup in the street to chat with a neighbor sweeping a sidewalk. When the BMW sped by, they both glared and yelled to some children, motioning for them to stay out of the street.

The next side street climbed a two-block hill. There, older kids jeered as the BMW approached, then threw rocks and garbage at the car. Their hate-filled gestures were visible in stark silhouette against the gray afternoon sky. Clare and Tommy made sure their windows were up and braced for a similar barrage. But when they passed, the kids ignored them. "Guess they used all their ammunition," Tommy said. "Where the fuck are these guys going?"

She didn't reply—she was fully occupied with not seeming to

be following the beemer. A mile further, she had to brake and slow to stay back out of view. The residences had thinned into a vast wasteland of rotting factories and shut down storage facilities along wide streets spotted with irrelevant traffic lights. In a different economic era the tri-colored sentinels no doubt regulated thousands of employees; but now two cars were the only signs of life. Far ahead, one light turned red and the BMW didn't even brake for it. By the time Clare reached the intersection, the light had turned green and then red again.

The beemer disappeared over a slight incline. When Clare and Tommy reached the top of the rise, the road ahead was empty. Clare sped up, slowed at an intersection, peered down the side street. Nothing. No one. She sped up to another intersection. Nothing. No one. The next intersection yielded the same result. They started driving in circles, loops, hoping to see the BMW parked somewhere.

The longer the car was out of Clare's view, the more she dreaded seeing it again—speeding straight at them or swerving into place directly behind. These vast empty streets left them incredibly exposed.

"We lost 'em. Only car for miles. God fucking damn it!"

Tommy's litany of swearing ceased mid-blue-syllable when Clare asked fearfully, "Did they know we were following them?"

"Nah. They would have driven differently. Turned more often, doubled back, stuff like that." Was he feigning that assurance?

"I think it's time to call Beaudine—and warn Bianca."

"Bianca might be safer not knowing, for now. Until Andy's locked up—I mean, what if she acted scared around him? He'd know why. Beaudine? Yeah, if we can reach him soon. Wherever Andy and 'Glenn' were going, they were in a hurry to get there. Which makes me think we've got to act fast, too. But fuck if I know what else to do. Except go find a phone."

Clare turned the car around, attempting to retrace their route; fighting an escalating agitation: on top of everything else they were hopelessly lost! She must remain calm. Was Tommy lost too? Calm, stay calm. If she asked and he said yes, could she bear it? Turn here? No not here either! Remember, Clare—calm. Turn here? N—yes? YES. There were the kids with the garbage, interrupting their play once again to watch the approaching car. Once again, the kids did not throw anything, though Clare saw many potential projectiles within their reach.

"What the—?" Tommy cried, so fast did she brake the car.

"They didn't throw anything at us again."

"Do we want them to?"

"Maybe they don't just attack any Anglos who pass by. Maybe they recognized the BMW. Or Andy or—" But Tommy was already out of the car, running to talk to the kids. Clare paused to take her keys but left the Nova double-parked.

The kids looked a little nervous and a lot curious as the strangers approached. Tommy smiled disarmingly while Clare politely requested, "May we talk to you?" The kids replied with blank stares. "About fifteen minutes ago a car went by, you threw things at it—it's okay, we don't mind, we'd like to throw things too." Still no response, although some of the kids began whispering among themselves. While she pondered other ways of winning their confidence, she realized the *sotto voce* discussions were all in Spanish.

She and Tommy exchanged a glance, then she smiled at the youngsters. "Do you speak any English?"

"Hi. How's it going?" the tallest girl replied.

Over the next few minutes, they determined that the kids knew a non sequitured assortment of English slang and advertising slogans. Which was superior to Clare's Spanish: she could order food and get directions to the ocean, the museum, and the library. Tommy knew a bit more than she, but none of his phrases could be repeated to minors.

Clare and Tommy were so clearly benign, so alarmingly somber, and so obviously frustrated by the lack of communication, that the kids became eager to break the impasse. In other circumstances, their efforts at pantomime would have been funny. But no one was laughing.

"This is nowhere. We're losing time," Tommy finally said. "We've gotta get an interpreter."

Clare looked around the neighborhood, saw no prospects. "I can start knocking on doors."

"We need a friend, somebody who'll trust us—'cuz who knows what we're gonna find out, or what we'll have to do about it?" He considered. "Dick speaks some Spanish but he's got swing shift this week. Who could you get?"

"Robert. He's fluent."

"Will he help us?"

"He has to."

It took another several moments to learn the location of a pay phone, back on the main thoroughfare. Tommy stayed with the kids, to make sure they stuck around. Clare took her car but had to park almost as many blocks away on the opposite side of the boulevard. She ran to the phone, then pointlessly plugged one ear against the haunted singing and strumming coming from the nameless bar next door; against the braking and revving autos at the corner signal; against the fast-paced conversations of pedestrians all around her.

Faintly, Robert's office phone rang. Or did it? The noise ceased. Or had it? Should she hang up and try again? What was that? At last—an irritated shouted "Hello!" penetrated. She spoke rapidly. "This is an emergency, don't hang up on me. I can't hear you, I'm at a pay phone on a very noisy street, please don't hang up." She waited, didn't hear a dial tone, eventually discerned yelling that sounded like Robert demanding "I repeat, what do you want?" She explained the situation, gave directions as best she could, begged him to hurry. "Will you come?" she kept repeating, but never heard the reply. She could only take hope from the fact that he'd remained on the line.

Next she spent a few chicken-sans-head minutes futilely hunting a quieter phone. She returned to the corner to find the original phone in use. Wondrously, the new user, a man calling numbers in the *La Opinion* classifieds, noticed her distress and handed the receiver to her. But her luck quickly reverted: from what she could discern when she called the Pasadena police station, Beaudine was out. A machine answered his home phone. She didn't leave messages—what should she say? She couldn't even give an accurate address.

When she got back to the kids, Tommy was playing catch with them. She told of her journey and joined in the game.

Thirty-odd minutes later, Robert found them. Clare was grateful when he drove up and their eyes connected: the look he gave hit her so hard, she was numb to him thereafter. He despised her and loathed Tommy: that was apparent in his refusal to look at them; in those clipped demands for information; in that hand that jerked up to halt additional speech from them, the instant he understood what they needed to find out. Of course, situations reversed, she doubted that she would have even answered her plea.

At first the kids were reluctant to answer Robert's inquiries, but slowly he won them over and eventually they were all shouting at once, raging against the BMW or its occupants. "El Malo . . . el Malo," Clare heard several times: it seemed to be a name, a name for someone these children hated more than Clare thought it possible for children to hate.

Finally Robert turned to inform a point equidistant between Clare and Tommy, "The men in the BMW work for someone who has taken terrible advantage of people in this neighborhood —hurt them dreadfully, maybe killed some of them—these children aren't sure; their parents stop talking when they realize the kids are listening. They do know there's a factory a couple miles from here where this man can be found; where these bad things happen."

"Did they give you an address to this factory?"

"No but they described the building and the general route to—" He paused as the children yelled protests across the street to a front door where an adult had appeared, apparently calling some of the children inside.

Then the man spotted Clare. He darted back into the house, slamming the door so hard it sprung back open. Clare gasped, belatedly aware of those eyes like black holes. "The man who attacked me. Who destroyed the labs."

Everything happened at once. Robert shouted questions at the kids, learned this was the uncle of three of them. Tommy and Clare yelled about getting help and ran for her car, then ran back to give chase instead. Robert dashed after them to join in. The kids trailed behind, sensing trouble and seeking to protect the Anglos' prey.

The tiny house across the street was empty—this was no surprise. Clare ran through living and dining rooms, past several stacks of mattresses. A large number of people lived in this cottage. Running out the open gaping kitchen door, Clare realized that in daylight the man no longer resembled a surfer despite his beachwear shorts and shirt. He was not tanned and blond. He was Latino—surely an illegal seeking to hide his origins—with bleached hair and mustache.

She stopped running to stand in the weedy backyard, listening to screeching tires and spraying gravel. Her attacker shoved the transmission of his ancient Falcon into gear and skidded out of the carport into the street and away. Clare, Tommy, and Robert sprinted down the driveway to the sidewalk—where the kids formed a protective wall, willing to fight to keep these treacherous strangers from giving further chase. Memories of Clare's attack grew diluted, distorted, as she faced these angry and defensive children. They clearly loved that man who so frightened her.

While she struggled to assimilate this, Tommy and Robert shouted their options. They knew where the man lived, they could come back for him later. Likewise, they would wait before attempting to reach Beaudine, or summoning some other cop who would have to be filled in to be of help. Now, before it got dark, they should use the kids' vague information to locate the facility where the bad things occurred.

They took Robert's car; it wouldn't be recognized if the BMW had spotted Clare and Tommy before. Once the three were enclosed, they recalled how unpleasant being together was. This kept them stiffly polite but otherwise was ignored. Briefly, Clare fretted about parking her car outside the deranged surfer's home, but she had no real choice.

Less than two miles away, they found it: a deserted warehouse complex up an alley, fenced by chain link topped with barbed wire—like any of the complexes in the area. A faded sign on the triple-locked gate posted phone numbers to call to learn of progress with the layoffs. Surely this, like the surrounding installations, had long since declared bankruptcy. Yet there, inside the grounds, was parked the beemer, two vans, and a twenty-foot U-Haul truck.

All four vehicles were parked behind a trailer some distance from the warehouse entrance, as though to be hidden from any casual passersby. Robert threw his car into reverse, backed out the alley and down around a truly vacant facility across the street. From here, they could observe without being seen.

The setting sun tinted the sky a ghastly orange; the metal buildings turned sickly yellow, moldy brown, lifeless black. Headlights slid onto the access road. Clare thought she discerned the dark hulk of a Mercedes entering the complex.

"I say we try to get closer," one of them whispered, almost inaudibly yet they jumped. Robert snapped off the overhead light and they opened their doors.

They'd crept across the street and halfway up the alley when headlights reappeared. They hurled themselves to the dirt. Flattened against the ground, nose pressed into soil, Clare fought the urge to gag. The earth had a sour chemical odor. She eased her head to the side, just as Tommy's breath tickled her ear. "Looks like Mercedes taillights."

"Over here," Robert called, so softly she sensed rather than heard the words. They scrabbled forward until they could sit behind a swatch of spiking shrubbery.

She heard scraping, discerned Robert tearing at the earth like a dog. "The ground's hard but I think we can dig under the fence," he breathed.

A mimed and whispered debate ensued about whether they should move forward—or retreat and leave the rest to Beaudine. Suddenly a vise gripped Clare's shoulder, a pipe throttled her throat, a dead fish covered her mouth, stifling her scream. *Click* —a slice of light darted, blinding Robert *click click* Tommy *click click* Clare—*click*. Utter blackness engulfed them. They were discovered. Found out. Caught.

"Don't make a sound, all our lives depend upon it," a voice murmured against Clare's ear. The arm around her throat jerked for emphasis. Robert and Tommy, kneeling nearby, were similarly gripped by other captors. "Do you understand?" They nodded and were released.

"Hugo?" she whispered, too astonished to fear him.

Click. The light illumined his face for an instant. *Click.* Her shoulder was tapped, her arm tugged. She followed his lead and crept back, out, around, behind. Now they were in back of a warehouse that was next door to the one upon which they all, apparently, were spying.

They were led to a VW bus. As soon as they were all standing under a thick black curtain, the van's doors opened. Inside was light, warmth, and low conversation between a man and woman who pored over documents that were fringed at one end as though pulled from a shredder. The bus was crowded once these two squeezed over to admit Clare, Tommy, Robert, then Hugo and—the other two captors! Clare did a double take when she saw their faces.

"Hello Dr. Austen," Matt Woods said. "We lied about the grant."

"But if we had any to give, we would unquestionably give one to you," Yvonne Hankoff added apologetically.

"It would seem we are all on the same side after all," Hugo intoned. "Else you would be inside those gates."

"And in the ninth circle of Hades," one of those at the documents remarked. Hugo made introductions all around but Clare was incapable of processing the new pair of names.

A light rap on a window, a low voice informed, "Vans moving out." So there was at least one more person still posted outside.

Hugo consulted his watch. "Another few minutes and we'll go in. There's a period after they remove the day's refuse, before night security is full on, when it's safest for us. I don't wish to be mysterious, I'll explain as much as time allows. It's horribly gruesome but you must join us. Otherwise you just might not believe me."

"You sure you're not trying to be mysterious?" Tommy demanded.

"We're members of an organization—which one, you don't need to know," Yvonne Hankoff began. "We use the grant giving and other ruses to collect information on particularly inhumane animal research."

"And once we know enough," Matt Woods continued, "We liberate the animals. But we don't move in until we can close the lab, not just rescue the current victims. We make sure we have enough evidence to force the media to pay attention, to force the cops to take action."

"Each serves to keep the other honest," Hugo noted.

"There's research being done next door? Why would anyone work out here?" Robert was puzzled.

Hugo consulted his watch, replied in a rush. "Exactly what we wondered. We'd gotten wind of primate experiments Colton was conducting on memory, brutal stuff indeed. But—"

"This is where Stanford Colton conducted research?" Clare was thrown to the far side of confusion. Too many shocks in too short a time: it became a tremendous struggle to hear, much less comprehend, as Hugo kept explaining.

"Yes. It took weeks to find his testing site, more weeks to

sneak inside. Once there, we had to completely alter our plan of attack. We didn't liberate, we collected proof—and tried to determine who was responsible, who was funding him. We had to be very careful, very complete, we dared leave no questions unanswered."

"But right away he was killed and they started shutting down the operation. Their need for secrecy has slowed them somewhat but it's almost gone and we still don't know who's behind it. If we don't find that out, Colton will be chalked off as a mad scientist and they'll get away with it. Maybe even set up shop again with someone new." If Yvonne could kill those responsible, there was no question she'd be happy to do so.

"What 'operation'? 'They' who?" Robert said with a particular type of irritation he exhibited when not following a conversation.

"Tekassist," Clare said, capturing the attention of all.

"To be continued," Hugo regarded her with frustration and excitement. "We've got to go inside. Now. Follow our leads, *exactly*. Lives are truly at stake."

Along the back of the facility, farthest from the street, where the building shielded the fence from the parking areas, a hole had been dug under the chicken wire and carefully hidden with bushes. One at a time, they crawled through. Once on the grounds, as they crept forward Clare noticed that the BMW, vans, and U-Haul were gone. Only one nondescript late-model American sedan was parked now. They inched around it, ran-crawled along the warehouse wall and slipped in the door.

Five of them crowded in a tiny anteroom while Yvonne scouted ahead, disappearing into a dimly lit hall. At last she returned and beckoned them forward. While waiting, Clare had time to anticipate all sorts of horrors, but nothing she could imagine could prepare her for the reality at the end of that long dark hall.

CHAPTER 18

Grand Mal

No longer would Clare mourn Stanford Colton's death. She hoped he'd been killed because of these experiments—and wished he'd passed on before beginning them. All those years admiring missing regretting. At some point, thanks to this new view of her mentor, she was going to have psychological hell to pay. But it would never rival the misery in this place.

In one small room, caged primates, cats, rats, and mice were in various stages of cranial dismemberment. Many were dead, the rest were dying: food dishes were dusty, water receptacles were green with scum. Here, some chimps and cats moved weakly, repetitively, as though trying to reenact behavior that had at one time won them food rewards. There, some mice writhed in pain. The rest simply lay in unnatural postures. Those still possessed of the proper brain regions panted in exhausted terror; those whose eyelids were not stitched shut stared fearfully or vacantly. A few strained their jaws to cry or howl; but as was common, their vocal chords had been cut to prevent such irritating noises.

Still, Clare had seen such sights in other research facilities. Only the sense of abandonment, of no longer monitored suffering, made this place unique. As though reading her thoughts, Hugo whispered, "We think he used these poor creatures to recreate the results of his primary experiments, so that he could publish his findings."

She didn't see what he meant until they reached the huge main room of the warehouse. And then she saw more than she could ever forget.

Yes, the test setups were the same here as in the smaller site next door. But here the test victims were humans. Latinos, the majority males.

In a nearby cage, three men performed weak repetitive movements; they reminded Clare of one cluster of chimps and cats in the anteroom. In another cage, Clare saw several old men writhing with strange twists identical to those certain of the mice had made. From Hugo's comment, Clare now deduced that Colton had experimented on humans, then tried to duplicate the results with other animals.

Neuroscientific advancement was ongoingly hampered, having to conduct nonhuman animal research to learn about the human brain. Clare had often heard Colton complain of all the gaps and limitations. Clearly he'd gone over the edge—to commit scientific cannibalism. But he hadn't gone so far over as to think his shortcuts would be sanctioned by his peers. And so he researched other animals after the fact: when he could duplicate the human results, he could publish the nonhuman experiments —with no one aware that he was working backward; with most everyone instead applauding his genius.

Contemplating how Colton had arrived here helped ease the impact of his lab. Morally, Clare found no difference between experiments on human and nonhuman creatures. But she could now fully sympathize with Jessie's terror, the day Clare had brought her in to her office near all those campus labs. For, as a member of *Homo sapiens*, the sensations of suffering here created a particularly visceral horror in Clare. To hear those men and women, with sutures and hollows where their vocal apparatuses had been, making those disemboweled moans. To see this group with eyelids stitched shut—christ, that one was barely a teenager! Or those two: naked, strapped down, immobilized save for rapidly darting eyes, windows to brains no longer comprehending their situation, aware only that it was unnatural, painful, and frightening.

For a moment, Clare also could not move. She could feel straps tightening against her own flesh, compressing her until she thought she would implode to escape the horrors she was witnessing. Her shaking released her from these bonds and she looked around, as through a long tunnel, an abyss at the other end.

A few of the subjects were dead; nearby discarded syringes made Clare guess that they'd recently received lethal injections. There were many empty cages in here, empty save for those syringes. Nearby, Matt found a syringe with a bit of fluid still in it. Holding it gingerly, intently, he returned to the anteroom—to put some small nonhuman victim out of its misery, Clare assumed. She knelt and groped between bars to grab a syringe. Her sleeve caught and she flailed wildly, every nerve cell in her body panicking at being caught here.

The sound of Hugo's even voice brought her back to rationality, as he called out to the three newcomers, "They haul away bodies and paperwork every night. They shredded the paper at first, but shredding was too slow. We believe they wish to 'disappear' all evidence as quickly as they can. Another few days and their wish will be fulfilled. Yvonne's just signaled that the guard has gone out to make his check of the grounds. We have seven minutes to get to that office across the way, take as much paper from the stacks on the floor as we can carry. Don't touch the top sheaves, and leave the stacks at the same relative height." As the five scurried to join Yvonne in the office, "Three minutes to return to our door. The guard enters around back, we count to thirty and exit—absolutely silently."

Clare nodded briskly, assuming her most clinical persona, to fight the screams building deep inside her. Under strictest personal control, she detoured to observe a man of about thirty, strapped in a chair. His hands hesitantly yet frantically lifted one cup then another of the three overturned on a platform before him. Clare had seen his test done on other primates: a panel door would slide open, the subject would watch a researcher place a food reward under one of the cups, the panel would close for a set number of seconds, reopen—and the subject would have time to lift one cup. If he remembered which cup hid the food, he was allowed to eat it. Win or lose, the panel would close and the process begin again. But now there was no researcher, no rewards; the panel remained open and the man in the chair would keep trying, until the last of his strength gave out, to find a morsel of food.

Clare's control wavered and her scalp crawled, its flesh burned in patterns mirroring the crisscrossing surgical incisions on the man's shaved head. The incisions were in various stages of healing and scarring. She consulted the chart hanging outside his cage. A series of operations had been performed, removing new slices of his temporal lobes each time, to determine what sorts of memory functioning became impaired with each excision. She studied the man's sallow face, positioned her fingers near her eyes to exclude the beard growth on his jaw and chin, yet include the hooked nose, broad cheekbones. Those deep set black eyes under that wide forehead. Yes. He looked enough like the "deranged surfer" to be his twin.

"Clare hurry," Tommy galloped her way, using his right hand to balance papers nested precariously in his sling. He followed her stare to the man in this cage, stepped back in confusion. "Wait, what's he doing here? No, it can't be, we just chased him."

"I'm afraid this is a brother or cousin."

"No wonder the guy trashed a lab," Tommy whispered as Hugo waved them to silence and speed. Tommy collapsed against the cage bars. Clare had to drag him several feet, before he could continue on his own.

They were all too slow getting out. They'd barely crossed the anteroom to the hall before the guard was back inside, making his rounds. They crouched in the dark, heartbeats pounding in dangerous syncopation with the guard's heavy stroll and airy whistling. Clare swallowed a gasp: it was one of the blond fake cops who'd tried to enter her office, purportedly hunting the deranged surfer. She wondered if Bruce the vanished security guard was also part of this operation.

The blond fake cop's circuit of the anteroom was nearly complete when Matt Woods teetered and his top file folder hit the ground with an explosion. Yet somehow the stroll and whistle did not waver. At last there was a shriek of metal, echoing under Hugo's hiss, "He's in the third room. Go!"

The night air was no colder than that inside, but Clare shook so hard she ran erratically: there was a whole other room. In fact, running beside the outer wall, she realized that they'd been through less than a fourth of the building.

Back at Hugo's bus, all but Robert climbed inside quickly. He first had to finish his hacking dry retches, made worse by the effort to keep quiet. When he joined them, he looked humiliated as well as ill. Hugo handed him a handiwipe, then dabbed his own face with another, more in sympathy than in need. They had to wait another moment, for an odd clacking to subside: Tommy was shaking so violently that his jaw kept snapping his teeth. Fleetingly, Clare felt alarm—when would her own reaction set in?

"Tekassist," Hugo prompted her, which helped divert her alarm. "What is it and why do you think it funded Colton?"

Clare explained how her research with Tommy had led them to Le Gym's parking lot, there to sight Tekassist brass and ex-employees. Hugo and cohorts were baffled to learn that one of these had killed Colton, in whom they'd invested so much. But there was no time for imponderables.

Hugo returned discussion to Le Gym. "We'd followed a car from here to that gym, two weeks ago. It seems to be a front, perhaps good for money laundering (although that's a wildish guess, really). Or perhaps to keep their most scurrilous activities harder to trace back to the source. We couldn't learn much, nor trace the owners—there are dummy corporations and so forth, we haven't had the resources or expertise to sort through it all yet." He paused to make notes.

"Those people in the warehouse. Are they—were they—illegals?" Tommy asked.

"Yes, we have a fair bit of proof of that; and we're trying to convince relatives of the victims to talk to authorities. They're quite reluctant: some fear deportation or lack trust that justice could be done; most still hope to retrieve their loved ones and fear that talking will prevent it."

"They don't know everything, you see," Yvonne added. "Until we could be sure of helping, we decided to not reveal what we've seen inside. How could we tell those families their loved ones would be better off dead—but then offer them no recourse? Those outside know something is wrong but of course who could imagine such depravity? When the subjects were initially 'hired,' they were told only that they'd be working for a scientist; and that there'd be risks but their families would be well cared for while the subjects 'worked' inside."

"And the families have been paid—rather well, by illegals' standards—though never as much as initially promised. What nobody knew was that the hirees would never be allowed to leave. That if the experiments didn't kill them, they'd be 'sacrificed' for brain autopsy. My favorite vivisection euphemism, by the by. Those Tekassist bosses you named did the roundups for volunteers and they were oh so clever. They warned that the work was top secret and if anyone was caught snooping, everyone would lose their jobs. Also, they said that the work assignments would last at least three years—and it's not been that long, so very few on the outside are frantic at this point."

"Except about the rumors," Matt continued. "Which started after one man managed to sneak inside and saw his half brother doing tricks for food rewards. He goes insane whenever he talks about it and he's incoherent anyway, from years of contact with industrial pesticides. They can't decide whether to believe him. Unfortunately, they won't tell us who he is; they're very protective of him. The only reason they trust us at all is because they're so unsure what to do next. A woman recently tried to sneak in to find her husband and she vanished. That led to talk of storming the place with arms; we convinced them to let us try our way first."

"Then Colton was killed and we ran out of time. Now we've been wondering if we were right to intervene," one of the document examiners said.

Yvonne snapped, "More innocents would have died. We discussed that."

Hugo read Clare's reaction. "No, fighting among ourselves hasn't helped. But it can't seem to be avoided. The pressure and doubts have been so enormous."

"Have you been able to learn why Tekassist would want to fund Colton?" Robert inquired.

Facing an answerable question bolstered Hugo. "To an extent. We found paperwork—notes really—in Colton's hand, indicating his backers owned any future commercial applications of his work. His only concern was that a portion of the profits be channeled back to fund additional research."

"The bulk of his research was in memory. While I'd have to study his operation more thoroughly to guess where this work was leading, I'd imagine it could have lucrative applications," Clare said.

"How nice for everyone. Except those beings whose memories were sacrificed for the cause," Hugo noted sourly.

"Where do they take the bodies once they stack them in the U-Haul?" Tommy demanded.

"Somewhere in the desert. Other cars are so rare on those routes, we can't follow the deliveries to the precise site. Or sites, given the volume of burials."

Clare exchanged a glance with Robert. Was he also recalling their recent desert hike? They'd loved that Saharan stretch of dunes, joked about all the bodies that were supposedly buried there. Southern Californian deserts were legendary for hiding corpses. Apropos nothing except a brief respite from horrors, her thoughts flashed to beaches, which she had never enjoyed. Beach sand seemed used, tawdry, in a way that desert—beach sand. Damnation and of course. The <u>sand</u>.

Someone had just asked her a question, all were waiting for her response. "The bikini picture," she said to Tommy. "Sand. Sandy. Andy."

"Fuck. Andy! Andy goddamned Williams. 'Mooooon River,'" Tommy crooned, as he had the night his right brain had used that as a clue.

The others looked baffled or irritated. Clare began an apology for the digression, Matt Woods waved it away. "It gets to us too. Sometimes we can't stop telling jokes, singing campfire songs, anything to avoid what we're facing here. But time <u>is</u> running out. And what I'd asked you was, do you have any other information we can use?"

"I'm not sure. I do know where you can find the half brother who started the rumors in the barrio." She explained about the deranged half brother né surfer, while Yvonne and Matt took notes. "But surely it's time to turn this over to the police."

"Yes, but that doesn't end our work," Hugo replied. "We cannot take any chances. Above all, Tekassist <u>must</u> be implicated. Despite what we've uncovered, they could still slip away, when the blame gets laid."

Robert and Clare looked skeptical, so Yvonne elaborated. "We've found much documentation of legitimate research.

We're afraid they'll hide behind that, claim they had no knowledge of Colton's mad activities."

"On the other hand," one of the others added, with a casual irritation that suggested longstanding dispute, "if we don't move now, they'll get away with it anyway."

"Here's what we must do," Hugo commanded, terminating bickering. "Tonight we will take everything we've learned and compiled to the police and the media. Simultaneously, we will locate the half brother and determine if he is able to corroborate what we've seen. Further, we will station observers outside Le Gym—what a ghastly name—and outside this facility, so that, if word of our activities reaches Tekassist before the authorities do, their interim reactions will be chronicled. For, even if they aren't tipped off that something's afoot, we'll need some time to show this facility, to convince and prove, before we can get either reporters or police to the spa."

"My wife works at Le Gym," Tommy volunteered with a grimace. "We're not getting along so hot but for something like this. If we need her help she's available. She'd probably notice more than somebody hanging around outside."

"Excellent," Hugo nodded. "It could prove quite useful to have her in place as a witness, once the screws begin to turn."

Before Clare had time to assimilate what was happening, Hugo had assigned tasks: Matt and Yvonne to the barrio; his other two associates to the media; Hugo and Robert to Beaudine; Clare and Tommy to Le Gym. No questions? Then good luck and great speed.

As the VW bus doors were eased open, Robert took Clare's hand. "For God's sake, be careful," he managed to say, his voice breaking repeatedly. She squeezed his fingers and jumped outside, not daring to think about what lay before her. Not daring to think at all.

Luckily, when Clare and Tommy arrived at Le Gym, there was no sign of the BMW or the Mercedes, and many staff parking spaces, including Andy's, were empty.

The gym's glass entry doors were soundproof, it turned out. As soon as Clare stepped inside, she could no longer hear her own thoughts. Funky Top 40 blasted from the aerobics room, martial arts grunts exploded from the weights room. At the smoked glass reception desk lounged a blonde teenager in a halter top, tight shorts, leg warmers, and high heels. Tommy shouted several times. Clare heard "wife" . . . "Bianca" . . . over and over. Finally the girl understood and waved red-clawed fingers toward the back, mouthed the words "Office C."

They strode past the aerobics room, where a man and woman led a fast-paced class for couples. The instructors had microphones, took turns counting the beat and making entendres about the exercise positions. "An a one an a two an a. This is a good one to try in the privacy of your own homes. But for all of you who just met your partner in this class, don't do this one 'til your third date."

Down a hall, past the steam-opaqued sauna door, it was comparatively quieter. Tommy paused outside the door to Office C, gave Clare a quick kiss, knocked while entering the office: he'd never be able to hear a "come in," anyway.

The door swung wide, exposing Bianca on a chrome and leather loveseat—all wrapped up in a black and hot pink clinch with Andy Stuart. The two jumped apart, then moved closer when they saw who was disturbing them. Andy wiped his face, studied the crimson smear of lipstick on his fingers, then put his hand out in a warning as Tommy stormed toward them. "Hold it, bud, you made your choice."

Tommy played the jealous husband as though he were a natural for the part. He grabbed Bianca's arm, dragged her halfway across the room. He threw a verbal knife that pierced Clare's gut. "There's nothing between us. She came with me to prove it to you." Why had this been the only ruse they could devise, in case Andy happened upon their talk with Bianca?

Andy looked angry, Bianca looked doubtful. Tommy swept her into a short but strong kiss then held her lopsidedly against his bad arm, while whispering his affections. Andy stomped from the loveseat to the chrome and leather desk. He jerked open the middle drawer, yanked out a black and hot pink address book, and grabbed the phone. "You're not supposed to be back here. You don't leave right now, I have to call security."

"Surely we can settle this like adults," Clare tried to sound calm, tried to play the part of the other woman here to testify to save the marriage. She had to say something. Otherwise Andy might hear Tommy whispering to Bianca.

"Go get a barbell, a knife. A weapon. Don't let Andy see it when you come back and don't ask questions, don't say a word, just do it. Life or death." He released her with a final kiss and a possessive pat on the butt, then sauntered to the loveseat and flopped down. "Sure let's talk like adults. I could use a drink, honey, can you score one from the snack bar? Anything but carrot juice."

Bianca nodded and crossed the room, frowning a bit. Clare dropped her coat and fussed noisily, retrieving it, in an effort to keep Andy from seeing that frown. Then Bianca reached the door: slammed it, locked it, and pivoted swiftly to guard it, while announcing, "Andy, he knows. He told me to go get a weapon."

"No problem, we've already got one." Andy lifted a gun from the still-open desk drawer, trained it on Tommy then Clare in turns, smiling smugly.

His wit was lost on them. They could only gape at Bianca. "Yeah I was part of it," she shrugged at Tommy, then qualified: "I didn't *help*, except with trying to find out what you knew. But you wouldn't tell me. If you knew how hard I tried to protect you! Until I stopped wanting to try." She glared at Clare then at Tommy, whose lack of response propelled her to further justification. "I did it for both of us. You think you're happy with that starving artist shit but you wait a few years and you'll be sorry. I was going to get us some of those big bucks. Except there won't be any now."

"Because you killed the golden goose," Clare said to Andy. "It doesn't make sense. Why did you kill Colton?"

"Sit down. Please." The gun waved Clare to the loveseat, from which Tommy still gaped at Bianca. *Andy, he knows.* It wasn't clear that he'd heard anything since.

"Why'd I kill who?" Andy replied amiably once Clare was seated. "I don't have to tell you anything but what the hell. We'll call it a last request. How've you been Clare, anyway? Always good to see you."

"Why did you kill Stanford Colton if he was your access to the big bucks?"

"He flipped out, why do you think."

"You didn't know he was experimenting on humans?"

"Humans. That sounds funny. Of course we knew that. But he got excited about what he was finding out, brought that Haffner guy out to see his work. Everybody knew it had to be kept quiet. Haffner was going right to the cops, you could see it all over his face."

"And that was why you were waiting for Haffner with a fire poker when Colton dropped him off."

"That was some busy day. I had to run right over to take care of Stan before he told somebody else. Except you locked me out so I had to come back the next day. You can be a real pain sometimes, you know that, Clare? I mean I like you but sometimes."

He'd been on the fire escape the night she'd found the door open. She started to shudder at how close she'd been to a murderer, laughed instead. She was much closer right now.

Everyone but Tommy reacted to her laugh. He was still immersed in the news of Bianca's complicity. He didn't even notice when Clare glanced at him. Perhaps that was why one or both sides of his brain had resisted their experiments so often; perhaps he'd realized all along, somewhere in his brain, that Bianca was involved—and couldn't face that knowledge consciously. Branding himself—or Robert—as a killer was the closest he could get to admitting the truth.

Andy said, "So. Heard any good jokes lately?" Bianca snorted, looked up briefly from examining her nails for flaws and chips.

"What about Lalitha?"

"What's a laleetha?"

"The physics professor you murdered."

"Oh her. Yeah, that one was tough. They wanted it to look sort of like the Haffner job but not totally. Anyhoo. She was killed same as the bum. So nobody would start wondering too much, what the connection was between the other two. The real murders. Is that smart or what?"

Lalitha had died to camouflage the motive for the murders of Haffner and Colton. That couldn't be true, she must have learned too much, as Haffner had. To kill for no reason required an amorality far beyond simple murderous intent and—what was she thinking? Tekassist had funded Colton's research.

"That's not just smart. It's brilliant," Clare replied.

Andy relaxed into his chair, petting the gun and musing, "I thought we should've done a couple more deaths—even more confusing. Slightly different style every time, too, that's important. Is it true they drained the fish ponds when they found the pieces of the bum? Hey, fish have to eat too, you know?"

Tommy reacted now, albeit bizarrely. "What fish ponds?" he said.

"There are two cement ponds on campus, with koi and water lilies. Apparently Andy got creative, disposing of Larry's remains." Clare spoke with too much venom. Bianca winced as though fearing reprisal. Yet Andy's pleasant mood only improved when he heard "creative." The psychopath as artiste.

"Why weren't we killed?"

"Until now, you mean?" Andy chuckled.

Clare dared not tell him that the jig was up, the police were closing in, lest that news enable Tekassist to defend itself. Yet at some point she could say this, and surely then their lives would be spared, during Tekassist's scramble to save itself. The assumption was logical, but didn't feel convincing, when she listened to Andy chuckle.

"There was a lot of fighting about what to do with you two. You had clues to the main death. If you got snuffed, that could make Colton's death look like it mattered, when he was supposed to seem like just one of the gang. But it would be a drag if you figured out who did it, so why take the risk? You two caused us some worrying, for sure. Thanks for helping us decide. Only one thing to do with you, now. Right, Bee?"

"Shut up, Andy," Bianca said to her nails.

"Show them the bruises you took for them, baby."

"Fuck off, sweetheart."

At this, Andy chuckled again, a sound that made Clare queasy.

Tommy continued to stare at his spouse, seemingly oblivious to all else. At last he looked away, to tap his earlobe and inquire of Andy, "You wear that diamond in your ear the night you got Colton?"

"Yeah. Half a carat. Cubic zirconia though. Don't tell anybody, haha."

"I saw it that night," Tommy explained to all and none. "But I didn't know what I saw, until now." Of course! All those clues about ears, which Clare had solely interpreted to mean he'd heard the killer.

Now Tommy couldn't look at Bianca but with that catch in his voice, he could only be talking to her. "You were in on this from the first."

She nodded at her nails. Bianca wasn't happy, that was obvious. And the way Andy looked from his lover to her husband, Clare sensed that, even if Robert and Hugo and the police rescued them right now, Tommy would end up shot. Clare tried to distract Andy with desperate cordiality. "You set the fire at my apartment building, didn't you? That was especially clever work, even for you. The police don't even suspect arson. You've got everybody fooled."

For some reason, he reacted unpleasantly to "everybody." But just then the doorknob rattled. Bianca looked to Andy for guidance. He stiffened, relaxed when a key sounded in the lock. A moment later, the Mercedes owner entered.

"Hi Mr. Bloomington. They know," Bianca greeted him.

Taylor Bloomington motioned infinitesimally for Bianca to shut and lock the door. She leaped to comply. "How much do they know and who have they told?" he questioned Andy. His Antarctic tone froze every atom in the room.

Andy flickered with terror, as he realized he'd conducted himself all wrong during the interview. "Not much but enough. They haven't told anybody—unless they're lying so hard they need to be interrogated."

"Get them out of here," Taylor negated Andy's suggestion.

"It's too late to kill us," Clare announced, realizing that once they were taken away, nothing she said could save them. "The police know everything."

"Yeah, they're on their way here now, that's no jive," Tommy added.

Andy sneered. "And a big cop is standing right behind me with a gun, right?"

"They know about Colton's research, and your involvement," Clare turned to Taylor.

With a smile like liquid helium, he replied, "Then we'd better hurry, hadn't we?" He turned to Bianca. "Bring Andy's car around."

"Bob's using mine for—you know. The situation." Andy was close to the vest now that his boss was listening. "You'll have to get yours."

"We're not using mine for. This." Bianca wavered under Taylor's gaze but repeated defiantly, "We're not using my car."

Taylor tried the look a moment longer, then chiseled a paternal smile up into his granite cheeks. He tossed her his keys. "Hurry up, I want to get home at a reasonable hour. But don't speed! Even on the way back. You don't want any record of where you've been," he instructed Andy, speaking slowly and clearly.

Andy stuffed the gun into the front pouch pocket of his Le Gym sweatshirt, waved for Tommy and Clare to stand. "Let's go for a ride." He put his arm around Clare, pressed the gun into her side.

"I'm not bluffing. The police are on the way," Clare tried not to shriek.

Tommy shouted, "If you kill us now, you'll—"

"Good-bye." Taylor silenced all sound and all hope.

The hall was miles long and yet after less than a second's walking Clare could see the glass entry doors, the blackness beyond. She closed her eyes and let Andy propel her forward. Just ahead, Bianca held Tommy's hand, leading him out.

Clare would never see Jessie again. The agony of this realization was only slightly quelled by the knowledge that Robert would take good care of the cat. She hoped Jessie wouldn't be one of those animals who pined away for her human and died. Unless of course there was a heaven.

The sound system was blasting a ballad. The aerobics instructors were putting their couples through a lewd final cooldown. In a space between songs, Clare heard Tommy yell, "Did the light just flash?"

She opened her eyes to see him swing around, put hand to head. Bianca watched with alarm. "Not now, not now," he moaned, then started to shiver and was soon on the floor, twitching mightily, then babbling, flailing. Curious exercisers migrated from the aerobics and weights rooms to observe. This seizure was much worse than the others of recent. In other circumstances, Clare would be very worried about it.

"He's faking!" Andy yelled at Bianca, shoved the gun hard into Clare. "Under control folks, she's a doctor." He held and waved Clare's arm. Then, having called attention to himself, he had to release his hold on her arm and push her forward to give Tommy a doctor's care.

Clare stepped to the side and just a bit back, as though to study the patient. But in reality she was trying to look at neither Tommy nor Andy nor Bianca nor the onlookers—at nothing but that pouch pocket. A door slammed far down the hall. Oh God if that was Taylor coming.

She darted a glance around. Bianca was watching Tommy: unsure, herself, if he was faking. Suddenly blood gushed from his mouth and Bianca screamed, battered at onlookers, screeching that they must give him room, give him air. This caused a commotion that made Andy pace in place. Then Taylor's voice called Andy's name, and Andy's head twitched in the direction of his boss.

"He's got a gun," Clare yelled, crystal clear above the din—as she lunged and grabbed at the pouch. "Help me, he's got a gun." She shoved one hand in each side of the pocket. Her move was so unexpected, she was able to hold on and get the gun pointed down, toward Andy.

"Watch out, you'll shoot my balls off," Andy screamed.

Then everything happened at once. In a streak of movement, someone slid around Clare, held an arm at Andy's throat. He choked, briefly slacked his grip on the gun and Clare ripped it away from him. She backed to a wall, aiming at anyone and everyone. The moment stabilized and she had time to pluck the torn pouch pocket from the gun barrel and look around.

Tommy was no longer on the floor. It was he who had jumped Andy. Now he released Andy with a knee to the kidneys, then reached for the gun. Clare held on to it. Their eyes met briefly and his shock that she hesitated in handing it over compelled her to do so.

"See the thing is," Tommy joined her at the wall, tapped Andy's head with the gun, "she'll only shoot if she has to. Whereas I never miss an opportunity."

Everyone stood frozen except Andy, who was shaking with rage. Clare heard whispered debates about whether the right people had wound up with the gun. "Call the cops," Bianca screamed to the receptionist. Bianca screamed? Clare had to look to make sure.

Someone flew up the hall. Taylor. "Stop him! Don't let him get away!" Clare yelled and a chartreuse bodysuit tackled him. Since Bianca had screamed for the cops, the crowd had become firmly supportive of Clare and Tommy; they formed a wall of sweaty flesh around the two miscreants to preclude further escape attempts.

The two, not the three. Bianca stood cooing beside Tommy. "You were faking, oh honey I was so scared. And you bit your lip on purpose, you didn't have to do all that." She reached up to wipe the blood away. He yanked his head back out of reach. "I wouldn't have let them hurt you," she said with wounded eyes. "I would never have let them."

He obviously wanted to believe her. But he jerked his head for Bianca to return to the middle of the circle, where Andy fidgeted, looking for someone to slug; where Taylor appraised the crowd impassively, looking for an out.

Various authorities arrived, the three were taken away, the crowd was dispersed. Clare and Tommy were being questioned by uniformed police when Beaudine appeared with Robert and Hugo in tow. Hugo and Robert hugged Clare; Beaudine touched her shoulder for an instant, before taking charge.

Clare was glad to answer police questions: anything to avoid contemplating Tommy. His grief about Bianca's betrayal was too strong. It infiltrated every answer he gave, action he took, reaction he made. Clare was sure this was normal and to be expected, but it was too much for her. Especially since, when he looked at Clare, he barely recognized her.

Finally at some point it was all over and she could leave.

Eventually, she would be affected by the day's events; this was unavoidable. There were many dreadful truths to face. She would collapse or howl or cry. Then some day she would recover; except, perhaps, in her dreams.

Outside, news camera crews lurked. So far, they only knew about the horrific research lab and a mysteriously related battle for a gun at Le Gym. They were not aware that these news items had connection to the campus murders, nor to Tekassist. The police had finished making evasive statements and now Hugo's people held the limelight. Clare thought Hugo demonstrated tremendous acceptance and compassion, the way he tried to hustle Robert and her through the camera gauntlet, to keep them from being media-linked to those animal rights crazies all true scientists loathed and/or feared.

Despite his efforts, however, Clare soon had glaring lights blinding her while disembodied shouts demanded her reaction to this shocking story still unfolding. She heard a voice very much like her own replying, "If humans were paid well and genuinely informed about potential risks, would experiments on them be less ethical than on other animals who participate without choice or compensation?"

"Oh my," she heard Hugo say in the brief stunned silence that followed. Then Beaudine appeared and the reporters forgot Clare existed. Hugo stayed behind to make sure Beaudine stated things correctly. Robert continued walking Clare out to the parking lot.

Distantly, Clare felt invigorated—in some respects, making that brief speech seemed braver than any action she'd taken that day. Then a piercing sudden realization deflated her sense of accomplishment: she was in shock. For some reason this made her start to cry. Christ. She'd cried more in the last two weeks than in the prior five years. Robert held her—comfortingly but uncomfortably—and they kept walking.

A blue car pulled up in front of them. Wasn't this the Honda that had followed Clare and Tommy earlier on? Yvonne Woods was driving. She and Matt were taking Tommy out to West Covina to stay with Ilsa and Dick.

"Your car used to follow us," Clare said hollowly.

"Yes, we wasted a lot of personnel time that way. We thought you were allied with Colton." Yvonne sounded rueful.

Clare didn't respond. Tommy had rolled down the back window, reached out a hand to her. Robert released her and she stepped forward, touched Tommy's fingers briefly. "I'll call you," he said. "But I've got some shit to go through first, that I've got to be alone for."

She stepped away. He watched her as the car pulled out of the lot, turned, drove away; she sensed this although she couldn't look at him any longer. They'd been through so much together in such a short time. Yet it was all superceded by Bianca's betrayal. Clare really wasn't sure what might remain between Tommy and herself, now that all this had transpired, expired. No, she didn't know what to expect. Or want.

By the time she took the few steps back to Robert, Hugo was bustling their way. He led them to his car, with which he would drop off Clare, then Robert. "Someday we must get together and—finish the evening," he suggested. "There's much I'd like to say or ask, but not now."

"I can see benefits to that, yes," Robert agreed. Clare simply nodded.

"But I must say, Clare," Hugo added, "earlier this evening, you made it rather plain you disapprove of methods in my organization, however much you might agree with the sentiments behind. It's lunacy, then, to let the media connect you with the animal liberation movement, by comments such as those you made. Which, incidentally, were far more extreme than anything I'd dare to say." He chuckled, a rich jagged rumble that made Clare feel warm.

She sat silently, her last bit of strength having now abandoned her.

"For us, a most important effort is the detailing of alternative research methods, which our people present to the scientific community. But most of ours are lay persons, trying to convince specialists. If you could assist with that effort, now that could be a tremendous boon."

"Yes," Clare whispered. "I could do that. I'd like to."

"Splendid."

They continued in silence, Robert directing Hugo's drive. When Hugo stopped outside Robert's apartment, temporarily occupied by Clare, Robert touched her shoulder. "Are you sure you don't want us to come in with you?"

His concern had no strings attached, yet Clare couldn't stop herself from flinching at his touch. Hugo observed and said, "Yvonne and Matt have room if you—"

"No. Jessie can't be moved again and I really need to be alone, right now."

They accepted this and perhaps believed her. The car idled below as she climbed the stairs, unlocked the door, turned to wave good-bye; then it drove off without hesitation.

If Jessie weren't inside, Clare might have fled, to avoid crossing that threshhold. She dreaded being alone inside; she feared her memories. When she could no longer hear Hugo's car, she turned and looked out at the few dim stars, nearly obliterated in the city's light. She felt depleted and exposed, drained of everything that mattered. Her blood had turned to air and was evaporating into the cold night sky.

Once she was completely empty, she felt a distinctive sort of relief—the kind that occurred after her most disastrous experiments, at the instant when she acknowledged that her methods were not working, had not worked and never would: the instant when she admitted that it was time to start anew. A short sharp meow sounded faintly from inside. Clare smiled and went in to feed Jessie.

PART 5

Epilogue

CHAPTER 19

Lucid Dreaming

"Dammit Robert, I was counting on you." He was supposed to pick up the dessert on his way home, but as usual got so caught up in his work that he returned home strictly out of habit. Now their dinner guests were due to arrive and the special double anniversary cake was left to grow stale at the long-closed bakery. Above all, Clare was mad at herself: so upset about such a small problem. They hadn't fought for weeks.

"I'll go buy an ice cream cake, be back before you know it. We can freeze the anniversary cake on Monday and that'll give us an excuse to reconvene next year."

"Good point." She kissed him hurriedly but warmly, then resumed setting the table, first removing Jessie, who was lounging like a centerpiece in the middle.

She heard voices at the door—as Robert was exiting, Tommy and Bianca were arriving. After hugs of greeting all around, Robert served them beers then said, "This time I'm really going." He stopped at a shrill high mechanical buzzing.

"Oh no, the smoke alarm! I forgot to turn down the oven."

The other three ran with Clare into the kitchen. Billowing white smoke engulfed them and they dissolved. The smoke thickened, solidified into a white mass with plaster swirls.

Clare continued to stare at her ceiling as she groped to turn off her alarm clock. Now that was a nightmare. Yugh. She felt a presence on the bed alongside her. "Morning, Jess." As always, it was not known how long the cat had been awake, staring at Clare, before the alarm went off.

She followed Jessie into the kitchen, sidestepping unpacked boxes. Another move. They'd relocated more in the last year than in the last decade prior. At least this time she had a small house, complete with small fenced yard for Jess.

The glories of a weekend. Jessie ate as vacuumously as usual, but Clare breakfasted with great pomp and leisure. She should be unpacking, of course. She continued perusing the morning paper instead, getting all she could of the balmy morning air before it mutated into a summer scorcher afternoon.

At last she heard a key in the lock. The door opened and Tommy's legs appeared, the rest of him hidden behind boxes. He dropped these and the floor shook. Good thing Jess was on bug patrol outside: she would have reacted as to an earthquake and hunched growling in the hallway for hours.

"Hi honey I'm home," he shouted, then threw his head back and cheered. They ran toward each other, failing at their attempt at slow motion but achieving the desired corniness nonetheless. They laughed and kissed and laughed some more. "Man, what a drag I couldn't be here with you before now."

"Agreed but it couldn't be helped." Ten days ago, while Tommy was out packing his belongings in West Covina, Dick's brother got hurt in Denver and Dick had to fly out there, leaving Ilsa weak with a summer flu. When Tommy had offered to stay until Dick got back, that was that. He could visit Clare; but their first nights together in their new, shared abode had to be postponed.

Amazing—after all the agonizing, doubts and second

thoughts—how correct their living together now felt. They'd spent most every night together for months; yet taking that final plunge had caused great tension. Once they decided to share a home, everything changed—becoming uncomfortable and troubled, only gradually reviving. They hadn't worked out all the kinks yet, Clare knew; they still had more acclimatizing to do. But life wasn't perfect and neither were they. For that matter, she'd be suspicious if there weren't any problems.

At this she snorted, and after resistance, she gave in to Tommy's demand to know why. He then groaned and said, "The really sick thing is, I thought I'd make you more, you know, happy-go-lucky. Instead you've got me brooding. I was just saying to myself on the way over here, I know this one's for real because so much shit goes wrong and we have to work so hard to fix it."

"Yes we do," Clare said softly, engulfed by pleasures: love, desire, camaraderie. Some doubt, too, yet not nearly so much as at one time. And a certain amount of guilt; presumably that would pass, if—no, *when* Robert became less lonely. Well, perhaps he was feeling better than she assumed. After all, they'd both been lonely that last year or so, though still together. And now they didn't talk much—it was still too awkward. Although, just yesterday he'd called to say how happy Mrs. Manning was, now that she had custody of Niels. The amount of time Robert spent visiting Mrs. Manning seemed to prove how unsettled his—

"What's with the sad look?"

"Nothing, I just thought about unpacking." She considered further, fought the usual fight against disclosure, then exposed what she'd really been thinking.

"Yeah, I get that. I was thinking about Bianca on the way over here. If I can feel bad for her you must really hurt for Robert." They walked each other into the backyard, sat on the crabgrass and watched Jessie the minute lion stalking microscopic prey. It was her second day out in her new yard and she loved it.

Clare plucked idly at a weed. "Are you going to the hearing?"

"Still can't decide." Bianca—out on bail, living with her sister—had a court date this week and claimed it was crucial that Tommy attend. He didn't want to go but Clare suspected he would. Bianca's few friends had deserted her once she was named an accessory to such heinous acts.

At several points during the last months, Tommy had vowed to thereafter treat her as dead. It was Bianca who had trapped them in that elevator, in hopes that it would disturb him so greatly, he'd have a seizure and forget the last day's events—which included Colton's murder. She believed she was doing him a favor. After all, others at Tekassist wanted to kill him. And the longer he and Clare kept experimenting to solve the murders, the stronger that Tekassist sentiment grew. That was why Bianca had lied and pretended she'd been threatened by a man in her home; that was why she claimed her car was being followed. That was why she had left them those notes. STOP OR YOU DIE. She'd stolen Lalitha's hair clip from Andy—he'd gripped it while murdering Lalitha, then run away with it still in his hand. Only Bianca knew he'd kept it as a souvenir. When he discovered his grisly memento missing, he knew he had to go to Taylor. Andy got in serious trouble for keeping evidence linking him to the crime; but when Taylor found out about Bianca's warning notes, he ordered her execution. Andy's one good deed was to convince his boss that Bianca had learned her lesson and a simple beating would suffice as punishment.

These days, Bianca was proud that she'd done so much for Tommy—and even for Clare. It really hurt her feelings, how everyone seemed to despise her. Some people have mental disabilities; Bianca had moral ones. What had she done that was so bad? She didn't hurt anyone. She just went with the flow, to get a little security for herself and her man. Her man Tommy, that was. Her man Andy she visited in prison—his judge refused to set bail.

Meanwhile, Taylor had posted his $1.5 million bond and fled

the country. Any day now, extradition proceedings would begin. All they had to do was find him first. Clare doubted they ever would. With each new legal twist, it looked less likely that justice would be served on any of the Tekassist bigwigs so clearly responsible yet so murkily involved. For that matter, Clare doubted she'd ever even learn who Andy's accomplice had been.

Tommy squinted and demanded, "That cactus wasn't out here before, was it? I would've noticed—it's the best thing in the yard. And I like the yard."

"It's a housewarming gift from Yvonne and Matt. Hugo sent Jessie a natural pesticides kit."

"Good old Hugo. Always did have a thing going with Jessie." He grew serious. "Man, if they don't get off."

"I know. But I think they will."

The activists also had a trial coming up: despite noteworthy reluctance, the D.A. had pressed charges. The law said that Hugo and his compatriots should have instantly notified the authorities when they learned the truth of Colton's lab; no matter that they kept silent in hopes of bringing all involved to justice.

Tommy looked up from coaxing a ladybug onto his finger. "Nine months ago today, you realize? Nine months since I gave myself this scar inside my lip and you got the gun away from Andy because he'd rather move to death row than get his balls shot off."

Clare could imagine laughing about that, someday. "That was one of the high points, in retrospect. Here's the proof that it was all so long ago: yesterday, leaving the lab, I walked by Sid Stein and he said hello. It pained him, but he managed it."

Tommy whistled then laughed. "Now that was a high point for me—his expression when you told him he'd been a suspect." Sid had been pompously congratulating her for assisting in her small way in apprehending the killer. She couldn't help it: she let him know about their suspicions, even the call to his father. Flabbergasted, he let slip a grain of truth about his whereabouts that weekend he'd disappeared. "Poor guy couldn't even shack his own grad student in peace." Clare supposed she should regret it: thanks to her, within hours the news that he and Deirdre had snuck away for an amorous weekend was spreading all over campus. Not as quickly as the Sid-fueled rumors about Clare; but then truth never traveled as fast.

They lay back on the grass, closing their eyes against the still searingly blue-white sky. Today shouldn't be more than a first stage smog alert. Clare browsed through her memories of the events surrounding the murders, pleased to discover how much less they prickled and pained her each time she reviewed them. Certain moments like the discovery of Lalitha's body would haunt her forever; but overall she'd recovered well. Briefly, she dared recollect that Thanksgiving weekend, those utter depths of despair. If she ever got that low again, she hoped to at least remember that she'd been there—and left there—before. Twice, now. But surely she could redirect so that she never led herself to that place again. She was trying to learn, anyway, which was a vast improvement on her previous methodology to ignore what she couldn't face and hide from what she could.

After a time Tommy asked, "Think you'll ever hear from Cynthia?"

"The longer it goes, the more I think not."

He opened his eyes, turned to watch her watching him. "I try to pretend she's okay, but I can never quite manage it."

"I know." The day after they'd confronted Cynthia Bates, she'd disappeared, leaving several notes that explained yet didn't. She felt pressured by all their expectations. She could never live up to them and the effort was weakening her control, loosening her grip on her inner demons. She feared they were driving her to do evil. And so she had to leave.

Expectations? They? Demons? Evil? It baffled all except Cynthia. And so she abandoned her husband—with whom there were admittedly problems; her children—whom she loved above all else; and her medical support—which might be required to keep her alive. Since then, no one had heard from her and the few leads to her whereabouts had led nowhere, months ago. Several times, Clare and Tommy had discussed their role in pushing her into action; and only intellectually could they take comfort in the signs that it was a decision long formed, a plan slowly implemented, based on irrational, unstable fears that had gone unrecognized by everyone else who knew Cynthia, too.

The sun was no longer tolerable. They moved into the bedroom—the only room with air-conditioning. Jessie was already on the bed, waiting for them to close the door and shut out the summer heat. They stripped down and sprawled alongside Jess, holding hands.

Clare fought back fears about the future, regrets about the past. For now, at least, the three of them were safe inside the present. There was nowhere else she'd rather be.

Bibliography

The brain experiments and information in this book were taken from the following sources. In applying the facts of neuroscience to this fictional situation, as few liberties as possible were taken. Any inaccuracies that may have arisen should in no way be attributed to the authors, contributors, or works below.

Benson, D. Frank, and Eran Zaidel, eds. *The Dual Brain: Hemispheric Specialization in Humans*, UCLA Forum in Medical Sciences No. 26. New York: The Guilford Press, 1985.

Bogen, Joseph, M.D. "Educational Aspects of Hemispheric Specialization." *UCLA Educator*, Vol. 17, No. 2, Spring 1975, pp. 24–32.

———. "Concluding Overview," *Epilepsy and the Corpus Callosum*, edited by A. Reeves. New York: Plenum Press, 1985.

Diamond, M. C., A. B. Scheibel, and L. M. Elson. *The Human Brain Coloring Book*. New York: Barnes & Noble Books, 1985.

Fincher, Jack. *The Brain.* New York: Torstar Books, 1984.

Franco, Laura, and Roger Sperry. "Hemisphere Lateralization for Cognitive Processing of Geometry." *Neuropsychologia* No. 15, 1977, pp. 107–111.

Gazzaniga, Michael S. *The Bisected Brain.* New York: Appleton-Century-Crofts, 1970.

———, and Joseph E. LeDoux. *The Integrated Mind.* New York: Plenum Press, 1978.

———. *The Social Brain: Discovering the Networks of the Mind.* New York: Basic Books, 1985.

Gleick, James. *Chaos, Making a New Science.* New York: Viking, 1987.

Hooper, Judith, and Dick Teresi. *The Three-Pound Universe.* New York: MacMillan Publishing Company, 1986.

Jaynes, Julian. *The Origin of Consciousness in the Breakdown of the Bicameral Mind.* Boston: Houghton Mifflin Company, 1976.

Levy, Jerre, C. Trevarthen, and Roger Sperry. "Perception of Bilateral Chimeric Figures Following Hemispheric Disconnection." *Brain* No. 95, 1972, pp. 61–78.

Restak, Richard, M.D. *The Brain.* New York: Bantam Books, 1984.

Sacks, Oliver. *The Man Who Mistook His Wife for a Hat and Other Clinical Tales.* New York: Harper & Row, 1970.

Segalowitz, Sid J. *Two Sides of the Brain: Brain Lateralization Explored.* Englewood Cliffs, N.J.: Prentice-Hall, 1983.

Sperry, Roger. *Science and Moral Priority: Merging Mind, Brain and Human Values.* New York: Praeger Publishers, 1985.

———, E. Zaidel, and D. Zaidel. "Self Recognition and Social Awareness in the Disconnected Minor Hemisphere." *Neuropsychologia* No. 17, 1979, pp. 153–166.

Springer, Sally P., and Georg Deutsch. Left Brain, Right Brain, Revised Edition. New York: W.H. Freeman and Company, 1985.

OFFICIALLY DISCARDED
BY LA CROSSE PUBLIC LIBRARY

JUN 1992

LA CROSSE PUBLIC LIBRARY
La Crosse, Wisconsin

Borrowers
Each borrower registering will be assigned a number to which the books will be charged, and will be held responsible for all materials charged to this number.

DEMCO